FALL INTO YOU

DYLAN MORRISON

This is a work of fiction. Names, characters, businesses, places, events and incidents are either the products of the author's imagination or used in a fictitious manner. Any resemblance to actual persons, living or dead, or actual events is purely coincidental.

Copyright © Dylan Morrison, 2025

The moral right of the author has been asserted.

All rights reserved. No part of this book may be reproduced or used in any manner without the prior written permission of the copyright owner. This prohibition includes, but is not limited to, any reproduction or use for the purpose of training artificial intelligence technologies or systems.

To request permissions, contact the publisher at rights@stormpublishing.co

Ebook ISBN: 978-1-83700-145-3
Paperback ISBN: 978-1-83700-148-4

Cover design: Dawn Adams
Cover images: Dawn Adams

Published by Storm Publishing.
For further information, visit:
www.stormpublishing.co

For R, without whom I would have been someone entirely else, and for H, without whom I would have done something entirely different. Thank you for changing my life.

PROLOGUE

Born unsettlingly quiet on 1987's very last October day, William Josiah Robertson IV had to be forced to scream. His mother used to tell the story when he was a boy, always a note of chiding about her tone—"After all that trouble to have you, it would've thrown a real wrench in things if you'd bailed out on us"—but he'd found it in himself to wail in the end. This was, by all accounts, quite a relief to everyone, because in addition to arriving a little short on breath, William Josiah Robertson IV was brought into the world intended for a very specific destiny.

The previous William Josiah Robertsons, all three of them, had each scrapped and scraped their way through a rugged, outdoor childhood, and been forged, one by one, into Bill Robertson, the owner and proprietor of Robertson Family Farms. The first Bill Robertson had founded the place more than a hundred years ago, using the money he made fighting in WWI to purchase the land; he'd planted acres and acres of apple trees, and huge fields of other crops besides. The second Bill Robertson, his son, had taken over operations in the late 1940s, and turned the place into the gem of Glenriver, Ohio.

2   DYLAN MORRISON

Situated a few hours south of Lake Erie on the eastern side of the state, Robertson Family Farms was able to draw tourist traffic from neighboring cities like Columbus and Cleveland, especially in the autumn. Bill Jr. opened a market, which became a sort of general store, and leaned into the beauty of Ohio's breathtaking fall foliage by creating a whole calendar of events to encourage visitors.

Eventually, Robertson Family Farms was covering most of their annual expenses on their autumn seasonal traffic. Between hot mulled apple cider handmade on the property, a pick-your-own-apples operation, hayrides, a corn maze, a bakery, a petting zoo, and a huge selection of pumpkins to choose from, people were coming in from all over by the time the *third* Bill Robertson was handed the reins in 1979. He looked the part, certainly, tall and broad-shouldered and quintessentially mascu-line, just like the Bill Robertsons who came before him. But his business sense was limited, and his temper legendary, and under his stewardship, little problems seemed to become big ones in the blink of an eye.

William Josiah Robertson IV was supposed to be the answer to those problems. He was supposed to grow up a little rough and tumble, with a big laugh and an easy charisma and a deep well of natural leadership and courage; he was supposed to face the world with the cheerful, boyish audacity that would, in time, yield a proper Bill Robertson, of the sort who was meant to inherit the farm.

But from the first, the youngest William Robertson was a Will, not a Bill. Where he was supposed to be rugged and stal-wart, he was sensitive and soft; where he was supposed to be strong and hale, he was scrawny and weak, easily injured, often ill. He *was* smart, that much was true, but smarter than anyone wanted him to be, or knew what to do with. "*Too* smart," as his father had commented whenever Will made a suggestion that

FALL INTO YOU 3

he particularly didn't like. His parents had hoped for a Bill Robertson with charisma and panache, a head for numbers and business and the bottom line; instead, Will was awkward and offbeat, with a head more suited for charting the meadow plants visited by various species of butterfly.

He tried, though. Will tried. He did his best to grow into the man his family needed him to be. But the older he got, the more obvious it became to everyone that there simply wasn't a Bill Robertson within him.

When Will left Glenriver at eighteen, in the middle of a night he'd spend the next sixteen years attempting to forget, he'd known two things for certain. The first was that he'd *never* be Bill Robertson, not if he spent his whole life trying. A Bill Robertson, after all, was meant to find himself a nice June, or Jessica, or Jillian, with an eye towards settling down and producing the Bill Robertson to come; no matter what else happened, that would *never* be Will. He'd known that about as long as he'd known anything, and while he'd done his best to do his familial duty and look away from it, he didn't figure there was any point in pretending anymore.

The second thing Will knew, as he walked down the farm's long gravel driveway for the last time, was that it *would* be the last time. Eighteen years was enough to spend trying and failing to bloom in the wrong sort of earth; he wouldn't ask an apple tree to grow in soil that couldn't drain, that left it so drowned by what it was meant to draw in, to live on, that its fruit rotted on the branch. Will left it all behind—the town, the farm, the weight of his family's expectations. The ways in which it had all gone wrong.

But no matter how far he got from that long, gravel driveway, from the ancient outbuildings half-rotted with decay, from the old farmhouse and the long, neat lines of gnarled apple trees, he could never quite outrun the looming specter of Bill

Robertson. Even decades later, long since settled into a life more suited to the person he is, some nights Will can almost feel the man that he was supposed to be hovering behind him, breath harsh against the back of his neck, waiting with dwindling patience for Will to turn around and face him.

ONE

"William," Selma says, her voice crackling through the car's speakers from the less-than-stellar phone connection, "why in God's name you are driving to, of all places, *Ohio*?"

"I was actually born and raised there," Will says. He changes lanes, and in spite of using the turn signal, his rental car's dodgy lane-detection feature beeps angrily at him before it shuts off again. "You don't have to say it like it's a curse word. And don't call me William; nobody calls me William."

He can practically hear Selma rolling her eyes as she says, "That's because you don't *know* anyone but me. And you didn't answer my question."

"I know people," Will mutters, sullen. "Lots of people. People I work with; people who live in my building; *you*, unfortunately. A whole collection of exes—"

"You know what I mean," Selma says. He can hear the faint tapping of her nails—always long, always painted a different color—against the polished oak surface of her desk. "You'd think you lived in the middle of nowhere instead of Chicago. You *never* leave that stupid lab, you haven't been to a single one of my networking events—"

"Which are for lawyers," Will points out. "Because you are a lawyer. But I, Selma, am not a lawyer—I've never been a lawyer—I'll never *be* a lawyer—so I don't see why I should network with them."

"Because you could *meet one.*" Selma groans, but Will, knowing where she's going, also groans; the effect has a brief choral quality, like they're complaining in harmony. "A nice *responsible* man, you know, with a *good* job and a *clean* apartment and absolutely *no* lizards—"

"Seriously, why can't you just have a couple of kids?" Will demands, nearly missing his exit in annoyance. He's reached the part of this drive where he *almost* remembers where he's going, but not quite, and he barely makes it onto the correct state route. A truly unsettling billboard that was definitely *not* there sixteen years ago—a single, contextless green eye, ringed with half of a pair of cat-eye glasses—stares bone-chillingly down at him as he continues, "That's who you're supposed to be like this with, you know: your own children. Not *your middle-aged friends who are older than you—*"

"You're not middle-aged," Selma says, clucking. "Don't say that; I'm only three years younger, so if you're middle-aged that basically means *I'm* middle-aged, and if that's what you're saying, I'm sending someone to have you killed."

Will rolls his eyes, glad she can't see the amused smile playing at the corners of his mouth. "I don't know what you're talking about, Sel—you're twenty-nine. You've been twenty-nine for years now. But I, I'm sorry to tell you, will turn thirty-five on Halloween night—"

"Ahhhh!" Selma's fake scream is nothing to write home about, but Will can't quite suppress a chuckle, anyway. "The horror! The ancient, wretched horror! I can't bear it!" Her voice drops into a more serious tone as she adds, "I know that, and it's part of my point. You're too *old* to be going out with guys who steal your wallet—"

"That was one time—"

"Or leave you stranded at a rest stop in Lake Forest—"

"There were extenuating circumstances—"

"Or *let his iguana loose in your bedroom while you're sleeping*—"

"Well, okay, he..." Will starts, and pauses. That had been Anthony, Will's most recent ex; he doesn't, honestly, have much in the way of excuses to make for Anthony. Weakly, he has no choice but to go with: "I mean, she was a pretty laid-back iguana, at least?"

Selma sighs. "Why are you driving to Ohio, Will? When I met you in that bar—what was it, ten thousand years ago now?"

"Couldn't be more than five or six," Will lies. He falters, briefly, as he drives past another strange billboard, with what seems to be: "Good Lord, is that the *other eye?*"

"What?" Selma sounds more put-out than worried when she adds, "If you're hallucinating eyeballs, okay, you're *way* past the point where you should have pulled off to the shoulder—"

"No, no, nothing like that," Will says quickly, shaking his head as if to chase the thought away. As he passes beneath what does, indeed, appear to be the counterpart to the first weird eye he saw, he reminds himself that Ohio is a bizarre place, and, also, that they were talking about something else. "Just, uh, really odd billboards out here. But I was saying, it can't have been that long ago that we met, Sel, because you were, what, twenty-three then? And you are now twenty-nine, so—"

"When I met you in that bar *before recorded time began,*" Selma says, cutting Will off by way of drowning him out, "you had four shots of tequila, and then, totally unprompted, you told me that Ohio was the world's armpit and you'd never go back even if someone offered you the unlikely sum of 'ten bajillion dollars.'"

"Why do you remember *that,*" Will complains, as he flips a

8   DYLAN MORRISON

brief middle finger at a Mercedes that cuts in front of him, "but never what time I tell you to meet me for lunch?"

"Well, it *was* the very first thing you ever said to me," Selma says, in tones that ride the line between sarcastic and sentimental. "So I suppose it made an impression. And I don't forget what time you tell me for lunch, Will; I just don't show up at that time unless I feel like it."

"Faaaaantastic," Will mutters. "Why did I call you, again?" Then his mouth drops open slightly as he passes yet another wildly strange billboard; this one features the rest of the face that goes with the eyes, though only the face, and shot from very close up. In the white space on either side of the woman's head are the words NEED TO CLOSE? CALL CATHERINE ROSE. But there's no phone number listed, Will notices. Not even a website.

"I think it was a cry for *help*," Selma snaps, pulling him back to the conversation. "Because I can't think why else you'd dial me up, tell me you're halfway to your hometown, and then refuse to explain! *Why* are you going to *Ohio*, Will!"

"Oh," Will says, his mouth going suddenly dry as the purpose of this phone call circles back to the forefront of his mind. "Did I, uh... did I not mention, last month, that my—my dad died?"

There's a sharp, sucked-in breath on the other end of the line, and then a long pause. Eventually, tightly, Selma says, "You know, it must have slipped your mind. I sort of think I'd *remember* something like that."

Will winces out at the highway. "We weren't... close, or anything. I hadn't talked to him in—"

"Oh, shut up, you don't need to tell me your tragic backstory," Selma snaps. "I *am* still your best friend, even if you don't bother to keep me informed about the most *basic*—" She cuts herself off, takes another breath, and then, in a tone that sounds quite carefully modulated, says, "Sorry. I just mean—you should have told me, that's all. Are you, like... okay?"

"Oh, sure," says Will, who's actually had the sneaking suspicion for some years that maybe he's *never* been okay, at least not in the way most people are, and never will be, either. But his voice is breezy as he adds, "It's not like it changes anything about the relationship, right? He didn't speak to me before; he doesn't speak to me now. It's just a... detail adjustment."

"A detail adjustment." Selma's voice is flat. "And what stage of grief is that, do you think?"

"Realism?" Will shrugs, even though there's no one else in the car to see it. "Look, it's not—it doesn't have to be a whole thing. I didn't call you to cry or anything. Bill was alive, and now he's dead, and my life will carry on more or less like it did before; case closed."

"You know, I loved being an only child," Selma says, in the tones of fond reminiscence. "I used to think about it all the time, how glad I was my parents didn't make me suffer some snot-nosed little brat. Now I wonder if you might be cosmic punishment for my hubris. My universe-assigned little brother."

"I am, again, *older than you*," Will points out, not that it will matter. He knows that really, she's doing this to avoid saying something like, *Will, your emotional constipation makes me want to rip out all my hair and then yours*, and he appreciates her containing it.

"So you're going back for the funeral, then?" Selma says. "A little late, isn't it, if he died last month?"

"Oh, no, I... wasn't invited to the funeral," Will admits, wincing a little on the lie. Or, well, it's—it's not *quite* a lie. But it's not quite the truth, either.

The truth is, a month ago Will received a call from an unfamiliar number. He'd answered it, even though he doesn't usually answer calls from unknown numbers; the voice on the other end had been unknown, too, one Will could swear he'd never heard before. It was deep and male and hesitant as it said, "Uh, hello, is this—is this William Robertson?"

"Speaking," Will said, cautious. "But if this is a spam call, I should warn you, I'm not interested and I don't want it and you're wasting your time with this number."

"Uh, no," the caller said, and cleared his throat. "Not spam. It's—uh—look, sorry, I'm. I'm calling to tell you your father is dead. That's probably not the best way to do that, but I'm not... I'm not an expert at, uh... at telling people their fathers are dead?" A pause. Then: "Uh, I'm... very sorry."

Will was silent for a moment, less out of grief than surprise; it didn't quite seem *possible*. Though he was more intimately aware of the impermanence of life than most, he'd realized in that moment that part of him *really thought* Bill would be storming around the farm forever, searching for something with which to find fault. That's why he'd said: "Sorry—you mean— Bill? Bill Robertson? Is dead?"

"That's what I said, isn't it?" The voice, for some reason, had started to sound a little annoyed; Will had found that quite irritating. After all, it was *his* father who'd died. And he'd been even more annoyed when, dryly, the voice had added, "I guess I figured you probably already knew his name."

"I was only checking you had the right person," he'd snapped back, nettled. "It would be silly to get down to mourning my father if you were calling to report the death of a *Greg* Robertson, wouldn't it? Not that I have so much mourning to do; he isn't much of a father. Or... God. Wasn't much of one, I guess." Briefly, Will had felt the floor give out under him, the wrongness of that sentence skittering up his spine and chilling him stone-cold. Then he gathered himself enough to add, tightly, "Thanks for telling me he's dead—good to know. Was there anything else?"

At this, the voice had taken on a note of disgust. "You don't want to know what happened? Or about the funeral arrangements? Or anything? *Seriously?* He was your father!"

And this, unfortunately, had been a step too far for Will. Perhaps it was a little glimmer of grief remaining for an old man he himself had lost more than fifteen years before; perhaps it was the audacity of *this* man, whoever he was, to say this to Will at this moment. He'd lost control of his temper; he'd snapped, "Who even *are* you? You're right that he was *my* father, so I think *I* get to decide how I feel about him dying, thank you *very* much! In fact, you might say I'm the *only* person who does, since I don't have any siblings and my aunts and uncles are dead, and the last funeral I went to was my mother's! Where, by the way, my father demonstrated for what must have been the thousandth time that he wouldn't spit on me if I was on fire, so! I don't actually care about your opinions, whoever you are, and you can bury him yourself if it means that much to you. Good*bye*." And then, furiously, he'd hung up.

It had taken Will some time to cool down, but he had, over the course of several days, begun to feel rather badly about the whole incident. After all, it was probably some hospital worker, who in all likelihood simply had the misfortune of being there for Bill's... well, for whatever had managed to take him down, in the end. A rage-induced heart attack remains Will's best guess, and probably one triggered by something that most other people wouldn't be remotely bothered by.

Regardless, it wasn't the person on the phone's fault that Bill wasn't ever exactly Father of the Year, and, guiltily, Will had tried to call back and apologize. But the number had been disconnected, and so he'd shoved the incident to the back of his mind and tried to forget about it.

Not interested in explaining all this to Selma now, Will says, "Anyway, honestly, after my mom's funeral, I wouldn't have gone even if they had invited me. I was planning to just roll on with my life, but..."

"But?" Selma's tone has a dangerous note of foreboding in it; nevertheless, Will has no choice but to forge ahead.

"Well," he hazards, grimacing dramatically and tightening his grip on the steering wheel for fortitude, "it turns out that, um... I may have... uh... inherited the farm? After all?"

"YOU INHERITED THE FARM?!" Selma shrieks this so loudly that one of the rental car's speakers refuses to render it, spitting out static before settling down again. "The farm you—that your dad... But you... *When?*"

"Uh, I mean, technically when he died," Will admits, "but I, um... missed some phone calls and letters and stuff, so I didn't find out until two weeks ago? And..." Will swallows hard but then forces himself ahead on the theory that he might as well rip the whole Band-Aid off in one go. "I'm going back to Ohio because there's someone who wants to, uh... buy it? So I wanted to give you a heads-up since you are—technically, you understand—my lawyer. Since I will, uh... want you to look over the paperwork, and everything. If you don't mind."

There's a pause. In this pause, Will passes below yet another utterly absurd billboard—he has to wonder how much this Catherine Rose woman is spending on billboards. This one doesn't have her slogan or her eyeballs or her face on it: It's *just* the outline of her cat-eye glasses against a completely white backdrop, hovering huge over the highway. Will's slightly horrified to even recognize them as an ad for this woman, but he has to admit, he does.

Then a series of odd, breathy noises begins on the other end of the line, the sound slightly reminiscent of Darth Vader.

"Sel?" Will says, a little concerned in spite of himself. "Did I actually kill you here? Why are you breathing like that?"

"I am... Lamaze breathing," Selma says, through what sounds like gritted teeth. "It's helpful... for stress relief."

"Why do you know Lamaze breathing?"

"Because I dated a pregnant woman in 2014," Selma snaps,

FALL INTO YOU   13

all traces of Lamaze breathing abruptly abandoned. "You *wouldn't* remember this, because you were lost to me in studying for one of the stupid letters after your name, but she was wonderful. For three months, anyway. After that she tragically rolled right on back to Terrible George, who we can all agree deserves fate's cruelest agonies—"

"Oh, sure, death and ruination to Terrible George," Will agrees readily, despite, indeed, remembering almost nothing about the year in question beyond winning the university record for "Most Often Found Asleep in the Library."

Selma takes a deep breath, and then picks up her sentence as though Will hadn't spoken at all. "—and because he was never around, I used to take her to Lamaze class, and also it *doesn't matter*, because the Lamaze breathing isn't *helping*, because what do you *mean* you *inherited an enormous piece of property* and you are on your way to make a *land deal* and your *father died* and I haven't looked over *anything* and—"

"Look, Sel, I'm sorry, I know you're going to hate this," Will says, and makes an unhappy face out at the road. "But I did, uh, mostly make this call to loop you in, so you wouldn't, um, kill me? For not telling you about it? But I think—I think this is one of those things I just sort of have to handle... myself?" As he expected, Selma makes a furious, wordless noise of disagreement. Hastily, before she can start talking and inevitably, as she always does when she puts her mind to it, convince him to see it her way, Will continues, "But you know what's so wild, is that if you look in your mailbox when you get home from work, some lunatic will have left you a gift card for a spa weekend! On him! To apologize for dropping all this on you last minute! At that stupid expensive place you like so much even though he's told you a thousand times that you can get a better, cheaper massage at *his* favorite spot across town! Crazy, that guy. No impulse control at all. Speaking of crazy, service out here is nuts, sorry about this

14   DYLAN MORRISON

and, uh, me. Call you later?" He hangs up on the sound of her outraged squawk.

Will doesn't relax until his phone stops buzzing with calls and messages from her, which takes about fifteen minutes. Only when a full sixty seconds has passed without a remonstrative rattle from the cupholder does he let out a long breath and turn up the radio. He and Selma have been friends a long time, and she knows he has a tendency to isolate and withdraw when things get intense. She doesn't *like* it, but she'll forgive him, the way he forgives her for what she tends to do when things get intense, which is usually more along the lines of getting into a fight at a Cubs game.

A thin tendril of guilt reminds Will that the *reason* Selma doesn't like it when he does this is because she cares about him, and wants to help. He pushes it down and lets himself sink back into the drive.

He's always liked to drive, from the very first time he learned. He must have been—oh, ten or eleven, probably. It hadn't been a real car, just the farm's old tractor, barely clinging to life and only going about fifteen miles per hour on its best day. Still, the principles were roughly the same, and the first time he got behind the wheel of an actual car, he'd known that it was for him. His father's worn-down old pickup had complained every mile of every drive, but Will had loved it anyway: When he was behind the wheel, he was briefly but beautifully in control of the world around him.

Will doesn't need a car in the city; he chose his current place quite carefully, about seven years ago. He walks to work, which is six blocks from his apartment, and to the grocery store, which is four blocks from his apartment, and, in theory, to the gym, which is nine blocks from his apartment, although he almost never bothers to go. Selma's apartment is about three minutes from his, and most of their favorite bars and restaurants are within easy walking distance. Anywhere else Will goes, he

FALL INTO YOU   15

takes public transportation, or, if he has to, calls a taxi, and it's not like he goes that many other places, anyway. His life is small, with limited variables and little, at least outside of his upsettingly poor taste in men, that can upset his equilibrium. That's the way he likes it.

But it's nice, now, to turn up the country station that broadcasts across the top half of the state and drive the long and only semi-familiar run of Route 90, catching occasional glimpses of a distant Lake Erie through the tree line. Though it's only barely October, still weeks to go before the very last green leaf gives it up and blushes, all the trees have at very least begun to flirt with their autumn colors. The golds and oranges and maroons rush past Will in a blur, tugging at a thread in his chest he does his best to keep clipped short and covered. There'd been a time when it meant something to him, this part of the year, that was deeper and more complicated than an appreciation for the beauty of the season. There'd been a time when Will thought his life would, in one way or another, revolve around it, and it aches more than he would have expected to be here, a few weeks shy of thirty-five, decades into a very different existence.

In spite of this Will's glad, as he guides the car through the labyrinthine highway system that skirts the edges of downtown Cleveland, that he decided to drive. Will doesn't relish the idea of being stuck in Glenriver, Ohio any longer than is necessary, and when he'd had to face down the reality of visiting, the thought of being at the mercy of an airplane, or a taxi driver, or *anything* but his own whims and urges to flee... rankled. But now, even after he merges onto the yawning gray sprawl of Route 77, one of America's most boring highways, Will is glad to have a steering wheel under his hands, an engine purring in front of him.

The ongoing onslaught of Catherine Rose billboards tempers the relaxation somewhat, but only somewhat. Very much in spite of himself, they start to grow on him. When he

16   DYLAN MORRISON

hits a run clearly inspired by Burma-Shave, a series of billboards all in a row, each printed with one word (NEED—TO—CLOSE? —CALL—CATHERINE—ROSE) until the final one, which is again that extreme close-up of her face—Will has to admit, he laughs. He can't help it. And credit where it's due: While her marketing has not given him any real sense of what she does, it's made him upsettingly interested in finding out.

Of course, there's quite a lot he's interested in finding out. He's realizing only now, in the tail end of the drive, that he's not even sure what the plan is once he gets to the farm. Someone named Zane had set it all up through a relentless series of phone calls, always identifying himself with some long title that boiled down to "Important, High-Ranking Assistant To Someone You're Supposed To Have Heard Of." Whoever it was, Will hadn't heard of them, nor of the company Zane mentioned as the party interested in buying his father's farm, which had some silly name that sounded like something out of a nursery rhyme. He'd been glad someone was interested in buying—no, that's not the truth. If he's honest, he'd been glad someone else was steering the decision-making process. When Zane gave him a date and time for a meeting at the property, sent over information on the hotel reservation and car rental, Will had agreed, even though the date was a Friday, and it would mean taking time off work. He'd marked his calendar, and let the necessary people know, and packed a bag that sat by his front door for a week and a half before being scooped up, at last, this morning. But it's dawning on him right now that while he knows he's meeting *someone* at the farm at three, and that the goal of that meeting is Will selling, that's... about all he knows. Zane told him more, he's sure, he just, well... hasn't retained much of it.

He considers calling Zane, and decides not to. The thought of confessing to that intense, tightly wound man that he hasn't been listening to at least five phone calls is a bit much for Will

FALL INTO YOU   17

to take, just now. He'll have to hope whoever it is does the polite thing and introduces themselves.

Once he's made it past the Cleveland suburbs, Will abruptly finds himself in better-known territory, highway exit signs changing from half-familiar to grounded in specific memories. There's the Akron exit, where Will's father had blown a flat on the way back from the county fair and screamed blue murder the whole time he was changing it; there's the sign for North Canton, next to which Will had forced his mother to pull over so he could be violently sick at age fifteen, after which he had been relentlessly accused of underage drinking right up until the moment he ended up in the hospital with acute appendicitis. He smiles, not entirely happily, when he passes Canton proper—in high school Will used to end up there on weekend nights, sneaking out after his parents were asleep to meet up with guys who were probably too old for him in bars that probably should have turned him away. He's not far from Glenriver now, and the peace he'd found in driving abruptly abandons Will, leaving him instead with what feels like a writhing ball of snakes in the pit of his stomach.

He turns off on the exit that will eventually lead him to the farm, even the muscles in his forehead tensing as he drives down the objectively picturesque road. The trees are showing off, towering and brilliantly colorful, alive with trilling birds and chittering wildlife busily preparing for winter; Will should be happy, really. He should feel some connection to this place, the various ways in which its beauty is singular and sewn into the very core of who he is.

He doesn't. He feels like he should have stayed in Chicago, but it's a bit late for all that now.

As he reaches the bridge over the Glen River, Will has to pull over briefly to the side of the road. It's... He's fine, of course he's fine. He's an *adult* and this is just a *visit* and it's his farm now, anyway, at least for a few more days. Everyone who could

18   DYLAN MORRISON

tell him otherwise is dead and buried and there's no reason to be feeling this way at all.

Still. "Okay, Will," Will says to himself, a little embarrassed at needing to hear it out loud. "It's just a couple days, right? It's just a couple of days. You're going to go to the farm, and Dad's not going to be there, and Mom's not going to be there, and it's going to be fine. Okay? It's going to be fine, and you're going to be fine, and all you have to do is *keep it together* and not *freak out.* You can do that, can't you? Keep it together for a few days? You have to meet with this person, and walk around a little, and send the paperwork to Selma, and sign it. That's it. Okay, Will? Okay."

As personal speeches to the self go, this is not one of Will's more rousing efforts. But it's enough, at least, to force him to put the car back into drive and pull it over the bridge, into the place where he was born.

Glenriver isn't a particularly intimidating town. That's part of what makes it so galling for Will to be afraid of it; it's like being afraid of a basket of kittens, or a little old woman showing off her quilting collection. Surrounded by the Glen River on three sides and a large, privately owned forest on the fourth, it's the sort of place that belongs on the front of a postcard. The houses are far apart but quaintly old-fashioned, with the heart of the town centered around a white, high-steepled church that's also the town hall and community center, and as Will drives down the main drag, he finds he can hardly see what is for what *was.* He's here, now, driving his tetchy little rental car, but he's four and ten and sixteen, too, skinning his knee on that patch of sidewalk and picking up a splinter off that wooden fence, making a hash of a variety of sports in that large, open field.

When he reaches the turnoff for Robertson Family Farms, the bizarre, off-kilter sense of déjà vu is so intense that Will feels as though he might choke on it. The sign marking the route

FALL INTO YOU   19

to the farm is new, but Will blinks and it's replaced by the ancient wooden one his great-grandfather constructed. That thing had been a hazard, more than half-rotted, always harboring bees or wasps under its peeling blue-and-white paint, but Will's mind can't quite seem to accept that it isn't there anymore. It seems impossible that it could have fallen without the whole place falling, too—as though the farm should have crumbled up in the absence of this defining piece, the way a whole building can go if the wrong support beam buckles.

Will pulls into a parking spot and tries to get a grip on himself. It's just a place! A location! It doesn't have to be all this —this—this *other stuff*, not if Will doesn't want it to be. This can just be a quick weekend getaway to make, as Selma put it, a land deal. That sounds professional, doesn't it? Like something someone with his life together would do? So that's what Will's doing, and nothing else. He definitely isn't, for example, sitting in the parking lot of the family farm, near tears over a sign he once harbored very real fantasies of burning to the ground. That would be ridiculous, and pathetic, and not logical at all.

Holding firm to this thought as his guiding principle, Will gets out of the car and takes a deep breath. The air that rushes into his lungs might as well be laced with some sort of drug; he feels a sharp spike of euphoria as he drags it in, clean and crisp and scented with the faint, grassy sweetness of fresh-cut hay. Maybe he *can* hack this, unwieldy sign-based emotions aside. He'll take a moment to appreciate it, to *enjoy* something about being in this godforsaken place, and then he'll be able to—

A hand closes on his shoulder before he can finish the thought.

TWO

Will flinches, jumps, turns; he's half expecting to see his mother, for all she's been dead more than a decade now. The thin, bony hand on his shoulder has a similar weight and grip strength to June's, but the resemblance fades even as Will's still turning around—the hand releases him as he moves, whereas June's grip would have clung, underscoring the unhappy, bitten-lemon expression that always accompanied it.

And the woman who stands before him looks nothing like June Robertson ever did, although she does strike him as familiar, for some reason. She seems to be about the age Will's mother will forever be in his mind, hovering in that unknowable area between about forty and roughly fifty-five, but that's about as far as the commonalities go. For one thing, June had been a wispy person, everything from her body type to her thin dark hair seeming to have been sketched as lightly as possible into the world. This woman is—compact, Will thinks, is probably the right word, although he doubts very much it's the one she'd choose for herself. She can't be taller than 5'5", though her pale blond hair, piled high on her head in a stiff hairdo reminiscent

FALL INTO YOU 21

of a beehive, gives her another few inches. Between that and the spiked heels she's wearing, her hair, at least, is looking down at Will, though her eyes are still a little below level with his. In a crisp black skirt suit and a deep fuchsia top with a dramatically ruffled collar, she looks ready to give a TED Talk.

Will glances from her outfit down to his ancient, mud-spattered boots, his rattiest pair of blue jeans, and a maroon sweater he fished out of a Goodwill bin sometime in his early twenties, feeling oddly underdressed in spite of knowing full well that it's *her* clothes that are impractical for the setting. His gaze catches, as he glances over her again, on her cat-eye glasses, and as he stares at her, the gears begin to turn, and—

"Oh my God," Will says, hoping the sense of ringing horror doesn't show in his voice, "you're the woman from the billboards."

"Guilty as charged!" The woman's voice is so booming and jolly that it seems to suggest she's heard a joke Will wouldn't understand at all. And though her grin is broad, Will finds the friendliness in it a little off-putting. Somehow, it doesn't quite fit on her face. "Catherine Rose! When you need to close, you call me. Great to finally meet you—you *are* Will, right? I'm not wasting my time talking to some random nobody?" She laughs, the chuckle seeming genuine, as though she considers this a joke.

"Ah," Will says, not at all sure how to reply. "I can't say I'm *not* a random nobody, but. I'm definitely... Will? Thanks for, uh, the car, and the hotel room, and everything."

"Oh, no problem at all, happy to do it," Catherine says, waving an easy hand. "Honestly, my team handled all that; I can't say I've got the time. Hope the hotel's not *too* awful—once you get about twenty minutes out of Cleveland, it's all pretty much trash, but I told my assistant to do his best for you."

"Oh," Will says, trying not to let his mouth twist in distaste;

22 DYLAN MORRISON

it's not like it should matter to him if this woman insults Glenriver or the surrounding areas, since he isn't a big fan, either. "I —I haven't stopped by the hotel yet. I wanted to... start here, I guess, and then, uh, deal with that after."

"Sure, sure, whatever," Catherine says, and cracks her knuckles. "Okay! Not that it matters, my firm is *so* busy that we hardly noticed, but: You're the one who ignored our communications for a few weeks, right?"

"*Ignored...*" Will says, irritated and trying not to show it. "... might be a strong word? I wasn't doing it on purpose, I had a bit of a breakthrough at work and wasn't—super available." The more honest version of this would be: *For reasons that I'm sure are totally psychologically fine and normal, two days after I learned that my father was dead, I decided to try a totally new avenue of inquiry on one of my experiments and basically didn't leave the lab for a week and a half, except when my friend Selma dragged me out and shamed me for smelling bad until I showered. Sorry I missed you!* Will decides it's probably best to keep this to himself.

"Oh, sure," Catherine says, nodding. "We all know how that is. What line of work are you in? Something high stakes, I assume, if it's taking over your life like that? Let me guess." She looks him over, tapping her chin thoughtfully. "Investment banking? Insurance?"

Will grimaces. "Uh. Botany?"

Catherine's expression visibly dulls. "Ah." Then, as if being reset to factory default, her smiles winches back up to full brightness, and she says, "Well, Will. How much did my staff tell you about the project we're helping to spearhead here?"

"Uh," Will says again. "Not—much? I know it's something to do with the company that bought out the Shiver a few years ago—" He pauses, and, noticing Catherine's brow crease in confusion, adds, "Sorry, the Glenriver Shiver; it's this music festival that runs out here every fall? And—"

FALL INTO YOU 23

"I *know* about the Shiver, Will," Catherine says, sounding weary of him already and holding up a hand. "If I look confused, it's because you were supposed to be fully briefed on all of this, but that's a matter for me to take up with my team later. You were supposed to have a call? To go through all the basics? So you and I could just walk the property, work through the vision, and wrap things up?"

Now that she says that, Will does have a vague memory of receiving an invitation to such a call, from someone called: "Uh, Zane? Would have been the person sending those invites?" There had, as Will thinks about it, maybe been a few. When Catherine nods, Will shrugs apologetically at her. "Yeah, I may have, uh... been a bit too wrapped up at work to be... super great about getting back to old Zane. Sorry."

"Ugh," Catherine says, eyeing him sharply, then glancing at her watch, before she turns on her heel and starts walking toward the far orchard, away from the large, one-story building that houses the farm market. "He told me it was all set, but— *fine*, I'll do it myself. Let's walk and talk, though, all right? Time is money."

"Only if your definition of money is 'distance over speed,'" Will mutters to himself, but quietly enough that she won't hear him. In his experience, it's not the kind of joke that people tend to enjoy.

He hurries to keep up with Catherine, who despite being shorter than him and in much more punishing shoes, manages to walk quite a bit faster than Will's natural gait. Kicking himself for it a little, he wishes Selma was here after all—she would have been if he'd given her any more notice. She would have wormed her way into his rental, or already have been sitting in the parking lot when he pulled into the farm, leaning against the hood of her stupid flashy car, smirking at him. He'd been very sure he didn't want that, but it would be helpful to have her keen eye, her understanding of how to *deal* with

24   DYLAN MORRISON

people. She'd know what to say to this sharp, intimidating woman to get the answers Will needs out of her, and, also, she'd probably have a better sense of what those answers *are*. She'd understand implicitly how to ask the sorts of questions Will's probably supposed to be asking, and her tendency to take over the conversation would leave Will free to freak out in the privacy of his own mind.

Selma, however, is back in Chicago, because Will worked very hard to ensure that this would be the case. So, with no other options, he has no choice but to turn to Catherine and say: "Uh. You were going to brief me?"

"Right, right," Catherine says, and sighs. "At least it's pretty simple, so Zane didn't set us back *too* much. The Shiver is owned by a company called Nimbletainment. You'll have heard of them, of course—they're *everywhere*."

Will has not heard of them, but he suspects that the "everywhere" to which Catherine refers simply doesn't extend to his lab facilities, his apartment, or the small handful of bars and restaurants he and Selma tend to frequent. It's not as though he goes much of anywhere else. Still, for the sake of politeness, he nods, and says, "Sure."

"Well, obviously the Shiver is wonderful," Catherine says, in tones that indicate she thinks it's a plague upon society but wouldn't want to upset anyone by saying so. "But Nimbletainment has big plans, big visions for it. The new, improved festival grounds, with the extra space and amenities from this farm—well, Nimbletainment thinks we could put this little town on the map."

"And the town... wants to be on the map?" Will asks this a little doubtfully; on the map is not a place he, himself, ever wants to be. When Catherine stares at him blankly, as if the answer is so obvious as to be inherently rhetorical, he adds, "Um, also... sorry, but—you work at Nimbletainment, then? Your billboards weren't exactly clear on what you... do? Other

FALL INTO YOU   25

than, well, *close*, I guess." *Whatever that means*, Will adds, to himself.

Catherine, however, beams as though Will has paid her a fabulous compliment. "I *do* close, that's true, Will. Thank you so much. But no, I don't work at Nimbletainment per se; I'm a consultant, and they're a client." Catherine's tone changes, to one Will thinks is maybe trying for tactful and hitting a note closer to cloying. "The truth is, the company has been hoping to make this deal happen for a long time—they really have a vision for this place. But it won't work without this property, and they found your father, ah, a bit of a challenge to communicate with, over the years. They brought me in hoping I could get matters resolved." She pauses and, this time in tones of modesty that ring utterly and entirely false, adds, "I have a bit of a gift, you know, for working with what you might call... difficult personalities."

"Ahhh," Will says, trying to sound amused, and not bitter. "Let me guess: It was all going so well until suddenly, for some mysterious reason no one else could quite understand, he threw a huge fit and blew the whole thing up? My father is—uh, was—famous for that. The old Bill Robertson charm."

"Ah, no," Catherine says, after a surprised beat. "Actually—sorry to speak ill of your recently deceased father, but he was a real flake. He *claimed* he wanted to sell, and that was easy to believe, since he'd have been crazy not to." She gives Will a speaking look at this point, and then sighs heavily, as though she finds the whole thing rather tragic. "But then he'd get partway through the process and stop answering calls, or claim he didn't have any idea what we were talking about. He ran the little scam a few different times before we realized he was messing with us; we stopped taking his calls, after that."

"Oh," Will says, blinking. "That's odd. Not how he used to be, or at least I don't think so." *But then again*, he adds in the privacy of his own mind, *I haven't actually spoken to the man in over fifteen years. Perhaps he found it within himself to change, at all, in any way!* Then, without meaning to, he finds himself thinking of his grandfather's bitter final years, the way things had started slipping away from him slowly at first, and then faster and faster. Discomfited, he mutters, "Been a while, anyway, so. Not like I'd know."

"Yeah, well, old folks," Catherine says. "They can surprise us." At this point, the asphalt of the sprawling parking lot, built large to accommodate big events, gives way to grass; the ground is a little damp, likely from the recent rains that left the Glen River so high. Will can feel the earth dip slightly beneath his boots, but somehow Catherine's spike heels don't seem to sink into the ground at all as she continues, "My own grandfather, you know, was famous up in Cleveland for his crusade against art programs in the local schools; he said it was a waste of public funds, ran for City Council on the platform several times, the whole thing. It wasn't a popular stance, I can tell you that; people *hated* him." She laughs, as though she finds this quite amusing, before she adds, "But do you know, when he died, we went into his garage and found hundreds of little whittled sculptures? The old coot was an artist himself! It just goes to show you never really know anyone."

I think it just goes to show your grandfather was a hypocritical old jerk, Will doesn't say. What would be the point? He also doesn't see any reason to inform her that his own grandfather, Old Bill, had also been something of a whittler, to say nothing of being something of a jerk. The old man hadn't taught *Will* to whittle, of course—he hadn't taught Will much of anything, except how to keep his footfalls soft and silent as he walked past the living room where Old Bill spent most of his time. No, actually, that's not fair; Will had also learned from him what channel *The Price Is Right* was on, and to never, ever turn it off.

Will had never found Old Bill's lack of warmth particularly surprising, since the shriveled-up geezer had always made it quite clear that he found even Will's *father* lacking, in terms of carrying the mantle of his handed-down name. This meant that Will, to his grandfather, was not a person so much as a mystifying anomaly, if one who happened to be occupying the space where a person was meant to exist. He'd never been cruel to Will, exactly, he'd just been... nothing. Vacant. Blank. The few times Will had heard Old Bill express an opinion of him, it was muttered to Bill under his breath, barely audible and clearly not positive.

Catherine draws to a stop, Will pausing next to her, as they reach the fence that encloses the primary apple orchard. Technically—last time Will checked, anyway—Robertson Family Farms encompasses three apple orchards, two large planting fields, and the grazing pasture attached to the barnyard, as well some other land, not put to agricultural purpose. The grove of trees they're standing in front of is the first and biggest orchard, the one the very first Bill Robertson planted back in the 1920s, and the vast majority of its trees are a few years past their hundredth birthdays. Barring the occasional stand that's needed replacing due to rot, or beetles, or flood damage, this orchard is the same as it was during the Cold War, and the Watergate trials, and the full run of the Golden Age of Hollywood.

And yet... something's not quite right. Something's *different.* It takes Will a moment to place it, and then he realizes: It's the *fence.* All his life, the fences that ran within Robertson Family Farms were the slapdash wooden ones you see all over Ohio, built either with two-by-fours purchased at the nearest big box hardware store or whatever actual logs were nearest to hand. None of this wood was ever treated or painted, and so it all took on the unpleasant brown color of a soaked paper bag, looking a little bit wet even in the peak of an August drought. Periodically, throughout Will's childhood, he'd been woken at the crack of dawn on an otherwise unassuming morning and told it was Repair Day, and he and his father, or whichever unfortunate

28   DYLAN MORRISON

underling Bill had managed to stick with the job, would go around the property replacing pieces of the fenceline that had cracked or rotted out. It was hard, unhappy, splintering work, but there was no getting out of it, not even for school—whenever Will tried that argument, Bill always pointed out that for what *he'd* be doing with his life, the farm *was* his school, and he'd better start getting his grades up.

These fences are... not like that. They are intentionally and professionally constructed, recently painted a fresh, crisp white, with a wide flat piece on top on which a person could lean, or set a drink. Craning his neck, Will realizes that all the fences he can *see* from here are the same, crisp and white and slotted together like puzzle pieces. Had *Bill* done that? Surely not; his hip was already giving him trouble when Will was a teenager, and anyway, he'd never cared about things like this. Bill wouldn't sink money into a proper fence that he could instead have spent on some get-rich-quick scheme that never panned out—it would have been too practical.

"Will," Catherine Rose says, in a deep, heady voice, dragging Will away from his thoughts. "I want you to imagine with me. Can you do that?"

"Um," Will says, not at all sure he can, "okay?"

"Picture this." Catherine sounds, now, as though she is narrating a very bizarre commercial. "It's time for the annual Glenriver Shiver, a festival haunted for years with stories of freak weather events and terrible cold! The festival with the most documented cases of hypothermia on record—"

"Is that true?" Will says, surprised and interested. "Based on what dataset, do you know? I didn't even know that was a metric anyone was *tracking* for music festivals—"

"*But*," Catherine continues, talking right over Will as though not having heard him at all, "instead of finding themselves in the middle of a terrible, unpleasant, regrettable festival experience, they find themselves instead at the new, *improved*

FALL INTO YOU   29

Glenriver Shiver. A festival with amenities, you understand? People can come and pick *apples* during the day, with a professional photographer to make sure they catch the moment for their socials, or they can come for a soak in the state-of-the-art hot tub facilities Nimbletainment will be building, or catch some music *without* freezing at the festival's brand-new, first-of-its-kind, temperature-controlled amphitheater. Whatever your vibe, the Glenriver Shiver will be able to cater to it after these fantastic improvements!"

"Sorry," Will says, turning to stare at her. She sounds so much like she's regurgitating a weird commercial that he half expects her to rattle off a toll-free phone number to call, but instead she smiles toothily at him, leaning in ever so slightly too close. Something about that smile seems to be draining Will's life force; weakly, he continues, "I, um. Just. This seems like a lot to do for just... one festival?"

"*Great* question, Will," Catherine says, although Will did not, strictly speaking, ask one. "But actually, the company has big plans for this town. Big plans. With the ability to expand the festival ground, add more stages, Nimbletainment could be bringing live music into town all year long. That's tourist revenue for businesses; it's guaranteed world-class entertainment for the locals right in their own backyards—it's a no-brainer, really. If your father hadn't been so determined to get in the way, the town would've been reaping the benefits years ago."

Will scuffs his right boot against one of the pristine fenceposts, slopping mud up against the side, as he considers this. Certainly, the last part rings true—God knows Bill loved to cause a problem, be the holdup—but something about the rest doesn't quite sit right.

Then again, he's not sure he cares. What he knows for sure is that he doesn't want to be here, in this town or on this property in particular. He doesn't want the trees hurt, or to screw up

30   DYLAN MORRISON

the local economy—his childhood memories of the place might not be the best, but he isn't a total monster—but it doesn't sound like he's at any risk of doing that by selling. If something feels a little weird, does that really have to matter? After all, it might just be Catherine Rose, who is clearly fairly weird herself.

Seeming to sense his hesitation, she throws an arm around Will's shoulders. "Walk with me, William."

She spends the next hour leading him through a property he absolutely knows better than she does, nearly walking them into a dead end or a patch of poison ivy roughly seven times. But throughout she's chattering, barely letting Will get a word in edgewise, about Nimbletainment and their gift for improving a town with music, about what each part of the place will look like when they're done, about how all the apple trees will of course be allowed to continue to flourish, and be looked after. He hardly has a chance to take in the land he grew up on, let alone get a sense of what's changed here—it takes everything in him to keep himself paying even the vaguest attention to what she's saying without graying out from sheer, overwhelmed boredom.

Still, the more she talks, the more Will allows the nervous little voice in the back of his head, the one screaming that something feels off and it's all too good to be true, to relax. He's probably paranoid; this woman really seems like she has things under control. How else would she be able to generate so much to say about it?

As they're looping back around to the parking lot, Catherine's phone rings. She shoos Will towards the market, saying, "Go on, go in, look around! We wouldn't be changing too much in there—the company loves the old-world charm. I have to take this—Bethany, hi!" That last is clearly directed into the phone, and she turns on her heel and walks off, her conversation quickly veering towards what could not more obviously be a personal call.

FALL INTO YOU   31

Will stands awkwardly in front of the door for a moment, his hand reaching out briefly towards the handle before it drops to his side, fingers twitching until he curls them into a resolute fist. It's just a door—it's not even the same door, he realizes, as it was when he was growing up. That one had been red and peeling, with the ghostly remains of dozens of little painted apples around the trim, less recognizable as fruit with every passing year. There'd been two small glass windows set near the top; for years Will had been too short to see through them, and the day he finally could, he found they were so filthy that looking through them was like peering into another time, warped and sepia-stained and somber.

This door is a bright, cheerful yellow. It has one enormous window in the center, which is lightly and expertly frosted. The paint job around it is crisp and fresh and professional, and while the large glass pane is intentionally opaque, it's clean. Hanging in the center of the window is a little wooden sign on a hook, clearly hand-painted, that reads, WE'RE OPEN! and then, below, in smaller letters, IF NO ONE'S INSIDE, C'MON IN ANYWAY; WE'LL BE RIGHT BACK.

Will stares at it. It's so... friendly. And it's hung like it's designed to be flipped over; curiously, Will lifts it slightly with two fingers to peer at the other side. It reads, WE'RE CLOSED! but again, there's an additional message in smaller letters below: IF YOU COME IN NOW, TECHNICALLY IT'S BREAKING AND ENTERING, JUST SO YOU KNOW.

In spite of himself, Will finds a smile tugging the edges of his mouth. It's... charming, which is a word he didn't ever imagine he'd use about anything on Robertson Family Farms. "Chilling," maybe, or perhaps "decrepit," or even "so unpleasantly loaded for me that looking at all of it makes me feel like driving my stupid rental car north until it careens into Lake Erie." But "charming"? No. And yet... it's such a bright, inviting door. Such a *cheerful* little sign, and not cheerful the way

32   DYLAN MORRISON

Catherine Rose is cheerful, which has a certain edge of "You'll have a good time with me or else." Someone made it by hand, clearly took their time about it, sanding down every edge and painting every letter with painstakingly clear brushstrokes, even the tiny ones. It reminds him, oddly, of the new fences, every aspect of it carefully thought out.

His hand flexes at his side, uncurling from a fist so tight he can feel the half-moon fingernail dents it left behind on his palm. He reaches out; he opens the door.

The first impression he has of the market as he steps inside is—bright. The old market had been dimly lit by a handful of hanging lamps, industrial gray metal shades that each housed a single bulb, which were forever flickering and going out. More than once over the course of Will's childhood, he'd gone into the shop to open it and flipped the switches only to have *none* of the lights turn on, which, depending on the cause, typically triggered a tirade from his father about either the worthless, cheap lightbulbs or the worthless, cheap power company. And it had been all done in old, dark wood, anyway, the wood Bill Senior, the very first Bill Robertson, had used across the farm. Old Bill must've liked it; he'd repurposed a lot of it from an unused barn on the west end of the property, which was more of a ruin than anything else. Maybe the wood had been nice in the '20s, or the '50s, or whenever, but by the time Will was introduced to it, it seemed to actively absorb light and energy both, leaving anyone who spent too long within its presence tight-lipped, drawn.

But the market now is—God, are there more windows? There's so much light, and the walls are—still wood, Will realizes, blinking, but much paler in color, and accented with white trim and...

Will stops dead in the center of the room, his mouth dropping open, immediately forgetting to track on the innumerable changes to the once-familiar space he's standing in. None of it

FALL INTO YOU 33

seems important anymore, because there is, impossibly, an honest-to-God Bill Robertson standing behind the counter.

It's not Bill *himself*, of course; he's in the ground, or at least Will certainly hopes he is, along with all his predecessors. The man doesn't even look like Bill, or Old Bill, or Bill Senior—the Robertson men have thick, dark hair that only grows up and back, like Will's, and long, rectangular faces, like Will's, and heavy eyebrows that tend towards scowling over dark brown eyes, like Will's. This man has dirty blond hair that hangs loose nearly to his chin, tucked casually behind his ears, and a square face, with the jaw to match, and deep green eyes that seem to sparkle with cheerfulness. He would never be mistaken for a Robertson, at least not by anyone with a basic understanding of a Punnett square.

And yet... somehow, intrinsically, Will knows that in the broad strokes, this man embodies everything a Bill Robertson is meant to represent. Unlike Will, he is tall and broad-chested, though admittedly not to the degree of either Will's father or grandfather. Still, he wears his patched flannel shirt as though he earned every hole and fray, and it clings a little against the strain of his forearms. He looks like he doesn't mind working up a sweat—he looks like someone Will wouldn't mind working up a sweat *with*—and, *whoops*, Will is veering wildly from center. The man looks... correct behind the counter, in a way Will never did. In a way that, if Will's honest, even Bill never did— he was scowling more often than he wasn't when he worked the shop floor, and this guy is *smiling*.

Oh, God, wait, correction: This guy is smiling *at Will*. It's a warm, open, inviting smile, too, a smile that says, "I'm here to help." Maybe he's no Bill Robertson after all.

"Hi," the man says. He tilts his head a little, and, his smile going smaller and more amused as he meets Will's eyes, adds, "You look lost. Were you hoping to buy something, maybe? The

34   DYLAN MORRISON

apples are up here, and if you go through that door and around the corner, Glenda can help you with the baked goods."

Who on earth is Glenda? Will doesn't say this—probably Glenda is some teenager who will work the counter until she gets bored or won't put up with the abuse anymore; that's how it always was when he was a kid.

"Uh, no baked goods," Will says slowly. He takes a few hesitant steps forward, almost as if he's in a dream. As he gets closer, he realizes the man is wearing a nametag in the shape of a tree; under the roots, the name CASEY is written in a hand that matches the sign on the door. "I'm sure they're great, I'm just—realizing I haven't had a ton to eat today. Probably better to have a meal before I eat a bunch of sweets." He could strangle himself—why did he say that? What possible reason could this man have for wanting to know that?

But for some reason, the man—Casey, apparently—continues to smile in response to this. If anything, the expression seems to deepen slightly, crinkling his eyes at the corners. Will notices, his mouth going a little dry, that his flannel shirt seems to shift with the man's slightest movement, as though the muscles beneath are moments from escaping containment. "I see. In that case, it's an apple you want—nice healthy choice, right? That's here at this counter. Step right up."

Will releases, very belatedly, that he is *still* standing more or less in the center of the room, an accidental island in the sparsely populated waters of the shop. He'd taken a few hesitant steps forward and just... stopped, again, standing immobile as other customers moved around him, transfixed by this person who he's half-convinced is a hallucination his stress-addled mind is using to conceal from him the fact that he has finally snapped. Hurriedly, he strides up to the counter, where he stops again and looks down, blinking.

When this had been his father's place they'd sold apples in clear plastic bags, crowded up against one another and

FALL INTO YOU   35

inevitably bruising. It was cheapest, Bill said, even when Will tried to point out that the bruising led to rotting and the rotting spread from apple to apple and they'd lose less, waste less, if they tried another method. Bill never wanted to hear it, and Will had given up after a while.

But the apples on this long, flat counter, separated out by variety, each type accompanied by a hand-painted sign describing its flavor and best uses, are not in bags. They're in little cardboard boxes, separated out by layers of thin green foam, so that none of them are touching.

"A little overwhelmed by all the choices?" Casey asks; Will's eyes jerk back up to his, startled, even though he could hardly have forgotten the other man was there. "I can give you a little breakdown, if you like."

I'm already having a little breakdown, thanks so much. Will keeps this within himself by the skin of his teeth. Instead, although it isn't much better in the scheme of things, he says, "Oh, no, uh. Thank you, but I actually—know a lot about apples. I'm, uh... an apple scientist."

This time Casey's smile breaks wide, spreading out into a huge grin. Will blinks at it, a little dazzled in spite of himself. "Sorry—you're an *apple scientist?*"

"I mean," Will says hurriedly, suddenly painfully aware that "apple scientist" is not a real job, and he might as well have announced himself as a dog whisperer, or a psychic detective. "I'm a—botanist, that's what my degree is in and everything, but my work is focused on apples. Well. Mostly apples."

Casey whistles. "Well, I call that lucky. Listen, in your professional opinion—how do the apples look? I've put a lot of work into them, but I wouldn't call myself a professional, just a dedicated amateur with internet access; I'd love an academic assessment."

Distantly, a little part of Will that has been honed through many nights at many bars, and many stern talkings-to from

36   DYLAN MORRISON

Selma, holds up a little sign. The sign reads: WILLIAM, YOU BIG IDIOT, THIS MAN MIGHT VERY WELL BE FLIRTING WITH YOU, in handwriting that, to give Will's imagination credit, does look quite a lot like Selma's.

As always, Will ignores it. He looks, instead, at the apples, his eyes skipping from McIntosh to Evercrisp to Winesap in increasing amazement. "They look... *good.*"

"Well, thanks," Casey says; when Will glances up at him, slightly stricken, Casey flashes him another bright grin. "Diiii-idya... want one?"

God, it's a good smile, an upsettingly, fracturingly good smile, and Will could look at it all day, except... his gaze is drawn, helpless, back down to the apples. They *shouldn't* look good, is the thing. They should look like Robertson Family Farms apples, which are small and often underripe and some-times mealy, or punishingly tasteless. The big draw when Will was a kid hadn't ever been the apples—it had been the bakery, and the hayrides, and the corn maze, the maple syrup and especially the cider, both the nonalcoholic kind that was essentially whole-grain apple juice and the harder, alcoholic stuff, which Bill brewed himself and sold out of the animal barn on Friday and Saturday nights. Even inconsistently watered apples grown in soil with the wrong pH and nitrogen balance could make a decent enough cider, assuming you were willing to throw in enough sugar to cover the flavor gaps.

These apples, Will can tell immediately, were neither inconsistently watered nor grown in incorrectly balanced soil. They are large and perfectly round and marred with neither bruises nor the unsettling pitting that's evidence of beetles and worms. They look like apples that would come in—in—in one of those fancy *fruit* baskets Selma's always bringing in around the holidays, where each individual piece of produce is wrapped up in several layers of tissue paper, and looks so perfect Will's

FALL INTO YOU 37

always almost afraid, before taking a bite, that he'll find himself sinking his teeth into wax.

"Oh boy, maybe you really do need to eat something," Casey says, laughing slightly. "You're staring at these apples like one of those cartoons, you know, where a wolf is looking at a bird and seeing a roast chicken dinner. Here." And in one long, fluid motion, he plucks an apple off the top of the nearest basket, tosses it into the air, picks up a paring knife from the counter while the apple is *still falling*, catches the apple, and lops off a single, perfect slice in two strokes so fast Will barely sees them. Then he holds out the slice, balanced between his thumb and the blade of the knife, for Will to take.

Will takes it. He takes a bite. It's a Pink Lady, his *favorite* stupid apple—he knows it immediately, the second it touches his tongue. God, even here, when he'd been a kid, the Pink Ladies had been good—it was a newer apple then, only invented in the '70s, but Old Bill had taken a liking to it and grafted the varietal onto some of the strongest trees. They'd been small, but they'd been flavorful, crisp and sour and sweet, never disappointing like the Red Delicious or the McIntosh. But *this* one... God help him, it might be the best-tasting apple Will's ever had. It's sweet at first, so briefly it hardly counts, and then sour enough to pinch at the back of his cheeks, and then sweet again, rich and light, like an apology for being so sharp.

"And you grew this *here*?" Will demands, when he's eaten the whole slice without entirely meaning to and swallowed hard a few times. "Here on this farm?"

"Sure did," Casey said. He looks a little pleased with himself now. "I gather it passes muster?"

"I..." Will says, his eyes flicking from the apple in Casey's hand to Casey's face. "I... You, I mean... How on earth did you fix the *soil*? Did Bill do that? They shouldn't... for them to look... and the *taste*. It had to have taken *years*!"

And Casey's face... changes. Something shifts, nearly

imperceptible and yet, somehow loud in the sudden quiet of the room. For a second, Will imagines he can hear the sound of a door slamming shut.

"I'm sorry," Casey says, and his tone is guarded now, in a way it wasn't a second ago. Suddenly, it's familiar to Will, although he couldn't quite say why. "What?"

Catherine Rose, naturally, chooses this moment to walk through the door.

THREE

"Will!" Catherine calls, her heels clacking against the lacquered hardwood floor. "*There* you are, I've been looking everywhere for you!"

"You told me to come in here," Will points out; Catherine doesn't seem to hear him.

"Well, nothing to be done about it now. I see you've met the —oh, whatever you are," Catherine says, waving a dismissive hand at Casey. "Assistant shop manager, wasn't it? Not that it matters for much longer, I suppose."

"I'm the general manager, actually," Casey says, tightly. "Of the entire farm. Not that it *matters* for much longer, I suppose." He turns to Will, and now his eyes are hard. "So *you* must be Will Robertson, the class act who couldn't be bothered to bury his own father. And yet, somehow you found the time to come back here and sell the land, huh? In your busy life as an apple scientist? Funny how that works."

Suddenly, Will recognizes Casey's voice; now that it's shot through with annoyance and resentment and disgust, it pulls him instantly back to the night he first heard it. Forgetting the weeks of guilt afterward, forgetting the way he'd tried to call the number back to apologize, Will feels his own lip curl up in irritation as he snarls, "Oh my God, and *you* must be the jerk who called to tell me my *father* was dead and then *lectured* me about not wanting to *know* enough—"

"Well," Casey exclaims, both his hands flexing in frustration, "maybe you didn't! Maybe I thought someone ought to tell you what the right thing to do was, since you obviously couldn't work it out for yourself—"

"How *dare* you," Will gasps, reeling back a step, feeling the blood drain from his face. He's never been the sort of person to say things like, "How dare you," or "Who do you think you are," or other dramatic lines from glamorous old movies. It just... isn't necessary, he's found, in life, where people are mostly a little dim and a little grating and a little unpleasant, and it's best to grit one's teeth and get on with things. But something about this man, in this place, while Will is tired and hungry and on edge— the words pour out of him before he can stop himself, before he can think of containing them. "How *dare* you say that to me! What on earth could you *possibly* know about it? You think, what—you think *working* here gives you the right to tell me what the best thing to do was? After the death of *my own father*? I don't think 'Hello, just wanted to let you know you're an orphan and, also, a terrible person, goodbye,' gives you the moral high ground here!"

"You're the one who hung up," Casey snaps, flushing. "I wanted you to consider the possibility that you owed it to the old man to—"

"Oh, who do you think you are!" This comes out louder than Will means it to, loud enough that there's absolutely no way to play it cool and conceal how upset he's allowed himself to become, so he has no choice but to jut his chin and stand behind it, as though it was intentional.

"I think I'm the person who fixed the soil!" Casey yells back, throwing his hands in the air. "You said it must have taken

FALL INTO YOU   41

years! Well, it *did*! Six years I've poured into this place while you were off, I don't know, studying some *other* apples, and now you're going to let these *vultures* come in and—"

"Boys, boys," Catherine says, one of her hands settling in a firm grip on Will's shoulder again, pulling him slightly back. "I think that's enough of that, don't you? We're all friends here, right? We all want what's best for the lovely little town of Glendale—"

"Glenriver," Will and Casey snap together, and then glare at each other.

"Glenriver, right, right, I misspoke," Catherine says, waving a hand. "But we're all on the same team, is my point."

"I'm not interested in being on any team with either of you," Casey snaps, folding his arms across his chest. "And I'm not interested in helping you, either. Technically, I can't make the *owner*"—he says this word as though it's poisonous—"get off the property, but I have the right to refuse service to *anyone*."

"Oh, fine," Catherine says, as though not remotely bothered by this hostility from a man who had, until about five minutes ago, seemed to be the embodiment of good-natured ease. "Be like that, if you insist. We have other things to do, after all. Come along, Will."

"I'm not a dog," Will snarls, still glaring at Casey. Casey is still glaring back, and for some reason, suddenly, Will can't bear the thought of letting him win this particular contest.

But then, even as she's saying, "Of *course* you're not," Catherine is dragging him backwards by the shoulder. This particular move is so reminiscent of Will's own mother that he jerks and twists away on sheer instinct, breaking eye contact with Casey after all. He does catch Casey's eye again, very briefly, as he's turning back towards the door, and for a second there's something startled, almost knowing, in the expression. Then it shutters and closes again, and Will scowls at him as he

42   DYLAN MORRISON

turns away, not dropping the expression even once they're outside.

"What *was* that?" he demands, when he's slammed the yellow door shut with a ringing finality that reminds him of his father and, as such, immediately shames him. He ignores this and plows ahead: "You said the whole town was behind this! That there was unanimous support!"

"There *is* unanimous support," Catherine says, in a tone that she clearly means to be soothing but sets Will's teeth on edge. "There's just one or two holdouts, that's all."

"That's not unanimous support," Will hisses furiously, as she hurries him over to the parking lot. He hisses it because if he doesn't hiss it, he will absolutely shout it, and he can't go reminding himself of his dad twice in one minute. "Unanimous means *everyone*, it's from the Latin—it basically *is* the Latin—for *one mind*. That means *everyone agrees*, Catherine! That's what it means!"

"Everyone *does* agree," Catherine says, again in that entirely unsoothing tone. It's the heavy peppering of condescension, Will thinks, that makes it so grating. "Casey Reeves is—well, he's a disgruntled employee, to tell you the truth. Rumor has it he was running some kind of long con on your father, trying to get him to hand over the farm. Who can say if *that's* true, of course." Her tone now suggests that *she* could say, if she wanted to, and if she wanted to, she'd say that it *was* true, but she wouldn't want to ruffle any feathers. *God*, Will wishes Selma was here; he's not built for all this, confronting his past and arguing with horrible, beautiful men and wrangling these weird, passive-aggressive business conversations. It turns out what he would really like is to be alone in his apartment in Chicago for between twelve and seventy-two hours while Selma just... makes all of this go away.

"Kinda wish he'd succeeded," Will mutters, glancing over at his underwhelming rental car. "He has a lot of nerve to tell me

FALL INTO YOU 43

what a terrible son I am, or whatever. Is he always so..." *Hot? Frustrating? Infuriating? Deeply in need of having a pie thrown in his face? Devastatingly, excruciatingly hot?* "...unpleasant?"

"He certainly has been every time I've encountered him," Catherine says, shrugging, "but you never can tell down here in the sticks." Will bristles reflexively; she doesn't seem to notice. "*You* know, right? You got out—Chicago's a fun city, but I like the speed in Cleveland better, personally. But I grew up in a little backwater like this, too, and I swear, it *does* something to these people. You can't take it personally, you know; he's angry his little scheme didn't work out, that's all. He'll probably try to run it on you next. You should go downtown while you're here, talk to some of the locals. You'll see—people want this for Glenriver. When the Shiver blows up, it's going to put this little town on the map."

"Hm," Will says, chewing the inside of his lip. Crazily, there's a part of him that wants to spin around and march right back into that market and *keep fighting*, which is just... *Why?* Will has proven over the years that he is neither a lover nor a fighter. He is, if he's anything, a flight risk; in the face of confrontation or conflict, he has the marked tendency to bolt.

"*Listen*," Catherine says, reaching out again to pat Will on the shoulder. Will's flinch this time must be excruciatingly noticeable, because even Catherine picks up on it; she pauses with her hand in midair for a bare second and then smooths it up over her own hair, as though this had always been her plan. "Why don't we pick this back up on Monday? You can take the weekend to think about it. I could show you the rest of the property, but you do, after all, already know it. You take the afternoon instead, go check in to that hotel—it's not close, you know. If I'd put you close, you'd be staying in the Motel 6 you passed on the highway on the way here."

Will doesn't care at all for this woman's casual classism, the way she seems to dismiss this town that Will had—well, yes,

44   DYLAN MORRISON

okay, she did have a point about him getting out. Will had dismissed it, too. But it had been Will's *right* to dismiss it; he'd been young and alone and badly hurt and—and none of that is relevant to the truth that, in spite of himself, he's quite glad he doesn't have to stay in that particular Motel 6. It's not a place he's ever, even once in his life, passed as either a driver or a passenger and thought, *It looks like nice things happen in there.*

"Yeah," Will says, instead of any of that, and glances one last time back at the yellow door. "Yeah, that's... that's a good idea. I'll take the weekend and think about him—that! It!"

"Sure," Catherine says. She smiles in a way that Will thinks is meant to be winsome; it comes off slightly threatening. "Just promise you won't take too long, okay? Monday's fine, but like all great deals, this *is* a limited-time offer. My client has put a lot of time and energy into making this happen, but they're frustrated, Will, if I'm honest, and getting ready to cut ties. They've made it clear to me that we can't get things wrapped up by the twenty-fourth—that's two weeks from Monday—well. Let's just say it would be a real disappointment to the people of this town, who are so excited about this opportunity."

Will swallows, a pit opening in the hollow of his stomach. He wants to sell—he *came* here to sell—but the idea of so much riding on his decision rankles. He's always found he has more success making choices that are just for himself. Fewer chances, that way, of disappointing anyone.

"Noted," Will says, ashamed of how thinly it comes out. Clearing his throat, he adds, tone firmer, "I'll do my due diligence this weekend, ask around, and get back to you. All right?"

"Right, right, diligence, of course." She's looking at her phone. "You do that. My office will call you to set up the signing, okay?"

"I didn't say I was ready to—" Will starts, but she's already walking off towards her own rather nicer car, heels clacking again against the asphalt.

FALL INTO YOU   45

"Monday, honey, I've got a meeting!" she calls, even though she could not possibly have generated a meeting so quickly, and then she's climbing into the sleek black sedan and speeding away in flagrant violation of the 15 MPH—CHILDREN PLAYING signs around the parking lot. Signs that, Will is realizing abruptly, and with an accompanying internal scare chord, he's never seen before.

God, he has to get *out* of here. The whole place gives him the sickening sense of being in one of those *dreams* where everything is almost right until you realize it's *not*. It's starting to make Will feel like he's in the opening scenes of a horror movie. He knows things have reached a point beyond rationality when he's starting to expect the scarecrows to start hobbling towards him wielding chainsaws.

Resolutely, he turns his focus away from the yellow door and the market and the fences and the signs and everything, *all of it*, because he, Will, has had enough. He's had enough! Who cares that there's some stupid hot guy working behind the counter of the shop! Who cares if he liked Will at first until he realized who he *was*, and who cares if Will can still taste his uncannily, horribly, *upsettingly* perfect apple on his stupid treacherous tongue! Who cares if being smiled at, and even *scowled* at, by that rude, unpleasant Adonis made Will's mind dive directly for the gutter? Will is *hungry*, is all, and wound so tightly now as to be nearly at a snapping point, at risk of leaving shrapnel all across these more or less innocent fields. It doesn't matter. It doesn't have to matter, unless he *wants* it to, which, obviously, he doesn't. He's going to get some food, is what he's going to do. Once he's eaten, he'll see, as he usually does, that most things aren't worth feeling upset, or angry, or anything much at all over, and certainly not this... this... this *Casey Reeves*.

He puts the car in gear; he drives away. When he passes a fast-food restaurant, without noticing which one it is, he pulls

46   DYLAN MORRISON

into line, orders a burger and fries, and mechanically eats as he follows the GPS's guidance to the hotel. It's a bleak, unsatisfying meal, and while it does make Will feel a bit less shaky down in the marrow of himself, it doesn't make him feel any *better*. In fact, if anything, it makes him feel *worse*, each empty bite seeming to land on the smoking pile of coals at the pit of his stomach, catch along the edges, and then go up in flames entirely. By the time he's swallowed his last fry, the conflagration in his chest is in danger of burning him down.

It figures, Will thinks, as he drives what turns out to be nearly forty minutes to a business-class hotel in an Akron suburb, that Bill did this. It just *figures*. Somehow, from beyond the grave, Will's unbearable jerk of a father has managed to build a Will-specific torture device, a diabolical trap set to ensure maximum suffering. Will's wondered for weeks now why Bill did it, left him the farm after all that talk about how he was turning away from his family and dooming the entire Robertson name and unfit to call himself Bill's son, after well over a decade of total radio silence; in his weaker and more self-punishing moments, he'd allowed himself to imagine that maybe it was a goodwill gesture, if more or less the definition of "too little, too late." He'd allowed himself to at least consider the possibility that time and age and sixteen years to reflect had moved the man, or, at very least, inched him a little to the left.

But now that he's met Casey—now that he's seen, in Casey's eyes and expression and tone of voice and general, utter rejection of Will, what impression of him Bill must have given—Will understands what's happened here. It's as he suspected in his more rational moments: Bill left him the farm as a gesture of *bad* will, one last twist of the knife. He'd wanted to force Will to come back one final time and look at it, the mess he'd created by leaving, the ruin of Robertson Family Farms, and he'd even found a strapping young man to play the part of the person Will was supposed to be.

FALL INTO YOU   47

Except... except the farm *isn't* a ruin. Will scowls at a NEED TO CLOSE? CALL CATHERINE ROSE! billboard as he passes it, trying to square this disquieting fact with the rest of the sharp, angry story he's woven for himself. Will's not being here hadn't left a mess. In fact, as far as Will can tell, the whole place is in better condition than it has been in at least thirty-five years. Was *that* the twist of the knife, then? That someone else had come in and done it better than Will ever could have? Surely not; Bill wasn't that conceptual a thinker. He had trouble working up a plan to clear a field for planting, much less set a complicated emotional trap for a person he never knew as an adult.

Abruptly, Will is exhausted, aching down to his bones with the desire to be asleep. He left his apartment before dawn this morning, since Catherine insisted she couldn't meet any later than noon, and the drive from Chicago was more than six hours; it must be catching up to him now. It's only 5:30 p.m., but when Will reaches his hotel, he checks in without processing much of the conversation, wanders around until he finds the room that corresponds with the number on his key, and lets himself inside. He collapses on top of the covers, his shoes still on, and falls unceremoniously asleep, his head only half on the pillow.

When he wakes up, jolting as though he's been shocked, it's 2:30 a.m. This is incredibly disorienting for several reasons: The first is that Will typically goes to bed at 10 p.m., falls asleep at 11 p.m., wakes up briefly around 1 a.m. and then again around 4 a.m., before finally admitting defeat and opening his eyes for good around seven. He wasn't always this way, but ever since his thirtieth birthday, his body has largely refused to offer him the long, blissful stretches of unconsciousness with which he used to while away particularly unpleasant hours. So to wake up in an unfamiliar hotel room, on top of the covers, still dressed in yesterday's clothes and shoes, with a crick in his neck from the angle of his head on the pillow and the fuzzy-headed

48   DYLAN MORRISON

almost-hangover of long, uninterrupted sleep, is... disquieting, to say the least. For a slow, unhappy moment, he runs through possibilities of how he got here and dismisses them quickly—who would drug and kidnap him, for example, and for what possible ransom?—before the events of the previous day fall into his head in one huge, unbroken block, like a brick plummeting from a high-rise.

Will groans, rolling onto his back, and throws a hand over his eyes. Then, feeling silly and overdramatic, even alone and unobserved in his hotel room, he gets up and gets re-dressed to go... well... nowhere. This is because he realizes, as he pulls his shoes back on, that there's nowhere *to* go. At 2:30 a.m. in Chicago, the bars would be closed, but Will could still go out and get a hot dog, or a cheesesteak, or what would admittedly probably be a slightly odd selection of items from the nearest all-night grocery store. But in this part of the country, the world is truly quiet in the small hours of the morning, nothing open and no one about, nothing to do but listen to the crickets sing and the owls trill, the occasional haunting scream of a fox.

Remembering that this room is on Catherine Rose's tab, Will selects a bag of M&Ms from the minibar and rips it open. He eats them all, one by one, as he paces around the room, thinking.

The thing is... the thing is... the thing is that it's not *right*, for Casey to have acted like that. It's not *fair*. That's why Will can't get over it, is ruminating on it angrily as he stomps around shoving M&Ms into his mouth; it's not for any other reason. It *certainly* has nothing to do with Casey's chiseled face, or his well-muscled chest, or his broad, long-fingered hands, or any dreams Will might have had about any of those things! It's because Will has a sense of justice and decency, that's what it is, and Casey's out here—out here *assuming* things, about people and events, assuming he knows what he's talking about when he *doesn't*. Will is the one who knows what he's talking about! *Will*

FALL INTO YOU   49

is the one who had to grow up on that farm, up to his eyeballs in other people's problems and expectations and failings, never an inch of room for him to be himself. The *audacity* of Casey to suggest he knew a single thing about it, that's what's stuck in Will's craw. The audacity, and nothing else.

Will spends the next few hours iterating new variations of essentially this same thought, in a dizzying assortment of different configurations. Casey's audacity is the problem, until it's his rudeness, until it's his stupid smug face, until it's his audacity again; then it's righteous indignation on behalf of Will's father, which admittedly he can't sustain; then it's righteous anger on behalf of the town, which feels like it has more of a foothold. It's—yes—Will is simply, out of *concern* for *Glenriver*, offended that Casey would—would have the *audacity*, oh, it's all coming together now—to be so rude about something that will benefit the community! With his stupid smug face! There it is, the unifying theory of "Why Casey Doesn't Merit Another Moment of Will's Thought," packaged up nice and neatly. No reason to think about it any further at all.

Unfortunately, by the time Will draws this conclusion, it's only 4:24 a.m. Groaning, he allows himself to look at his phone for the first time in about sixteen hours; there are an absurd number of missed calls and messages, but they're nearly all from Selma. Will, honor bound by a pact of more than a decade that he's fairly certain Selma doesn't hold up her end of, dutifully deletes every voicemail left between 11:45 p.m. and 4 a.m. without listening to them. There are, however, enough of them that he winces, and when he scrolls through the messages, he sees that Selma seems to have played out several stages of grief in a one-sided argument, cycling through anger and bargaining and back to anger and then briefly to depression before landing, grudgingly, on acceptance: The last message says:

50   DYLAN MORRISON

> Proof of life, please, you incredibly stressful bastard. I will send a Marine if I don't hear from you by 0800.

Will chews on the inside of his lip, weighing his options, before finally he types:

> Hi, I'm alive. Sorry to vanish on you—it's all kind of a lot. Not trying to be a stressful bastard; you really don't have to worry about me. All under control here. Please don't send a Marine if by "a Marine," you mean "your brother, Vaughn," you know how I feel about Vaughn. If it's a different, hotter Marine, though, feel free.

He sends it before he can think better of it, before his treacherous thumbs add something dangerously true, like, *I wish I'd asked you to come with me*, or, *I met this really hot guy, but we became Mortal Enemies before I could figure out if he was flirting with me, do you have a solve for that?* or, *Turns out I'm a little more cut up about this whole thing than I expected, ha ha, I know you love being right.* Then he silences his notifications and shoves his phone deep into the pocket of his jeans, and, feeling obliquely as though he's being chased, picks up the keys to his rental car and quits his hotel for the parking lot.

The lack of sleep has taken a toll. Will drops the keys when he climbs into the car, and dawn hasn't quite found it in herself to stretch her first rays of weak, wakeful light into the sky. It's so dark he has to turn on the overhead light to search for them, not that it helps; it barely casts any light at all, and in the end, Will has to pat around for the keys under the seat, unearthing several receipts the previous driver must have lodged there in the process.

Will starts driving not entirely sure where he's going, just turns on the radio to the old country station and starts down the road, singing along tunelessly to songs by Garth Brooks and Charlie Daniels he hasn't heard in years. He's not that surprised, though, when between the aggressively and unsettlingly watchful eyes of Catherine Rose, he finds himself zipping past landmarks on the way to Glenriver. A little part of him has been here on this road all these years, left behind after one drive too many, stretched out thin between the double yellow lane lines. He's dreamed the last stretch of the trip, off the highway and down the long, winding road to the bridge, so many times that when he finally reaches it he feels tingly and barely awake, as though any moment he's going to blink and find himself back in his hotel room, face still half-pressed against his pillow.

As he did yesterday, Will pulls off the road before crossing the Glen River, but unlike yesterday, this time he gets out of the car and walks up to the barrier separating road from riverbank and hops up onto it. For about ten minutes he sits there, watching the water flow, fast and churning, brown with disturbed sediment, and oddly high for the time of year. Or, at least, it would have been, once up a time; Will supposes he wouldn't know anymore. Maybe this is perfectly normal for October these days. It's not as though anyone would have told him if it wasn't.

Despite this sour note, it's peaceful, sitting next to the water. It puts Will in a reflective state of mind, and then a determined one. If he wants to know whether or not Casey had any right to say those things to him—more importantly, he wants to know whether or not the town will benefit from the sale of the farm—well, then all he has to do is follow through on Catherine's suggestion and *ask the townspeople*. He's here, isn't he? If he thinks about it, that's probably exactly what he came here today to do. That, and nothing else.

It's too early, though, to go visiting businesses and knocking on doors—most businesses, anyway. Abruptly, it occurs to Will

52   DYLAN MORRISON

that there's one place he could go, and he finds to his surprise that he's smiling slightly as he hops off the barrier. He gets back into his rental car and drives it over the bridge, and it's only a few minutes down the road to Mike's Diner. The original Mike had died some generations back, but the current Mike—the fourth or fifth in a row, Will can't remember now—keeps the same eye-wateringly early hours as his forefathers. He'd been in school with Will, a few years older, and once or twice they'd shared the strange confidences of two young men born into names and fates they wouldn't necessarily have chosen for themselves.

Still, though, Will had congratulated Mike on social media when he'd taken over the diner a few years ago, and when Will walks in this morning, though Mike's eyes widen briefly behind the counter, the expression settles into a smile as he says, "Will. Good to see you; I was sorry to hear about your old man."

Will bites back, *I wasn't*, thinking mostly of the disgust on Casey's face and, if he's honest, hating himself a little for it. Instead, he says, "Oh, thanks. It—he—well, you know how it is, with family." He has to forcibly contain a sigh at falling back on this particular chestnut, the sort of Midwestern classic he's heard trotted out over the years to cover a horrific multitude of sins.

But, as expected, it makes Mike break out in a sympathetic grin, shake his head. "Boy, do I ever. Listen, you take a seat wherever you like, okay? I'll have someone bring you some coffee—you know what you're getting?"

For all it's been more than a decade, Will could still recite the menu at Mike's Diner after several drinks, long after he'd lost track of saying the alphabet backwards or reeling off all the Latin names for the various species of apple. It's not a menu that's subject to change—classic diner staples, all day breakfast and overstuffed deli sandwiches, an ever-present meatloaf special and a rotating selection of pie. As a child, Will's order had always been two eggs and hash browns, because his father had always said he was allowed to order two eggs and hash browns; he's opening his mouth to ask for it before he remembers that he's an *adult*, with his own money and no one's preferences to cater to but his own, and smiles.

"I will have the Daybreak Special," Will says, relishing the words as they fall out of his mouth. "With sausage links, and fried eggs, and buttered rye toast, please. And—you guys got pie yet this morning?"

"You know it," Mike says, his grin a bright, brief slash across his face. "Blackberry today; it's excellent, if I do say so myself."

"A slice of pie, too, then," Will says, with a firm nod. "And a big mug of coffee, whenever you can—I'm not awake enough to eat all that yet."

Mike laughs, and nods, and waves him off, and Will settles in, after a moment of hesitation, at the booth in the far corner his father always used to choose. Bill had liked it because it afforded him a view of the whole place, allowed him the chance to people-watch in glowering silence; Will, on the other side of the booth, had only been given the opportunity to watch him. His stony face had not changed much in eighteen years of observation, becoming more weathered and wearied, perhaps, but never any softer.

Today, he sits in what he still can't help but think of as Bill's seat, sips his coffee when a waiter runs it over, and watches Glenriver wake up. His breakfast, when it comes, is hot and greasy and too much; he eats about half of it, then lingers over the pie, savoring each sweet-tart bite against his tongue, as the diner fills up with people. There are parents and children, single diners on their harried ways to work, sharply dressed office professionals and people clearly on their way to a more outdoor-oriented job. Will finds himself flush with a sudden understanding of his father's distant, vacant stare on those mornings they breakfasted here together—Will has to give it to

54   DYLAN MORRISON

him, it's pretty interesting. Will himself doesn't think he'd find it more interesting than, for example, his own child, but still, he can see the appeal.

He'd half expected these people would scream on seeing him, or treat him the way Casey did, when he figured out who Will was. But most of them don't look twice at him, and those who do—the ones who recognize him—mostly blink, and then smile, and nod.

By the time Will has swallowed the last bite of his pie, and left a hearty tip for Mike and his staff, it's 7:45 a.m. The shops will be open by the time Will makes it over to them, and he feels ready, with a full belly and a few less confrontational encounters, to start asking questions. He's going to get to the bottom of this Casey Reeves situation once and for all, and after that, his conscience will be clear, and he can head back to Chicago, as planned.

And, well, sure, when Mike says, "Good to have you back, Will!" Will turns around and replies, "Good to be back, Mike." Sure, he does that. But it's just... polite, isn't it? It doesn't have to mean anything at all.

FOUR

It's... an interesting morning.

Mike's Diner is at the very top of the long, sloping hill that serves as Glenriver's main drag, the appropriately named Main Street, running straight through the heart of the town. Will starts out by walking slowly down one side of its retail district, then back up the other, observing and peering into the windows of still-opening shops with interest. Some of the stores are the same as they were when Will was a child; Cardinal Bakery is still standing at the intersection of Main and First Streets, its cheerful red logo chalked onto the front window as it had been when he was a boy. It's a lovingly painted version of the state bird, after which the bakery was half-named—it's run by the Cardini family, whose matriarch had enjoyed the pun. His father's favorite hardware store looks exactly as it did the last time Will remembers looking at it, down to the chipping paint on the sign. The bike shop where Will had handed over years of scrimped and saved allowances remains, too, as do the toy and candy stores he'd spent his childhood hungrily staring into, and the bookstore he'd lurked inside for much of his adolescence. And, of course, Gunderson's Grocers stands at the far end of the

56   DYLAN MORRISON

street, so achingly familiar even after all these years that Will can hardly stand to look at it.

But there are new stores, too. A number of new stores. More new stores than, if Will is entirely honest, he feels should be allowed. He understands logically that Glenriver is not a snow globe, stilled forever in the moment Will last bothered to pick it up, turn it over, and give it a good shake; he knows, too, that life goes on, wherever you are, and whatever you've left behind. He's built his life on knowing that—at the end of the day, it's most of why he'd left this town in the first place. Will could have stayed in Glenriver, if what he'd wanted was to wither into a gnarled, unrecognizable version of himself, watching the years he could have spent thriving slip through his fingers the way apple blossoms always seem to float off on the wind all at once on the one day all season you're not paying attention. But he had understood, achingly and horribly and too well for someone who had, at the time, been so young, that the time would pass either way. That whether he chose to submit to standing still or made the grueling effort to move, the world would continue to revolve around him, as it had around Will's father, and Bill's father before him. It had been that, more than anything, that had forced Will's hand—more than he'd wanted to please his family, more even than he'd wanted to live up to his name, Will had abhorred the thought of watching his life pass him by without his ever once getting what he wanted from it.

And yet... God. Will supposes some part of him *had* thought that Glenriver would stay the same, that the *farm* would stay the same, preserved in life just as in the thick, clouded amber of his memories. Some small, stupid part of him, not subject to the rules of logic or the rigors of adulthood, had held onto Glenriver as he'd left it, marked it down as a sure, immovable thing. If someone had asked him yesterday, he would have described the town as perhaps slightly cursed and certainly utterly unchangeable, a fixed constant even when you wished it would prove itself capable of a bit of growth, small and uninspired and stifling.

But, much like Robertson Family Farms, the little town of Glenriver seems to be committed to showing Will its good side this weekend. The new stores—a clothing boutique, a Thai restaurant, a coffee shop, and a place called Lucas Ice Cream, which has a sign in the window that reads, SOUP SEASON—NO ICE CREAM. SOUP! SOUP! SOUP!—are all places that Will thinks he'd enjoy shopping in. And, to his surprise and amazement, a number of the stores, new and old, have little queer pride flag decals in the window.

It's not that Glenriver had been anti-queer when Will was growing up, exactly. That wouldn't be characterizing it quite right. It was more that, at least in this part of Ohio in the '90s and early 2000s, queer people were like... elephants. Everyone vaguely knew that they existed, if somewhere far away and rarely thought of, and no one would ever have said that they *shouldn't* exist, at least not out loud. In the right context, an elephant could be quite interesting, after all. But if one were to show up in the town square, or otherwise announce themselves to the populace, well. People would have every right to find that a little dangerous, wouldn't they? An elephant on a rampage in the innocent town of Glenriver, where people were trying to live quiet, normal lives? This simply wasn't the place for one of those—they'd be better off in a different environment, with more of their own kind. Certainly, no one would ever have considered putting signs in their windows that said, ELEPHANTS WELCOME, or otherwise done anything to indicate they were open to the possibility of inviting them into the community. If nothing else, their neighbors would have had something to say about it.

But it seems this, like the selection of shops, and the height of the Glen River in October, and so many other little, inconsequential details that Will has lost count, has changed since the last time he visited. As he completes his first circuit and starts venturing into stores one after another, he's surprised and then oddly touched to see a number of clearly queer people, in singles and couples, popping in and out of the various buildings, chatting and laughing and waving hellos to their friends and neighbors like everyone else. It's almost unmooring, and Will wanders in and out of several establishments before he remembers that he came here with a purpose in mind.

Nobody recognizes him at the bike shop, or the hardware store, or any of the other places Will stops by. He recognizes a few of them, but over fifteen years on and not expecting to see him, he catches a few assessing glances, nothing more. Will's glad—it's easier to strike up conversations as a random stranger, and then pepper in the fact that he's an interested party in the sale, than it is to explain exactly who he is and how he's involved. Feeling a bit like a spy in one of those novels he used to read in college when he was supposed to be covering great works of literature, he asks each person he talks to, working his way subtly up to the topic, for their thoughts on the Nimbletainment Corporation and the Glenriver Shiver. Only then, as carefully and neutrally as he possibly can, does he turn the topic to Casey Reeves.

It's... well, it's an odd little series of conversations, if Will's going to be honest with himself about it. Everyone Will talks to is chipper and friendly right until the point Nimbletainment comes up; after that, they *still* seem chipper and friendly, but in a more brittle way. Will gets the sense, in each successive chat, that the person he's talking to is choosing their words very carefully, not wanting to take a step out of line and into dangerous territory.

But those words they do choose are fairly consistent. They're grateful for the Shiver and Nimbletainment; the traffic from festival week covers a huge portion of their sales every year; expansion of the festival can only bring good things for the

FALL INTO YOU 59

town; they're personally invested in seeing it through. That last part they all say more or less exactly that way—personally invested in seeing it through—and Will chews on that as he walks from store to store to repeat his little data-gathering exercise again and again. He wonders if it's a slogan Catherine Rose, who must practically *think* in them, attached to the project to convince people to get on board, or if it means something deeper, more literal. It's the kind of thing Selma would probably know how to find out, and he puts a pin in it for when he can next face talking to her properly.

And on Casey Reeves... Well. Will's not sure how to parse those answers at *all*.

First of all, nearly everyone he asks assumes he's asking out of *attraction* to the man, which is deeply mortifying. Will stumbles through a furious, flaming-cheeked protest three times before it occurs to him that the way people are bringing it up is more informative than it is personal. They all say things like, "You wouldn't be the first to go sniffing around that tree," and, "Oh, Lord, you too? Seems like everyone who goes through that farm comes out with an eye on snagging him. I wouldn't hold your breath, though; in all the years he's been living here, no one's ever seen him out with anyone."

There is—Will begins to gather as he progresses through his visits—a somewhat fervid tone to the gossip about Casey's love life, as though he has been elevated to the status of local celebrity on merit of, as best Will can tell, a mixture of sheer mystery and raw animal magnetism. Finding clues to the man's preferences and passions appears to have become the town's collective crossword puzzle, and Will gets the sense some of them are beginning to lose track of the objective line. Noah Anderson at the bike shop, who Will recognizes from the years he used to work at the town's since-shuttered video store, clearly doesn't remember him at all, but he still does not hesitate to lay out in great detail an incident the previous summer where he saw someone who *might* have been Casey across the room at a gay bar in Columbus. All Will had said to prompt Noah's telling him this story was, "Hey, so, I met this guy Casey? Up at the farm?" But the man tells it with confidence, as though he's told it many times before to many rapt listeners, who all filed the information away with great interest to consider at length later.

Will, of course, does listen raptly and file the information away with great interest to consider at length later, but he feels a little guilty about it. Or, at least, he does until he remembers that he *hates* Casey, who is a *horrific* person, to whom he owes nothing at all. Then Will feels fine. Perfectly, utterly fine.

Anyway, in all cases, the conversation stays weird even after Will forcibly turns things away from such topics as, "Well, *I* heard he doesn't date because he has a secret family in Iowa," and "I swear half the traffic to that farm in the summer is folks hoping to see him out working with his shirt off. It's disgraceful, really, what young people get up to!" Once he's established that he is, in fact, asking business questions, for business reasons, and is simply looking for a character read in the context of the Nimbletainment deal, the tone shifts every single time. Half of them say, "Oh, well, Casey's the best," or "His personality, you mean? Nicest guy in the world, real helpful," or something along those lines before their faces freeze. The other half freeze up straight away, looking at Will as though he has caught them in a trap. And eventually, one by one, they all come up with similar, very careful responses: Casey's passionate, but misguided. Casey means well, but he's got the wrong end of the stick here. Casey's heart is in the right place, but he should learn when to leave well enough alone. Casey's doing the best he can in a tough situation, but unless something changes, we might all be better off if he lets the whole thing go.

That last one Will hears from old Mrs. Cardini, who had seemed ancient even when Will was a child and now seems to

FALL INTO YOU   61

have shrunken down into the oldest and most essential version of herself. She's not working the bakery counter, just sitting at the table in the back holding court, but she *does* recognize Will when he comes in, gimlet-eyed old woman that she is. She cackles, and invites him to sit, and answers his questions as the rest of them did, but with a sharp gleam in her eye that seems to be entreating Will to understand what she's not saying.

Unfortunately, the unspoken request alone is not itself a cipher key, so Will's left turning her words over and over in his head as he walks up the road, eating a blueberry streusel muffin Mrs. Cardini had insisted he take, on the house. Unless *what* changes? What will happen if Casey *doesn't* let it go? He'd tried asking Mrs. Cardini, but she'd clammed up immediately and started pushing pastry on him, so Will had no choice but to leave it for now.

There's something here, though, some thread of this he's not understanding, or being told, or both. Will doesn't like it. He's never enjoyed the sensation that there's some critical piece of information floating around outside his field of vision—that sort of thing will often tend to crash into him from behind at the worst possible moment if he doesn't keep an eye on it.

He stops, warily, outside of Gunderson's.

If Robertson Family Farms was the backdrop of most of Will's bad childhood memories, then this grocery store and the rambling, spacious apartment above it were the backdrop for most of his good ones. Will had been born only three days before Meredith Gunderson, the third of six Gunderson siblings, and they'd become fast friends in elementary school. When Will could get away from the farm—a little easier to do, he found, with each passing year—he was often at the Gundersons' apartment or messing around with Mere in the back room of the store. Her parents had been cheerful and kind and permissive, and Nancy, her mother, had always heaped an extra

62   DYLAN MORRISON

helping of whatever they were having onto Will's plate when he stayed for supper.

Once, when Will had been about eleven, he'd dropped a plate while setting the table for dinner. He'd panicked immediately, almost hyperventilating, knowing in his own house a mistake like that would set someone off on a tear. Nancy had stared at him and then she'd nodded, and then she'd picked up another plate, grabbed Will by the wrist, and pulled him out onto their back patio. Making direct eye contact with him, she'd held the plate up in the air, shrugged, and dropped it, not blinking or flinching when it shattered across the ground. "It doesn't matter," she'd said, "okay? They're only dishes." Will had just nodded, wide-eyed and solemn, and helped her clean it up, and that night when Nancy dropped him off, she'd asked Will to wait in the car for a minute. He'd watched, confused and more than a little afraid, as Nancy spoke to his mother, hard-faced and gesturing emphatically, for several minutes before coming back and sending him inside.

Nothing had really changed in Will's house after that—all June had said was, "Stop being such a nervous nelly, you're making people think we treat you bad"—but he'd never forgotten it, either. The flash of anger in Nancy's eyes as she said good night to him, the way she always offered him a hug before she sent him off home, had sat in the pit of his stomach, an anchoring weight, all through his childhood. It still sits there even now, as he stares up at the semi-familiar facade of the store, updated and repainted over the years, but still the same in the essentials.

He'd never called Meredith, after he left. Never written, never stopped by. She'd been the first person he ever came out to, a gawky teen out of place everywhere but in her living room, and she'd been surprised but sweet about it, kind and discreet where she could have been cruel. He'd owed it to her, probably,

FALL INTO YOU 63

to give her an explanation, but he just... couldn't seem to face it, not at the time, and the longer he waited, the harder it got.

But Nancy had been there, at June's funeral. She'd come into the service late, like Will did, and stood in the back, like Will did, and about halfway through, she'd shuffled up next to Will and taken his hand. She hadn't said anything; she hadn't needed to. Her hand had been as cool and dry as Will's eyes, but for all he held his composure, he couldn't quite bring himself to let go. For an hour, they stood like that, and then she'd walked with him out to his car, and given him a brief, firm hug, like she used to when he was young. "You take care of yourself," she'd said, which was a simple kindness. A platitude. But it was the closest he came to crying that whole stupid day, sitting there in his car with his throat catching as she walked off into the fog.

Will takes a breath. It's just a store. He'll go in, and if he sees Mere, great, and if he doesn't, great. It doesn't have to be a whole thing; he's already *here*, right in front of the place, with a question he needs to ask of whoever happens to be in charge these days. It might not even be Meredith—in fact, it probably isn't. One of the other Gunderson siblings had probably stepped in when Jake and Nancy retired, if they even have retired, and it will be one of them Will has to face. Or, better yet, it'll be some member of staff. He needs to go in, and find out what's what, instead of standing out dithering his way into a panic attack. That, as he knows all too well, will not help anyone.

He goes inside. The store *smells* as he remembers it, of smoked meat and fresh herbs and rich, earthy spices, all balanced against the sweet, perfumey notes of the floral section up front. He takes a huge lungful of air and feels transported back in time as he weaves through the aisles, hardly seeing the product on the shelves. And then he steps up to the information desk, and Jamie Gunderson is standing there, preserved in time, not a day older than the fourteen-year-old he was when Will last saw him standing here, more than a decade ago.

Will's saying, *"Jamie?"* before logic catches up to eyesight—this can't be Jamie Gunderson, Meredith's youngest brother, because Jamie Gunderson has to be at least *thirty* by now.

This kid is just his absolute spitting image, down to the way he grins easily at Will, and shakes his head, and says, "Nah, he's my uncle. I'm Todd Weaver, actually, but—Ma! Some guy's in here calling me Jamie again!"

"Ooh, a blast from the past?" a semi-familiar voice calls from upstairs. "Be right down!"

The voice almost tips it, but—it's aged, naturally, changed a little, so on that alone Will's not 100 percent sure. But her footfalls on the stairs... Will heard those a hundred times, learned to track them automatically the way he'd learned to track his parents' through the farmhouse. His gut is clenching with anticipation, muscles seizing up with a desire to run that he clamps down on with everything in him, as Meredith Gunderson herself emerges from the stairwell. She's older, certainly, curly auburn hair a little shorter, features more settled, but she's still got the same round, expressive face, the same kind brown eyes.

To her credit, she stops dead the second she sees him. None of the hesitant glancing or double-taking Will spotted amongst the townsfolk here—Meredith's eyes widen, and then fill with tears, and her mouth drops open before she covers it, belatedly, with one hand.

Finally, she says, *"Will?"*

"Um. Yeah?" Will says, and shrugs, and winces, feeling abruptly and utterly fifteen years old. "God, look. There's a lot I should say, probably, and I don't, uh. Think I know how to say most of it? Or where to even start? So, I guess I'll start with: sorry. I know it sucks that I, um. That I... haven't been in touch."

She starts to move towards him, and he braces himself—for what he's not entirely sure even as he's doing it. Is he expecting

FALL INTO YOU   65

her to slap him? Push him back out the door? He thinks he'd probably deserve that after more than a decade, but it doesn't seem her style.

Instead, to his absolute shock, he realizes that she's hugging him. Quite hard, in fact. Hesitantly, his arms lifting as though against some great resistance, he hugs her back, not entirely certain he's doing it right.

"You *stupid jerk*," she says, releasing him, after a moment. But she's smiling as she says it, and when she does thwap him, it's lightly on the arm with the end of an overlong knit pullover sleeve. "You couldn't have written me a letter? A postcard? 'Hey, Mere, FYI I'm alive, Love, Will'?"

"I'm sorry," Will says again, groaning on it a little. "I didn't mean to... I know I should have. It was all so—"

"Oh, stop, stop," Mere says easily, flapping the sleeve at him and then wiping her eyes with it. "You don't have to explain it to me—I get it. You had to get out of here, and didn't want to look back, right?"

Will blinks, startled, though he shouldn't be, by her easy empathy. She was always like this, more perceptive than she had any right to be, so quick to forgive things Will would have spent years castigating himself for that it made him feel a little silly about being so upset. With a sheepish smile, he says, "I mean, I was going to blame being a teenage imbecile with more anxiety than social skills, not to mention an incredibly poor relational model, but something like that, yeah."

Grinning at him, Meredith says, "You sound like you've been to see a therapist, Will. Could be wishful thinking, of course—I'd send this whole town to therapy if I could."

"Ugh, you only say that because *Dad's* a therapist. It's gross; get a room if you want to be in love with him. That's my *dad*," Todd comments, rolling his eyes. Then, his tone abruptly dropping into a wheedling one, he adds, "Speaking of therapy, you know, this was a really intense Jamie mix-up. So many emotions

66   DYLAN MORRISON

flying around for my tender young ears to hear! So maaaaaybe you could let me off the last fifteen minutes of my shift so I could go meet up with Luke and the guys?"

Meredith rolls her eyes at Will, as though the lost years never happened, and they are still at the same level of easy camaraderie they were in high school. "That depends on whether or not Will—sorry, that's Mr. Robertson to you—"

"Oh, God, no it's not," Will says, horrified. "Will's fine— Will's great. I'm in town for a visit, okay, not trying to be *Mr. Robertson.*"

"Hmm," Meredith says. "Fine, but you mind your manners otherwise, Todd, all right? And *if* Will doesn't mind covering the store with me until Winnie clocks in for her shift, then yes, you may go to—"

"Thanks, Ma, thanks, Will!" Todd cries before she can finish her sentence, not waiting for Will's approval, just vaulting directly over the desk and dashing for the door.

"Oh, for crying out—" Mere starts, annoyed, but cuts herself off when the door slams behind Todd with a laugh. "God, you know, it used to drive my mother nuts when Jamie did that; I always thought it was hilarious. I get it now."

"How *is* your mother?" Will braces himself again; it's been ten years since June's funeral, and Nancy's not the youngest woman. It's always possible the worst has happened.

"Oh, she's good," Mere says easily, with the warmth and lack of tension of someone whose relationships with their parents are largely positive, and not, at least for the moment, riddled with the grief and horror of either significant childhood trauma or serious health problems. "She and my father got a place down in Georgia —she likes the peaches, you know—and they stay with us here in the summers, but they spend most of the winter down there. The cold gets to my dad's sciatica these days, otherwise. You just missed her, actually; they left last week. She'll be sorry she didn't see you."

FALL INTO YOU   67

"Tell her I say hello, will you?" Will says, a little wistful, and Mere promises she will.

The conversation turns, as conversations have always seemed to for the last ten years or so, to the basic niceties of two adults with busy lives catching up. Meredith tells Will about her husband, Sandy, who she met in college and eventually lured out to the sticks from the teeming metropolis of Columbus; they've got four kids, three boys and a girl, Todd being the oldest, the youngest having just entered third grade. She hadn't intended to take over the store—she'd gotten a bachelor's degree in business administration, with big plans of starting her own clothing line. "But," she confesses, flushing a little even to tell it all these years later, "the truth is, I never cared much about fashion—it just sounded glamorous when I was eighteen, you know?"

"Sure," Will says, waving a hand. They've passed off control of the shop to Winnie by this point and settled into what was once Mere's parents' living room, but is now clearly hers. She's redecorated it entirely, stripping out the '70s chic-gone-shabby-chic wood paneling and colorful carpet for soothing forest green walls, a fuzzy shearling rug tossed across the hardwood. Her couch is a little plush for Will's taste—he tends to err on the spartan side when it comes to decor—but it's comfortable, and cozy, and *her*. "When I was eighteen, I thought I was going to be... Well, at eighteen, I wasn't sure *what* was going to happen." He reaches up unthinkingly to rub a thumb against the scar along his left cheekbone, then drops his hand and swallows, hard, when sympathy wells in Mere's eyes, blinking the emotion away from his own. "But at twenty, when I started college, I was sure I was going to be an engineer. I wanted to build rocket parts."

"Your tone makes me think that's not where you ended up," Meredith says dryly. "What *do* you do for a living? I won't lie,

68   DYLAN MORRISON

I've tried looking you up on LinkedIn with no luck—the curiosity is killing me."

"Oh," Will says, blinking again. He's never kept up much of a social media presence; the single account he has, he'd created to decline an invite to his ten-year high school reunion, because it had been the only option provided for doing so. Resultantly, he has only three contacts on the app: Mike's wife, who had organized the event; Mike, who had presumably heard about it from his wife; and Selma, who had found and friended Will out of amusement before he even finished telling her the story. "I never set up one of those. A LinkedIn, I mean. I'm not much of a social media guy; I was nothing but school for about a decade there, honestly, and I think I missed my window. I ended up studying, uh... botany, actually." He clears his throat, Casey's comments about going off to study some *other* apples still rattling around in his brain, and neglects to get into specifics. "Plants are a lot more interesting than rocket parts, as it turns out. Or, I think so, anyway. I don't have anything against the rocket folks, just couldn't be me. Anyway, I got a job in the lab I work in now while I was completing my PhD, and just... stayed. Worked my way up. I'm the Primary Investigator now, running my own study—the boss, basically, which is weird to say, I guess. Still doesn't feel like it could possibly be true, you know?"

"You seem pretty professional to *me*. And good for you, honestly—I'm sure that lab's lucky to have you, you always were a genius. But I do know what you mean," Mere says, with a little grimace. "Some days, I can't believe *I'm* the Gunderson keeping Gunderson's going—it feels like maybe a stress dream I started having in the tenth grade, and any minute I'll wake up."

She's joking, so Will laughs, but then, painfully aware of the life he himself barely escaped, says, "You're happy, though, right? I mean, you—it's not... I don't know, you don't feel—stuck in it, or anything, right?" Cringing slightly, he adds, "I don't mean—it's great, obviously, that you're here! You seem amazing,

FALL INTO YOU   69

you have this beautiful family, the store's never looked better, I only wanted to—oh, God. I don't know."

Mere's eyes soften, and she claps a gentle hand on Will's shoulder. Her tone very kind, she says, "I'm going to forgive you for what an insulting question that is, Will, because I understand why you're asking it. *Yes*, I'm happy—I spent a year convincing my dad to give up the reins, you know. When I graduated, I came back here for the summer; I was supposed to meet Sandy back in Columbus in the fall, after he finished—oh, I don't remember now, some internship or summer trip, or something. Anyway, after a couple weeks here, I realized I had about a million and one things I wanted to change, and I started getting after it, and one thing turned to another and I realized: I liked doing it. I didn't care about fashion, but I did care about this place, and keeping good food affordable and accessible for the people around here." She shrugs, and adds, her eyes sparkling, "And, you know, it made August blow his lid, which didn't hurt."

Will can't help but laugh; August, Meredith's oldest brother, had been a terror for rules and restrictions, always insisting he was in charge in any situation. The thought of Meredith pulling rank on him in the family store is truly hysterical, and she tells Will several entertaining stories to that effect, then updates him on the various Gunderson siblings, all still alive and in various states of wellness and wealth. By the time she wraps this up, it's lunchtime, and Will accepts when she invites him to join her, a recently returned Todd, and the rest of the kids for lunch. Sandy, her husband, stops in too; he's a skinny, cheerful guy with shaggy light brown hair who gives off an outdoorsy energy Will can't quite quantify. Still, he likes the man a lot, and Meredith's kids are funny and interesting and a credit to her.

All in all, he doesn't get around to asking about Casey until the very end of the visit, when Will looks down at his watch and

70   DYLAN MORRISON

realizes, to his shock, that it's nearly two in the afternoon. He apologizes for overstaying his welcome, though Mere waves this away as nonsense, and then, hesitantly, he says, "Listen, before I go—I'm, uh, dealing with the farm? My da—uh, my father left it to me? And, you know, I don't think I want to... keep it, or... live here. There. No offense," he adds, hastily, holding up his hands. "Glenriver's great, just—"

"No, I get it," Meredith says, though her voice is sad. "For what it's worth it's—this town is a different place than it was then. We've all put a lot of work into it. And the farm has changed a *lot*, in ways I think would honestly surprise you. But... I get it. If I were you, I don't think I'd want to live here after all that, either."

Will swallows, looks away. But his voice is calm when he says, "I assume you know about the Nimbletainment thing? With the Shiver?"

"Oh, yeah," Meredith says, and Will notices her face go slightly guarded. *Even her*, he notes, *and after all this talk. Why?* "Probably nobody in town who doesn't. You're planning on selling, yeah? No shame in it—a lot of folks are, if it all goes through."

"Are they?" Will says, slightly confused. But, not wanting to seem like he's dodging her question, he adds, "And, I mean, yeah, I think so. It seems like the simplest solution for everyone, and it sounds like the town is behind it? But... I don't know, something feels... well... *off*, I guess. And then when I went to the orchard, I met, uh... Do you know Casey Reeves?"

Meredith flushes slightly, though her tone is light enough when she says, "Ha. I think you'd be hard-pressed to find anyone in this town who doesn't. You'd think he was some kind of movie star, the way people talk about him." When Will, without entirely meaning to, raises a curious eyebrow at her, her flush deepens, and she says, "*I* don't know any of the gossip, obviously. Sandy and I don't partake in that kind of thing; it's rude to say something behind someone's back you wouldn't say to their face. And, anyway, Casey..." She pauses, a moment of uncharacteristic hesitation playing around her mouth, before she says, "Casey's—a friend. We haven't seen him that much lately, but that's not his fault. He's our friend." Her eyes softening slightly, she adds, "He's done a lot of good for the farm, and for Glenriver. And your dad liked him a lot; you know he wasn't exactly the softest touch."

"Hmm," Will says, trying not to sound bitter and, he suspects, failing. "Well, as far as I can tell *everyone* likes Casey Reeves, so. I guess even Bill wasn't immune to his charms." *Just me*, he adds, in the privacy of own mind. *One more way I don't quite fit here.*

"My man CASE," Todd bellows, abruptly, from the next room. Proving Will's point, he gets up off the couch and lopes over to them, grinning, and holds out his phone. "That dude's the best. He runs these youth wilderness camps in the summer, *so* dope, it's like kayaking and fishing and all *sorts* of stuff. Anyway, I toasted three phones on his watch and then he got me this sick cover. He said it's the one people in the *military* use."

"He said your phone needed military-grade protection to survive you," Mere says, rolling her eyes and laughing on it a little.

But Will's brow furrows as he looks at the case on Todd's phone, which appears to be quite expensive. "What, he— bought that for you? Out of the goodness of his heart?" Seems a little at odds with the snarling man Will met yesterday.

"He said it was an act of mercy for my phone," Todd says, grinning. "Casey's cool, man. He gets it." Then he lopes off again, out of the room and down the stairs, off to parts unknown.

"From the mouth of babes," Mere says with a sigh. She gives Will a slightly awkward little shrug. "The truth is, Casey's great, and I think he did a lot for your dad. But the whole thing with the festival—the rest of us know which way the wind is blowing, you know? One way or another, in a situation like this, the house always wins, so we might as well get our cut before it's too late. But Casey... He's not from around here. He wants everyone to band together and let idealism win the day and that's not how it goes, you know?"

"I'm not sure I do," Will admits, but before he can ask any more questions, Todd's calling, "MA! The meat guy's here! He's got meat questions! I'm vegan suddenly!"

"You ate a roast beef sandwich an hour ago!" Mere calls down the stairs after him.

"Stop disrespecting my dietary choices, *Mom*," Todd howls back, and things descend, from there, into mild chaos.

Will chooses this moment to make his escape, saying a quick goodbye to Meredith and cutting out the back, striding with purpose back up the hill to his rental car even as he tells himself he doesn't know where he's going. He keeps telling himself that as he pulls onto the road, and down the winding, residential streets, houses spaced far apart and decorated with various flags and hangings. Some of them, he's noticed, are queer flags, and it warms his heart, even as he tells himself he's not taking a familiar route at all.

It's only when he pulls into the parking lot of the farm that Will lets himself admit that this is where he was headed the whole time.

FIVE

Will cuts the engine, grimacing when he hears it whine slightly as it settles down. He climbs out of the car and stretches, even though it hasn't been more than a fifteen-minute drive. He pats his pockets, checking that he has his wallet, phone, and keys. He straightens his shirt.

He stares at the bright yellow door of the market, which yesterday had looked inviting and today reminds him that yellow is a color that often indicates poison in nature, for so long that he begins to feel a little awkward about it. Then he turns on his heel, and instead walks sharply towards the first apple orchard.

He'd barely gotten a chance to glance at it yesterday with Catherine; she'd walked so quickly in spite of those terrifyingly high spike heels. But the first orchard, so called because it was the one Original Bill had planted back in the early days of the farm, deserves more from Will than a passing glance. He's missed many years of its life, but it was there for nearly the first twenty years of his, a large, familiar grove of old, silent friends.

When he gets to the gate, however, a dark-haired teenager

74 DYLAN MORRISON

in a yellow T-shirt the same color as the market door is standing there. There's a tree-shaped nametag affixed to the shirt, similar to Casey's, but this one says NOEL, and then, in smaller but somehow more pointed handwriting, THEY/THEM. They smile both brightly and somewhat falsely at Will and say, "Hi there! Welcome to Robertson Family Farms. Are you here to pick your own apples? To get a bag you can visit the market, just back—"

"No!" Will says sharply, and then, when the teenager's customer service mask flickers in badly concealed alarm, wants to bite his own tongue off. He recognizes that expression from people dealing with his father; he's not interested in carrying on that particular family legacy. More softly, he says, "Sorry, uh. I'm sorry. I'm not looking to pick the apples. I'm—" He pauses, considering his choice of words. He *could* say he's the owner, of course. That's... true. He knows, logically, that it's true. It just doesn't *feel* true, and he doesn't want to be a jerk about it, and, anyway, it's not like it's going to be true for long. In another day or two, he's going to sign the paperwork and never set foot here again, exactly according to plan. No point putting on airs, or assuming his father's stupid mantle, for what will amount to less than forty-eight hours.

His hesitation must come off wrong, however, because Noel abandons all traces of customer-service voice and settles into what must be their more natural disaffected teen personality. Crossing their arms over their chest, they demand: "Look, man, are you some kind of creep or something? Trying to pick up women? Because we're not going to be having any of that at all, I'll get Casey out here so fast—"

"God," Will says, a horrified laugh spilling out on the word, "no, no, nothing like that. I wouldn't be picking up women, anyway, but I'm not—uh, I'm not here for that. I... grew up here? My dad just died? Bill—"

"Oh my God you're *Will Robertson*," Noel gasps, putting a

FALL INTO YOU 75

hand to their mouth. Then, dropping it abruptly, they say, "Oh my *God*, does Casey know you're here? Oh my God, he's going to *flip out*, he's—"

"Whoaaa there," Will says, holding up a hand. He tries, frantically, to think back to what motivates teenagers; all his brain offers up to him is "information" and "currency," but hey, any port in a storm, right? Lowering his voice and pulling out his wallet, Will says, "Look, here's the truth—Casey knows I'm here, in town, but I'd rather he *didn't* know I was here right now. So I will give you..." Will riffles through his wallet, wincing. "...uh, well, twenty... six dollars, it looks like, if you'll keep this between us. Okay?"

"Gee, thanks, mister!" Noel says, with an oddly wholesome enthusiasm, accepting the money. They let Will pass without another word, waving him off cheerfully as he goes.

Knowing from years of experience that the first several stands of apple trees will be packed with guests but the rest will go largely ignored, as visitors don't typically want to walk that far, Will hurries along the heavily trafficked dirt paths until he's bypassed the tourists, then starts cutting between rows and trees. He walks slowly and carefully between them, noticing each brush of a finely toothed leaf or ripe, swollen fruit, stepping easily away from lazy, sugar-drunk wasps. By this time of the year, the ground is littered with apples—there are signs now, Will notices, encouraging guests to toss any bruised or half-eaten apples to the ground, to help support the soil and ecosystem. They hadn't needed those back in Will's day; guests hadn't needed to be told twice to chuck a moldy, mealy, or worm-filled apple.

God, the apples look good. It had been remarkable in the market, but the improved health of the trees, at least compared to what Will remembers, is incredibly stark. Whatever he might feel about Casey, it's good to see the old grove looking so lush,

76   DYLAN MORRISON

like it's growing for the joy of it instead battling against adverse conditions.

He stops, surprised and a little annoyed to find himself blinking back tears, in front of his favorite apple tree. It's a Melrose tree, although of course Will hadn't known that when it had become his favorite; it had been the one with the lowest bottom branch, and thus the easiest one for him to climb as a short, scrawny six-year-old. And there had been, in the heart of the tree, a perfectly forked little wooden seat, which, in a happy accident of branch growth, always seemed to fit him perfectly, even as he got older. Will could sit there amidst apple blossoms in spring, hidden through the summer by the dark, saw-edged green of the leaves, and always, from August through nearly to Thanksgiving, in reach of an easy snack. It wasn't always a ripe snack, of course—the Melrose, like Will, was really a child of October—but even the tiny, half-finished apples were sweet and tart, quietly satisfying.

They're ripe now, swollen nearly to the point of dropping everywhere he looks; someone on staff will probably be out in the next few days to clear them, he realizes, a little startled by it. It washes over him that while he knows exactly what will happen to these apples, who exactly will be doing it is a strange, yawning mystery. Every Melrose before him will be picked, then sorted and separated, the best sent to the market, the bakery, or into cold storage for later sale, and the rest divided by quality for cider production or to supplement the animal feed— but by whom? Once it would have been Clive and Denise, or Tara and Jed, or Samson and Kyle, or... Well. Will doesn't remember them all, the rotating cast of farm staff who'd been hired and fired on Bill's capricious whims. Still, he'd always *known*, while he was actually *here*, who they were at any given moment. It's oddly unmooring to realize he doesn't; more than the changes to the farm, the town, the yellow market door, Mere's *children*, it drops on Will the weight of how long he's been gone, on how much has carried on, come and gone, without him.

He can't bring himself to climb it—it will hurt too much if the seat no longer fits—but, eyes stinging, Will pulls an apple off the tree and takes a bite. He remembers, as he chews and swallows, that it's the state apple of Ohio, chosen sometime in the '40s. As a young man, Old Bill had ripped out fifteen Baldwin trees to put these in against his own father's advice, which Will only knows because the ensuing fight had entered family lore. Will thinks now that the Melrose is an appropriate representative choice: so sweet at the front of the bite that you can almost forget the note of sharp, puckering sour at the back.

It's a good apple, though, and Will chomps quite happily through it as he makes his way out of the first orchard. To avoid the indignity of being caught having picked an apple after all by Noel the Easily Bribed Teen, Will decides to avoid going back through to the main gate. He cuts, instead, through the back of the first orchard, and into the little collection of sheds, silos, and other storage outbuildings that various Bills have had constructed here out of lack of interest in considering anywhere better to put them. Many times over the years, as Will grimly drove one of roughly seventeen loads of feed grain per season clear across the farm on their wheezing, ancient tractor, he'd wondered why no one had, for example, considered *building the feed silo next to the barn.* But critical thinking was not encouraged, at least not from Will—it was the sort of idea that, if voiced, would, at best, result in his being told to watch his mouth.

He's grimly pleased to see these are roughly as he saw them last. That they haven't collapsed is honestly impressive; not a one of them was in solid condition even when Will was a kid. Some of them look like they're one good storm or heavy snow away from becoming the Ruins Formerly Known as Bill's "To

78   DYLAN MORRISON

Repair" Shed, and Will considers peeking inside a few of them and decides better of it. Some doors are better left unopened.

He winds instead through the third orchard, planted in the '80s, shortly after Will's father took over operations. Bill had been ambitious, but not necessarily a genius—his big idea had been, more or less, *more apples*. It had worked out for him. Farm visitors, who had never managed to pick their way through even the first and second orchards, had not, as Bill had expected, spontaneously generated a new demand to meet the extra supply, but he'd found buyers in the end. The third orchard was closed to guests all through Will's childhood, promised along with the overflow from the other groves to grocery stores in Columbus and Cleveland, as well as to a few local school districts. It was these sales, more often than not, that had kept the lights on, the water running, and the staff paid when Will was young, as market traffic had been variable at best.

As expected, it's empty, and as Will approaches the farmhouse from the back, he has to stop and take a breath. Here's something else that looks the same as he left it—after everything else that's changed here in Glenriver, Will's been bracing himself all day to see the old place painted over in a bright magenta, or covered with a complicated mural of bees.

But instead it's the same. Just the same. The same blue paint, which was maybe a nice robin's egg once, but has faded and peeled over the years into a dusty, pallid color, like the sky on a half-gray day. The same tattered red, white, and blue hangings draped over the whitewashed wooden railings of the wraparound porch, which Bill had hung up over a Memorial Day weekend that must've been thirty years ago now and never bothered taking down. The same thin, yellowing lace curtains visible through the same dirty windows.

But no, Will realizes, squinting. That *is* different: The windows aren't dirty at all. Not one of them is streaked with dust, or fingerprints, or long dribbles of dried bird poop, or a cheeky message along the lines of WASH ME! left by a member of staff who didn't realize Will would end up catching the blame. Someone has cleaned them, and recently. It certainly wasn't Bill, since he'd avoided the task successfully and actively even when he wasn't in his eighties and approaching his extremely timely death. Casey might have done it—certainly rumor, vibe, and Noel's immediate suggestion of getting him suggests he is the one behind most of the improvements—but Will can't imagine why he would have. He puzzles over it as he climbs the steps up onto the porch, moving unconsciously towards the back door, which his whole family had always used as though it was the front.

The windows might be clean, but the porch furniture is the same, Old Bill's rocking chair dust-coated and clearly calcified in place after all these years, but obviously left alone, even now. Bill's rocker, too, is coated in a thin layer of brownish dust, which gives Will a moment's pause. The man hadn't died that long ago, not long enough for a layer like that to form, and Will can't imagine any version of his father not sitting in that accursed chair for at least an hour or two a day, rocking back and forth in a foul mood, chewing bitterly on his preferred tobacco.

He takes a breath; there's no point thinking about that now. What's past is past, and Will's here to do... well, to do whatever it is he wants to do here, exactly. He's still not sure even now, as he pulls his wallet out of his pocket and, his fingers trembling a little, reaches deep into the recesses of a rarely accessed flap.

He pulls out a small, standard metal key, of the type available in any hardware store. It's unremarkable to look at, nothing about it that would suggest any real significance, but Will has transferred it from wallet to wallet for nearly twenty years, feeling small and silly about it each time. He'd just wanted... He'd wanted to remember where he came from, maybe. He'd wanted to feel, in whatever stupid, insignificant way, that there was still some thread tying him to the place that had meant so much to him until, abruptly, it had meant so little.

He takes a deep breath, inserts the key in the lock, and turns.

It opens.

The tumblers give easily, in fact, none of the frustrating sticking and jiggling Will remembers from opening this door in his youth. And when he turns the knob and pushes the door open, his heart pounding frenetically in his chest, the hinges don't whine or squeak at all. It's the first time in his life he's managed to step into this vestibule totally silently, not a single creak or groan to announce him, not one voice snapping, "*There* you are," or "You're not supposed to be back yet!" or "Get those filthy shoes off your mother's rug before I make you regret it."

He stands for a moment in the stillness, letting his heart rate settle out, his breathing slow. Bill's dead, and June's dead, and Old Bill's dead—they've gone, and their opinions and expectations and standards for Will have gone with them, buried under dirt and past and withering away, even now, to nothing. There's no one in the house but Will, save the ghosts, and those walk with him, anyway, and did even when his parents were alive. There's nothing left here for him to be scared of, and he might as well, after all these years, give himself the closure of walking these halls as an adult.

Feeling bold and brave and, if he's honest, a bit like he might throw up, Will sets about exploring. He's surprised, and then puzzled, and then downright mystified by what he finds.

The living room, first of all. The furniture is the same—the blue chintz sofa June had insisted on keeping under a plastic cover even though it had been out-of-date fifteen years before Will was even alive is still there, as is the brown leather armchair Bill had loved to doze in while whatever Cleveland sports team was playing that night competed and lost. But the ancient box television is gone, replaced by a sleek modern one.

FALL INTO YOU   81

If it was that alone, Will could understand; after all, at a certain point even the ugly behemoth of a television he'd grown up with would have been bound to kick the bucket, having been in regular use since roughly 1982.

But there's a *gaming system* hooked up to the television. Will stares at it, and the collection of games stacked next to it, with the bewilderment of a man who has just discovered a pile of loose shrimp in his medicine cabinet: What are these *doing* here? How did they *get* here? *Why?* Will knows that people *can* change, although they rarely do, but he simply can't imagine anything that could have happened to his father that would have caused him to turn, in his old age, to the sweet embrace of digital adventure. Will had, more than once, seen the man brought to apoplectic frustration by the shop's basic digital credit card machine; he didn't seem the type to play *Elden Ring*.

The bookshelf in the living room, too, is unsettling. The various nonfiction books about wars, farming, and maritime disasters, Bill's three primary interests, are still there, but among them—God help him, there are *fiction* books on this shelf. This would be strange enough on its own, since Bill had never held with fiction and encouraged Will not to, either, but some of them are books Will himself counts amongst his favorites. Some of them are *queer* books.

Will is capable of a lot of things. He can read and understand a complicated genome sequence; he can make a passable French omelette and a pretty solid lasagna; he can assess a pile of graduate student exams in less time than it takes him to finish a cup of coffee. But he can't, to any degree, picture his father reading even one of these books. The very thought is almost bloodcurdling in its essential wrongness.

He sets the books aside as beyond his rational understanding and prowls through the rest of the first floor. The kitchen, at least, is more or less unchanged, the old microwave still clearly the only element in regular use, the freezer full of frozen dinners and the fridge full of beer and hard cider. The dining room, too, is the same, dust thick over the large, rarely used dinner table. That had been a wedding gift, Will knows, from Old Bill and Jillian, Will's grandmother. Maybe that's why Bill had never liked using it, and they'd eaten nearly all their meals at the cramped, wobbling breakfast table in the kitchen. It is, Will realizes now with a bit of a pang, quite a beautiful dining set—black walnut, if Will doesn't miss his guess, and with intricate carving work along the sideboards and thick table legs, in the detailing of the chairs. Old Bill would have gathered the lumber himself, probably, after a storm took down one of the big, behemoth trees near the farmhouse, which were always dropping those huge, ground-staining fruit pods in the weeks leading up to Will's birthday. He glances out the nearest window and smirks, satisfied, to see a number of them on the ground even now.

He drums his fingers on the tabletop, thinking about how Old Bill, ever the whittler, must have carved it himself. Even when he'd forgotten essentially everything else near the end, he'd whittled simple figurines and spoons, still scattered on windowsills around the house. There was love in that, wasn't there, of a sort? And yet Will had never heard the old man *express* love, not to his father or his grandmother, and certainly not to him. It just... wasn't the sort of thing the Robertson men got up to.

Looking down at the table, Will wonders if maybe it didn't all have to go *somewhere*. If maybe Old Bill had put it all into his woodworking, all the affection he couldn't show, all the things he couldn't bring himself to say. By all accounts, the original Bill had been that way about the farm—even when Will was a kid, generations later a town legend was still making the rounds about the night Old Bill was born. The original Bill had, indeed, famously been up all night, but not at the hospital with his wife: He'd been out in the apple grove, trying to protect

FALL INTO YOU 83

some young saplings from being nibbled to nothing by area wildlife.

Will wonders, knowing it's too late to ask the answer, where his own father had put it all.

Sighing, he steps away, turns towards the stairs, and finds as he climbs them that his tension is mounting with each one. He's not sure what he's expecting to find, or afraid that he'll find, at the top; it's hard to know which would feel worse. If he finds his old bedroom changed, turned into an office or a sewing room or whatever, he thinks that might not be... amazing, as an emotional experience. But the thought of it as a mausoleum, preserved forever as though Will died in a tragic prank-gone-wrong like that Gramlich kid did when Will was in middle school—that's awful, too, in an equally disquieting way.

His was the first door at the top of the stairs growing up, and so it's the first one he has to face. It's closed, and Will takes a deep breath before gripping the knob, bracing himself for it to be locked. It turns, though, and on an exhale, Will pushes the door open...

Will *pushes* the door *open*...

Will struggles, in vain, to push the door open, getting it about half an inch off the frame before it's caught against some heavy obstacle. Annoyed, Will huffs, repositions, leans his shoulder against the door, and *shoves*, really putting his weight into it. Something moves, and the door gives way; Will stumbles at the sudden shift and only barely doesn't face-plant, jumping to straighten himself even though no one is here to see him.

He looks around. In spite of himself, he starts to laugh.

Will had feared an utterly changed room or an utterly unchanged one; what a foolish, laughable idea. Either option would have required from his parents either a willingness to address a situation head-on or the ability to leave a thing alone, and that simply wasn't in Bill's or June's cards. What Will should have expected is exactly what he sees—his room *is* more

84   DYLAN MORRISON

or less as he left it, somewhere underneath many years of accumulated boxes, old clothes, extra tools, forgotten kitchen appliances, various manuals for an assortment of devices, and other detritus of the modern home. Without Will here to defend the territory, this room had simply continued bearing on with its original purpose: containing things his parents had no idea what to do with, and would prefer didn't clutter up the rest of the house.

He shakes his head and leaves, shutting the door behind him. There's nothing in there he wants, at least not badly enough to go digging for it.

The next door is his parents' room, and it's open. Will stops in the hallway before it and stares. That is certainly... quite different. Upsettingly different. Chillingly different, even. The bed doesn't look like it's been slept in for some time, but the decor is such a radical departure from Will's memory that, feeling some shame, he pinches himself in hopes that it's a nightmare, without luck.

In his childhood, this room had *art* on the walls. It wasn't tasteful art, of course—as Will recalls it had been framed illustrations of ducks wearing little hats and bonnets, and other things of that ilk—but there'd been *something*, anyway. Will knows he isn't imagining it, because he can see the ghostly outlines of their former places on the wallpaper, demarcated in the slightly altered fading.

That's gone, now. The decorative throw pillows, gone, the cedar chest at the foot of the bed, gone, the porcelain figurines lining the shelves across the front window, gone. The shelves themselves are gone, Will realizes, as he steps further into the room; he can see the grooves in the windowpane where they used to sit, if he squints. Even the bedspread is gone, replaced with a thin white blanket that Will can tell, if he touches it, will be itchy.

He touches it. It's itchy.

FALL INTO YOU   85

"What did I expect?" Will mutters, knowing there isn't any point. No one is here to answer him, and no one could tell him the answer to that particular question even if they *were*, and anyway, he's only trying to distract himself. He doesn't really care about the texture of the blanket, or the missing paintings, or the lack of throw pillows.

Will cares about the Post-it notes.

The *reason* Will cares about the Post-it notes is that the room is covered in them. Papered, really. Unable to help himself, he glances between a few of them, wincing; the messages they bear vary. Some of them say things like, GET MILK! or DON'T FORGET YOUR GLASSES! which, okay, normal enough for a man in his eighties. But others say things like, 1971—NEW CABLE FOR PUMP 3? and STOLEN MAIL—DATES —6/7—7/19—4/22—5.

So: dementia, then. Will could waffle about it with himself, could try to pretend it was something else. A psychotic break, or a spike in paranoia due to a medication mix-up—after so many years in the cloisters of academia, socializing only with other people deep in the recesses of a scientific pursuit, Will's imagination on this front is vast. He could come up with enough explanations for this horrible wall to rival the writers of *House, M.D.*, if he wanted to.

There just wouldn't be any point. Old Bill died of Alzheimer's, after all; the original Bill Robertson had died of it, too, or at least everyone assumed, in retrospect, that he had. According to family lore, he'd refused to see a doctor, but certainly by all accounts, he'd exhibited the classic signs. It's genetic, and highly heritable, and Will watched his grandfather trickle away like rainwater from a slowly leaking bucket, less and less of him left each day. He's known since he was a teenager that it would probably kill his father, and, eventually, him.

There was a day, sometime in his late twenties, where that

86   DYLAN MORRISON

had really hit home for Will, the weight of it. It probably would have been sooner if he hadn't kept himself so busy, always buried in some research project or another. But he'd graduated, and he'd taken a weekend off, and he was sitting on a park bench staring at some pigeons splashing in a fountain when he thought, *Someday, I'm going to forget what this feels like.* It was a clear blue day, bracingly cold for the time of year —still pristine in Will's memory for now. At the time, it had made him feel an uncomfortable rush of sympathy for his father, and the years he, too, had spent waiting for the axe to fall.

Will realizes abruptly that his eyes are filled with tears, that standing in the middle of this room is starting to make him feel profoundly like screaming. He backs out quickly, trying to walk the fine line between not letting himself absorb any other details without wishing to *forget* any of what he's already noticed.

Once Will is back out in the hallway, in spite of feeling a bit foolish about it, he allows himself a moment to slump slightly against a wall. He wants a second to let his heart calm down, to feel less like he's in a horror movie. For God's sake, his mind is playing such aggressive tricks on him that he almost thinks he hears the back door shutting! He needs to take a few nice deep breaths and then...

Hell. It *wasn't* Will's mind playing tricks on him after all; the sound of unfamiliar footsteps across the first-floor vestibule is too loud and unmistakable to be memory messing him around.

Will glances wildly around him, trying to decide his best move. He knows a dozen ways out of this house, but every workable exit from this floor is through one of his bedroom windows, and there's no way Will could get to any of them right now without displacing the junk and making an enormous racket. If he could get to the bathroom, down at the end of the hall, he *might* still be able to shimmy his way out of the little window over the shower, but it's only a maybe. It was a tight fit when he was sixteen, and that was a long time ago.

He hears the footsteps approaching the stairs, and someone —burglar, intruder, whoever they are—whistling softly. Panicking, Will decides the bathroom is his best move and takes two hesitant steps towards the other side of the hall before the old house betrays him: a loud creak emanates up from the ancient pine floorboards, mockingly louder for Will's slow, hesitant footfall.

The whistling and the footsteps downstairs both abruptly cut off. Will swallows.

He glances around wildly for something to use as a weapon, now that confrontation seems all but inevitable. The framed photographs on the little wooden side table are too small, not heavy enough to do any real damage; the table itself is too large to be easily wielded; the lamp atop the table, too, is a bit too heavy to be workable, and anyway his mother would kill him if it broke—

Aaaand she's dead, Will reminds himself, somewhat hysterically, as he hears a single, ominous creak from below. *Nearly a decade now, isn't it? Focus!* His eyes light upon a broom leaned up against the corner of the hall, and he hurries over as quietly as he can and snatches it. It's not particularly heavy, but it will have to do, and after an awkward second of wrangling, Will lifts it in a two-handed grip, bristles up over his head, ready to attack.

He creeps over to the top of the stairs and peers down; he can't see anyone on the landing, but the turn beyond that is blind. Nothing to do but press forward.

He moves down one stair...

...and then the next...

...and as he goes, he tries to tell himself that he doesn't hear the softest, faintest creaks every time he moves his foot, or the equally soft creaks filtering back in reply from below...

...until he is, after what feels like hours, on the last stair left before the landing.

Will takes a huge breath, tightens his grip on the broom, and, with a slightly strangled war-cry that he would never have expected himself to release, jumps down onto the landing.

He crashes immediately into Casey, who has chosen this moment to do the exact same thing from the other side.

SIX

"AHH!" It takes Will a second to figure out who's screaming; then he realizes it's both of them. He snaps his mouth shut and reels for a second instead, reaching out a hand to steady himself on the railing so he doesn't tumble down the stairs and break his neck. Out of the corner of his eye, he sees Casey doing the same, which, horribly, is a relief.

Wait, *Casey*—

"What are *you* doing here?" Will demands, crossing his arms over his chest. Or, at least, he attempts to cross his arms over his chest; he forgets he's holding the broom and pokes himself aggressively in the side of the cheek with the handle, and has to settle for putting one hand on a hip instead.

"What am *I* doing here?" Casey repeats, incredulous. Will realizes, rather belatedly, that the other man seems to be holding one of Jillian's ancient parrot-headed umbrellas, left unused in the stand these last thirty-odd years. "I live here! What are *you* doing here?"

"You *live* here?" Will says, feeling his own eyes bulge. "You... I... This is my childhood home! Where I grew up! Those missing balusters in the staircase—" Will points a slightly trembling finger and then blinks, surprised, and continues, "Or, well, there *used* to be two missing balusters there, where I accidentally pulled them out trying to climb up the—oh, it doesn't matter! What do you mean you *live* here?"

Casey throws his hands in the air, which in the tight space of the landing causes him to, instead, thwack his hand hard against the broom handle. He hisses and shakes it, then says, "Oh, this is ridiculous. What were you going to do with a *broom*, and—I'm—just—come downstairs!" He wheels around and stalks back down to the first floor, Will hot on his heels in irritation and eagerness to put the stupid broom down.

The second Casey's feet are off the stairs, however, he turns back to Will, trapping him on the final step. "I live here! Who do you think fixed the balusters? Who do you think got the hot water back on, and the electric, and the gas—"

"The hot water and—you—God, can you at least let me through to put this *down*?" Will snaps. The house had *always* had hot water when he was growing up, and if the electric or the gas was out, it was never for more than a couple of days. How exactly had his father been living? "Or is it critical for this conversation that I be ready to sweep at a moment's notice?"

Casey crosses his arms, and, with a smirk, says, "I should make you take it back upstairs. It's the *upstairs* broom, as anyone who *lived here* would know."

"Oh, for the love of—" Will doesn't bother finishing the sentence, he just turns around and stomps back up the stairs, ignoring it when Casey groans and calls after him that he wasn't *serious*. When, to make a point to precisely no one, Will has carefully put it back exactly in the same position as he found it, he stomps back down the stairs and says, "There. The broom is back in its home and we can all die happy. May I pass now?"

"Christ, you are irritating," Casey mutters, but he steps aside with a sarcastic little hand gesture. "Look, are you *here* for something? Do you *want* something?"

FALL INTO YOU 91

"I want to know why you're living in my father's house!" Will says, taking advantage, finally, of the opportunity to cross his arms tightly over his chest. "Are you, like, squatting here?"

"What business would it be of yours if I was?"

"I mean, it is my house, technically," Will says, though the sentence is uncomfortable in his mouth, seems to leave a grating, unpleasant residue behind, like wet sand.

Casey rolls his eyes. "Not for long, though, right? You're going to sell out to Catherine Rose and that stupid company, like everyone else. Bill would be ashamed, you know—*he* saw all this for what it was... when he was seeing clearly."

"Gee," Will says, blinking wide, furious eyes, "do you think so? Do you think that Bill would be ashamed? That he wouldn't approve of me and who I've become? Gosh. That's something I'd *never* have worked out for myself, Casey, so really, thanks so much for enlightening me!" Abruptly solving the mystery of the gaming system, and then, somewhat more surprisingly, the queer books on the shelves, his mouth hardens. "You might be surprised, actually, by how many directions Bill's shame could run. If you'd known him the way I did, of course."

Will expects this to make Casey angry; instead, his brow furrows. "What does that mean?"

"Oh, what does it matter what it means," Will snarls, abruptly unwilling to delve even an inch further into that territory, never mind that he's the one who brought it up. He starts walking backwards towards the door. "It's not like you care what I have to say, right? Not like you bothered to try and *call* me before my father *died* to, I don't know, seek my opinion on his medical care? Inform me he was wasting away from the disease that'll probably—"

"For Christ's sake, *really*?" Casey snaps, though Will notices his face twists guiltily before shuttering hard. "You wanna go *there*? Don't act like you'd have had a damn thing to say, like you wanted to be involved! I remember how you were on that phone call—"

"Yeah, maybe that wasn't my *best moment*!" Will nearly shrieks this, too irritated to modulate his volume, shrillness, or tone. "But fine, sure, why *wouldn't* you base your entire opinion of who I am as a person on my very first reaction to the death of the man who gave me this—ugh!"

The "ugh" is not entirely intentional; it turns out to be the noise Will releases when he trips on some unseen obstacle that *shouldn't be there* and falls, hard, onto his ass. With a groan that's half pain, half embarrassment, Will runs a hand over his face, leaving it gripping over his nose and mouth to keep himself from screaming in annoyance, as he looks down the length of his legs to see—

"Why on *earth*," Will asks, in a low, dangerous voice, "is there a rug hiding a *two-inch hole* in my father's hardwood floor?"

"Because it was a twelve-inch hole!" Casey nearly bellows this, towering over Will, who is still flat on the floor, not quite able to muster the energy yet to stand back up. "It was here when I *got* here. Bill said there was an incident with a *bowling* ball, I didn't ask! But there wasn't enough spare wood to fill it after I finished all the other projects, and you know what, okay, there were a lot of projects, and I'm one person, and usually people aren't *walking backwards* over that weird corner of the floor. I was going to get to it eventually!"

"A bowling ball?" Will says, half-bewildered, staring up into Casey's twisting, angry face. With a hollow feeling in his gut, he thinks of the various accidents and incidents Old Bill had caused in the last years of his life, out of confusion, agitation, or both. Still: "My dad didn't even bowl!"

Casey's expression changes, morphing from one of irritation bordering on rage to one of sheepish realization. He must have noticed that he is, essentially, yelling at someone who has fallen

FALL INTO YOU 93

down and not yet gotten up, and he shifts, clearly discomfited. "Look, sorry about the hole. I didn't mean it to be a hazard, let me help you—"

"*No*," Will barks, suddenly full of energy again. He jumps up, bristling at the idea that he wants anything at all from Casey, let alone help. His body objects a little, but he ignores it. "Forget the stupid hole, it didn't... It doesn't... Look, I didn't come here to do this with you! I just wanted..."

God, what *had* Will wanted? Closure, maybe? A sense of peace? To confirm that both Bill and June were really, truly gone, and not playing a complicated prank on him, even though he knows, to his bones, that neither one of them could possibly have cared enough to bother with something like that? Maybe he'd wanted to see if any of it was still here: his teenage CD collection, his handful of classic comics, the books he'd loved enough to steal from the school library and claim had been lost in a farm accident.

"To bother me?" Casey suggests, his expression souring again. "You do seem to be pretty good at that."

This, for whatever reason, annoys Will so much that he forgets how to think for a minute. It's not the fact that he bothers Casey—that is an oddly satisfying piece of information—it's the total lack of *logic*. "I didn't even know that you *lived* here, man! How could I possibly be coming to bother you?"

"I'm sure you'd find a way."

"I could have just gone to the *market*, if that's what I'd wanted, why would I *ever* come *here* looking for *you*?"

"Oh please, it's easy enough to deduce that I'd be staying here—"

"Is it? *Is* it? Just because you're *working* here? A lot of people worked here when I was a kid, Casey, and nobody ever lived in this house but us!"

"Well, it's not like *you* were living here, or doing anything about any of the problems, and anyway, Noel *told* me you were sniffing around, so—"

This draws Will up short; he gasps. "After I *bribed* them? That little rat! What kind of respect for your queer elders is that, I ask you—*what*?"

A small smile is playing at the corners of Casey's mouth, though it's comically clear that he's attempting to suppress it. "Nothing, nothing. Just. Uh. You bribed Noel?"

"I *tried* to," Will mutters darkly. "Apparently, I didn't have enough cash on me, but the polite thing to do in that circumstance is *say*, really—"

"Oh, don't waste your money; you can't trust Noel," Casey says, with a little laugh. "Their grandfather died four times last year, and when I said, 'That seems like a lot of grandfathers, Noel, you maybe want to think of a different excuse this time?' they said, 'I don't see the point, Mr. Reeves; you know I'm lying, I know I'm lying, let's all get on with our lives, right?' And then they didn't come back to work for three days."

Will laughs in spite of himself. "God, *teenagers*. We get these interns at the lab, and you know, you'd think they'd care about this, be passionate? Every one of them has written some devastating essay about how better nutrition in early childhood would have improved their lives, and how deeply invested they are in the concept, and then they show up and all they want to do is find ways to get out of it."

Abruptly, Will realizes that he is just *talking* to this man, who hates him, and who, of course, he hates as well, because that's the only sane and natural reaction for a human being to have here. Obviously. So there's no reason for him to be *yammering pleasantly on* as though this is an old friend, instead of someone he nearly attacked with a broom a few minutes ago.

But before he can make his escape, Casey, brow furrowed, says, "Early childhood nutrition? I thought you said you were an apple scientist."

FALL INTO YOU   95

"Nobody is an apple scientist!" Will says this with a level of self-directed hysteria that he's sure comes across as slightly unhinged. Forging ruthlessly on, he continues, "It was a stupid thing to say, I just said it because... being here makes me... Oh, look, it doesn't matter. I'm a botanist, okay? And for the last ten years, I've been working on a project to grow apples infused with vitamin D."

Sounding cautious about it, like he's almost afraid of the answer, Casey says, "Why...?"

Will crosses his arms over his chest. He loves talking about his work, provided the other conversational party is, say, a fellow scientist, ideally also a botanist, and in the best possible scenario, also a botanist either focusing on work within his specific sector of bioengineering, or sharing his particular interest in the genus *Malus*. But talking about it with essentially anyone else is, more often than not, an agonizing, hair-raising nightmare. At best, Will comes across as boring; at worst, he has to endure a round of insipid-to-insulting questions, fired off at him by someone who mostly just wants to feel smart. And talking to this man, at this moment, in this house, he can't help but feel defensive, as though he's arguing for his funding all over again.

So he knows it comes out prickly, daring a challenge, when he says, "Because vitamin D is one of the most common deficits shown in children, *actually*, and it's worse for children from low-income families, or with inadequate nutritional access, or in places like *this* one, where the sun barely comes out from November to March! And, if you didn't know, deficiency in vitamin D can cause all kinds of problems for kids—bone- and muscle-growth issues, developmental challenges, they get sick more often, I could go on and on. Vitamin D doesn't occur naturally in apples, but they're a good source of other things kids need: iron, vitamin C, it's a long list. And they store well, too. So if we could create a cultivar that provides a daily dose of vitamin D, we could distribute them through school lunches, and share cuttings from the mother plant so it would be sort of— open access." Casey's staring at him, so Will adds, sharply, "We've almost cracked it, you know; you don't have to look at me like I'm crazy. The theory's solid, it's just about isolating the right—"

"I don't think it's crazy," Casey says, cutting him off. His eyes are wide. "I think it's *amazing*—can you really *do* that?"

"Oh," Will says, blinking. "I—I mean, yes. I think so, anyway. It's looking increasingly likely."

They stare at each other for a second; Casey's hair, Will notices, has a single twig caught in it, thin and easily missed. Briefly, he finds himself wanting to reach over and pluck it out, which is so wildly inappropriate that it throws him back, again, to the *reality of this situation*, which is that he is standing here with a man who he doesn't like, and who doesn't like him.

Casey must come to the same conclusion, because his face hardens again, and he snaps, "Well, that doesn't change the fact that you shouldn't be poking around in here when I'm not home. Bad enough that you're trying to strip away my livelihood —now you're after my house, too?"

"You—I—it's my house!" Will throws his hands in the air. "I don't—I just—I can't do this with you. I can't be here, it's too— just—good*bye*." And he wheels around without further cere- mony and stalks, in earnest, towards the door.

"Oh, okay," Casey says, his voice thin, needle-sharp. "Leave, then. I guess Bill *did* say that was your primary skillset."

Will stops dead a foot from the door. He should leave, right now. He knows that. He should *leave*. Nothing he allows to come out of his mouth, in this place, when his skin feels hot and too tight like this, ever leads to anything good. How many times, over the course of his childhood and especially his adolescence, had he stood in front of this door vibrating with this much tension, telling himself to just go? Telling himself it wasn't

FALL INTO YOU 97

worth the trouble of letting out whatever he was working so hard to keep in? Hasn't he learned *anything* in these past years? He should walk out, like he should have walked every time before, like he did, eventually, walk out.

Trembling, knowing even as he does it that it's a mistake, Will turns around.

"Do you know what," Will says. He means it to come out low, ferocious; instead it's high and reedy, little fault-line cracks around his vowels where emotion is spilling out. "I've had just about enough of being told what the old man thought of me, you know that? That's *enough*. Maybe the two of you braided each other's hair or exchanged friendship bracelets or *whatever*, and, like, *good for you*, but he and I, as you *clearly* know, weren't exactly the best of pals! And you can believe me or not, okay, but there was nothing I could have *done* about that, because he wanted me to be someone I just—wasn't! I wasn't that person! And now he's dead, so—"

Will stops, drawn to an abrupt, hideous halt. Bill is *dead*. He's *dead*. It's not that Will didn't know, objectively, that this was true; it's not that the relationship hasn't been dead for decades; it's not that he's under any illusions about the nature of death, or of the relationship. It was always going to end this way, with Will hearing about it after the fact, and having to pick up the pieces, fill in the blanks.

But—as Will had learned when his mother had died—grief has neither time for nor interest in logic. God, this had happened *later* with her, after the funeral, after Nancy; he'd been back in Chicago, a month and a half later, trying to order at a stupid bakery counter. She'd always loved a cherry Danish, which had annoyed Will's father, because cherries were one of the few things they didn't grow, and he'd seen a particularly nice one sitting there, and it had all hit him. That he'd never again see her eat another cherry Danish, or feel her tight grip close on his shoulder, or hear her mutter to herself as she strug-

98   DYLAN MORRISON

gled to solve a newspaper crossword. He had started crying, silently but unstoppably, right there in the middle of the bakery, and had to rush out past the other patrons, who had at least been very polite and Midwestern about it.

Will cannot—he *cannot*—burst into tears in front of Casey Reeves. It would be worse than bursting into tears in the middle of a Chicago bakery, which was at least relatively anonymous, and also over his mother; Will and June had, at least, kept vaguely in touch for a few years after Will left, until she decided it was too difficult keeping it from Will's father. Still, it was better than nothing, and better to cry over her than Bill, and better to cry in front of *anyone* than the tall, blond slice of *aggressive unpleasantness* who stands, ashen, before him.

"Will," Casey says. It's a very different voice, and, slowly, Will processes the expression on Casey's blood-drained face, the harmonics of his tone. The bottom is dropping out of his stomach even as Casey, quietly, says, "I'm sorry, you're right, he was your father and you're obviously—"

"Oh, *don't*," Will says, wrapping his arms around himself unconsciously, his voice clipped and wretched even to his own ears. "Don't say whatever sympathetic thing you're going to say, just—God, I can't. Leave me *alone*, all right?"

A line of irritation appears in Casey's forehead, but his tone is still struggling towards compassion as he says, "Man, listen, if you could chill for a second, you'd see that I'm trying to—"

"I know what you're trying to do!" Will's voice is shrill, now, embarrassingly so, but he doesn't care. "You're trying to say that you're *sorry* my stupid father is dead, because now it seems like I *cared* about him, but I didn't! I don't! So just—just—keep it to yourself!"

And then, without giving Casey another instant to reply, Will flees.

It is, once he's truly decided to go, a very quick escape: three steps to the door while Casey swears quietly behind him, six

FALL INTO YOU 99

more across the porch, eyes ahead, unstoppable. It always was that way, he remembers, wry even over his pounding heart, as he hurries down the porch steps, through the stand of black walnuts and maples, across the large open field that is used for various farm and private events throughout the year, and into the parking lot.

The weather has turned while he was in the house; what was, before, distantly threatening rain has now abandoned the concept of distance and is clearly moments from letting go of "threatening" as well. The air is swollen and slightly thick, and the faint, coppery smell of lightning is hard to mistake, familiar from a childhood getting caught in a variety of storms. He picks up his pace when he hears a rumble of thunder that sounds a little close for comfort, relieved to see his depressing beige rental exactly where he left it.

His relief, however, is short-lived.

When he throws himself into the front seat and turns the car on, the engine makes a... sound. Will is no expert in mechanics, unless those mechanics have the word "bio" in front of them and fall within a very specific school of research and thought, but he does consider himself possessed of basic common sense. And it's common sense that tells him the sound the engine makes is not a good sound. It's more a sound that might inspire someone to mutter the word "Uh-oh."

"Uh-oh," Will mutters, looking balefully at the dashboard. It doesn't pop up any helpful information, such as, "That noise was the result of the following problem, which is explained thoroughly and in layman's terms here," or "If you continue to drive this machine, you will perish in 17.35 minutes." Instead, it displays a little symbol that Will can't remember having seen before.

He hasn't driven a car more than a handful of times in the last sixteen years, and he's sure he *should* know what it means, but he doesn't.

In his rearview mirror, he sees Casey coming through the tree line, probably on his way back to the market. Will decides the engine is a problem for later—possibly but hopefully not 17.35 minutes from now—and that currently, his main focus needs to be on being somewhere, *anywhere* else.

He backs the car out of the spot, pulls it out of the parking area, and gets it about halfway down the tiny private road connecting Robertson Family Farms to the nearest major street, where the car sputters, makes a noise unsettlingly like a wheeze, and unceremoniously dies. The whole thing comes to a shuddering standstill, the engine whining into silence, the power flickering off.

And as Will stares at the now-useless dashboard, mouth open, stunned into shocked, overwhelmed silence by how much has gone wrong so quickly, he hears, on the car roof above him, the sudden but ferocious pitter-patter of the sky opening up.

SEVEN

For a moment, Will sits there, letting pure, unfiltered emotion caterwaul within him. He learned to do this first as a child, knowing from bitter experience that he was better off keeping his feelings contained, but he *really* perfected it when he started working in a lab. That's what taught him that, for example, sometimes it's four in the morning, and you're neck-deep in a delicate experiment extremely critical to the completion of your thesis, and at exactly the wrong moment, your useless lab-mate Larry, who is exploring an utterly asinine theory about giving caffeine to worms, decides to start blasting death metal at earsplitting volumes. At a time like that, a person might want to really *snap*, might want to shriek and scream and throw things and tell Larry to take his terrible music and his awful haircut and his stupid unethical jittery worms and get out of the lab before someone *killed* him.

But a person—or, at least, Will—couldn't do things like that. Will had to keep it together, and be a professional, and *not* get drummed out of a small, gossipy scientific community, which, from the earliest days and not exactly incorrectly, has always viewed Will as a bit of a weirdo. It's not that it was an unfair

102 DYLAN MORRISON

assessment, since Will had not exactly socialized much for the bulk of his academic career, finding more comfort in data and facts than he did amongst his peers. And so he got good, very good, at letting the scream he wanted to release build up inside him, swell in his lungs and catch in his throat, make it all the way to knocking against the back of his teeth in eagerness to be let out... only to grit his molars and swallow it, get on with the job.

He does it now, closing his eyes and letting the hysteria bubble and boil within him for as long as he can stand before pushing it down again. It's almost cathartic. Almost.

It lets him get on with things, at least, and Will sighs as he opens his eyes, takes a deep breath, and looks around the car. Nothing useful that he can see in the way of tools, and there hadn't been any information about who to call in the event of a breakdown; Catherine Rose's office set the car rental up for him, and had a driver drop it off the morning of Will's departure. He'd been a little excited about that, in spite of everything—the prospect of a driver bringing it by had made him anticipate something sleek and high-end—and he'd been more than a little let down by the sad, unpleasantly beige little sedan.

Will had felt guilty about that at the time, like he was turning up his nose at a privilege, a kindness. Just at this moment, however, he's quite sure that he should have called Catherine back and insisted the driver return with something else.

There's nothing for it now, though, and no helpful stickers or information vis-à-vis what to do if the car quits on you in the middle of a very unpleasant Saturday afternoon. On the theory that it's a practical option that delays him getting wet for at least another minute or two, Will checks the glove compartment, where there should be an owner's manual. He finds instead the manual for an entirely different vehicle in type, make and model, though it is, Will notes darkly, the same *year* as this car.

FALL INTO YOU   103

A mix-up at the rental place, probably; Will is beginning to think it might be less a rental place and more a really bad car thief with a lot of spare time on his hands. Regardless, since Will is *not* actually sitting in a souped-up pickup truck that runs on diesel fuel, he dismisses the little booklet as useless to him and pulls out his phone, turns to the internet instead.

Service is bad and slow, so the only thing he's able to get in response to his search query—"car dead why????"—is a half-loaded page of barely readable results. Still, the common theme is to check the battery, and Will decides this is good enough advice. How hard could a battery be to check?

Steeling himself, he gets out of the car.

The drenching effect is instantaneous. God, Will had forgotten about this, about the way it can *rain* here. It's not that it doesn't pour in Chicago; it's not called the Windy City for nothing, and is battered regularly with huge, terrifying storms, even weathers the occasional tornado. But in Chicago, you are always surrounded by *more Chicago*, tall buildings slicing the sky down into little slivers. If you got caught in the rain in the city, you could duck into a nearby store or restaurant, or under an awning, or hop in a cab, or hurry to the nearest spot to catch the train. And so, no matter how hard it was coming down, there was a certain impermanence to the weather there, a sense that it was merely in the background.

But out here, with nothing for miles to cut even a single line through the arcing dome of the sky, there's no background for the rain to fade into. The storm that pelts furiously down onto Will's head, plastering his hair to his scalp in seconds, is the foreground of the entire area around him, more urgently present than the farm or the town or even Will's dead car.

Thunder claps directly overhead and Will starts, remembering suddenly, as though pulling it from a dust-covered box deep in his mental attic, how much time he spent during his youth out in weather like this. He'd always hated it, to be cold and damp and miserable and know it didn't matter, that he had to finish his chores or walk home, no matter the weather. He hadn't even noticed himself pack that away, but as he walks around to the front of the car and feels rain dripping down inside his collar and along the line of his back, he realizes he can't remember the last time he let himself get caught in this kind of rain. Has he been avoiding it subconsciously, then? And if he has, then how much *else* is tucked away here on the family farm, under the floorboards in that old house, or hidden up in the rafters of the market, or buried down in the dirt amongst the apple trees' roots?

Will is distracted from this disquieting thought when he attempts to open the hood of the car. He pulls; it doesn't move. He pulls again; it doesn't move. He pulls again, and this time something moves, but it's something unfortunate, and it's in Will's back—the hood doesn't budge.

He swears, steps away, and remembers very belatedly that you have to *unlatch* the hood of a car before it opens, so it doesn't *blow up in front of the windshield on the highway and kill you*. Swearing again at his stupidity, Will gets back into the car, soaking the front seat as he does, and spends several increasingly frustrating minutes looking for the latch release. When he finally finds it, it's in such an obvious place that Will does almost lose it and start screaming, but he strangles it back, barely, and gets out of the car again.

The hood opens this time. Will props it up as well as he can, and then, staring down into the guts of the car, runs up against his next problem.

Will doesn't know how to check the battery. Will, to be perfectly honest, doesn't even know which of these various intimidating metal and plastic shapes the battery *is*.

"Are *you* the battery?" he asks the large metal block in the center. It doesn't answer; he reaches out to touch it and then yanks his hand away hastily at the temperature. Shaking it out,

FALL INTO YOU 105

he mutters, "Okay, no, that was stupid, you are clearly the engine. Also, *ow*." Will knows it's not a great sign that he's progressed to talking to the car, but he's also reasonably sure it's not a great sign that he can feel the rain starting to soak through his jacket and into the inner layers of his clothes, so. Perhaps best, in such a circumstance, to simply accept things are not great and carry on.

"Okay," he mutters to himself. "You're a scientist. You have a PhD, for God's sake; this is not that complicated. Process of elimination. A battery has a positive and negative end, so you have to look for—there!" Flush with his success, Will leans over what appears to be a plastic block with a positive and a negative symbol marked on either side.

The next step, however, eludes him. He stares down at the red and black plastic pieces on either side of the battery block, and starts, rather wretchedly, to laugh.

"Well," he says, not noticing or caring about the edge of hysteria slipping into it. "I've checked it! There it is! One battery! It's in there! Who needs a mechanic?" On the theory that perhaps it's like a phone and just needs a factory reset, he tries pushing on both the plastic pieces on top of the box, hoping against hope that they're buttons.

They are not buttons. They also are not knobs, although Will does twist them for a while, and have a bit of panic when the red one comes off in his hand, before realizing very belatedly that they are *caps*. He stares down at the bare metal bolt the red cap revealed, removes the black one, and experiences, deep in the horror chamber that is his current mental landscape, a montage of every time he's ever seen a pair of jumper cables in film or television. They have alligator clips at the end, don't they? Like something might need to clamp on a bolt?

At this point, Will starts laughing again, but there's nothing even remotely mirthful about it—it's more despair than happiness, the noise a body makes when it knows it won't be allowed

106 DYLAN MORRISON

to cry. Shivering, Will doesn't bother trying to contain it as he checks the trunk, and then the back seat, and then the trunk again for jumper cables. He doesn't find any, which doesn't matter, because there's no one else here to jump the car if the battery is dead, which he can't check, because he doesn't know how.

With the jaunty spirit of the well and truly doomed, Will pastes a bright grin on his face, walks back to the front of the car, and replaces the caps on the battery bolts. He also slams the hood shut with an unnecessarily forceful bang. Then he gets back in the car, rictus grin still in place, inserts the key into the ignition with a stiffness borne both of cold and distress, and turns the engine over.

The car doesn't do him the courtesy of emitting a single sound.

Will lets his grin fall first; then he lets his head fall, wincing as it squelches slightly against the steering wheel. He decides, in the proud tradition of his name, to give up.

He can't really give up, of course. However much he might like to, he can't sit here until the grass grows up over him and this stupid horrible useless waste of a car, until birds nest in his hair and hedgehogs build a home in his lap. He will, at some point, have to get up. Do something. Walk back, probably, to the Robertson Family Farms market, through its new, cheerful yellow door, and admit right to Casey Reeves's infuriating, unfairly chiseled face that he is a helpless idiot baby who can't even manage a simple rental car.

No, Will decides with a shudder. He simply can't do that; it isn't in him. It'll have to be the hedgehogs after all.

For a long time—he's not sure how long—he just sits there, his head against the steering wheel. But then, to his slow, crystalizing horror, he hears footsteps approach. And then, much worse, a voice.

"You know what?" God help him, it's Casey, walking up

FALL INTO YOU   107

from behind from the farm parking lot. Will thinks very hard about evaporating—surely, if nothing else, he's wet enough. "I can't sit in there looking at the tail end of your ugly car through the shop window, *waiting* for you to make up your mind about coming back in to mess up the rest of my afternoon. So tell me: What is it?" Will can see Casey's face in the side mirror now, dripping wet and twisted up with anger. "On top of everything else, you can't just leave? You had to wait, and make me come out here in the rain, to say whatever else it is you *have* to say about how terrible this place is and how much you can't wait to be rid of it? Is that it?"

Will does not like to lose control of himself. He was raised to bottle things up, to put them away on a shelf, and to stare at that shelf in resentful silence in his own private time. But as he climbs out of the rental car, wet and angry and upset and still seeing the image of those stupid, heartbreaking Post-it notes every time he so much as blinks his eyes, he is at the very end of his rope. And when he turns around, and takes in the full picture of Casey, dripping wet, clothes clinging to his thick thighs and broad chest like something directly out of Will's hindbrain *except* for the expression of total disgust on his face, Will lets that rope go.

"What is your DAMAGE," he yells, stalking towards Casey, whose expression changes from twisted rage to surprised confusion as Will approaches. "Can't you see my stupid CAR has broken down and I don't WANT to be here?" God, Will's voice is breaking; he tries his best to ignore it. "I'm sorry you HATE me, but you can just GO INSIDE! And leave me out here to drown!"

But then Casey yells back, "Well, why didn't you just SAY that then, or come back to the HOUSE instead of standing out in the RAIN? How was *I* supposed to know? You don't even have the hood open!"

"I closed the hood!" Will more or less screams this, even

108   DYLAN MORRISON

though Casey is close enough now that he doesn't need to shout anymore. "I closed the hood, because I'm supposed to check if the battery's dead, but I don't know how to check if the battery's dead, so there's no point! In having the hood open! And anyway, I didn't think you'd be particularly eager to help me, since you seem to be hoping that I fall into the nearest MANHOLE and—"

"If you'd have just *asked* me to help you, I would have," Casey cries, throwing up his hands. "Have you just been sitting out here in—honestly, what's *wrong* with you? Just because I don't agree with what you're doing here doesn't mean I'm a *terrible person. And* I know how to jump a stupid battery!"

"Well—then I guess—thank you!" Will's voice comes out as a strangled yelp this time, as some of the anger that was fueling him starts to drain away.

There's a beat, and then Casey, in a voice only slightly louder than what Will has come to understand is his usual register, says, "Why are we yelling at each other?"

Will stares at him, searching himself for an answer, and draws only a shivery, ice-cold blank. This time, when he starts to laugh, it's genuine, although the edge of hysteria is still there. And it's drowned out, anyway, that harsh edge, when Casey joins him, his deep, baritone laugh richer and more inviting than Will's, seeming to shake his own body. For just a second, it crowds out even the thunder.

"I don't know," Will admits, shaking his head and still chuckling, after a minute. "God—I don't know. Look, I'm— sorry, okay? I didn't come here trying to mess everything up for you, I'm not... This isn't... I'm not, uh." He swallows, hard, against the idea of admitting this, but something about Casey's bright, inquisitive gaze seems to pull it out of him: "I'm not exactly doing great right now, so. Uh. I'm sorry." Quickly, before he has to bear a reply to that, he adds, "Can you really help with the car?"

FALL INTO YOU   109

Casey pauses for a second, seeming to consider his answer. Then: "Yeah," he says, with a little sigh. "I've got a lot of experience with cars. But one thing I know for sure is that it's not a great idea to mess around with jumping a battery in a lightning storm. I think you should let me tow her back into the lot. We can do the jump once the weather's calmed down."

"And until then, I just... what?" Will says, trepidation mounting. "Wait around out here?"

Rolling his eyes, Casey says, "I mean, in the market, yeah. Or in the house, if you want. Might be better, and I do know it's... uh, technically yours, or whatever."

"Generous of you," Will mutters under his breath, regretting it immediately, but Casey's looking away, and a roll of thunder blots it out. He tries again: "Um. Thanks? If you really don't mind towing the car—"

But Casey's already jogging off, calling, "I didn't say I didn't mind! I said that I *would*," over his shoulder, which, Will notes, is not very reassuring at all.

He trudges soggily after Casey, his cold, wet clothes heavy and clinging. But he quickly realizes, watching Casey pull a dark blue vintage pickup truck out of the staff garage, that Casey has no need of him, and is capable of handling this process entirely by himself. Pointlessly—it's not as though there's any part of him left to keep dry—Will shuffles over to stand under the market awning. He can't bring himself to go inside, to step again through the yellow door to the strange, changed world within, but he can't bring himself to go back to the house without Casey, either. It's too... awkward. It feels, now that Will has a slightly better grip on the situation, like crossing a line, even though logically he knows he has more right to the house than Casey does.

Still, he stands there, shuddering slightly, cold to the point that he's stopped feeling it or thinking particularly clearly. He watches as Casey, in the distance, pulls up in front of Will's

110   DYLAN MORRISON

rental, hops out of the cab, pulls some hook-ended chains out of the truck bed, and starts setting up the tow. In spite of being every inch as wet as Will, his body language communicates the easy good cheer of an action figure, or perhaps a cartoon—Will bets that Casey's *whistling*, the bastard, and he just can't hear it at this distance over the rain.

A sharp voice, unsettlingly like Selma's, stirs from a cat-like sleep in the back of Will's mind. *Hmm*, it says, *let's try this again. Instead of simmering in needless resentment, have you considered approaching the incredibly handsome, apparently unmarried, devastatingly muscled man who labors cheerfully before you in a friendlier spirit? Have you thought about suggesting you work out some of this tension between you in a more productive way? Have you, even once, entertained the idea of saying, "Hey, Casey, thanks so much for helping with my car, why don't you let me repay you with a—"*

"Nope!" Will says aloud, through slightly chattering teeth. "Nope, nope, nope." That's enough indulging of his inner Selma; she can't be trusted. The real Selma is also a fountain of bad ideas, but sometimes they're bad ideas that turn out to be weirdly good ideas, and when they aren't, she's always there to bail Will out of the consequences. The Selma of Will's mind, however, is merely a reflection of his own baser impulses, and lacks Selma's discernment, taste, and understanding of the criminal code. He's learned a few times too many that he's better off not taking her advice.

He could call the real Selma, of course. She'd be bound to have something helpful to say, once she finished ripping him a new one for going essentially radio silent on her. But talking to Selma about something is always a double-edged sword, at least in Will's experience; she would be helpful, certainly, but it would come at a price. In getting the story out of Will, she'd get everything out of him, even the pieces of it he doesn't want to look at, or isn't ready to see. He loves her, of course he loves her, but he can't quite bear her just now. Talking to her always shows him too much of himself.

Guiltily, he pulls out his phone, spends a few slow minutes searching and battling the patchy signal, and then orders Selma a box of chocolates described as, "A variety of lewd confections to delight both the sweetest of tooths and the dirtiest of minds." He includes a card that says, "Made me think of you," then types and deletes a longer message three times, and finally places the order.

With nothing else to do, he just waits and watches until the car is safely in the lot, and Casey's pulled the truck back into the staff garage. He walks out, as Will had feared, *visibly whistling*, and wiping his hands on the tails of his still-soaked white-and-green flannel work shirt, but his expression drops into a scowl when he sees Will huddled under the awning. Of course.

"What are you still doing out here?" Casey demands, crossing his arms over his chest. "I thought you were going to go in, or back to the house—"

"I didn't want to be..." Will says, trying and failing to suppress a visible shudder. "...rude, or whatever. Just go barging in." He pauses, and adds, "I mean, uh. Again."

"Common sense just doesn't run in your family, huh?" Casey mutters. Giving Will's soaked, shivering form a brief once-over and shaking his head, he adds, "Come on, then!" He wheels around and starts stalking towards the house.

Will follows him a few steps behind. His thoughts, he notices, have slowed down considerably; though normally guilty of thinking about seventeen things at once, he is currently down to one at a time. They float past him lazily, in no hurry at all to make room for his next worry or idea or thing to say. One of them is the thought that he *should* say something, but after some intense consideration, he dismisses it on merit of not knowing what.

So he follows Casey, feeling meek and foolish and extremely ridiculous, back across the field and through the copse of trees and up the stairs and across the porch of the house he, less than an hour ago, so emphatically ran away from. As he steps through the threshold behind Casey, pulling the door closed behind him, he mutters, "Thanks."

"Don't mention it," Casey says, looking away, and sounding too uncomfortable to be saying it out of Midwestern politeness. "I wasn't going to, like, *leave* you out there. You were..." He pauses, and swallows, before continuing. "You were blocking the road."

"Right," Will says, for some reason feeling a little scrape of disappointment he can't quite place. "Traffic hazard. I get it." He rubs his hands over his arms, willing the soaked fabric of his sweater to dry faster.

Casey gives him a doubtful look. "Sorry, but what are you doing, exactly?"

Will scowls at him. "What does it look like I'm doing? I'm trying to speed up the drying process."

"By method of rubbing?" Casey shakes his head; for a second, it almost looks like he's trying not to smile. "That's not a recommended approach in any of the survival books, you know."

"Well, what other choice do I have?" Will snaps, nettled and cold and so uncertain of his footing here that he barely knows where to step at all, and so might as well be honest. "My clothes—these clothes, on my body—are the only clothes I'm wearing today! The rest of the stuff I brought is in my suitcase, which is in my hotel, which is forty-five minutes away, and if there's anything left from when I was a teenager, it's trapped behind Junk Mountain." He pauses, and, considering, adds, "And, I mean, in fairness, it has been a long time; it probably wouldn't fit me, anyway. So I have to make do with what I've got."

"If only someone had invented a machine," Casey says, in tones of mock thoughtfulness. "One that you could use to make wet clothes dry. Almost like a... hmm, what's it called... dryer?"

Rolling his eyes and, crucially, not thinking before speaking, Will says, "I would *love* to put these in the dryer, Casey, really, I would, but the thing is, *again*, they are the only clothes I've currently got, so unless you want me walking around the house naked—"

Will pauses. And freezes. And tries, in a second that drips slow and thick through his mind like so much molasses, to tell himself that Casey didn't hear it, or that he can somehow turn back time a crucial few seconds and wind the words right back into his mouth.

But Casey's cheeks flush, anyway, the flare of crimson surprising Will almost as much as the way his expression flickers, from annoyance to surprise to something Will's not sure how to interpret, but can't look away from. Their eyes meet, and for a brief and beautiful instant, Will's back in those first moments in the market, only *yesterday* somehow. He's looking up at this unexpected, unlikely man, and seeing in his cool green gaze a whole host of possibilities Will normally wouldn't even allow himself to consider.

Will hates Casey, of course. Maybe he didn't the moment they met, but from the next moment, and in every moment since, he's been insufferable and impossible; Will can't stand the man, no doubt. But it's occurring to him—he can't, in fact, make it *stop* occurring to him—that *liking* and *wanting* are not necessarily the same. That Will doesn't have to like Casey at *all* to wish Casey would push him up against the doorframe, redirect all the grating, frustrating parts of his unfortunate personality into making him Will scream at him in a new, more productive way. That what Will wants to do with his clothes is neither wear nor dry them, but let Casey pull them off him one by one, ripping them if that's what it takes, as they stumble together

114   DYLAN MORRISON

towards the nearest couch or bed or rug. That, in fact, the hungry look that has appeared in Casey's eyes is all the more thrilling *because* they don't like each other; because whatever happened between them wouldn't have to be nice, or polite, or considered, or appropriate. It's not like anything has been between them so far, and in every other respect that's been dreadful, but now it makes Will's whole body thrum with a sort of nervous, anticipatory tension that reminds him, distantly, of riding a roller coaster.

Then Casey's face shutters and, his voice suddenly remote, he says, "Yeah, probably for the best that you restrain yourself."

Whatever strange feeling was swelling within Will like a balloon pops unceremoniously, leaving the confetti of his burgeoning hope strewn across his mind. Without another word, Casey crosses the hall, climbs the stairs, and disappears up to the second floor.

"Well, great," Will mutters to himself. "That's just great. I'll stay here in the hallway then, freezing slowly to death, don't worry about old Will, nothing to see here—" A thud on the stairs cuts him off, and Will whips his head up just in time to see the source of the second thud hit the hardwood. Curious, he approaches, and in spite of himself, knowing it's idiotic and pointless and hardly worth it and setting himself up for embarrassment in any case, his stupid heart can't help but beat a little faster in his stupid chest when he realizes what he's looking at.

Casey has thrown down, from the second floor, a pair of sweatpants, a T-shirt, a sweatshirt, and a towel.

EIGHT

Essentially the entire first floor of the farmhouse is visible to the outside world, at least if you choose the right window; Will, resigned to his fate, scoops up the clothes and heads for the Lime.

The Lime had once been known as the Lime Green Powder Room. This, to the best of Will's handed-down knowledge, had been in the 1970s, when the house had been under Jillian's control—it was an era where a certain sort of woman in late middle age went wild and painted low-stakes rooms green, and when people still said "powder room" instead of "bathroom" or "toilet." Jillian had been shooting for a reasonable, respectable shade of sage, but what she had ended up with was a sickly, almost-neon green bathroom, which evoked nothing more than the sense of being in a chemical accident. Unable to afford a new round of paint, she'd quite emphatically insisted that the color was a very intentional selection of lime green, and things had proceeded accordingly. By the time Will was a child, the bathroom had been referred to as "the Lime" for so long that he'd thought, for years longer than was acceptable, that a lime was another name for a toilet.

116 DYLAN MORRISON

He walks in now, already pulling his sodden sweater and shirt off over his head, grateful to be rid of them. He makes quick work of stripping down and drying off, shimmying into the clothes Casey tossed down to him with a groan of gratitude —he'd almost forgotten what it was like to be both warm and dry. He sits down on top of the closed toilet for a second, taking a deep breath, reveling in the sensation of basic comfort. Looking down at himself, he starts to smile; he is, he realizes, wearing head-to-toe farm merchandise. Kudos to Casey, he's guessed Will's sizing right; every piece of bright red, clearly holiday-themed clothing fits him perfectly, and something about that is oddly satisfying, for reasons he's not prepared to consider. He settles, instead, for glancing around him with the smug self-satisfaction he'd never risk if anyone had any chance of seeing him.

It bears strange fruit, this little moment of smugness, because after a second, Will notices the Lime is... different.

It takes him a while to place it, but the color hits him first. The green is the wrong shade—the color that assaulted one's eyes while using the facilities in the Lime was not a good color, but it was unforgettable. If lime green could vomit, was the experience... or maybe if an olive and a yellow highlighter had a child.

The color on the walls now is green. Not the strange, unsettling green of before—this is a bright, clear yellow-forward green you'd find on the rind of an actual lime. It even shifts, Will notices as he looks around the small bathroom, yellower in some places and more chartreuse in others, like the skin of an actual lime.

Will stands at this point, and leans in close to be sure—oh, wow, there's *texture*. The particular stippled texture of citrus rind, worked into the wall. It must have taken someone *ages* to do, and...

God. "Someone." As if Will doesn't know exactly who it

FALL INTO YOU   117

was. As if Will couldn't just walk upstairs and ask him about it. "Hey, seems like you did something really awesome and interesting with an inside joke my family left alone out of amusement and then simmering resentment for fifty-odd years, good for you," might not be the best conversation opener, but it wouldn't be the worst, either. Would it be better or worse than, "Hey, it seems like you do all kinds of weird, interesting art projects around here—that's neat, don't you think? I think it's neat, anyway, unless that makes you hate me even more, in which case I feel totally neutral about it and forget I said anything at all." What about a good, old fashioned, "Hey, it seems like we got off on the wrong foot, is there any chance you're kind of a cool person? Because I'm not, but hey, if you are, that might be nice."

It doesn't come to that, anyway. As Will leaves the Lime behind, a pile of wet clothes balanced precariously in one hand and soaked shoes in the other, a knock sounds at the front door.

"Coming!" Will calls automatically, and then winces; it's not his house. Or, well, no, it *is* his house, technically, but no one is likely to be coming by for him. But Casey doesn't yell anything down, so Will decides he might as well follow through on his promise, however automatic it might have been. He leaves his shoes on the mat, and his clothes, after a moment's agonized thought, in a tight little ball on top of the shoes.

The knock sounds again, annoying Will; don't they know he's working on it? "I'm *coming*, you're going to *live*," Will snarls, not caring how much he sounds like himself at fifteen, but he does hurry the last few steps to the door.

It's Noel on the other side, because why wouldn't it be.

"*You*," Noel says, as though *they're* the aggrieved one of the two of them. Then, their jaw dropping open: "Oh my God, is that the new sweatset? For the store? For Christmas? He said we weren't allowed to see them yet! He said we had to wait until we put them out for the guests—I drew the design on that

118   DYLAN MORRISON

one, you know," Noel says, pointing proudly at Will's sweatshirt.

Will looks a little closer and realizes that what he'd thought was a Christmas tree is, in fact, a little apple tree, one fruit still on it like an ornament, strung loosely with string lights. In spite of being swindled by this child earlier this very afternoon, Will can't help but feel a certain fondness for them as he looks upside down at their handiwork. "I like it."

"Thanks," Noel says, grinning and then ducking their head, seeming abruptly to go shy. It only lasts a merciful half a second, though; after that they lean over Will's shoulder, stick their head into the body of the house, and yell, "Hey, Casey!"

A pause. Then, filtering down from what sounds like quite far away, "Yeah?"

"You know this dude's in your house, first of all?" Noel gives Will an apologetic look at this, as though sorry to blow up his spot. "In the Christmas sweats?"

"*Yes*, Noel. Is that all?" Casey's voice sounds closer now, like maybe he's leaning over the stair landing.

"No. Mrs. Baumcombe is at the market? She's here to pick up her order for next Saturday."

A pause. Then, wearily, as though knowing there's little point in saying it: "Is she aware that it's currently *this* Saturday?"

"Yes," Noel says, as solemnly as one can while yelling to a person on a different floor. "And yet. There she is! Hungry for the pies of next Saturday. Twelve of them, in fact."

Footfalls on the stairs; then Casey appears on the landing, changed into a pair of charcoal jeans and a new, less wet flannel shirt, this one grey-and-black plaid. Eyebrows up, he says, "Do we not have twelve pies we could give her now?" He makes eye contact with Will and, with an odd, hard to read expression, pulls a small lump out of his pocket and wiggles it at him, then tosses it over.

FALL INTO YOU 119

Will catches it, barely, and realizes after a second that it's a pair of clean, dry socks.

"Oh, easily," says Noel, not seeming to notice Will's wide-eyed, blinking surprise at all, and punctuating it with a wave of their hand. Will gets the sense that they're really enjoying themselves, and maybe thought about how they were going to present this on the way over here. "We have pies enough to fill her request and then some! But she doesn't want any of the pies we have. She wants *her* pies, Casey. That we're going to be baking. Specifically for her. And no one else. *Next* Saturday. When she ordered them." With a wide, beatific grin, they add, "I'm terribly afraid she wants to see a manager."

"Christ almighty," Casey mutters, reaching the bottom of the stairs. "Of course she does." He turns and, putting a hand to the back of his neck and not quite meeting Will's eyes, says, "You're welcome to hang out here, if you want, but there's more to eat at the market, so. You can borrow a pair of my extra boots, if your shoes are still drying out. Over on the mat by the door."

Feeling the heat of Noel's curious stare drilling into his skull, Will tells himself very firmly not to flush, or rub at the back of his neck, or go on any kind of face journey at all— teenagers can smell fear. He simply steps into a pair of Casey's workboots, which are worn and broken in and about half a size too big for Will, but should be fine enough for walking around in, and says, "Thanks."

"Sure," Casey says, without looking at him, and leads the way out of the house.

Will notices as they do it, that they're all, without having to talk about it, taking the Unofficial Market Employee Rainy Day Break Run Route. Nobody who had worked in the market when Will was a kid had wanted to spend a second of their break time in there if they didn't have to. He'd passed them outside in the parking lot, or, if the weather was particularly brutal, huddled up in one corner of the farmhouse's wraparound porch, praying

120   DYLAN MORRISON

Old Bill wouldn't see them and kick up some dramatic fuss. And if he did, the trick to get from farmhouse to market without getting wet was just a matter of knowing where to step in the tight little tree line, hugging close to it around the back end of the field, letting the trees shield you from the worst of whatever the sky wanted to throw at you until you could dash under the cover of the market's large awning.

Will finds himself oddly exuberant to be doing it now, hastily clamping down on his grin when he notices Casey looking him over assessingly. It's just... the familiarity, he thinks, that's all. Like singing a song you've forgotten over the years, only to realize, bar by bar, that all the words are still floating around inside you, packed away in a corner but never lost. Will is pleased, in spite of the hopes he'd had at the time, not to have burned away all he once carried of Glenriver and the farm, and the life he'd thought, once, was the only future he'd ever be allowed.

Maybe it's this spirit that carries him into the backed-up market, oddly crowded for such a rainy afternoon. Maybe it's this spirit that, as Casey picks up the frustrating pie thread with Mrs. Baumcombe and Noel steps back behind the safety of the apple display, moves Will not only to round the corner into the bakery, but to take a deep breath, and start walking towards the counter.

It's good to see the old bakery again, even if there's a line of irritated-looking people waiting to be helped. It's good to smell the rich mixture of apple and vanilla and caramel and butter, somehow just as Will remembers it and also deeper, more refined. It's good to hear the soft purr of the flame in the commercial ovens lick on and off, more soothing than any white noise machine.

But mostly, it's good to see Daphne Cardini-Johnstone right where he left her, new lines on her face but her hair that same shade of bottle-fresh auburn.

FALL INTO YOU   121

"Daph," Will says, drawing her attention away from her customer, as he takes a hesitant step into the disputed territory between "Customers Welcome" and "Only Staff Allowed." It's a question in more ways than one—Will has no idea, honestly, how this interaction is going to go. He's known Daphne since he was born, but she was his mother's friend and Bill's, more than she was ever his. She might react like Mere did, with tears and hugs, but she also might tell him to stick it where the sun dares not shine. Daphne could be like that, sometimes. Unpredictable.

She turns. She looks him up and down. She grins.

"Tell you what," she says, "About twenty years ago, you didn't show up for your Saturday shift and really messed up my weekend plans, but—better late than never, right? You, next in line; give Will your order, let's get this moving."

"What, did you just hire him off the street?" the customer demands. "Who is he?"

"Well," Daph says, cutting Will a sly sidelong look, "I'd say he's the owner, but rumor has it not for long."

"Oh," the customer says, relaxing even as Will tenses—*God*, he'd forgotten how quickly gossip travels in this little town. "Well, the *owner*, that's all right, then."

Thus mollified, he deigns to give Will the courtesy of his order, which is for several donuts, a pie, and one of the bakery's signature apple turnovers. Will packs it all up, marveling briefly at the new logo on the stickers with which he closes bags and boxes, which combines that of Cardinal Bakery and the new Robertson iconography. The bakery started running their production out of Robertson Family Farms sometime in the '70s, and Will knows it was Daphne who'd kept it going after Bill took things over on the farm side. Daphne's mother, old Mrs. Cardini, had decided within a few months that Will's father was fine enough as far as company went, but she couldn't work with him.

122 DYLAN MORRISON

But Daphne had seemed to enjoy working with Bill, finding his rudeness amusing and his tendency to fly off the handle entertaining and funny. She'd liked June, too, become good friends with her over the years. For a period of his life, Will had grown very used to seeing the two of them sitting together somewhere on the farm, whispering and then laughing hysterically. She was more or less famous locally, quite the gossip, and Will tries to steel himself against the barrage of questions he expects as he helps the next customer in line.

Instead, Daphne gives *him* information, interrupted only by the occasional violent lash of rain against the window, or boom of thunder so loud she has to repeat herself. She pours in such an enormous volume of talking—about who's gotten married, and divorced, and had babies, and tried and failed to have babies, and gotten fired, and gotten famous, and did you hear about the fire on Chesterfield Road, and on and on and *on*—that Will forgets to guard himself, or to think at all. He just packs up pies and turnovers and donuts and slices of apple cake, and says things like, "Wow" or "No kidding?" or "Oh, God, I would *not* have seen that coming." It's nice, honestly. More comforting than Will would have guessed.

But then, when the line winds down, Daph stops and gives him a sharp look over, seeming to be cataloguing his changes, nodding firmly when she's done. She pinches his cheek, strongly enough that it stings a little even after she lets go, but then pats it lightly, twice, as if in apology.

"Your folks missed you, kid," she says quietly. There's nothing hard in her tone, if you don't count the iron ring of truth. No judgement; just information. Good old Daphne. "They wouldn't have said it, your old man especially, but. They did."

Will stares at her for a second. Finally, because it's all he can think of, he says, "What am I supposed to say to that?"

FALL INTO YOU   123

Daphne shrugs, and gives him a strange, sad smile. "Nothing, baby. You're just supposed to know."

Will shifts, discomfited, wishing there was another customer to help. He's relieved when Casey rounds the corner, looking harried.

"Daph," he hisses tightly, his gaze landing briefly on Will and seeming to stick in irritation for a moment at his position behind the counter, before it slides on to Daphne. "You set aside twelve pies for her, right? When she came in? You're not selling off her pies while she whittles my soul into nothing?"

"Two blackberry, two blueberry, two cherry, two pumpkin, and four apple," Daphne rattles off, shaking her head. "Didn't know what she wanted 'em for next week and sure as hell don't know why she suddenly needs them now, but I've got 'em, if she wants them."

"She does," Casey says, pulling a darkly sarcastic little face. "And she doesn't! Because they're not *her* pies, you know—the pies that were made for *her*—"

Daphne cuts Casey off at this point, but Will doesn't catch what she says. Almost without meaning to, he wanders out from behind the counter and back towards the central market. He's oddly calm, not even jumping when the wind outside blows a branch into a window with particular viciousness as he passes, some part of him abruptly retuned to the wavelength upon which this place operates.

He knows Mrs. Baumcombe, despite never having laid eyes on her before, the second he sees her. Something about her outfit—the little pearl-lined pin sharply fixed to her sweater, perhaps—suggests she's a person who is constantly encountering shocking customer-service issues and never recognizing the single common denominator in all those unfortunate stories.

"Mrs. Baumcombe," Will says, in a booming, cheerful voice that isn't his own. Selma taught him this, admittedly with the help of quite a large amount of alcohol and through peals

124 DYLAN MORRISON

of laughter, the very first time he had to present an argument for study funding. She'd said a number of things that night, some of which were helpful and some of which were neither helpful nor repeatable, but the most useful was this dreadful but inarguable truth: With most people, most of the time, presenting a certain aggressively audacious confidence is 80 percent of the battle. "Your pies are all ready for you. If you'll give me your keys, I'll get them loaded into your car, how's that?"

"But," Mrs. Baumcombe says, blinking at him. "But the other man said—he said it would have to be *other pies* from today, not the ones made for *me*—"

"Twelve pies," Will says brightly. Out of the corner of his eye, he sees a blond head peek around the corner to watch, and doesn't let himself turn to look and see if it's Casey. "Ready to go! What car do you drive? Noel can take your payment right over here..." Will falters, realizing he's not sure if that's true; the ancient, horrifying monstrosity of a cash register that used to sit in here, taking up roughly one-third of the counter space, is nowhere to be seen. "I mean, probably, anyway."

Noel nods solemnly, but their eyes are entertained. "Oh yes. This is where the paying happens."

"But," Mrs. Baumcombe says, even as Will herds her over to the register. "I—"

"Do you *not* want them loaded into your car?" Will says, very innocently. "Because it's quite a rainy day. I personally wouldn't recommend it, but if you *want* to carry them all to the car yourself—"

"No, no, I want them loaded in," Mrs. Baumcombe says, looking a little baffled. She opens her mouth as if to argue further, but:

"That's settled, then," Will says. To Noel, firmly, he adds, "Ring her up."

"Sir, yes, sir," Noel mutters, sounding both impressed and

FALL INTO YOU   125

annoyed about being impressed. "Right away, Mr. Bossman, sir."

"Don't do that," Will mutters. "I'm not your boss." He turns away hastily, mostly looking for the blond head he briefly caught in his peripheral vision, although he's not at all sure whether or not he's hoping it will be Casey.

He doesn't find out, anyway. When he turns around, Casey is standing directly behind him, a stack of six pies in each hand and a bright grin on his face.

"I believe," he says, sounding very pleased about it, "I heard you advertise your car-loading services? I guess that's how you know we're under new management—I myself wouldn't have offered such a courtesy on a day like this, but hey, way to go the extra mile."

Will bites back a groan; he hadn't thought this far ahead. He'd been trying to get the woman out of everyone's hair, and had figured he'd try to finagle some way out of getting wet again if it came down to it. But, alas, there's nothing for it now. He's going to have to follow through because, clearly, Casey's not going to let him forget it.

That shouldn't matter to Will, of course. After all, he will be forgetting all about Casey in another day or two, maybe a week, once he leaves Glenriver behind. A month, tops. Six at the outside—nowhere near long enough, anyway, to make "He'd never let me forget it" much of an argument.

Will sighs, and squares his shoulders, and holds out his hands. "All right. Give them here."

Casey hands the pies over, the amusement on his face changing into an expression Will has a hard time identifying. Will nods, turns, walks over to the door, and—

—stops, mouth dropping open, as he watches a huge bolt of lightning strike down dead in front of the market, not even a hundred yards away.

The boom of thunder is loud and immediate, making

126   DYLAN MORRISON

everyone in the room jump; it's accompanied, barely a second later, by the blare of a variety of car alarms, spooked by the electric jolt.

"Jesus," Casey mutters, moving towards the shop's front windows. "That sounded close." To Will, as he passes: "You see what it hit?"

"You're looking for a lightly smoking fencepost, about forty yards to the left," Will says. The ease of the estimated distance surprises him; he's famous in his insular scientific community for insisting on double- and triple-checking even the most inconsequential guess before hazarding it. He's been told many times it's a sign of his brilliance, but equally often that it's the single most significant impediment to his brilliance, which Will has always found somewhat annoying, since he's pretty sure it's neither.

Once, in his undergrad years, someone had asked Will about it directly, his refusal to risk an estimate. It was, unhappily, before he'd quite gotten a grip on the critically important line between "Normal, relatable anecdote of a regular human childhood" and "A story that makes people look at you as though you have, with the enormity of the bummer you have conveyed unto them, peeled all the paint from their interior walls." So unthinkingly, laughing about it, he had told the story of the summer he was eleven, when Bill had asked Will to calculate how much lumber they'd need to replace the new fenceposts. He had gotten the math wrong and they'd ordered too much, far too much, enough that it was a significant expense. After he'd explained how Bill had screamed and raged, cycled back to the topic to blow again for months and months, never quite let it go even years on, Will had shaken his head, concluded the story with a shrugging, "Fathers, you know?"

No one had known, though. They'd simply looked embarrassed, and left Will to stand there with a new, unfamiliar shame sitting uncomfortably in the pit of his stomach.

FALL INTO YOU   127

Thunder rolls overhead, and lightning slashes through the sky again, somewhere close—God, what is Will *doing*? Standing here with his arms full of pie, staring out into the storm lost in reverie? It doesn't matter, anyway, about the horrible summer with the extra lumber, and it *certainly* doesn't matter that Will rattled off an estimate, any estimate, to Casey stupid Reeves. It doesn't matter at all.

Still: "On second thought, Mrs. B, we're going to hold on this for a second," Will says, setting the pies down on the nearest counter. "I think we should give it a minute to calm down out there—not sure you want to drive in that."

"That last strike hit the big red oak along the access road," Casey adds tightly, still looking out the window. "Think the whole left side's going to go, at least."

Will groans, stepping up to the window next to him without thinking. Sure enough, there's a harsh, blackened damage line splitting the tree, the left half of it nearly cleaved from the right. A strong enough wind, or enough time for gravity to do its work, and: "Crap. It'll block the whole road when it does."

"Do you think—" Casey starts, his voice low and serious, like for some reason he genuinely wants to ask Will's opinion on something. But before he can finish the thought, his phone rings. As he's fishing it out of his pocket, Will feels a tap on his shoulder.

He turns. Mrs. Baumcombe is glaring at him. "I must say, young man, you are *awfully* familiar with me! Taking my pies, *refusing* to take my pies, referring to 'Mrs. B.' Do I *know* you?"

Far more interestingly, Casey is now saying into the phone "Hel—whoa, hey, slow down. Just—I can help, take a breath and tell me slow."

"Probably?" Will says to Mrs. B, grimacing slightly. "Or at least, you probably knew my dad, Bill. He was... Noel, what is it?" The teen's face has gone ashen, and they're looking down at their phone as though it's told them the date of their own death.

128 DYLAN MORRISON

"I..." Noel says, blinking down at it. When they look up at Will, their eyes are wide, abruptly young in that horrible way of teenagers, who can't help occasionally throwing into sharp relief the reality of adulthood. One of the harshest lessons of that rocky transition is learning how much of who you are is shaped simply by what you've had to deal with. Will doesn't know Noel very well, but the look on their face is universal, and he can tell that whatever they just saw on that phone, it's something that is reshaping them right now.

"Mere! Jesus, all right, let me find the keys," Casey is saying, running towards the back of the market; half of Will is quite urgently tracking on that, ears particularly pricking at Mere's name. Mrs. Baumcombe is pulling on his sleeve, saying some other stupid, insipid thing—no part of Will is tracking on that *at all*, and he really hopes it won't turn out to have been important. Every spare thought that isn't wondering what on earth is happening on Casey's phone call is waiting to see what Noel's going to say.

Thunder rolls.

"You grew up here, right?" Noel says, in a small voice, eyes back on their phone. "So... so maybe you know. It's an urban legend, right? About that kid in the '90s? And the bridge? And the river?" A desperate, dangerous edge has entered their voice, as though they're holding back tears. "That didn't happen. A flood couldn't... It didn't happen, right? It's an urban legend? Tell me it didn't happen, man, okay! It's an urban legend—*say* it."

"Oh, God," Will says, drawn back to the hideous summer of the extra lumber for a new, worse, and far more pressing reason. He knows what's happened, or at least the broad, terrible shape of it, even before he sees Casey run past, keys in his hand, and hurry out the front door.

Will doesn't think; the cheerful yellow door doesn't even

have a chance to land in its frame before he's grabbing it and following Casey into the storm.

NINE

Will regrets his decision to leave the market more or less immediately.

The wind, first of all, has grown stronger in the last half an hour or so. It throws raindrops directly into Will's face with sharp, stinging strength, each splash just this side of a pinprick. He can hardly keep his eyes open against the onslaught, and he holds an arm up over his face so he can keep track of Casey, in order to chase him. Will curses the man for pulling on dark jeans and a black-and-gray flannel the last time he'd changed out of wet clothes—it's an upsettingly good look for him, obviously, but it does make him harder to track against the current landscape of bruise-like navies and threatening grays. Will himself, in candy-apple red, is the easier of the two of them to keep an eye on.

Still, he manages to follow Casey back to the staff garage without losing him, falling on his face, getting struck by lightning, or otherwise humiliating himself. He's pretty pleased with his efforts, until he swings his way up into the passenger side of the pickup and sees Casey jump.

FALL INTO YOU 131

"Jesus!" Casey snaps, visibly unsettled. "How did you... Oh, never mind, there isn't time. Get out of the cab!"

"No," Will says calmly, shutting the door and buckling his seatbelt. He should probably feel a sense of dread, the gut-clenching fear of conflict that always seems to rise any time someone is displeased with him; he finds, instead, that the deep annoyance on Casey's face is funny. "That was Mere Gunderson, wasn't it? She's a friend of mine. I was hanging out with her and her kids a few hours ago—and something's happened to one of them, right? So, I'm coming. You never know; I might be helpful." Casey is staring at him, mouth open, so Will, to prove his final point, adds, "For example, you might want to start driving now."

"You—oh, God, right," Casey says, seeming to jerk back to himself. He turns the key over in the ignition with more force than necessary, the engine whining at him a little as it rolls to life. He throws the shifter too hard and puts the truck into neutral instead of reverse, and has to correct before he can back up and pull out of the garage. Raising his voice a little to be heard over the abrupt din of rain against roof as he whips across the parking lot, he adds, "*How* did you know it was one of Mere's kids?"

"Noel," Will says back, shaking his head. "They asked about Walter Gramlich." At Casey's split-second glance of confusion, he clarifies: "There was a kid by that name who died here, when I was ten or eleven. A teenager more than a kid, really, I guess. There was some stupid tradition about jumping off the Glen River Bridge... God, you'd have to ask someone else for the details. All I know is, you got more points—or 'street cred,' if you want to call it that—the worse the weather was, or the higher the waterline—"

Will stops, drawn to an urgent halt by the vision growing nearer by the second through the windshield. The glorious red

132   DYLAN MORRISON

oak that they'd watched the lightning strike—it's coming up alongside them on the right, directly next to Will's spot in the passenger seat. The damage had looked plenty bad from back in the market, but from up close like this, in these more intense winds, the left and right sides of the trees look to be held together by hope more than anything else. Will could swear, as they barrel towards it at a speed he himself would not attempt in this weather, that he hears the wood let out a long, sickening creak.

Will is suddenly intensely aware of several things. These things include, but are not limited to: the inescapability of gravity; the rapidly decreasing distance between his body and the barely standing tree, which is nearly next to them now; the relative difference in size between a person and a centuries-old oak. The bulk of his awareness, however, is occupied by the undeniable fact that his body, like all human bodies, is basically a flesh bag of highly temperamental organic machines that don't tend to continue functioning after being smashed, crushed, pulped, or otherwise reduced to smithereens.

"Casey," he says, his tone threaded with barely contained panic, "I think maybe we should—"

"Yep," Casey says, grim, and guns it.

The car lurches forward—they're so nearly at the tree as to be basically upon it—and then, all at once, they're next to it. And while they should, within the space of a few seconds, be safely past it and on the other side, Will can tell it's going to go wrong an instant before it does. As he feels, from the passenger seat, the tire treads losing their grip on the slick surface of the road, he hears more than sees the tree give way. The sound is *enormous*, a sharp crack that seems to splinter through the air itself, and activates some scrabbling, primordial survival instinct in the back of Will's mind.

Then it's all happening too quickly to keep track of. The car is spinning—Will can see half the tree falling, in little glimpses at the peak of every turn, like a terrifying flip-book—the tree is landing, knocking off one of Casey's mirrors but otherwise missing the car—the car is *still spinning* and—no, wait, it's... not. Casey is hooting and hollering in delight and cutting the wheel and—

"Oh my God, did you spin out on *purpose*," Will demands, all one gasping breath. "You *bastard*, I thought we were going to *die*—"

"Eh," Casey says, the smallest edge of a smile stealing onto his face. "Nah. From that thing?" He shakes his head, and says again: "Nah. Couple broken bones, maybe, or neck injury if you're very unlucky, but you'd probably live." When Will makes an outraged little noise in reply, Casey smirks and adds, "Anyway, I wasn't spinning out; I was just spinning. Quicker to get out of the trajectory, in the circumstances. It's only spinning out if you're not in control."

Will decides to ignore this and cranes around in his seat to look at the damage behind them. Whistling, and then remembering his father used to do that and wishing he could wind the sound back into his mouth like fishing wire, he says, "Not going to be pretty getting back in, is it? Whole road's blocked off."

Casey looks in the rearview mirror as Will settles back into his seat, and swears. Then, tightly: "God. Well. Problem for later me, I guess." Pulling an unhappy face, and clearly mostly to himself, he mutters, "Really piling them up for that guy today, aren't I? Let's all spare a thought for him."

As Casey blows out a breath, and then throws the shifter back into gear and starts peeling down the road, Will does his best to regulate his breathing and heart rate. In fairness, it's a *bit* hard to tell the difference between his own pulse thudding in his ears and the rain still lashing down around them, or to hear the raggedness of his own breathing over the howling of the wind outside. It's possible that Will's doing a great job of regu-

134 DYLAN MORRISON

lating his response to that particular near-death experience. Perhaps he is completely calm, and simply can't tell.

I think being completely calm isn't usually a mystery to the self, says the cool, rational, Selma-esque voice in the back of Will's mind. *Also, critical note for you: He's driving very fast again, but you still don't know where you're going, or what on earth has even happened, so...*

"Look," Will says, a sense of dread stealing over him as he remembers what little he knows about what drove them out here in the first place, then deepening as he clocks how quickly the nearby fenceposts are starting to whip past. "I know we don't, uh... get along, or whatever, but can you *please* tell me what the hell is happening? Meredith and I grew up together, and I literally met all of her kids like three hours ago, and Walter Gramlich did very much *die*, so. If it has to be a no-questions-asked thing, then fine, happy to help, whatever it is, but if not... *what is it?*"

Casey sucks in a harsh breath. "Yeah. So—Todd? You met Todd?"

"God," Will says, swallowing hard against a sudden wave of nauseousness. "Yes, I met Todd. I liked Todd. He jumped?"

"Not exactly," Casey says, in a growl. "I guess he and some of his friends were out there daring each other to jump, but they all told her they didn't mean it, that it was just messing around, being stupid. But something happened, I guess part of the bridge collapsed or something, and the rest of them got clear in time but Todd didn't. Swept into the river." Casey glances at the clock, gnawing on his lower lip, and swears again, low, under his breath.

"Jesus," Will says, swallowing hard.

"Yeah," Casey says, shaking his head. "His friends couldn't quite agree, but one of them insisted he saw Todd trying to swim against the current; said he tried to grab for him, and missed. Mere tried 911, but EMS can't get over the bridge because it *isn't there*. So she tried me because Todd has GPS tracking on his phone that shows up on hers, one of those family monitoring things, you know, and a few months ago I got him this waterproof phone case because—"

"He kept breaking them," Will says, nodding along, too concerned about Todd to remember to be self-conscious about having already discussed Casey with other people in the roughly twenty-four hours since meeting him. "He told me you did, yeah."

"Thank God, right?" Casey says, with a slightly shaky laugh. For a second, he looks almost green in the dim light of the cab, but it might be a reflection from the lighting; when he speaks again, his voice is steadier. "Anyway, the phone is pinging somewhere on the perimeter of the property line— Meredith says it bounced around for a while, and now it looks like it's stopped right at the edge of the river. She hopes it's the edge of the river, anyway. She sounded pretty..." He trails off without finishing the sentence, but Will can imagine; no parent is going to sound anything but gut-wrenchingly frantic in that situation. Casey leans forward a little, obviously urging the car to pick up yet another few miles per hour of speed, as he says, "This is just the fastest route. She's on her way, but with the weather this crazy she's not sure how long—"

"No, of course," Will says, shaking his head, sick with worry for her, for Todd. "Someone had to go, in case—sometimes it just comes down to timing, right, and—you couldn't—of course you had to go."

"Yeah," Casey says, after a long, slow beat. "That's right."

Silence blooms out between them, yawning into the heart of the car even as they hurtle down the rain-slick road, barely able to see more than a few feet in front of them through the thick curtain of the downpour. Will tries not to let his newly acquired fear of hydroplaning to his quick and painful death show in his face or body language, contains himself to shifting a little against the worn leather seat covers when he notices the speedometer climbing into territory he wouldn't take it on a *sunny* day. Still, it's not an uncomfortable silence, except in all the ways that it is, because it's a fraught, uncertain moment, and those are always uncomfortable. But between them, in some little way, something that was tight and tense seems to uncurl a little, in spite of the circumstances—soothed like a panicky animal by the urgency of the task, or the hum of the motor.

It's a stolen moment of peace, though, too much to face to allow them much more than a breath or two of pause, and after a second, Will finally remembers to say: "Oh! *Where* are we going? You said edge of the property line, but I'm pretty sure—" He peers out into the wet, angry blackness that was once a familiar thoroughfare, trying to orient himself, then continues: "Yeah, I thought so—look, if we keep going this way we're going to hit that stupid forest, and unless things have changed a lot since I was a kid, the owners aren't going to let us cut through—"

"Oh, no, definitely not," Casey agrees, sounding sour. "*Not* a friendly bunch; I'm not interested in tangling with them today. Doubt they'd help us even for a kid's life, to be honest. But it's not going to be an issue—I know a shortcut."

"A shortcut?" Will pulls up his mental map of the farm, trying to think of how this could possibly be so. They pulled out of the market parking lot and turned left on the main road; Robertson property is passing them quickly by on the right. They're already beyond the outbuildings, the first orchard, *and* the cornfield, the final fence marking the property line wicking by, and all that's left between here and the forest is—

"Oh my God," Will says, as he sees Casey flip his turn signal and start twisting the wheel, "are you going to use the *private road?* It's blocked off, man! Look!" He gestures at the

FALL INTO YOU   137

length of metal chain, fitted in the middle with a PRIVATE ROAD: NO ACCESS sign, which is hanging from two posts on either side of the road.

"Oh no," Casey says sarcastically, rolling his eyes even as he guns the engine. "A single length of rusty chain! However will I defeat that with only the power of my *enormous truck*," and then he's driving through it as though it's nothing, the PRIVATE ROAD sign banging as it hits the ground behind them.

"That... did not occur to me as an option," Will admits, impressed in spite of himself. There's something oddly attractive about the man's sheer audacity, his willingness to do things that Will would never even consider trying himself.

"Shouldn't be private, anyway," Casey mutters. "It's not like it's somebody's driveway. Road's a road. Sometimes there's an *emergency*."

Will swallows, his thoughts sliding, the way he's been willing them not to, to what might be happening to Todd right now. Casey's must, too, because they fall into a tense, anxious silence, which lasts for the last few minutes of their breathtakingly fast drive.

Abruptly, Casey whips the wheel to the right, and they're barreling through a tight gap in the fence line that Will never would have seen, let alone cleared, in time. It puts them back on Robertson land, as close to the river as even the farm's dirt roads get, and Will expects Casey to stop the car. Instead, he continues to drive, urging the truck off the dirt road and through an already winterized planting field, directly towards a line of thin, scraggly maple trees, unhappy in their placements at the edge of an eroding slope. Will knows those trees were put there to denote the end of the plantable ground, and that beyond them sits a long, low incline down to the riverbank, and thus the *water*. If someone were to drive directly through one of the gaps between those trees, as Will is half-convinced Casey intends to do, then that person and any unfortunate passenger who happened to be with them would briefly fly through the air before crashing into the water. Will takes deep breath in and...

...releases it in one shocked, punched-out exhale when Casey throws the emergency brake, sends the car spinning sideways through the mud before it skids to a perfect stop mere inches from the tree line.

"Wow," Will breathes, not meaning to, so surprised to be alive that he can't help it. The skill it must take to drive a car so dangerously without crashing it—

But Casey's already out of the car, calling, "Are you coming or not?" over his shoulder, running towards the river. Will jolts back to himself and, hurrying to catch up, doesn't bother to close the passenger-side door. Casey didn't shut his door, either, or cut the ignition, so this leaves the car still on, engine humming, both doors wide. Backlit by the latest flash of lightning, it's like a still from a horror movie, as though someone has just finished abducting them. Part of Will—a young part, and, in another way, an old part—wants to hurry back and close things up before he can get in trouble for whatever mess is left, but he pushes that down, ignores it. The interiors will get a little wet, probably; it's not as though it matters. It's not as though it's really important.

Will dashes forward, working hard to make good time through the thick, sinking soup the storm's made of the ground, until he finally catches up with Casey, who, still running and annoyingly much less out of breath than Will, says, "I thought about calling out to him, but if he's in the water, is there any point?"

"He might not be," Will points out, even though he thinks his out-of-shape lungs might blow up like a pufferfish and kill him if he tries to scream Todd's name, just to put themselves out of their misery. "Maybe he pulled himself out. Can't hurt to try."

"Christ. Yeah, you're right," Casey says, his footfalls hard,

FALL INTO YOU 139

his neck telescoping left and right as he runs, seemingly *quite easily*, at a speed that for Will is an all-out sprint. They both scream out Todd's name several times, Will's lungs sending him a series of increasingly upset memos about it, but then Casey's voice cracks and he snaps, "I'm too close to this to *think* clearly. I keep cycling back to statistics about—" He whips his head around to give Will a desperate look. "I understand that you don't like me, and that's fine, I can't say I like you so much, either. But if you help me get Todd out safe, I'll—oh, *I* don't know. Clear out of the damn house, if that's what you want, or—"

"Oh my God, do I look evil to you? Did I grow some little goatee overnight I'm not aware of? I don't need an incentive for keeping teenagers from dying! Why do you think I got in the truck in the first place?" Will snaps, trying to rein in the part of himself that he knows is veering towards absurdity and hysteria because it doesn't want to face the sobering realities of the present. Giving himself a little internal slap, he says, "Look, I'm happy to help, but where are we *running* to? Did Mere give you coordinates? Or just—"

"She said back half of the property, across from that little picnic area on the other bank of the river." Casey reaches the edge of the river as he says this, the closest he can get to it without actively wading in, and doesn't exactly stop running; instead, he switches to jogging in place, whipping his head around to try to see as far as he can in either direction, as though afraid to waste a single moment being still. Will, a few steps behind him, thinks that's fair, but he does have to pause briefly and gasp for breath as he, too, looks around to orient himself. Casey sounds like he's starting to really panic, a thread of terror in his voice Will wouldn't necessarily have expected from him, as he says, "She sent me a screenshot, but it's just a radius, and I've never spent that much time back here, except dealing with the corn, and—"

140   DYLAN MORRISON

"Okay, there's two places he could be stuck, unless they've significantly changed this since I was a kid," Will says, certain now of where he's standing. You couldn't spend a whole summer fruitlessly dragging a section of river for a variety of tractor parts your father had drunkenly chucked in there and *forget* it. He shades his eyes and looks upriver, pointing as he talks so Casey can follow him. "See that bend? Past that, there's a grate, which filters anything big that gets thrown into the river —trees, debris, whatever. That's so nothing big spits out at the *other* place he could be stuck, which is at the property line." Will winces, and adds, "Have to hope it's the first option—the water fence at the property line is basically a net with hooks on it. And on a day like this—I mean, that grate's only so tall, and a lot gets past it when the waterline's this high. The backup at that water fence is probably... pretty gnarly, by this—"

But Casey's already running again; Will is sick with the urgency of the situation, but he'd be lying if he said his body was designed, or at least conditioned, for much in the way of thrilling danger, cardiovascular exercise, or becoming soaking wet and covered in mud for the second time today. It sends up a variety of objections when Will, too, begins running again, all along the lines of, *I am considering going on strike*, and *These conditions are not workable and I'll sue.* A kid's life is at stake, so Will ignores them, but it's more of a struggle than he's strictly speaking proud of.

When he was a teenager, he remembers suddenly, as thunder roars overhead and rain seems to blow directly into both of his eyes, Will could run for miles. He'd wanted to join the track and field team, had been practicing. The memory's there and gone again as quickly as breathing, popping into his mind incongruously the way things sometimes do, when the stakes are high and the chips are down and a little part of you can't quite bear to get with the hideous program. He'd forgotten all about it, the long hours alone, his feet thwapping hard

FALL INTO YOU   141

against the pavement and asphalt of Glenriver in order to be anywhere but at home.

His feet don't thwap now; they *squelch*, and it takes all the energy his thigh muscles can muster to scramble after Casey without pitching face-first into the mud. But even the desire to stop running doesn't ease the way the bottom drops out of Will's stomach when, as they reach the bend in the river, Casey groans, "Oh, *God*."

Will looks up, and grimaces. A little ways up the river, a large eastern cottonwood has toppled over just past the filtering grate, but before the water fence at the property line. It's obviously been blown down, an awkward skirt of dirt and ripped-up roots ringing the base of it and billowing loosely in the harsh wind, and is still tethered to the earth—barely—by the few larger flat roots that haven't given way. Otherwise, though, the cottonwood is mostly in the water. It is—or was, anyway—a tall tree, but not a *redwood*, so it doesn't fully span across the width of the Glen River, swollen and thrashing and furious. But it's most of the way across, at the perfect angle for the sway of the river to act as a horrible kind of leverage, and Will can tell even as he runs that the roots holding the tree to earth are losing their grip splinter by splinter. The whole enormous thing is obviously ready and eager to be swept back into the property line net and cause all sorts of problems.

And there, pinned to the center of the trunk by the sheer force of the rushing water, is Todd Gunderson.

All of Will's bodily complaints abruptly cease, except for a roiling sense of nausea that, counterintuitively, seems to make his feet move faster than they were before. His aching muscles, his overtaxed lungs, the little alarm trying to let him know that he is a bit colder than a person is supposed to get—all of it fades away, so much less urgent than reaching Todd as to be rendered unimportant. Will's mind, which had been pinging from thought to thought, fills with a fuzzy static he associates with hospital rooms, and devastating professional meetings, and phone calls where someone tells him his father is dead.

Todd is *really in the river*. He's alive, clearly, because you have to be alive to look that frightened, but it's a miracle he is, and how long he might be able to remain so is anyone's guess, and—God, Will would feel sick with dread for anyone, but he's only a kid, and he's *Mere's* kid. Before today, the last time he'd spent time with Meredith was when the two of them were barely older than Todd is now, and it makes it worse, somehow. All Will can see, as he pelts forward through the rain next to Casey, is Meredith's younger face, crumpling in heartbreak.

Will feels one of his legs sink in well past his ankle within the first few steps, but he wrenches it back up, ignoring the mud, trying to think of a plan as he goes. Resources—nothing— maybe some rope in the back of the truck but it's not *his* truck, or his dad's truck in *1994*; Will can't count on it. No time to go get anything else; Will's no arborist, but the tree can't have more than a few minutes left before it breaks free of the stump.

"TODD!" Casey bellows as they go. "WE'RE COMING, DUDE! HANG TIGHT!" While Todd's clearly both awake and scared out of his mind, he doesn't respond; Will thinks there's a decent chance he can't hear anything over the cascade of water, close as he is to the river's rushing surface.

Someone else hears them, though, or maybe just spots them, because suddenly Will can see, on the other side of the river, a tall figure wearing a lime-green rain jacket jumping up and down waving his arms. It looks like his mouth's moving, but— God, between the wind and the rain and the river he could be saying anything—

"Sandy," Casey says tightly. "Todd's dad—I know the coat. I don't think he can—oh my God, *phones*—" He fumbles in his pocket as they approach the riverbank, and as he struggles with that, and to scroll to the right number on the already rain-slicked screen, Will casts back to his still-percolating plan.

FALL INTO YOU   143

Okay—outdoor crisis—no supplies—that's the moment any reasonable adult botanist turns to vegetation. So he just has to remember which plants are around, which, God, Will knows this, he grew *up* here. Wasn't *Aesculus glabra* the first Latin name he ever looked up in the Glenriver library, wanting a softer, less sports-associated name for such a lovely tree than "buckeye"? Didn't he run a comprehensive three-year sample of every wild aggregate berry bush in the area, keeping detailed field notes on flavor, density, change over time? Hadn't he spent six months as a teenager testing the tensile strengths of vines of Virginia creeper that he subjected to various—

"Oh!" Will says, because suddenly, he has it. Casey is talking to Sandy, Will realizes, probably. He's not processing what's being said; he doesn't need to know, not right now. He needs to know where he can find some—ah, yes, there it is. It's never hard to find the Virginia creeper in this part of the state, not if you know what to look for, and Will spots some working its way around a tree a few yards away. Quickly, he turns on his heel and dashes over to it.

"Where are you going?" Casey calls; Will hardly notices. He's busy fishing around in his pockets for his pocketknife, before he remembers that this is a pair of borrowed sweats, and he doesn't even have his wallet. Shrugging, and resigning himself to the possibility that his hands might not thank him for it, he settles for pulling his sleeves over his palms as he reaches and grips the nearest tendril of creeper. He knows it's one of those plants that has the tendency to bite back, shooting out sharp little raphides of calcium oxalate whenever it's damaged, but the situation is too urgent to be concerned about sensitive skin.

"Jesus, I think this guy's lost his mind," Casey is saying into the phone, behind him. "Will! What are you *doing*, man? We've got to figure out a way to *get* him. I've got a couple feet of rope in the truck, *maybe*, but Sandy thinks—"

144   DYLAN MORRISON

"Working on it," Will grunts, pulling on the vine as hard as he can. It barely budges—too tightly wrapped around the tree—and then a thought occurs to him. "Hey—you got a pocketknife?"

Casey, sounding annoyed now, stomps into Will's eyeline and snaps, "This is not the time for *botany*!"

Grunting slightly in frustration and wasted effort, Will, with his full weight hanging off the stubborn tendril, turns his head without letting go of the vine. "It's a *rope*, okay? If we can get it off the tree, anyway. It's strong—should work—*pocketknife*—" At this, Casey blinks and then pulls one out, flipping it over in the air and opening it in one smooth movement. He doesn't hand it to Will, just holds it hovering over the plant, then cuts the vine in a single place where Will indicates to him with a sharp little nod.

It's exactly where Will wanted him to cut, exactly what Will was silently asking him to do, but Will undercounted how quickly the vine would give up. He also forgot that his full weight was still hanging from it. The creeper comes loose at once and Will stumbles back wildly, reeling, one step—two—he's overbalancing, and is going to land on his back in the mud, and—

Casey catches him, stepping behind him easily and solidly, like it's nothing at all.

"Oh," Will says, stupidly, as he registers the warm brick wall of Casey against him, the iron bar of his arm reaching to keep Will steady. "I... Thanks."

"No worries," Casey says, and for a second, his voice is low; then he seems to shake himself all over, stepping away, already winding the vine over his arm as fast as he can as he adds, "You good?"

"Yeah," Will says, blinking. "I... Yeah." Hurriedly, he starts pulling more of the vine loose, making it easier for Casey to wind up quickly. "These things can go to fifty or sixty feet, so I thought—tied around one of our waists—then the other one climbs out on the tree—scoops him up and brings him in?"

"Great," Casey says, sounding distracted. He's switched to looping the vine over his shoulder, gathering it into a large, loose coil before cutting it again. "Should be enough for that, anyway —come on!"

Together they race back over to the riverbank, where Todd is looking more and more petrified by the minute. Will doesn't blame him; the tree has started to make some really upsetting cracking noises.

"Sandy!" Casey calls over the rush of river and rain; Will glances at him, wondering how on earth he expects the other man to hear him across the water, and then realizes Casey's put him on speakerphone. "Will found—a rope, sort of. I'm going to go get him, and Will's gonna stay here in case—"

"No," Will says, the awful realization washing over him all at once, "it can't be you. It has to be me." Casey opens his mouth to argue, but they don't have *time*, so Will snatches the vines with his bare hands after all—oh, well—and, as he wraps it around his waist and ties it off, snaps, "Just think about it for a second, will you? You're bigger than me; I'm pretty sure you're stronger than me, too. If I get to Todd and the tree breaks, or we go in, you've got a chance of pulling us both back. Me? Nah. We'd all end up in the river together." He tosses Casey, whose face is creasing with obvious disagreement, the other end of the rope, such as it is, and says, "Also, and this is important: If you let me drown in there, I'm going to kill you, so I recommend you keep track of that end, all right?"

Then, swallowing hard and before Casey can reply, he turns around and hops up onto the felled, failing tree trunk. The way it's swaying in the river had been, from the banks, slight but somewhat unsettling—from here it's downright sickening, and he realizes immediately that he'll be thrown off if he tries to walk across it. Swallowing his fear as well as some of his pride and at least a third of his dignity, Will crouches down on the tree until he can lie basically flat across it, and pull himself along the trunk in a half-realized army crawl.

"You don't have to do this!" Casey's voice already sounds further away than it had from the ground, fading as Will inches further out over the water. "Whatever you're trying to prove, let *me* do it, you idiot, at least I know what I'm—"

"Shut up!" Will calls back to him. "Let me focus!"

At this point, Casey either listens to him—a miraculous first, if so—or, more likely, Will simply stops being able to hear him over the rush of water. Either way it's just as well. Grimly, as he inches his way across the tree to the spot where Todd's dark hair is just visible, Will thinks that he'd probably have fallen in by now if he could still hear Casey, sent to his death by an inability to keep himself from turning his own head to glare.

Will tries, as he goes, not to think of that summer after Walter Gramlich died, when it was all anyone talked about. Will tries not to think about the sound of the water or the creak of the tree or the furious rabbit-beat of his heart in his eardrums, thumping out the time. He tries not to think about the stinging sensation in his hands, irritated by the vine and now, he suspects, scraped bloody on the tree bark, or about the fact that he's not sure he's ever been quite this cold before. He tries to think, instead, about how it would feel to be Todd Gunderson right now, shocked and alone and scared, half-drowned, too deep in the nightmare of the experience to realize anyone is even there to help him. Will can't be scared right now, because if he were Todd Gunderson, he would want whatever adult was coming to help him to be strong. Hearty. Unafraid.

Will is, in fact, utterly, chokingly terrified, but he's reasonably certain pretending he isn't is at least half the battle.

He reaches Todd eventually. The tree is swaying alarmingly now, and Will slides sideways as far as he dares, half to get close enough to be heard over the water, and half out of a desire to

FALL INTO YOU   147

cling briefly to the tree trunk like a human barnacle. All he succeeds in doing is delivering a nasty surprise to Todd, who, not expecting a human face to abruptly appear next to his own in this situation, helpfully says, "AHHHH!" and then, in case Will missed it, "AHHHHHHHH!"

"Hey! Todd! It's me, Will, from lunch." Will basically screams this to be heard over the water before realizing, seconds too late, that it's a completely asinine thing to say in the circumstances, but there's nothing to be done about it now. "I'm here to get you out of this, okay?"

"You?" Todd says. His voice is a squeak of terror, which, while understandable, is not very flattering.

"Me," Will confirms, and then, in case it helps, adds, "and Casey. He's on the bank; he's tied to me with a—well—it's a vine, basically, but it'll hold. You're going to climb up, and—"

Todd whimpers, shaking his head, and cries, "I tried to *before*, okay, the current's too *strong*, it'll pull me back down—"

"I got you," Will says, and offers Todd a hand. "Come on."

The next few minutes are, not to put too fine a point on it, an agony. In spite of a strong verbal offense, Will becomes increasingly sure as he attempts to haul Todd up out of the churning river that he is going to fail miserably and doom them both to a watery grave. The current, as Todd warned, is incredibly strong, and Todd's also nearly Will's height, despite being decades younger. In the end, it's only on sheer spite that Will manages it—after so many years of refusing to go to the gym, it would be such an indignity to cause his own death and someone else's due to a lack of upper body strength. That, combined with several previous minutes' effort on inching Todd ever so slightly higher on the log, gives Will the burst of energy he needs. With a huge, grunting breath, he throws as much of his weight as he can into one last heave, and manages to get Todd onto the top of the log.

Both of them lie there, gasping, getting their breath back, for

148   DYLAN MORRISON

a second. But they don't have seconds to spare; the minute he has air in his lungs again, Will says, "All right! Come on! Let's go!"

"Don't want to," Todd says, in a small voice; he is, Will notices, clinging to the tree quite tightly. "Can't move."

Will takes a deep breath, wanting to sound reassuring and steady and not like he's going to *freak out* and start *screaming* if they don't get off this *precarious log* in the next *fifteen seconds*. That's what his father would have done—freaked out, and yelled at Will, and made it worse—and Will's surprised to find within him an untapped well to reach for now, of the sort of things he'd always wished the man might say instead. "I know you're scared, Todd, but it's all going to be okay. Casey's here, and your dad, and all you have to do is make it a couple more feet, all right? You don't have to stand up or anything; you can just crawl along the trunk, okay? And—here." Quickly, he yanks at the dangling vine until he can loop a section of it around Todd's wrist. "Now you're tied to Casey on the shore, and I'll be right behind you. You can do this, Todd; I know you can. Take it nice and slow if you need to, just get moving, all right?"

"All right," Todd says, in a small voice. "All right." And then, thank God, he starts to crawl.

He goes, in Will's opinion, a bit *too* slowly, but it doesn't seem the time to point it out. Still, as they inch their way back towards the riverbank, Will can't quite escape the knowledge that time is running short. The sways are getting larger—what little hold remains between land and tree is slipping away— they're nearly to the shore, inches away, Casey close enough that he could almost wade in and grab them, but any second now—

"Todd, jump!" Will calls, and Todd freezes, flinches; God, they don't have time to *wait*. With a snarling noise he wouldn't have expected himself to make, Will shifts his own grip on the tree, grabs Todd by the wrist, and, using his legs to generate as much momentum as possible, throws them both towards the riverbank with a desperate, frantic abandon. And as they fly through the air, arms windmilling, Will hears the tree let out one last groan of defeat, and, at last, leave the land entirely behind.

TEN

The drive back to the market parking lot isn't the *most* awkward car ride of Will's life. It is, however, second only to a van ride back from some field trip or another when Will was in ninth grade, during which he had been taking an innocent nap and woken up to the realization that Missy Pruitt and Kyle Jackson were hooking up in the seat next to him. He has to give it to those two: That was a worse situation than this one.

However, in that unfortunate instance, Will had decided his best course of action was simply to continue to pretend to be asleep. That option is decidedly not available to him here, and to be honest, Will thinks it would be an improvement if it was. They're sitting three across in the cab of Casey's pickup, Will in the middle because it felt rude to make a traumatized teenager suffer another indignity; Todd's dripping underneath the blanket Casey hauled out from beneath the passenger seat, not that it matters. It's not as though Will isn't basically soaked again himself, the brand-new, pristine sweatsuit transformed into a mud-streaked, rain-weighted horror. He's achingly aware that there is nothing between him and Casey but a few scant inches of space and some soaking wet fabric, but he's trying his best not to be. Instead, he's watching the water slip and slide in little droplets across the worn brown leather seats for something to do, since Casey's doing most of the talking.

The conversation... ranges. Sometimes Casey's stern, even harsh: What was Todd thinking, going out on that bridge with those kids, even if they were joking? Didn't he know better? Hadn't Casey taught Todd better himself, taught him to respect the power and danger of the natural world?

But then at other moments, Casey's softer. Gruffer. He's so glad Todd's okay; he doesn't mean to yell, it's just that it was such a scary thing; he hopes Todd will still come to him for help and guidance. His voice breaks once or twice, and Will has to look out the window and think, *If you pretend to be asleep, William, it will make you look even weirder than if you just don't make eye contact with anyone. No one wants to make eye contact with you, anyway! It's a moving car! Be normal! Be neutral!*

But Todd, somewhat understandably in Will's opinion, is surly and sharp and irritable and embarrassed, more prickly than Will thinks he would be usually. It's not really like Will has such a sense of him—some of the awkwardness of the car ride is the fact that, halfway *to* the car, Todd had turned to him and demanded, "Okay, seriously, *lunch guy*, why are you *here*, what is *happening*," which, while fair, had been demoralizing.

Todd and Casey, on the other hand, obviously have quite a close relationship, and one Will clearly doesn't know the half of. There's not much he can think of to say that wouldn't sound, at best, overly familiar and, at worst, incredibly stupid, so he mostly sits quietly and tries not to flinch too dramatically when Todd, unhappy and lashing out, snaps something like, "I mean, it's not like I've seen you *around* so much," or, "What else are we supposed to do with our free time, then, huh? You got any thoughts, Case?" It's obvious that these jabs land for Casey, for

152   DYLAN MORRISON

all Will doesn't have the context to understand why; it's clear in his face, the way his breath hisses in.

Do you imagine it's a sign of how normal and neutral you're feeling that you think you can tell how this man feels based on the quality of his inhales? The voice sounds like Selma's; the stupid voice always sounds like Selma's. Some days Will half suspects her of having installed a chip inside his head. *Here's a normal, neutral question: How are you feeling about how he looks in that wet flannel? The second wet flannel of the day? I mean, how many flannels can one guy own, first of all, but I don't want you to think I'm complaining, because me personally, my feelings on the wet flannels are—*

Will strangles this thought back with some effort before it can share those feelings, but, grimly, he doubts they would surprise him.

He's distracted, anyway, when they get the car back to the private access road they illegally came in on. Will had half expected there to be security guards or police there, to yell at Casey for driving through before; he can see now that that was stupid. Nobody cares about this silly little access road.

Also, no one is going to get across this silly little access road, because a large branch has fallen across it since they were last here, completely blocking it off.

"Only way back is the long way," Will observes, with a slightly nervous glance at Casey. It's not that he thinks Todd is going to die in here or anything, but he'd rather not drag this on for the poor kid any longer than necessary. "In this weather, working around the damage, it'll be fifteen minutes back to the main roads at least."

Casey drums his fingers against the steering wheel. Then an idea seems to occur to him, and he slants a look at Todd. "Hey, kid—you remember last summer when you helped me and Noel dress up the scarecrows for Halloween? And we—"

"Took the shortcut back?" Suddenly Todd is bright and

FALL INTO YOU 153

alert, his sullenness dropping away for excitement. Will, who remembers all too well being a teenager, doubts this is going anywhere he will like. "*Of course* I remember, I've only been *begging* you to take me again, you had to do it the *one week* my phone was too smashed to record!"

"Now, see, I was *going* to ask if you felt up for it, but I guess that's a yes," Casey says with a grin, throws the car into reverse, and turns it around, repositioning it so it's facing—

"Oh, God," Will says, as he notices anticipation start to change Casey's face, "Casey, *please* don't tell me you're planning on—"

Will doesn't bother finishing the sentence, because Casey has already spun the wheel to the right as far as it'll go, punched hard on the gas, and pitched the whole truck directly into the cornfield.

"I HAVE *NEVER* WANTED TO DO THIS!" Will has to scream to be heard over the sudden cacophony of corn leaves wicking by. Todd, now cackling next to him, seems to be recording out the window, not paying them any attention at all. "PEOPLE DO IT IN MOVIES AND I THINK 'STUPID. I'M NOT GOING TO DIE LIKE THAT. NOT ME!'"

"WE'RE NOT GOING TO DIE," Casey howls back, sounding, in spite of the circumstances, a little entertained. "IT'S THE FASTEST WAY."

Will grips the door handle as tightly as he can, fighting the urge to screw his eyes shut. "TO THE *OPERATING* TABLE, MAYBE."

"WOULD YOU JUST SHUT UP AND HAVE SOME FUN?" Casey somehow manages to sound oddly calm in spite of the circumstances and his volume. "ENJOY SOMETHING, FOR ONCE IN YOUR LIFE?" Then he cuts a quick, hard-to-parse look at Will—a look that he should, be instead, keeping on the *road*, or, in this case, the corn—and adds, almost daring, "OR

ARE YOU TOO MUCH OF A CONTROL FREAK FOR THAT? LIKE YOUR DAD?"

Will opens his mouth and then, not wanting to prove Casey right, snaps it shut. He folds his arms over his chest and glares out the windshield, prepared to experience, in fact, a number of things. Rage, for one, and terror, for another, and then possibly death by way of inconveniently placed scarecrow, although in Will's opinion that would be an indignity too far. Even his life has to have *some* sense of the mercy rule.

But he finds, to his surprise, that it's... pretty cool, to roll through the sodden cornfield as though it really is the sort of glossy, waving sea it sometimes appears to be in the wind, from a distance. It's a similar mechanic, now that Will thinks about it —the empty stalks, still green but stripped of their golden fruit, seem to become something else for being too close, just as they do for being very far away. Briefly, watching the now-fading leaves and left-behind strings of pale yellow corn silk brush endlessly over the windshield, sticking damply before being dragged away by the laws of physics, Will wonders if this is what it would be like to be an ant at the very bottom of a huge jungle, looking up through the layers of unbroken canopy above.

Abruptly, the windshield clears, and they're barreling towards the road and, oh, *God*, an oncoming car, which beeps furiously at them. Will grips the armrest again and does close his eyes this time, braces his body for impact, and—

"We didn't hit them, you know," Casey says, sounding quite grim and a little amused, as Will feels the car juddering towards a stop. "If you wanted to open your eyes or whatever."

Will opens his eyes; the truck is still moving, but it's on the nice, normal road now, no sign of its misadventure except the various corn leaves that rain has stuck fast against the windshield. Also, Todd appears to be filming him, snickering; when Will pushes the camera down, annoyed, Todd just shrugs and

FALL INTO YOU   155

says, "Be like that, then," and starts tapping at the screen, ignoring Will entirely.

"I want you to know," Will says shakily to Casey, as they cruise down the road at a speed that still, to Will, seems somewhat excessive, "that I've decided that I hate you. I hate you! Who drives into a *cornfield*? Don't you have any sense of—of— your own mortality, first of all, but also quite critically, *my mortality*, and—"

"Are you dead?" Casey seems quite amused to be asking, which makes Will hate him all the more. "You don't look dead to me, but I guess you'd know better than I would. Pretty sure *I'm* not dead, though—"

"You might be in ten minutes," Will mutters, no longer able to keep even the slightest bit of a grip on his tongue. "If you keep driving me so *insane*."

This makes Casey laugh, brief and choked off, and Todd mutter something under his breath that sounds like, "God, get a room." Casey doesn't appear to hear that, but Will certainly does, and it's mortifying enough to shut him up for the remainder of the drive.

As they near the farm, Will sees the access road in is still blocked, but as they're approaching from the north, Mere is driving up from the south. She pulls over to the side of the road when she sees their car and throws herself out of the driver's side, running over. Will gets out of the way as fast as possible and then it's all a blur: her hugging Todd, and yelling at him, and thanking them, and hugging them, and yelling at Todd, and hugging him again, and making him get into her station wagon.

There's a brief, strange moment that Will can't totally parse, a half conversation between Meredith and Casey that's cut off when they notice Will looking. Meredith says something like, "Look, that Town Council meeting—everything that happened, I know I could have been a better friend to—" and then Casey's

156   DYLAN MORRISON

waving her off before she can finish, muttering something about how she should forget it, and it doesn't matter now.

Then she's driving off, and Will and Casey are alone in the middle of the road, rain still pelting down. A large tree remains between them and the parking lot; there's not, Will is coming to realize, anyone but Casey to move it. It's always possible he has a larger staff running around than it appears, but Will's starting to get the sense that Casey handles most of the work here himself.

He stares, grimly, at the downed red oak, and for a second, it sways in front of him, like the one in the river. Will really, deeply, enormously doesn't want to deal with it right now; he can't imagine Casey does, either.

As if reading his mind, Casey says: "Christ. Look, I don't care what *you* do, but I don't have it in me to handle that right now. I've had enough close encounters of the wooden kind for one day. You can walk back from here, or you can ride into town with me; I'm going to see whether the whole bridge really blew out. Because, if it did..." Casey shrugs, and then looks at Will with a curiously youthful expression, like a kid lit up with excitement about something as simple as a piece of candy, or an interesting rock. "I think I want to see that, is all."

There's a beat, and then Will starts to grin. "You know what? Me too. Let's go."

This drive is mostly silent but, somehow, not awkward. Maybe it's the relief—of Todd being safe, of Todd being out of the car, of not having any barbs left to throw at one another— but whatever it is, it's nice. Will feels his muscles relax a little as Casey turns on the radio and twists the dial to classic rock, and then a little more when Casey starts humming along, under his breath, with the music.

When they get to the river, in spite of the rain, they both get out of the car. They're not the only ones to stand there, staring: Half the town seems to be with them, eyes wide, mouths slightly agape, staring at rushing, angry river water where the one bridge into and out of this town used to sit.

And on the other side of the river, standing in a row next to their line of temporarily abandoned cars, are all the citizens of Glenriver who happened to be on the other side when the bridge went. Will can see, on their faces, an echo of the realization that must be passing over his right now: Without that bridge, nobody here in Glenriver will be going *anywhere*, no matter how urgently they might want to.

"Well," Casey says, after a second, with a sidelong glance at Will. He sounds—something. Not quite resigned, but... something. "Looks like you'll be staying a while."

ELEVEN

It's not that Will sprints through the next week; that would imply he has some amount of say in the matter. It's rather more accurate to say that the week sprints *at Will*, bent at the waist as though intending to piledrive him, and then sends him flying through it like a sack of flour.

That he'll stay at the house until he can make it back to the hotel is implied, but never said; Casey clears his throat a couple of times on the drive back like maybe he's going to offer, but it always seems to die somewhere in the process. It's just as well, Will thinks—it's too awkward, the whole thing. What would Will say if he did offer? "Thanks so much for letting me stay in my childhood home, which I technically own, that's really generous of you?" A nightmare, no matter the approach.

But he does thank Casey, when Casey shows him the guest bedroom on the second floor, passing Bill's door—closed now, Will notices—with his head bowed. It's a nice guest room, far too modern and tasteful to have been June's or Bill's work, and Casey confirms it, looking pleased, when Will asks if he's the one who refinished what Will remembers as his mother's quilting room. But when Will says, confused, that he figured

FALL INTO YOU   159

Casey himself would be staying in the guest bedroom, Casey shakes his head, looking suddenly uncomfortable.

"Nah," he says, glancing away with an awkward little half shrug. "Used to, but—a few years ago, I finished the attic, made it into a separate suite, you know? The back stairs in and out are nice, and, anyway, it was just easier. Nicer, too, ultimately."

"Sure," Will says. Then, because it's been a long, unpleasant day and he's still more than a little damp and his brain-to-mouth filtering system is, for all intents and purposes, still bailing out an afternoon of rainwater, his mouth carries on without him and adds: "Although actually, I say that, but the last time I was up there, I was supposed to be cleaning it out as a summer punishment, and I think I was maybe seven, and my cousins had convinced me it was haunted, so. You know. I may not have the best memories of it."

Casey laughs, but then his brow furrows, and he opens his mouth like he wants to ask a question before closing it again, shaking his head. Instead of whatever it was, he says: "Look, there are some spare clothes in the dresser in there, just old work shirts and jeans, sweats from past merch runs in the market. Nothing fancy, and there's also obviously everything in, uh..." Casey drops his eyes to the ground, his throat visibly working as he swallows. "In your dad's closet. It's—I do know it's yours." He gives Will a brief up-and-down glance and then, flushing for some reason, mutters, "A lot of it would probably fit you, honestly. The vintage stuff, anyway."

"You can say 'Bill,'" Will offers, not entirely sure which one of them he's trying to be kind to. "I mean, he was my dad, but it was... complicated. Anyway, I'll probably stick to the sweats, if it's all the same to you; I was always scrawny for a Robertson, and I'd rather not... uh... Anyway. Thanks."

Casey cocks his head, his expression again tipping into curiosity, but then he shrugs, and stiffens, and says he's going back to the market to deal with things, and Will knows where to

160   DYLAN MORRISON

find him if he needs anything. Will can tell that the offer is begrudging, a little—that part of him desperately resents Will's presence in this house, in this town, in this family—but he appreciates Casey making it, anyway. After all, there have been plenty of people before Casey who resented Will's place in the Robertson family, and they, by and large, hadn't even bothered to try to be decent about it.

Once Casey's gone, Will pulls out his phone, wincingly ignores several missed messages from Selma, and calls Bartholomew, his overly enthusiastic second-in-command at the lab. Bartholomew is, in a word, thrilled to hear that Will has been caught in a natural disaster. Twice, when Will says something about expecting to be stuck here a week at least, Bartholomew asks hopefully if it might take longer. He also explains, at great length, that Will has never taken a real vacation, or even *long weekend*, in the four and a half years they've worked together, and so he, Bartholomew, has never truly enjoyed the sweet taste of ultimate power, except that one time Will got the flu. He actually says the words "the sweet taste of ultimate power," which concerns Will very deeply vis-à-vis what's going to happen to his work while he's gone, but when he points this out, Bartholomew assures him everything will be fine and that he'll email regular status reports and hangs up at once, so. Nothing there except to wait and see, Will supposes, given that he is completely and utterly trapped in Ohio.

It's at this point that Will realizes he could, if he wanted to, *take* a bit of a vacation. That life has, in a real way, offered one up to him on a plate. He could pick up one of the books off the shelves downstairs, or buy one on his phone, or turn on the television, and just... sit. Do nothing. Luxuriate in the odd sensation, possibly common to orphans the world over or possibly unique to Will's specific cocktail of dysfunctions, of having no one left alive to impress. Not that he was trying to impress his parents these last sixteen years, exactly, just—well

—there'd always been that little flame burning, hadn't there? In the center of his chest? The thought that maybe he'd encounter them again one day, Bill or June or both of them, and that more than anything, what he wanted to be in that moment, should it ever come, was: good. Doing just fine, thanks. Someone who could not possibly have been affected by what happened; someone who had never needed any help from them at all.

Too late for all that, now. He could let the little flame flicker and die; he could let his shoulders drop, let his guard go out on a quick smoke break. He could rest on his laurels, and take a beat, and let himself experience the sort of blissful, lazy abandon he's heard so much about from friends, colleagues, and television shows.

Will considers it for the time it takes to change into dry clothes. Then, his mind made up, he goes down to the market, to help Casey clear the tree out of the road.

This takes two days. In the middle of the first one, Mere shows up with a basket of food and a huge hug for both of them. She thanks them, and tells them they're both invited for dinner whenever they want it for life and, laughing only slightly tearfully, says if either of them ever needs a kidney, they're welcome to one of Todd's.

Will's very glad to have been able to help, but he expects that to be that. Mere surprises him, though—surprises them both, at least if the expression on Casey's face is anything to go by—and she asks to stay and run something past them. It turns out that she and a few of the other members of the local business council have cobbled together a rough census of who is trapped in Glenriver, and one of those members is of the town population stuck on the other side.

"I have a very good information source on that one," Mere adds, rolling her eyes, as she explains this. "Since Sandy's basically got everyone who can't get into town camped in the field off Main, on the other side of where the bridge used to be. He told me he's buying a *drone*, you guys. A *drone*."

"I mean," Casey says, a speculative look in his eyes. "It might be practical? Hauling things back and forth across the river—medicines, supplies, food—"

"That," Mere says with a little stab of her finger, cutting him off, "is exactly what I came here to talk to you about. Because he also said, and I need you to know that I know my husband, and he'll do this, that he's thinking about building a *trebuchet*. To *throw food to us*. And I just, you know what? I really, really need to find a way to make that unnecessary before he makes it *possible*."

Sandy's trebuchet plans aside, it turns out that between them, Meredith and Casey have most of the food in this town. Sure, Mike has some stuff in stock at the diner, and individual households have their pantries, but between the apples, produce, and frozen farm meat available at the Robertson Family Farms market, and the wide selection of household staples at Gunderson's, Mere and Casey are sitting on the bulk of the pile. Or, well, *technically* it's Mere and *Will* who are doing that, since, technically, this is Will's farm now. Will gets the sense that everyone is tactfully avoiding mentioning this; he knows he is.

But he and Casey are agreed, regardless, on Meredith's idea to pool resources, set up a generous rationing system that will make sure everyone in town has enough for at least a week or two, sort out the financials later. However, they both seem to think everyone in town will be fine getting the same selection of items, so long as that selection covers the basic necessities. Will, who lived nearly twenty years with Bill, many of them while working directly with the public from behind one of the market's counters, is sure his shock at this shows on his face; Casey seems to bristle at it, but Mere just waves a hand at him. "It's okay, Will—people will be flexible,

FALL INTO YOU 163

you'll see. You wouldn't have learned this from Bill, probably, but my parents always taught us that folks band together in a crisis, let go of the little things. Most folks, anyway." She chews her lip, adding, with slightly less confidence, "Although, now that you mention it, there are some people in town who can be—let's call it 'particular'—about their groceries—"

"Wait, why wouldn't he have learned that from Bill?" Casey demands, his voice suddenly sharp, but Meredith suddenly seems very occupied with a tune Will could swear she wasn't whistling a second ago, and doesn't reply.

Regardless, Will makes a note to build a quick survey form about preferences, allergies, long-held asinine grudges against specific brands, etcetera. The Gunderson ethos of optimism and community spirit is all well and good, but they grew realists out at Robertson Family Farms, so Will knows the data will start rolling in eventually. It's mostly a question of being ready when it does.

While they're working out the details and who will handle what, Will's phone buzzes; he only half glances at it, occupied with building a spreadsheet on Casey's borrowed laptop, his own being back at the hotel. However, when he notices the name is CATHERINE ROSE, he freezes like a panicked animal and silences the call, flipping the phone face down.

The voicemail she leaves him, when Will finally checks it that night, is breezy: "Hey, Will! Catherine Rose. Heard about the bridge situation; I called your hotel and they said you'd let them know, so I figure you got stuck in town. At least you have somewhere to stay, right? Anyway, obviously this puts a bit of a damper on our proposed timeline, since we won't be able to get over to you for you to sign, but! I figured it's been a couple of days, and a verbal contract's generally binding, so I wanted to touch base and see if you're ready to make yourself a very rich man. Get that nest egg together for your next... uhm... science

164   DYLAN MORRISON

project. Anyway, here when you're ready to close! Let me know."

Over the next several days, as Will settles into a new routine, her voicemails get less breezy.

In the mornings, Will gets up early, helps Casey load the truck with produce and eggs, and goes to Mike's, where he delivers some of the load and has breakfast. He likes watching Glenriver wake up, especially from the seat he'd always coveted as a child; something about it soothes him, settles him. He needs soothing and settling, because around the time he finishes breakfast, Catherine Rose usually hits him with her first call of the day. This one tends towards being bright and chipper, as though she's hosting one of those local morning shows, and has to make content out of cheerfulness and air. Something along the lines of, "Hi, Will! Me, Catherine! Another bright, beautiful day to call me back and let me know you're ready to commit to your future, can't wait to hear from you!"

Habitually, he ignores this call, and heads down the road to Gunderson's. The rest of the food is dropped off there, to be held in the grocery store's more ample fridges and freezers and be distributed on a schedule and rotation for which Will is maintaining the logistics. He spends most of the morning dealing with that, and then around noon Mere sends him back to the farm with lunch for himself and for Casey. On the drive back, Will generally receives his second Catherine Rose call of the day, this one always a little less cheerful, like she's really jonesing for another cup of coffee, or maybe lunch: "Will! Catherine. What could you possibly be doing, trapped in that tiny little town, that's so urgent you can't be calling me back? I know you're not trapped under a log without cell service, because you did manage to get in touch with the hotel we booked for you, right? Anyway. Don't forget this is a limited

FALL INTO YOU   165

time offer! Deadline getting closer every minute! Call me back."

Usually, at this point in the day, Will tracks down Casey to pass along the lunch Meredith sent for him. And then, one way or another, they tend to end up passing the afternoon together, whether Will means for them to or not. They're figuring out clearing the tree from the road the first few days, and after that, things just... come up. One afternoon, there's something wrong with the cider press, and Casey needs another pair of hands; they're interrupted doing that by Betsy Lundgren, who lives a few miles away, and has a storm damage issue she hasn't been able to resolve by herself. While they're there, three of her pigs get loose, and Will and Casey spend the bulk of the afternoon struggling to catch them in the mud, howling at first with frustration and rage but, eventually, with laughter. By the time they get home, they're both mud-covered and badly in need of a shower, but when they get there, a few other locals are waiting for them—well, for Casey, anyway—hoping to ask for help or advice.

And after that there's always something to do, every afternoon, and a number of the mornings besides. It's not that Glenriver doesn't have a mayor and a local government meant to handle emergencies, but, well. It's the same mayor that had been seated when Will was a child, and he'd been old even then, and the city council hasn't had much of a shake-up in the last few decades, either. They're a perfectly useful governing body if you're looking to get potential money for a potential bridge potentially approved in some potential future business quarter, but for in-the-moment crisis management, they're not what Will would call super helpful.

Casey, on the other hand, *is* what Will would call super helpful. He's so helpful, on such a broad swath of topics, that Will can hardly begin to catalogue them all. He watches in amazement as Casey handles damaged sump pumps and

166   DYLAN MORRISON

blown-out fences and flooded basements and broken windows, an old woman's car stuck deep in the persistent mud. Will helps, silencing Catherine Rose's late-afternoon-to-evening calls (painfully brief, always, as though she's been reconsidering her lunch message and determined the issue was volume of words— "Will! Catherine! Please return! Thanks!"). Or, at least, Will tries to help. Generally, whoever has called for Casey figures out pretty quickly that Will's the person managing the grocery situation, and the entire rest of the visit for him becomes either about accepting a donation of food from their freezer, which is lovely, or about explaining to them that he can't possibly be bribed into giving them special grocery treatment, which is annoying.

It doesn't seem to bother Casey, though—not just doing the work without Will's help, but doing the work at all. He whistles his way through most of it, unbothered by the jobs that get him dirty, undeterred by the tasks that leave him pouring with sweat. Will has, perhaps, taken to observing some of these tasks a little more closely than is appropriate, although not exactly on purpose. It's just... difficult, isn't it, to look away from a man with Casey's devastatingly muscled body while he's giving that body a workout. Will keeps finding himself drifting away in a haze while he watches Casey do things like tossing around heavy pieces of storm debris as though they weigh nothing. Worse, he's almost always, when he catches himself at it, in the middle of some horrible thought like, *Wish I was that sack of leaves and branches he just threw over his shoulder*, or *God, he should leave the logs for the beavers to sort out and toss me around instead.*

One afternoon, Will happens to catch sight of Casey out the window of the bakery while he's covering Daphne's break. Casey's in the parking lot, wearing work jeans and a thin, dirty white tank top, one of his ever-present flannels tied around his waist. He appears to be in the early stages of replacing the section of fence that was damaged by lightning strike, and regretting his previous thoroughness in driving the fenceposts down. As he struggles, attempting to yank the damaged wood from the ground, visibly grunting and cursing even though Will can't hear him from in here, Will loses track of what he's supposed to be doing; the bakery's empty, anyway, and doesn't, for the moment, feel important. Casey's muscles flex and strain as he attempts to pull the post from the earth, one of his calloused hands wedged in each of the empty fencepost slots, and Will watches the growing sweat stain on his tank top with a hunger that surprises even him, lost to the flow of time.

This is unfortunate because, after several minutes, Daphne returns, and clears her throat. At this point, the flow of time not only resumes, but viciously punishes Will for trying to pause it by dropping him right into one of the most embarrassing moments of his life, which seems about right. It's not even that Daphne *says* anything; she doesn't. But her face speaks wildly entertained volumes that make Will want to live the rest of his life in an underground cave, safe from the dangerous eyes of other people.

Regardless of the work he's doing, or who he's doing it for, Casey will never accept payment; he'll barely, Will notices with increasing concern and no small amount of desperately buried attraction, accept *thanks*. He smiles and laughs with everyone, always remembering their pets' names and where the last time they saw one another was and, if they're regulars at the market, their favorite kind of apple. It's honestly remarkable. Will's known some of these people since literally the day he was born, and he doesn't have half the rapport with them that Casey does, even if there's an odd, off note thrumming through it sometimes that Will can't quite identify.

Will knows about people, how they move separately and how they move together. He knows the way only an observer can know, the knowledge sharpened with the remove of the

168 DYLAN MORRISON

scientist. He's been lonely, and that's been difficult, but it's been educational, too. It's allowed him a perspective that he has, until now, appreciated as unique and useful.

Casey breaks this perspective. Casey, just by existing and acting like this, takes this perspective, spits on it, and throws it out an upper-story window.

The problem is that he's so... nice, Will thinks. Not to Will, necessarily—the two of them have achieved, in these last few days, a détente Will would describe as "pleasantly neutral"— but to everyone else, he's too nice. People aren't *nice* like this, not real people, who walk around in the world interacting with others. Who has the time, or the energy, or the inclination, or the will, to be that nice? To help every neighbor who asks; to really listen when someone comes in and complains about something stupid at the market; to head out at least a few nights a week to solve for some issue and not, if Will's any judge of the creaks and groans of this old house, return until late?

It's too much for one person, that's all, or at least for one person based on Will's understanding of people prior to meeting a certain flannel-loving reckless driver. It makes it hard to imagine Casey's a real human being as opposed to a robot invented at Bill's request, even though Will is all too intimately aware, sharing houseroom with him, that he's an honest-to-God flesh-and-blood man. A flesh-and-blood man who is sometimes wandering around in a towel after a shower; a flesh-and-blood man who hums to himself in the mornings while he's getting ready, the sound filtering down to Will's bedroom from the attic; a flesh-and-blood man who never seems to find time to eat dinner, not that Will is paying attention to that.

Paying attention or not, Will finds himself puzzling at that last piece on Sunday evening, a week and a day after the incident that wiped the bridge out. The estimated one week of repair is now being reported as two, and Will, sitting at the kitchen table, should be thinking about that. He should be

FALL INTO YOU 169

making a new plan, or, at very least, dinner, not thinking about *Casey's* dinner. He should be calling Selma, something he has put off for so long now that she must surely be apoplectic.

A sharp pang of guilt distracts him, and he pauses the entire train of thought to send Selma another apology gift. There have been... several, in the days since he learned he would be trapped indefinitely here on the farm. It's not that he thinks he can buy her affection; he knows Selma doesn't work like that. If her affections could be bought, her parents would have managed years ago. But if she knows Will's alive, and thinking about her, and sorry for going ghost mode, and just in that place where he's basically bricking it and turtling up and unable to have an honest conversation without absolutely freaking out, she'll understand. Will hopes she'll understand, anyway. Their friendship has only survived this long because she very generously has before.

He sends her a pair of leather Chicago Cubs driving gloves, with the note, "Because I'm sure I'm driving you crazy. Sorry, for that and the pun. Love you."

Guilt semi-assuaged, his thoughts return, as they tend to lately, to Casey. This time it's not a particularly wholesome turn, and he jumps, hoping he's not blushing, when Casey slouches through the door as if summoned. "Oh! You're back. I didn't hear you come in."

"Hey," Casey says. His voice is lower than usual, a tired, drawn quality to it. He drops into the chair across from Will heavily, puts his elbows on the table, and rests his head in his hands. Some inner part of Will twitches—June had the unfortunate habit of delivering a hard, unforgiving flick to the back of any elbow that she happened to see on this table—but he doesn't comment as Casey adds, "I'm surprised you're here already. I thought that thing at the cider mill would've taken you hours."

"What, the contracts issue?" Will says, his eyebrows going up. "No, I was done with it an hour ago."

170   DYLAN MORRISON

Ruefully, Casey snorts. "Of course you were. Would've taken *me* hours, anyway."

"I mean..." Will says, in what he hopes are generous tones. Casey seems to be in a dark headspace; that's not like him, and Will stares for a second, warring with conflicting internal impulses. Half of him is screaming that it's never a good idea to stay at this table, in this house, with someone in this mood, but the other half wants to do something *insane*, like reach out and squeeze Casey's shoulder.

Better he find something to do with his hands. Will stands, and starts puttering around the kitchen as he says, "In your defense, I'm pretty sure I was the last person who sorted that filing cabinet, so I had a leg up. My labels were still in there and everything—my teen handwriting, I have to say, probably didn't help anyone else who tried to use it very much." Deciding he might as well solve one of his own problems, Will starts rummaging around in the cabinets for likely-looking things to eat as he continues, "I redid it so it's easier to navigate, and I did find that Bradley contract you were looking for—stuck between two files with something that smelled like maple syrup, horribly enough. Still legible, though, and that guy who called is full of it, like you thought. He sold Bill all that equipment flat out, no rental agreement. Probably figured he could squeeze a few more dollars out of the place, since the old man was famous for losing track of the paperwork."

Casey mutters something colorful under his breath, but then, lifting his head briefly to make eye contact with Will, says, "That's great, actually. Thanks. You leave it—"

"In your office at the market? Yeah," Will says easily. He doesn't have to be easy about it—he could point out that, really that it's Will's office, because it's Will's market, because it's Will's farm, but there's no point. Casey knows all that, and it would be rubbing salt in the wound to point it out. Anyway, Will doesn't want to. This tentative peace they've managed to

FALL INTO YOU   171

cobble together is... strange, certainly, but nice. It wouldn't be worth it, to go upsetting the equilibrium over something that, at least to Will and at least right now, doesn't matter very much at all.

"Thanks," Casey says again, with real feeling, and drops his head back into his hands. "One less thing to deal with; thank you."

"It's... really fine," Will says, eyeing Casey's bent head in mild concern that he would, if Casey were to look up and catch him at it, have to pretend was disdain, or perhaps smelling something odd. Selecting a few things from the cabinet and moving on to the fridge, he adds, "Uh, not to be weird, or whatever, but... are you like... good?"

Casey laughs, short and bitter. "Define 'good.'"

"Well, that's not a promising answer," Will remarks, mostly to himself. "But, sure, you asked, fair enough: adjective, at least in this instance, meaning favorable or positive. Are you currently feeling favorable or positive?" When Casey snorts, but doesn't respond, Will grabs several items from the fridge as he adds, "It can also mean morally correct, if you'd rather answer that question. I can't imagine you would, but it's there for you as an option."

"Is *anyone* morally correct, really?" Casey asks, sounding a little bleak. "Do you think there's such a thing? Or are we all doing our best and not getting there, most of the time?"

For several long moments, as he finds and removes a pan from the cupboard next to the fridge, Will tries to think of something to say other than what he is thinking, which is, *Yeesh.*

"Yeesh," says Will eventually, not feeling great about it. "Did someone like break your spirit on the way back from—uh —where—well, wherever you were, anyway." God, Will had almost asked Casey *where he was*, as though he has any right to know; sharing houseroom with the man is playing tricks on Will, and that's all there is to it.

172   DYLAN MORRISON

He focuses, because it's high time he did, on making dinner. He's lucky that there was a natural disaster, and that he and Casey teamed up with Meredith. If he'd tried to do this even a few days ago, the contents of the fridge as Casey kept it would have left him with a choice between a variety of gross frozen dinners and a spoonful of questionable mustard. But, as it is, they were sent, like everyone else in town, a bag full of staples and supplies and, because they'd both filled out their dietary needs and preferences through Will's hastily constructed little electronic system, Will knows there's nothing in that Casey can't or won't eat.

He finds himself turning to a dish he used to make a lot in college, which involves, essentially, boiling pasta in one pot and cooking together olive oil, white beans, garlic, red pepper flakes, and a can of tuna fish in another. It's not anything he cooks from a recipe—now, as then, it's a meal of convenience more than one designed to impress. As Will works through the motions of the opening steps, he thinks that it's a pretty good summary of his general cooking philosophy: Will is a functional cook, and that's all he's trying to be. He does his best to save what brilliance and creativity he possesses for the lab; at the stove, he's satisfied if it's tasty, and, broadly speaking, not too terrible for him.

Will's so wrapped up in getting things going that he half forgets Casey's there, and only just doesn't jump when Casey says, "I was with Todd, actually."

It takes Will a second to process that Casey is picking up a conversational thread Will thought he abandoned several minutes ago; then it takes him another second for the content of the sentence to sink in. When it does: "*Oh.* How, uh. How did that go?"

"Oh, you know," Casey says, and Will cocks his head, surprised to hear an edge of bleak despair in his tone. "He wanted to talk about how he's having nightmares, which is fair. I would be having nightmares, too, if I were him. I am having nightmares *about* him, about what would have happened, so I get it. It's not that I *mind*, right, talking to this traumatized teenage kid about what happened to him, God knows I've done it before, I don't mind! It's just that everyone in this town, all of them, for months and months, have been so polite, and so awkward, and so distant. 'Hey, Casey!' and 'Hiya, Casey!' but never anything more. And now, all of a sudden, it's so urgent for all of them to talk to me, and ask my help with this thing, or that thing, or the other thing, and while I'm there, can I help with this issue they've been meaning to ask me about, but it's been so *awkward*, and oh there's *another* problem, and meanwhile it's not as though there isn't always something that needs doing *here* and I—" Casey cuts himself off, his chest heaving, and Will raises his eyebrows down into his pan as he stirs. When Casey speaks again, his voice is tightly controlled. "I feel. As though it might be nice. For things to... stop. For a minute or two. That's all."

Will stares at Casey, whose head is still in his hands, who is not looking at Will. Will stares at Casey and tries, for an upsettingly long moment, to place the sharp sense of confusion within him, the abrupt but utter sense that he, Will, is at sea. What's so confusing about that statement? Why should it make him feel unmoored, lost? Casey is obviously feeling exhausted, worn thin, overtaxed, and it's perfectly normal that he should be. After all, it's a natural disaster they're living through right now, and, surely, they're all feeling worn and overtaxed...

A wave of realization washes over Will; it's almost nauseating in intensity, and he turns back to the nearly finished dinner, draining the pasta and combining the ingredients essentially on autopilot. Casey might be feeling worn and exhausted, pushed to the brink by these strange circumstances, but Will is not. Will is feeling—good. Really good. The best, maybe, he has felt in... It couldn't be years, could it? Could that possibly be right?

He tips the pasta into two bowls as he tries to disprove this theory within himself, carding through memories for a comparable sense of fulfillment and calm and coming up worryingly blank. When was it, the last time he felt like this? God, has Will *ever* felt like this? And what does it mean, if he hasn't? If this is the first and only time?

Throwing a handful of Parmesan on top of each bowl, Will sets one down in front of Casey as he walks back to his own vacated chair, too distracted by this disquieting moment of realization to be self-conscious. "Here, eat. Nothing ever feels as grim after pasta."

Will sits down, too, and sets his own food on the table, and then looks up to see Casey staring at him over his steaming bowl like a trapped animal. Will stares back at him, guilt and confusion and a horrible certainty raising the hairs on his neck, climbing like bile up the back of his throat. He focuses, dizzily, on the way the light from the overhead lamp catches in the soft green of Casey's eyes and thinks he doesn't know what he wants at all, and maybe he's never known.

"Thank you," Casey says, like he really means it, like he can't believe Will's done this simple thing for him. And God, hell, maybe Will *does* know what he wants, but he would prefer, actually, if he didn't.

TWELVE

Will spends the next several days in a panic.

It's not, of course, the correct panic. A smart person—a *sane* person—would be panicking about being stuck in Glenriver for another week as the emergency bridge repair drags on, trapped without access to essentially any of his worldly possessions. Or, if not that, perhaps they would be panicking about Bartholomew at work, who responded to Will's phone call informing him of the delay with something like a witch's cackle; that would be a good reason to panic. They could panic about their phone burning from ignoring so many calls, as between Selma and Catherine Rose, Will's is surely nearly at its limit. Will could, if he wanted to be reasonable about it, panic about the sale of the farm falling through, although given the ever-increasing volume of Catherine Rose's phone calls, he doubts he could convince himself to worry it might.

Regardless: He's not panicking about any of those good, reasonable, rational things. No; instead he is panicking about stupid Casey, and his stupid *eyes* and *face* and *hands* and what, exactly, is so *wrong* with Will, that he could have spent so many days in this house with him and *not realized*. God, it's so embar-

176   DYLAN MORRISON

rassing he could throw himself off the top of one of the apple trees. This would only be a dramatic gesture, because Robertson Family Farms has always favored dwarf varietals, which Will knows full well only grow about ten feet tall for maximum apple-pickability, but *still*.

It's just that Casey's unacceptably hot, and the situation has gotten out of hand. Or, well, no, it's not *just* that he's horrifically hot, Will *knows* Casey's hot, has had a firm, unyielding grip on that little detail from the very instant they met. It's that he's... Being around him is so *easy*, even when it's messy, or stupid, or horrible, or so frustrating that it makes Will want to tear all his hair out. That doesn't any make sense—how can something be easy but make him want to tear all his hair out?—but that doesn't stop it being true. It's almost like...

When Will was a child, the earliest years of his life he can remember, there had been this dog on the farm, Bear. He hadn't been the Robertsons' pet—that had been made very clear to Will from the first, that this was a working barn animal, like the cows and the pigs, not his friend. But Will had befriended him, anyway, sneaking pieces of chicken into his pocket at dinner and hurrying outside on short little legs to toss them, one by one, to the drooling dog. Bear was some kind of mutt, border collie somewhere in the mix, at least if Will's memories are anything to go by. He was a serious creature, not much for affection. But he liked Will, and as Will got older and was able to wander further and further from the farm, sometimes Bear would come with him, following him curiously, leading him back home if he got lost. Some of Will's best childhood memories are of afternoons in the woods with Bear, who was always calm and patient and never yelled at him. Even if Will was stomping around after a fight, or running through the woods crying, Bear would trot steadily after him, reliably centered in his own canine head-space, not bothered at all. It had always given Will this weird sense of peace, knowing there was someone alive, even if they

FALL INTO YOU   177

were only a dog, with whom he could just *be*. Whose opinion of him wasn't hinged upon how pleased they were with him that day.

Anyway, being around Casey is like that. It's really starting to give Will some trouble.

Like—the other night, Sunday night. Will was in a bad mood; he'd decided, somewhere around midday, that he'd like to try to access the stuff in his old bedroom, and spent some time attempting to clear out the junk. The attempt had been fruitless, frustrating, and emotionally excoriating, and he'd stormed downstairs around four in the afternoon streaked with grime, wild-eyed, and brimming with a vibrating, unhinged energy.

When he'd walked past the living room, Casey had raised an eyebrow and said, "Uh, hey. You look weird."

"Do I look weird?" Will had said, hearing the manic edge in it and not caring very much. "Ha ha! Perhaps I do. Do you know how people usually look, though, when they've found a box of... um, I'm going to go with 'intimacy aids,' in their parents' house? In their own former bedroom, no less? Because listen, I mean, maybe this is normal—"

"Oh, *God*," Casey said, laughing on it. "Bill—*eurgh*. I don't want to think about *that*, I have to say."

"*You* don't want to think about it?" Will said, sinking down to perch on the arm of the cushy wing chair near the door. "How do you think I feel? I suppose there's no chance you're going to tell me they're yours and free me from a lifetime of horror?"

Casey snorted. "Nah, man, I don't keep anything in that junk pit; I tried cleaning it out once and Bill about bit my head off, so. I've left it alone ever since." Shaking his head, still laughing on it a little, he added, "Listen—want to watch the back half of this movie with me? Think about something else?"

"What is it?" Will asked, a little interested in spite of his horrified mood, and had brightened somewhat when he realized

178 DYLAN MORRISON

it was one of his own favorite Mel Brooks films. And then he'd just... watched the movie with Casey, both of them seeming to enjoy the rare chance to do nothing, laughing together and smiling at one another occasionally before looking away. What *was* that? What was Will supposed to do with that? All his previous boyfriends—not that Casey is Will's boyfriend, or anything like his boyfriend, or even remotely interested in filling the position, *obviously*—but still, the people Will has dated in the past have been pretty clear about not enjoying Will in his less-than-centered moments. Whether implicitly or explicitly, the message that has always been made clear is that Will, in less-than-optimal mental condition, is less-than-optimal company.

But Casey isn't like that. He's just not. Will's come to realize over the last few days, turning the whole thing over and over in his mind, that Casey wasn't that way even when they were fighting with one another, that very first day. He hadn't dismissed Will, or ignored him, or called him impossible, or acted like he wasn't worth the trouble of taking seriously. He'd been mad at Will, sure, and said some less-than-great things, okay, but he'd *fought*, at least. He'd done his best to say his piece, and what's more, he'd respected Will enough to engage with him, from that very first minute. Is that what it is—why Will can't stop thinking about it?

Whatever the reason, it's getting worse. On Wednesday morning, Casey laughs at a shirt Will's wearing, says, "God, I haven't seen that in forever, I can't even remember why I stopped wearing it now," which is when it finally clicks for Will that he has been *walking around in Casey's old clothes* for the better part of a week and a half. This is so upsetting to him that he does, at long last, find himself digging through Bill's closet for any alternative options, and he pulls on and buttons up a green-and-blue tartan flannel without much hope before stepping over to the mirror, expecting to see it dwarf him.

FALL INTO YOU 179

Instead, surprised, Will sees... Well, it's no Bill Robertson staring back at him, certainly, but. The shirt fits. It sits flat and unbunched over his shoulders, across his chest, as though it was cut for him. It was, actually, always a little tight on Bill, back in the old days. Will remembers realizing as a teenager that Bill must have bought them that way on purpose, and finding it a little amusing. But it fits him, the overall silhouette slightly slimmer than the one Bill cut in his prime, perhaps, but not by enough to really matter. He meets his own eyes in the mirror, taking in his high cheekbones and dark hair, his father's nose, eyebrows, and long, rectangular face over his mother's thinner lips and weaker chin. Then, feeling better about it than he would have guessed, he walks downstairs still wearing the flannel, feeling like maybe, after all, there was some glimmer of the family potential in him all along.

Of course, then Casey smirks when he sees Will, and says he *knew* Bill's shirts would fit him, and Will experiences what's surely the least heterosexual series of emotions and impulses to ever occur inside of said shirt, so. Maybe not.

All in all, it's not the worst way Will's spent a few days; in fact, even factoring in the number of hours he spends absolutely panicking to himself, it might be one of the better weeks Will's ever passed. Which is probably why the bottom drops out of his stomach when Casey comes home on Thursday night and says, "Good news—they're finally got a repair date set for the bridge. Guys on the crew said Saturday for sure; they're covering the overtime themselves out of pocket, because they feel bad they've had everyone trapped so long."

"Oh," Will says, trying to sound calm and casual and not like the very thought fills his veins with ice water. "Well. That's, I mean. That's great, right? Everyone can get out of town—or into town, I guess, if we're talking about the folks on the other side of the river. And I can, uh, get out of your hair." As if summoned by the specter of her impending access to him, Will's phone begins to buzz in his pocket with what he's sure is today's tenth phone call from Catherine Rose. Even a text begging natural disaster amnesty hadn't deterred her; the woman is like a hyena.

"Right," Casey says, his voice distant. "My hair. Right." There's a long pause, in which Casey's gaze seems to be fixed on something far further away than the fridge he appears to be staring at, and which Will spends briefly but fervently considering taking a career turn towards unlicensed bridge demolition. Then, more brightly, Casey says, "We should do something, you know? To mark the occasion."

Will has several enterprising suggestions, none of which are remotely appropriate. He swallows them, trying not to wince, and says, in an impressively normal tone, "That's a good idea; what were you thinking?"

Casey shrugs, his face very casual, but his eyes dancing in excitement. "What do you think about a bonfire? We probably could do with one, anyway, a lot of dried out husks and other stuff that we could stand to clear out of the barn, and conditions are certainly safe for it right now, after all that rain. Get some drinks, some food, have it out in the field by the market—if, you know, that's... workable."

There's a loaded pause, and this time Will can't totally suppress the wince; he knows what Casey's saying, or what he's not saying. He means that he knows it's Will's land, and thus Will's call whether or not they set a big fire on it and invite the town to come enjoy its light and warmth. It's good of him, an allowance of sorts for things to sit easier between them, but it makes Will feel as though his intestines have had an unlikely Gorgon encounter and are being slowly turned to stone.

"Sure," he says weakly, after a second, instead of adding insult to injury by uttering the words "stone intestines" in front of what surely has to be the most attractive man the state of Ohio has ever produced. "I mean, who doesn't like a bonfire?

And I can talk to Mere and see if she'll help me throw together a plan, get the word out—it's not like anyone can have anything better to do, right?"

"Exactly," Casey says, grinning. Then the expression goes smaller, more thoughtful, as he adds, "And, anyway, I think with something like this, it's all about how people remember it, right? When I was a kid, there was this crazy mudslide one year at a festival we were at, took out half the hill behind the main stage, it was bananas. So much rain, flooding, obviously mud everywhere, ruined equipment—a nightmare. Whole thing got shut down after the first day. But, at the end of that day, the bands came out and played a few crazy, off-the-cuff sets, and everybody danced and drank and ate what they could before the crews came to clear it out, and I still run into people who remember that as the best show they ever went to, mud and all." He shrugs, throwing Will a slightly rueful glance, and adds, "Or, you know, maybe it was all the drugs everyone was probably on; what do I know? I was nine."

You were NINE? Will thinks, wondering what on earth Casey would have been doing at an outdoor music festival in a mudslide at nine years old, but not sure this is the moment to ask. Instead, striving for a light, jovial tone, he says, "I'm not saying we should drug the town, you understand, but I do think we could probably achieve getting several of them slightly tipsy and showing the rest a moderately good time. But, if the bridge will be ready Saturday—" Will swallows, hard, against the realization of exactly how soon that is. "That pretty much means we'd have to do it tomorrow, right?"

"Yeah," Casey says, and grimaces at Will good-naturedly. "Insane, do you think? Not possible in the timeframe?"

Will considers. He should say yes, that it's impossible, that it'll be slapdash and chaotic and no one will remember it fondly and that it would be better not to even try—that's what he'd

182   DYLAN MORRISON

usually say—but instead, what comes out is, "Nah. I think we got this."

Will is not, in fact, sure that they got this. It is, at best, a wildly optimistic summary of his general opinion, and, at worst, an outright lie—but, to his surprise and pleasure, it turns out they do. Meredith handles spreading the word and helps Will figure out who to speak to about bringing food and drinks; everyone Will reaches out to is happy to help, and Will realizes fairly quickly that it's because Casey was right. People want closure at the end of something that shifts their lives around, even if it was only for a few weeks. People are eager to throw their lot in with anything that feels like a bookend, a way to mark this chapter of upheaval as closed.

Will never had closure when he left Glenriver. He told himself he didn't need or even want it, that it was pointless to wish for it, that it wasn't important; he told himself he could draw the line in the sand for himself, and that line could count as enough. He told himself he could carry on without it, and that the yawning, empty space inside himself where he ripped out a section of his internal circuitry so its virus wouldn't poison the entire machine would knit itself closed, maybe, new sinews weaving together from wire and steel, so long as he didn't interfere too much.

It never did, though. The hole stayed, sparking and hissing, every bit as impossible to miss as the faded spots of wallpaper in Bill's bedroom, where paintings used to sit. Will's staring at it— through it, really—even now.

At least seeing it is better than not seeing it. At least Will *can* see it, even if how he does choose to make use of that particular ability is to pretend, immediately and with increasingly poor results, that he can't. He throws himself into the bonfire preparations instead, zipping around town in the farm's old pickup truck because it's easier, with the big bed and every-

FALL INTO YOU   183

thing, than using his terrible but long-since-jumped rental car. It's not as nice as Casey's truck, and makes a wheezing noise sometimes on the big hill on the far side of town, but it feels like an old friend, for all it must have arrived at the farm years after Will left. Its chipped red paint, the way the fake leather peels up off the seats, evokes the oddly specific comfort of certain sorts of wear, the way something can age in the same shape as things did when you were a child. It was Will's father, after all, who broke this car in, smoothed down the ridges on the radio dial from rolling it under his thumb, picked at the edges of the leather as he sat in the parking lot of the feed store; just because Will wasn't here to see it doesn't mean he doesn't know.

It's funny, though, after all those years of hearing that he was a Will and not a Bill, after all the heavy, unpleasant conversations about expectations and duty and falling short—it's funny, how many of the older citizens of Glenriver jump, or put their hands to their chests, or shake their heads when they see Will get out of that truck in one of Bill's old work shirts. How many of them gasp, or mutter, "The spitting image," or yell, "Thought you were your old man for a second there—how you been, Will? Long time!"

Will's not sure if it feels good or bad; it certainly feels *something*, makes some unwieldy, choking emotion bubble and roil within him. He can't quite tell what would come out of his mouth if he were to let it surface: sobbing or screaming or a long sigh of relief, or maybe really *uncomfortable* laughter, the kind that goes on far too long.

He keeps it inside, whatever it is. In that, if nothing else, he's managed to be his father's son.

But he's in an odd mood, all told, by the time cars start arriving in the parking lot Friday night. The whole day he's been manic and macabre by turns, delighted about the party one moment and then gripped with dread the next; tomorrow

184   DYLAN MORRISON

the bridge is going to be repaired, and then... then... what? What is Will going to *do*? He can't very well continue to live in the house with Casey, avoiding Catherine Rose's phone calls, until such a time as some convenient representative of the Universal Public Good arrives and says, *William Josiah Robertson, I declare you UNFIT to handle conflict. Shut your mouth and step away from the delicate interpersonal situation with your hands up; I am here to relieve you of your duties.*

Will *would* be relieved, honestly, to hand all this off to someone else—it occurs to him, abruptly but quite emphatically, that this would be so much easier with a partner. Not even Casey, necessarily, just *someone*, some other, more objective person whose only remaining parent had not recently shuffled off their mortal coil. Someone to whom Will could go and say, *Listen, listen, I know the whole time I lived here, I dreamed about getting away, and the minute I did, I never looked back, but this town isn't the one I left behind, somehow, and I'm not at all sure I'm the person I was when I walked away, either. Does that make sense, do you think, or am I going insane? Does grief do this, to the best of your knowledge, put a new film over the lens of your life, make everything appear to be a slightly different color? Is this a condition in which someone should make a large real estate deal—probably not, right?* Someone to throw this kind of question at would be, honestly, a godsend.

An image of Selma, larger-than-life and looking so irritated that Will actually grimaces at his own imagination, blooms behind his eyes. Swallowing hard, he nods to himself—tomorrow, then. He'll talk to her tomorrow.

For tonight, he goes to greet Mere, one of the first to arrive, all the kids in tow. She grins at him but is pulled away by Casey before they can talk. Todd gives Will an awkward half hug and then skitters away to talk to Noel, who, to Will's amazement and deep amusement, blushes tellingly at being approached.

FALL INTO YOU 185

The rest of the children are shepherded off by Daphne Cardini-Johnstone, who has emerged from behind the market bakery counter to hold court in the kids' play area, where a number of members of the Cardini family are keeping a vague eye on the proceedings to ensure none of the town children kill one another or themselves. Hazily, Will finds he remembers this from town gatherings of his own youth, the loose network of Glenriver families who took the "it takes a village" approach. Old Mrs. Cardini, now that Will thinks about it, had bandaged more of his skinned knees when he was a child than his own mother had. Nancy Gunderson, too.

Nancy's still off in Georgia, but old Mrs. Cardini's sitting at the playground with Daphne, having arrived about three hours early to poke around the market bakery, pass judgement, and gossip. Will takes her a cup of hot cider and kisses her on the cheek, and she swats him away and says, "Oh go *away*, William; if *you've* gone and become a gentleman, I will die of old age," but he thinks she's pleased, even so.

Most of the rest of the town trickles in over the next hour or so, as the sun sets. They are still missing the section of the populace trapped on the other side of the bridge, but before darkness falls, Mere hurries over to Will with a beer in one hand and her phone in the other. When she gets close, she turns the phone proudly to face him. "So, okay, I told Sandy about this idea, and he liked it so much they're doing one on the other side of the river, too! See?"

Will peers at the screen, a slow grin spreading over his face as he sees the loose circle of tents in the distance, the large pile of dead wood and branches being added to even as he watches. Oddly touched, he says, "God, that's—amazing, actually? I'm glad he thought of it."

"Yeah, I liked it, too," Mere says, shaking her head with a fond smile at the screen before she tucks the phone back in her pocket. Then—maybe, Will thinks with trepidation as it happens, it's the beer—she throws an arm around him, pulling him in for a tight hug. "I'm glad you came back here, Will," she whispers, fierce. "Even if you drive away tomorrow and I never hear from you again: *Thank you* for coming back."

"Oh," Will says, unexpected tears pricking at the corners of his eyes. "That's... Sure. Of course." He clears his throat, and then, slightly raggedly, adds, "And you're not going to—to never hear from me again, God. I'm not a stupid teenager anymore; I know about social niceties now."

"I'm holding you to that," Mere warns, stepping back and wiping her own eyes. "See if I don't!"

Will smiles brightly at her, and opens his mouth to say—oh, he doesn't know what. He's as interested as anyone to hear what it's going to be, whether a promise to return and visit, or a confession that he's suddenly not sure he wants to sell, or even *leave*, at all. Mere isn't Selma, obviously, but she *was* Will's very first best friend, and he trusted her enough then for it to carry over now, in spite of all the lost years between them. She might be biased towards Casey and Glenriver, but then again, wouldn't Selma be biased towards Will doing the right thing, the *sane* thing, and sticking with the life he's spent two decades building in Chicago?

He doesn't get to find out, anyway, what he would have ended up saying. A hand lands on Will's shoulder, its grip warm and familiar, and Will's voice shrivels back down into his throat when he realizes that it's Casey's. If nothing else, Will would like to do his very best to avoid discussing his feelings for Casey, which are messy and complicated except in the ways they are upsettingly and graphically simple, *in Casey's actual earshot*, so. For the best, really, that the surprise of being grabbed by the man seconds before going maudlin and confessional has left Will feeling as though he swallowed a series of furious frogs.

"*There* you are," Casey says, smiling at him, when Will half

FALL INTO YOU 187

turns to face him. Glancing quickly at Mere and then looking back at Will, he adds, "Sorry to interrupt, but I was wondering if you'd mind helping me with something?"

"Oh," Will says, trying to gather himself at speed and finding it a bit like trying to scoop sand with a sieve. "I—sure, yeah. Or, uh. I don't mind, is what I mean."

"Great," says Casey, beaming at him. Will smiles back, helpless not to in the face of Casey's expression, though his own goes somewhat queasy when, out of the corner of his eye, he notices Meredith suddenly looking very amused.

If other people are able to tell how I feel about this, Will thinks with sudden, crystalline clarity, *I will walk north until I am fully submersed in Lake Erie and see if there's any truth to the rumors of lake monsters. They can have their merry way with me! Take me away, boys!*

"Can I," Will says, as he waves an awkward goodbye to a now-grinning Mere without making eye contact with her, then starts to follow Casey through the gathering crowd of the party, "grab a drink, maybe? I think I might really need a drink."

"You can get one where we're going," Casey says. As they pass it, Will looks wistfully at the bartender's table he himself, six hours before, stocked with his own favorite brands of alcohol; he considers ducking over while Casey isn't paying attention and at least grabbing a beer. But Casey must sense it; he looks over his shoulder at Will, and snorts, and then reaches over and grabs Will's wrist like it's nothing, like he doesn't even think about it. "Come *on.* After the two weeks we've had, I think we can do a little better than one of Jared Eckles' mixed drinks."

Casey's hand is warm around his wrist, the meat of his palm flush against the suddenly rushing estuaries of Will's veins, his fingers flexing a little with every step; Will can't think about that. If he does, he'll stop talking, and stop moving, and just

188   DYLAN MORRISON

stand here like stone, transfixed. If nothing else, Casey would be bound to notice that. So...

"You said Jared was a good bartender!" Will protests, outraged. He does so in a hiss, so that Jared won't overhear them and be offended. "This morning! I said we needed a good bartender, and you said Jared *was* a good bartender—"

"You said you needed *a* bartender, and I said Jared was *a* bartender," Casey corrects, slanting a grin over his shoulder. "Which he is! He's a fine and affordable bartender, who will get you serviceably drunk on cocktails that taste fine at the beginning of the night, and then progressively less good as he, himself, gets drunker." At Will's little squawk of outrage, Casey adds, in relenting tones, "He's also the only game in town, unless you want to hire in one of those companies from Akron to send somebody down. And he's fine, really; nobody here will mind or be surprised by any of Jared's drinks. I just... think we might be able to do a little better, that's all."

God, he still hasn't let go of Will's wrist, is pulling him through the crowd now. Somewhere, somebody's started playing some music over the speakers—Noel, probably, since the music is decidedly teenage for about twenty seconds before the track is abruptly switched to something more upbeat, and involving fewer swear words—and as they walk, people around them begin to dance. Some are just bobbing loosely to the music, but others are pairing off, laughing and swinging one another around, happy in that way music and a warm night and good company can bring out in people. It's so simple, and yet to Will always feels so monumental, so important. Maybe it's because he grew up without much of it, and struggles now both to find it and to be part of it when he does track it down, the way an animal raised in captivity can forget the basic instincts it was born with. Perhaps it's because it *does* feel like a basic instinct human beings are born with, some intrinsic part of the experience for as long as people have been people: the urge to

FALL INTO YOU   189

gather, and dance, and laugh, relish the simple joy of being with others.

God, I've been lonely for a long time, Will thinks, and then, out loud, says, "You know, I think I need that drink quite badly now."

"Is Noah Anderson's dancing really so disturbing to you?" Casey asks, his eyes sparkling with amusement.

"No, it's not that—" Will starts to say, but then he follows Casey's leading gaze to the owner of Anderson's Bike Shop, who is doing something that is clearly an attempt at the Worm, but might, generously, be called the Unfortunate Piece of String. He corrects himself: "Uh, sorry, it *is* actually that. What—?"

"He does it at every party," Casey says, in as low a voice as he can while still being audible, with an amused little shrug. "Thinks he's killing it. Nobody has the heart to tell him—ah, here we are." He drops Will's wrist at last, and Will looks up in surprise at the large pile of wood they had thrown together this afternoon, sitting ready to be set ablaze.

Will eyes it dubiously. "You put a bar in there while I wasn't paying attention?"

Casey laughs, but something about the quality of it draws Will's attention; his gaze flicks sharply away from the woodpile, up to Casey's face. He looks—nervous, Will realizes, after a second. It takes him a moment to place it because he's so unused to seeing that emotion from Casey; isn't sure, now that he thinks about it, that he ever has before.

"Sort of," Casey admits, and pulls something long and thin out of the little bag of supplies he tucked next to the woodpile early in the afternoon. "We have to light it with something, and it would be a little symbolic, and I was going to show, uh... Bill, to be honest with you, a while ago, but he wasn't, uh... he wasn't always—"

"I get the sense he wasn't always... super with it?" Will says, very carefully. They haven't talked about this—Will hasn't asked because, if he's honest, he hasn't been entirely sure he wants to hear it—but the agonized shift in Casey's tone seems to pull the words from his mouth as though caught on a wire.

"Yeah," Casey says, on a long, low breath. "Yes." He pauses, and then, unceremoniously, sticks out his hand and offers Will the bottle for inspection. "Anyway, it's ice cider. Like ice wine, except apples, and not grapes. It's not easy to make; you have to freeze the apples, and it takes *way* more apples than regular cider does, and then it has to ferment and age, and it took me a while to work out the flavor balance the way I wanted it, get the mix right. But the alcohol content is way higher than regular cider, and not a lot of people make it, and I thought it might... bring in more money, you know, then the standard hard cider does. It's a more specialized product, right? And it's *good*, or, I think it's good. If you don't think it's good, that's fine, but it took me a few years to make, so maybe *don't* tell me—"

"Oh my God, stop talking about it and give me a *taste*, if that's how you're going to be," Will says, his eyes wide as he stares from Casey to the bottle.

Casey laughs, and shakes his head, and pulls two little shot glasses from a side pouch in the bag—just two. Will eyes them, his analytical brain whirring. It's not like Will just happened to stumble upon him out here, or like Will was the first person Casey could find to try this with him; Casey planned this. He put the bottle and the glasses here hours ago, he came and *found Will*, pulled him all the way across the party, sought specifically him to share this moment with.

A little dizzily, Will tries to remember the last time someone did that, and is embarrassed to realize that the closest thing he can think of is Selma inviting him to cheer her on in the Chicago marathon. It's not that it hadn't been an honor, in a way, to stand in one spot for three hours with Selma's girlfriend at the time, a woman who was very passionate about essential oils, in order to eventually hand Selma a bottle of Gatorade and watch her run away, but it hadn't felt quite so... personal.

This *does* feel personal, in a way Will's not sure how to parse—or, at least, in a way Will can't help but parse in a singular and very particular fashion, one that will make him look very, very foolish if he's wrong. To Will's eye, it seems... well, it seems like *something* of a romantic thing to do, doesn't it, dragging him out here, making such a point of sharing this with him? It doesn't seem, for example, like something you might do with someone you *really* thought of as your loathed enemy, or upon whom you wished, to list only one of the things Will imagined Casey wished for him only a few weeks ago, slow death by aggressive foot infection. It seems like the sort of thing you might do if you wanted someone to... If you wanted them to think...

Thank God, Casey is handing Will one of the shot glasses before he can finish that thought. "Thanks," Will says, and then holds his breath as Casey leans close to pour Will's shot—is he leaning closer than necessary, Will wonders, or does he just feel a little drunk every time he's inside the bubble of Casey's personal space? Either way, it's over before Will can work out an answer, Casey stepping back to fill his own glass and set the bottle carefully down on the nearest flat patch of earth.

Will wrestles back the urge to close the space between them again, saying instead, "So, um. Are we toasting?"

"It's your farm," Casey says, with a shrug. His voice is pained, Will notices, but differently than it was around this topic a week ago. Less angry; more wistful. "So maybe you should make the toast."

Will meets him shrug for shrug, then gaze for gaze. "Ah, but it's your cider, right? And I've never been much of one for toasts, anyway. I've always been happier letting someone else handle it."

Casey holds his gaze for a long moment, an assessing quality

192 DYLAN MORRISON

slipping into his expression that Will notices there, just sometimes, and usually from the very corner of his own eye. Then, slowly, his mouth quirks, and he lifts the glass and says, "Okay, then. Here's to absent friends, and twice to absent enemies."

"Ha," Will says, his own mouth twisting, before he can stop himself. He shouldn't, really—he's not even quite sure what Casey means by saying it—but it's one of his own favorite toasts, and it feels, in this moment, apropos. He thinks of Catherine Rose; of the Casey he met two weeks ago who seems like a distant memory; of his family, and his father. He wonders, wanting to laugh, which of them he's drinking twice for.

But he would drink twice, would drink four times, quite happily. The ice cider is *good*, the flavor suggesting an unholy union between apple juice, woodsmoke, and deep, nearly burnt caramel, and Will savors it in little sips rather than throwing it back. "*God*," he breathes, when he's done. "I've never had anything like it, it's—*wonderful*."

"Right?" Casey says, grinning brightly at him. "It's a Canadian thing. I spent a few summers up there, long time ago, that's where I first tried it—so people down here mostly don't know about it. But I was going to, before it all... Before everything. I thought I'd present it to Bill or... whatever, you know, and see if we couldn't set up a real operation here. I ran the numbers and I thought it might make us more, maybe a lot more, than the traditional cider alone." He pauses for a moment, his face tight, and then the expression smooths out as he sighs. "But things played out differently, and that's life, right? You can't know how it's going to go. It seemed a waste, though, after all that work, not to at least try the prototype, and it's yours now, technically. I did it all in the farm's name, so."

"Casey," Will starts, gobsmacked, not sure where to begin. But before he can say anything, Noel and Todd are bustling up, demanding to know if it's time to start the fire yet, and saying people are asking when the fire will be starting, and pointing out that the sun is down and they're right here and have they considered starting the fire?

"Fine, fine," Casey relents, laughing, and it's quick work after that. He and Will each take a box of long camping matches out of Casey's bag and get to work catching pieces of fatwood on fire, which they slot into the larger woodpile once a proper flame gets going. After a few minutes, the faint crackling of a few pieces of wood burning starts to grow into the louder roar of a proper fire, and Casey yells, "Stand back!" and then tosses a slow arc of the ice cider towards the flames. It's not a lot, just enough that the short-lived cascade of liquid catches the fire-light before the alcohol brightens it considerably, a blinding flare that seems to solidify the blaze.

There isn't time, after that, to circle back to who owns the ice cider, or all Casey's hard work, or the fact that with every passing day Will becomes more sure that selling this farm to Catherine Rose's buyers would be a godawful thing to do to someone who seems, reckless driving habits aside, like a pretty excellent person. There's dancing, instead, and more drinking, and so many people and conversations that Will can't quite keep track of them all. There's singing and laughing and a late-night slice of cherry pie from the trunk of someone's car that is maybe the most delicious thing Will has ever eaten in his life, and Will can't make the space to go back to it. He's having too much fun with Casey, who makes him feel so *present*, so *alive*, that it's hard to remember the Will he was just a few weeks ago, lurking at the edges of Selma's parties, getting into emotional showdowns with his ex-boyfriends' untamed lizards. It's not as though they don't have time, after all. It's not as though, just because the bridge is being repaired tomorrow, they have to get into all of this right now.

It's a good night, a golden night, a night that makes a painful, aching hope—the kind of hope, Will thinks, that really does kill you—throb like a fresh bruise in his chest. When, even-

194 DYLAN MORRISON

tually, he and Casey walk home together, they are bathed both in the edge-softening moonlight and the hazy wash of yellowish lamp-glow from the motion-activated lights on the side of the market, forever triggered by bugs and so on most of the night. Will thinks, for a second, when they reach the porch, that maybe Casey might lean closer, into Will's space, and change the rules again, between them. He pauses at the foot of the stairs, turning to face Will, a smile crinkling the corners of his eyes as their gazes lock. Then Casey's falls, sliding down slowly over Will's body, and his smile falls, too, into a headier, more intent expression. It makes Will's mouth go bone dry, the moisture seeming to migrate to his suddenly sweating palms. Casey steps forward, and for a single, blissful second, Will thinks he's going to feel one of those long-fingered hands against his neck, sliding up the back of his shirt, and—

"Night, Casey! Night, Will!" The voice is Todd's, and slightly pointed, and hugely effective. Casey steps back with the same calm efficiency he did three days ago when they'd encountered a swamp rattler in some brush they were clearing together, his face carefully blank. Will, certain his own face is flaming red, glances over with at *least* as much venom as a swamp rattler to see Todd passing, affecting an expression of exaggerated innocence, with Noel, who's looking highly amused.

"Good night," he calls back through gritted teeth. Mortifyingly, he thinks he hears Noel snort as they walk off with Todd.

And, worse: "God save me from *teenagers*," Casey mutters, turning away and hurrying up the steps. He's not looking at Will; Will, amazed, wonders if he's *embarrassed*. If maybe those damn kids really *had* interrupted him, crashing into this moment he spent all night building. It certainly seems that way when Casey adds, "They're more trouble than they're worth!" and disappears into the house before Will can reply.

He's retreated up to his bedroom by the time Will gets inside, and after some consideration, Will decides to leave it

FALL INTO YOU   195

alone for tonight. If Casey wanted to talk, he wouldn't have gone up to the attic, and Will can let it lie, for now.

The morning, he decides, is the moment for him to act. Before all of his neuroses and doubts and unfortunate quirks of personality have completely woken up; before he can talk himself out of it. He'll just—he'll—tell Casey everything, maybe, or perhaps just go for broke and pin him up against the kitchen counter—better yet, let Casey pin *him* against the kitchen counter...

Abruptly, Will finds himself standing in front of the door to Casey's attic bedroom, gnawing on his lower lip as he stares at the polished wooden surface. It's slightly ajar, the door—it often is—but Will has never gone upstairs, or even knocked. Casey, he's noticed, has maintained a similar tacit boundary ever since the first night Will spent in the guest room, giving his private living space a wide berth. He can't speak to Casey's reasons, but it had seemed to Will like a bridge too far, to ask for passage into a space that was entirely Casey's own. The house, the market, the farm: Will has a claim to all of that, if an awkward and uncomfortable one. But the last time Will saw the attic it was just unfinished rafters, and loose insulation, and more spiders than he felt was compatible with his continued presence there. Whatever's up there *now* is Casey's and only Casey's, and even in his most irritated and self-righteous moments, Will's felt honor-bound to respect that.

And... it's not that he *doesn't* feel bound by honor just now. That's not it at all. It's that there's a corner of him, not particularly impressive in size but quite doggedly stubborn, insisting that those teenagers *did* interrupt Casey in a delicate moment. Insisting that he, Will, is standing in front of the bedroom door of the *single most attractive human being* with whom he has ever shared *air*, let alone houseroom, on the last night before his own excuse to stay here is swept away like the Glen River Bridge. Insisting that if there's even a *chance*, even a glimmer of possibility, that those damn kids really did cut Casey off seconds before he could lean in for a kiss, that Will would be wasting the opportunity of a lifetime to walk past, call it a night.

He tries, for a second, to walk past anyway. But his feet won't move; he's every inch as rooted to the hardwood floor as the trees out in the orchard are to the earth, somehow both fixed in place and growing. He takes a breath; another one. What could it hurt, really? What harm could it do, at this point, to see what would happen if Will just reached within himself and found the courage to ask for what he wanted?

Will reaches within himself. He lifts a hand. He knocks.

There is a pause. Then, "One second," Casey calls, in a voice Will can't read at all. Surprised? Pleased? Panicked? It's not enough *data*, those two words—three syllables—God, Casey's making crashing noises up there like he's knocked something over... wait, is he taking the steps two at a—

"Hi," Casey says, ripping the door open to reveal a small landing, a set of stairs ascending into the attic behind him. He sounds slightly breathless, and for a moment he looks thunderstruck, as though the world has shifted underneath him. Then, slowly, he starts to smile as he leans against the doorframe, affecting a casual pose. God, *hell*, he must have been partway through changing for bed—he's wearing a pair of loose pajama bottoms, which Will notes with distant amusement are printed with a pattern of little radishes... and, as far as Will can tell, *absolutely nothing else*. Raking a hand through his thick blond hair, his voice threaded with an invitation that thrills Will as much as it frightens him, Casey says, "Diiiiiidya want something?"

"Did I... want something." It's a question, technically, but Will doesn't say it like one. He's forgotten how to ask questions, and maybe also how to *produce saliva*, if the sudden dryness of his mouth is anything to go by. Casey's shirtless body is more distracting than Will would have expected it to be by such a wide margin that it's a little disquieting. It's just a *torso*, first of all, and Will has seen it *before*: in fleeting glimpses as Casey exited the bathroom after a shower, and in far less fleeting glimpses while Casey was just wearing a tank top. And those tank tops are practically nothing! Gossamer thin, some of them! No one alive, surely, is more aware of this fact than Will! But somehow none of that has allowed Will the chance to really... take it in, to catalogue this part of Casey the way he's catalogued everything else. It shouldn't be surprising. This is the torso that makes sense for someone who throws around sacks of feed as though they're full of feathers—no beefed-up vanity muscles, just a solid wall of strength—but being so close to it short-circuits the bulk of Will's brain.

Actually, maybe it's more accurate to say that it reroutes most of the energy in his brain... somewhere south.

The little part of Will remaining up top to run the ship thinks, *You've been quiet too long – words, William! Surely you've heard one or two in your life!* It's not particularly helpful in terms of pulling any *up*, but his mouth opens anyway: "I, um. I just wanted..." Helplessly, his eyes flick from Casey's warm, open, inviting face to his chest, which also looks, to Will, warm, open and inviting. "Sorry, uh. I mean, I want..."

All at once Will realizes this is *humiliating*, that he is making a *fool* of himself standing here babbling, all but *drooling*, like he's... he's... one of the stupid gawking *townspeople* who talk about Casey like he's a piece of meat! Like he's *Noah Anderson*! It's shameful, is what it is, and Will should be ashamed of himself. He should have to do the Unfortunate Piece of String as a punishment.

But when he drags his eyes, with some force, back up to Casey's face, there's a smile on it that Will's never seen before. It's a *good* smile: one that has a lot of delightful things to say, very few of which would be repeatable in company.

"Jesus, I'm... sorry," Will stammers, scrabbling to hold onto what he's supposed to be saying in the face of that promising expression. "I don't—I'm. I probably should've thought through what I wanted to say before I got up here, huh? But I didn't, so." His gaze drifts down again for a moment; he wrenches it back up. "Now I'm struggling with the, uh. Talking?"

"I wouldn't worry about it. There's some problems you don't solve with talking." Casey starts shifting his weight, leaning off the doorframe and towards Will, one arm snaking out. "Anyway, I figure I know what you want."

All the times he's pictured Casey kissing him—and it has, if Will's going to be honest about it, been quite a few—he's imagined being kissed as though by a hurricane, all force and power and too much at once to keep track of, a marvel of nature you can't help but admire until the moment it rips you apart. But Casey doesn't rush. Casey kisses Will like they've got all the time in the world, like the bridge repair's been cancelled, like tomorrow's never coming. He splays the hand that isn't holding Will flush against himself along the side of Will's neck, fingers sliding against the tender skin underneath Will's ear. The sound Will makes into Casey's mouth at this particular sensation is less than dignified, but far from making Casey back away, or snort in mockery, or roll his eyes, Casey tightens his grip and moves them both, spinning them so he has Will up against the stairwell wall.

Some time passes; Will couldn't say how much. Who could possibly say how much? The minutes burn merrily away, hissing and crackling as they go, thoughts and logic and hesitations going up in smoke right along with them. He doesn't pause when Casey says, "You wanna come up?" He doesn't question himself, or the moment, or whether he's making the best objective choice, the choice that runs the fewest risks in the circumstances. He's busy following Casey up the stairs instead, and being interrupted halfway through to be thoroughly kissed

FALL INTO YOU   199

against the banister before, eventually, Casey grabs him by the wrist and growls, "C'mon."

As Will's being pulled along behind him, he can't help but remember the *first* encounter he and Casey had on a stairwell, which was somehow only the Saturday before last. What would have happened if it had all played out a little differently? If Will had come out to the farm first that morning, instead of going to Mike's for breakfast, and caught Casey fresh from the shower, still dripping with a towel slung around his waist? Would they have screamed at each other and stormed away angry, the way it happened in reality? Or would the tension, Casey's bare chest, the thin light of the early hour, have tipped things past the breaking point? Maybe Casey would have tossed him up against the landing wall, snarling, all that white-hot frustration pouring out of him as passion—

"Will?" Casey's staring at him, eyebrows up, when Will breaks out of this filthy train of thought at the top of the stairs. For the first time since he opened the door to the attic, he looks a little uncertain. "You good? We don't have to do this, you know, if it's too—"

"No, God," Will says, flushing. "Nothing like that. I was just..." He pauses, embarrassed, and then realizes that in the circumstances, he's not sure he needs to be. "I was thinking about, um. How it might have gone differently the last time we were in close quarters on a set of stairs?"

Casey blinks at him for a second; then he smiles; then he laughs. "What," he says, chuckling, "you mean if I'd said, 'Is that a broom handle you're poking me with, or are you just happy to—'"

"Oh my God *don't* make *that* joke," Will says, half-groaning on a laugh of his own. "Jesus Christ, I can't believe you said that, I *hate* you—" He freezes, a deer in the headlights, abruptly sure that he's gone too far, made it weird, misread the moment, said the wrong thing, or otherwise killed the mood. God knows it wouldn't be the first time.

But Casey's smile goes dark and purposeful again, and he steps close, right into Will's space, until there's only a single electric inch between them. "You hate me, huh?" he says, his voice low. "Go ahead, then. Prove it."

Will launches himself forward like he's leaping for shore, the very last dregs of his higher thinking skills swirling down the drain. He's pretty sure he fails, over the next few hours, to prove that he hates Casey, but that's all right; it's not like he was ever really trying to.

Will wakes up slowly, stretching out, cat-like, against the sheets. He's alone in the room, but after a night involving quite a lot of exercise and very little sleep, he's stiff in more ways than one. Downstairs, he can hear the distant clattering of Casey puttering around. Reassured that he hasn't been abandoned in the night, he tries to doze for a few minutes, but finds he can't quite manage it. He's too interested in the attic, which he had not observed closely last night, but which in daylight is so different from his memories as to feel like part of a different home. It's bright and open, the walls covered with framed vintage band posters and photos from all over the country, more light filtering through than Will would have imagined possible.

Fairly quickly, though, he starts to feel like his curiosity will overwhelm his good intentions if he doesn't get out of here, and he'll cross the line from observation into snooping. He pulls on a pair of Casey's sweatpants on the theory that it isn't *too* presumptuous, since most of the clothes he's been wearing recently are *Casey's anyway*, and goes downstairs. He finds Casey in the kitchen, making breakfast.

Well. He's attempting to make breakfast, anyway. He is, as Will has learned over these last few weeks, not much of a cook,

FALL INTO YOU   201

so what he appears to be doing is heading towards burning a variety of breakfast items, but it doesn't matter. Standing in front of the stove, barefoot in boxers and a T-shirt that reads IDAHO: Big Potato Country, he's hot to the point of practically burning *Will*. He'd eat the food even if Casey reduced it to ashes, and with a sense of fellow-feeling.

Still: "You want some help with that?" Will's voice comes out huskier than he means it to, not sure yet what the vibe is going to be between them, but when Casey looks up, he smiles, so that's all right. "The, uh. Breakfast, I mean."

"Sure," he says, stepping aside slightly to let Will access the range. "If you don't mind." Casey passes him the spatula, his hand brushing against Will's for what's *surely* longer than necessary. His body heat, the nearness of him, the way he could reach down and grab Will's arm, pull him close, is... distracting, to say the least. Will's sorry when he moves away, although he does, at least, finally notice he's just stirring *air*, and lets the spatula descend into the potatoes.

"I don't mind," Will says, and looks up into Casey's warm green eyes. "My pleasure, really. The least I can do, after last night." The phone starts ringing in the other room; without breaking Casey's gaze, he asks, "Do you need to answer that?"

"Eh," Casey says, still looking directly at Will. "Let it ring. They can wait, whoever they are."

Will smiles at him, and Casey smiles back. The phone works through its ring cycle and finally clicks over to voicemail as Will, pulled toward the broad plateau of Casey's chest like an iron shaving to a magnet, lists forward, all his hesitation and rationalizing and self-control falling away towards—

"Pick up, Will! I know you're there! Pick up!" The voice is shrill and furious and loud even over the answering machine in the other room, and Will knows it immediately as Catherine Rose's. "You think you can just avoid me forever? Well, you *can't*, Will, the deadline is in *two days*, and if you think I'm just going to let you ghost me like your stupid father always did, you have another thing coming! I am Catherine Rose, goddamn it! I *close*. It's what I *do*. If I have to call up everyone you might be staying with, or come back to that *backwater* and hold the contract under your hand *myself* until you *sign* it, then that's what I'll do! Call! Me! Back!"

Will freezes, abruptly a pillar of ice, as panic radically diverts the path of his morning.

THIRTEEN

The last time that answering machine sent Will stumbling headlong into a panic attack, it was—God, nearly eighteen years ago, and Will reels a little to realize how old that makes him. But he'd been seventeen then, which had felt at the time like a bright, worldly, professional age, the sort of age that certainly merited full access to the wonders of adulthood. Thinking back on it from the ripe old age of nearly thirty-five, Will feels a bit sick about the decisions he felt capable of making at seventeen, but the wonderful and terrible thing about *being* seventeen is you don't have to worry about things like that yet. You haven't quite been alive long enough to look out for your tricky patterns, or brace for unfortunate impact, or think through all the potential consequences.

Will hadn't been thinking through all the potential consequences, for example, when he stopped in at his high school's annual college fair, urged by his science teacher, Mr. Zajac, to at least consider it. He hadn't been bracing for unfortunate impact when he'd given that nice man at the Dartmouth table his home phone number, said it was fine to call whenever. He *would* have been bracing, if he'd understood more at the time—

Will might have been seventeen, but he wasn't stupid. He'd never have been so cavalier with the number if it had been, say, a military recruiter; Bill himself had, against Old Bill's wishes, attempted to join the army in his own youth, and washed out quickly and entirely. Old Bill had loved to bring it up and laugh, even years later, when Will was a boy.

Will didn't know, at seventeen, that college was going to be such an issue. He just didn't know. Bill had never mentioned college as an issue. Bill had never mentioned college at all, which, in retrospect, Will knows should have been his first clue that something was amiss. Bill was like that, without middle gears, when it came to things that were bothering him—he either avoided a topic entirely or went *way* too far.

It was the last day of school, he remembers now; he can almost hear the strange cackle of nesting ovenbirds, their call oddly like someone crying "Teacher—TEACHER—teacher," as he walked cheerfully home. He'd been in a good mood, glad to be done with the hustle and grind of homework and classwork and petty teenage social dynamics for a few months, but his steps had gotten heavier and heavier as he'd approached the farm. They always did, somehow, even on days when he was looking forward to being at home, as though the place had an internal gravity that drew him down to earth that much harder with every shifting step.

Regardless, his good mood had shattered when he'd gone inside. Bill had been standing there, next to the answering machine, the expression on his face a bitter harbinger of the approaching storm.

He'd said, "Will? You got something you want to tell me?"

Will had swallowed; God, that was a diabolical trap to set for anyone, but especially for a closeted teenage homosexual. The honest answer to that question would have curled Bill's hair, so instead Will had said, "Uh. I'm... not sure. You got something you want me to say?"

FALL INTO YOU   205

Bill had grunted instead of answering, and then pushed play on the machine.

"Hey, Will." The tinny voice was only half-familiar; the college fair had been weeks before. Will didn't place it until: "This is Robin, from the Dartmouth admissions team—we met at the college fair last month. After our conversation, I took the liberty of poking around a little, on your end and mine. Obviously, it's early days yet, and there's a lot that would still need to happen, but it does seem like you're exactly the kind of student we're looking for, and I'd love for you to get the chance to get to know the campus better. Maybe we could set up a visit? A couple of interviews, while you're here? You can call me back at —" But Bill cut off the playback before Robin could read off his number.

And just for a second, even with that storm cloud expression on Bill's face, even with the glitter of malice in his eyes and the anger just in the motion of stabbing his finger down on the answering machine buttons, Will had felt *good*. He'd felt wildly, crazily, beautifully, blissfully good, on top of the world, on top of the *galaxy*. He'd talked to Robin for nearly forty minutes about the chemical structure of chlorophyll and things he'd like the chance to learn about in gene sequencing and the experiments he'd been running for years around the farm, and when nothing had come of it, Will had thought, *Oh, well*. It's not as though he didn't have a life path intended for him, whether he thought he could hack that life plan or not; it didn't matter if his teacher thought he should go to college, not if college didn't think so.

But for that moment, in the foyer, even below the shadow of Bill's thunderous mood, Will had thought: He *liked* me. And: He *looked into it*. And: I could go to *Dartmouth*.

And then Bill had said, his voice low and rumbling, a threat, "And where in the hell are you thinking we've been keeping a hundred thousand goddamn dollars to send you off to some

206   DYLAN MORRISON

fancy college?" And suddenly Will's joy, which had been spreading its wings to take flight, was stuck to the floor like an insect with a poisoned pin, barely a chance to thrash as it died.

Will can't remember the argument now; he doesn't have to. It was the first time they had it, sure, but they had it many, many times. Will wanted to go; Bill didn't think that he should. Will could figure out the money, get scholarships, take out loans, whatever; Bill didn't understand why Will even wanted to go, what he thought he'd be getting by putting on airs like that, when what he needed to learn was here, and as soon as possible. Will thought he might be meant for more than this; Bill thought this was *exactly* what he was meant for, had been born for. Will didn't think it was Bill's choice; Bill didn't understand why on earth Will thought he got any choice in this at all.

"It's in your name," Bill had shouted eventually; Will remembers that. "William Josiah Robertson, same as mine, same as my father's, same as his father's! And if you're going to be William Josiah Robertson, by God, then you're going to do as William Josiah Robertson does! He runs this farm! He lives in this house! He doesn't go to Dartmouth!"

"I didn't *ask* to be William Josiah Robertson," Will had snarled back, not that it had mattered. Not that it had moved the needle, or changed Bill's mind.

It's strange—not the way the memory washes over him, but the way it, and the emotion that Will knows is supposed to accompany it, judders on its usual track. All these years, no matter how far away he got from the farm, no matter how many therapists he spoke to, Will has felt deep, grinding shame whenever he remembered this day, and all the other days like it. Even knowing rationally that his father had been wrong, that Will's intelligence and scientific aptitude would have left him unsatisfied simply following the family path, that it was *Will's life*, and thus his decision to make... still, unavoidably, the guilt. Still, Bill's face would loom in his mind, spittle flying from the sides

FALL INTO YOU 207

of his mouth as he bellowed about duty and family and what it meant to be a Robertson, as he explained that Will was selfish and impulsive and hard of both head and heart. And part of Will, down to his bones, would whisper: *Listen, buddy, not trying to bum you out here, but are you* sure *the old man doesn't have all that right?*

But today, that part of Will appears to be out to lunch. Instead of hearing the old litany, choking abruptly for air in an ocean of outsized remorse, Will blinks and finds himself imagining *himself,* as he is now, standing at the answering machine, looking down at the gawky seventeen-year-old he once was. Whatever internal mechanism is at work here, it's fairly merciless in terms of the accuracy of the remembered pimples and blemishes, not to mention the way his ears wouldn't quite fit his face for another four or five years. Stick-skinny but with baby fat around his cheeks, wearing some band T-shirt he'd destroyed so thoroughly that it was totally unreadable, a tragically desperate attempt at stubble making a patchy appearance along his neck—not, Will realizes, a little stunned at the thought, someone any reasonable fully grown person could mistake for another adult.

As if in response to this thought, the imagined version of himself begins to shrink down; he's fifteen, the horrifying at-home frosted tips as good as carbon dating, and then thirteen, his hair buzzed short after an unfortunate incident with some very sticky, over-boiled cider that had splashed onto the mill ceiling, partially dried, and then dripped at exactly the wrong moment. Eleven now, and abruptly shorter, not yet having hit the growth spurt that, when it did come at twelve, still did not make him tall enough to satisfy his father—nine, wearing that weird lime-green bucket hat he'd found at a thrift store in Canton and decided was the height of fashion.

God, and when his mind finally settles on an image, it's Will at *seven,* with both of his front teeth missing, in that brief but formative period where he'd whistled on nearly every word. It wasn't even for some interesting and fun reason, both of them going at once—it would have been different if he got in a fight, or hit in the face with a baseball bat. But he'd just bitten into an apple, like he'd done a hundred times before, and *both* of them had simply come away with it, as though having made a pact to quit together, when the moment was right.

For the first time, it occurs to Will to wonder whether he, himself, today, can think of a circumstance in which he'd scream at a child of this age. Not just his own child, to whom one would think he'd have a particular attachment—at *any* child of this age. At, quite frankly, *any* of the children he has found himself imagining in this long, anguished moment, rooted to the spot as though turning into another of the orchard's many trees, exchanging muscle and sinew for fiber and pulp.

He wouldn't, is what he concludes, a little startled by it. He would not yell at any of those children, not in any circumstances, not unless their lives depended on him doing so. Even then, he'd probably try to find another way. They were just *children*—they couldn't be expected to process that kind of aggression, to not take it personally. It wouldn't be *fair*, to treat them they like they were adults just because it would be *easier* if they were, or because he, himself, didn't have the emotional intelligence to do any *better*...

"Will, hey." Casey's voice is low, warm with a concern so alien to the world of Will's childhood that it wrenches him back to the present with the immediacy of a rip cord, the parachute of Casey's attention billowing out to catch him before he can land too firmly in the past. "Are you okay? Sorry to say it, but you seem like maybe you're freaking out a little." Tightly, Will nods, not trusting himself to speak without hyperventilating, sobbing, or otherwise exhibiting humiliating symptoms of a panic attack. But Casey just says, "I thought so. Take a few deep breaths with me, okay? I'm a deep breathing expert, believe it or not. I've been told I don't look the type, but I went through an *extensive* meditation phase, and I still keep up a pretty consistent practice..."

Casey keeps talking for several minutes, calm and relaxed, about breathwork and clearing one's mind, not seeming bothered at all by the fact that Will's deep breaths are occasionally verging on gasps. Though his heart is still hammering with adrenaline, Will realizes as he starts to come back to himself that Casey's arm, which was reaching for his water bottle the last time Will clocked it, has wrapped itself around Will's shoulders at some point in the proceedings. It's a sign of how deeply he'd fallen away from himself that it didn't register immediately —even scrabbling like this, still half-panicked and trying desperately to let it go, now that he's noticed Casey's arm around him, he cannot shake a white-hot awareness of every place they're touching.

"I..." Will says eventually, feeling slightly queasy. He swallows; his mouth is dry. "Sorry, I—she—I'm sorry. I didn't mean to—lose my grip. *Sorry.*"

"It's really okay," Casey says, soft. Then, his voice taking on a slightly rumbling quality, he adds, "Does she always talk to you like that?"

"Oh," Will says, waving a hand and trying to smile. He gets the sense he doesn't quite pull it off. "Not... exactly. Most of the time there's just kind of the implication that she might? This is the first time she's actually, uh. Yelled at me." Will swallows, and, guiltily, adds, "That I know of, anyway. I kinda stopped listening to the voicemails a few days ago, because they started getting really intense, so. Maybe she's been screaming for days." He shakes his head, abruptly annoyed with himself, and straightens up. "And anyway it doesn't *matter*, it's not about her, it was just—unfortunate timing, that's all. It's just that being screamed at, like that, in this house..." He shudders in spite of the warmth that seems to radiate from Casey, as though caught

210   DYLAN MORRISON

up in that golden hair is a little piece of the sun itself. "It... brings stuff up, that's all."

"Hmm," Casey says. Regrettably, he steps away from Will, flips off the still-lit stove burners under the now lightly smoking breakfast Will entirely forgot he was cooking, and leans up against the nearest counter, bracing his weight on his palms. He seems to be thinking about something; Will, still trying to get a handle on the mechanics of normal breathing, leaves him to it.

Finally, Casey says, "God help me, there just isn't any other way around it."

Will stares at him, confused. "Around what?"

"You gotta tell me about what happened with you and Bill," Casey says, and then sighs. "And I gotta tell you what happened with *me* and Bill. We can't just keep avoiding it like it's not going to come up—that never works out, not for anyone." He makes a face when Will immediately grimaces. "Oh, I *know*, don't give me that look! You think *I* want to talk about it? I've been avoiding it for a *reason*, the whole thing is so awkward, I'd rather chase Betsy Lundgren's stupid *pigs* around again, but." He gestures at Will, and then at himself. "It's obviously bothering you, and I *know* it's bothering me. When I thought you were just going to leave and that was going to be it, that was one thing. But after last night—well. I don't know how *you* like to navigate this sort of situation, but me personally? I'm not one for tiptoeing around issues until they blow up in my face. Only smart move is to barrel right at it, headfirst. Get it over with so we can get on with things."

In spite of some lingering anxiety, Will can't help the little smile that steals over his face at this assessment, since it's such a clear summary of Casey's whole personality. Will, himself, has never once thought the smart move in basically *any* situation was to barrel right at it headfirst but: "Yeah, God. Okay, you're probably right." He takes a breath, trying to steady himself, which becomes a huge, cracking yawn. Then, hating how

FALL INTO YOU 211

faintly it comes out, he says, "Sorry, can we... I heard you, right, good logic, we're agreed, but... um. It's early? And I burned breakfast? So. Maybe I could get some coffee first? And food... of some kind. Just because, I mean, I want to talk about it, but I'm kind of..." God help him, the edge of all that buried emotion is tugging at some rarely touched vocal cord, and Will winces when Casey's expression softens at the sound. "I'm *fine*, just, not super awake, is all. Okay? Is that okay?"

There's a beat, and then, softly, Casey says, "Sure, that's okay. Tell you what—we'll both go. Cardini's? I'll drive if you go in."

"God, yes," Will says eagerly, wanting to cement this path before it's lost to him. It's too eager, maybe, because it makes Casey laugh, but Will doesn't care—fifteen minutes later, he's sitting in the front seat of Casey's pickup, his window halfway down to let the cool autumn air rush over him, music playing gently over the radio. After a minute or two, Casey says, "Oh, that's funny," and turns the volume up, starts singing along. It's one Will doesn't know, but it seems to be about a man called Casey Jones who is driving a train in some unfortunate drug-related circumstances and needs to make some hasty choices. It's catchy, and Casey himself—the real one, that is, not the one from the song—has a nice voice, a rich, uncomplicated baritone that he doesn't seem to think about too much. Will feels himself relax by increments as he sings along, although the words themselves don't tell a particularly happy story.

When it ends, Casey huffs out half a laugh, shakes his head, and says, "I was named after that song, you know. My middle name is Jones and everything."

In spite of himself, Will's mouth drops open very slightly. "You're kidding."

Pulling up to a stoplight, Casey slants him half a smile. "What?" he says, making his eyes wide and innocent. "Do you

212   DYLAN MORRISON

not think that every child should aspire to driving a train while high on cocaine? That's very limiting of you."

Will snorts out half a laugh, and then, before he can stop himself, says, "Honestly, the things I aspired to as a child *are* nearly that grim, so. When I was eight, it was the great dream of my life to replace all the busted-out fences on this farm—driving a train, even blitzed out of my mind, would have been reaching for the stars." It's too honest, the sort of thing Will wouldn't say to anyone but Selma, and he has to bite his cheek to keep from wincing when he finishes spitting it out.

But Casey, to his surprise and, honestly, pleasure, meets him beat for beat, not a moment of hesitation before he says, "Yeah, I know how that is. I think when I was eight what I wanted most in the world was to see Jerry Garcia play live, which in and of itself wasn't a terrible aspiration, except that at that point he'd already been dead for years, and I didn't have any idea who he was. I knew that's what a person was *supposed* to want most in the world, just like the right answer to 'What do you want to be when you grow up?' was 'I want to be chill, man.'" Casey must notice the confusion Will's sure he's not managing to keep off his face; he laughs, not entirely pleasantly. "I had a very different childhood to yours. Not that I know so much about yours, but I think it's a safe bet, anyway. Mine was pretty... pretty far from the standard, or at least that's what I've been reliably told. It all feels fairly normal to me." He shrugs, his eyes fixed firmly on the road ahead of him. "Best I can tell that's almost always true, right? Even for the people whose childhoods were *really* traumatic—you talk to them and they say it was whatever, no biggie, nothing to worry about, let's change the subject. I guess you get used to what you get used to, right?"

"I went to undergrad with this guy who was obsessed with the idea that human evolutionary success was entirely a result of adaptability," Will says, shaking his head to remember it. "Luke Graves—he was interesting, honestly, but he *would* go

FALL INTO YOU   213

on. But the idea was that what made a human being a human being, on a fundamental level, was the ability to look at almost any given situation and figure out a way not just to get on with it, but to forget there was ever a time before it was *normal.*"

"He sounds like he was a real hoot at parties," Casey says drily.

Will chuckles, shaking his head. "Actually, proving his point, you... got used to him? A little something to eat, a little something to drink, a little light existential chatter with Luke—oh." He realizes, abruptly, that Casey has parked the car outside Cardinal Bakery, and is looking at him patiently across the gearshift, no longer driving at all. "Right, uh—you drive, I get. You want anything in particular?"

"Eh," Casey says, with an easy grin. "So long as there's coffee, I'm good; anything else is a bonus."

Will feels a little spike of odd, irrational irritation at this, laced with a fondness that's strangely hard to bear. He swallows back the urge to say, *But I asked you what you* want, *isn't there anything you'd* like, *can't you* ever *make it easy for* anyone *to do* anything *for you?* And, instead, smiles. "You got it."

Still, spike of irritation aside, he's in a good mood when he walks through the Cardinal doors. An oddly good mood, to be honest, given the way his morning started and the way it's likely to go after this. Will can't imagine he's going to have a good time dragging up the past for Casey, who is, in all likelihood, going to take Bill's side. That will be both *really* embarrassing and, if Will doesn't miss his guess, a lampoon through the balloon of silly, desperate hope he's been trying frantically to keep tethered to the earth with fraying rope. Even Will is not so self-punishing as to imagine he could stomach building something on ground that profoundly cursed.

But that's later, after coffee, after breakfast. This might be Will's last morning in Glenriver for some time—a thought that makes him feel brittle and half-sheared, as though the next

214   DYLAN MORRISON

strong wind is going to send him toppling—and he is, by God, going to enjoy it. This, right now, is Will's golden moment, his final chance to savor the way these last two weeks have felt before it all goes wrong, and, for his sins, he is going to let himself have it.

He's humming under his breath as he walks to the counter and waits in line, a tuneless, half-remembered version of the song Casey was named for, heard only once but rattling around still in his head. When he reaches the front, he cracks a couple of jokes with the people working the counter, and doesn't have to think about the order at all—he's been in here with Casey enough times, after all. Left to his own devices, Casey usually orders a maple latte and a bear claw, but the bear claws are sold out by the time Will reaches the front, Saturday mornings being what they are. Instead, he orders Casey's latte, as well as a brown sugar cardamom one for himself, and gets them each one of the apple turnovers that are being freshly placed in the case as he watches. As he waits for the order to come up, he tries to drink in the smell of this place, the specific color of the paint on the walls, without allowing the thought of why he's doing so to make him maudlin.

But as he's walking to the door, a paper coffee carrier with their drinks in one hand and the turnover bag in the other, old Mrs. Cardini waves to him. "William! You weren't going to leave without saying goodbye, were you?"

Will was, in fact—he hadn't seen her—but he shakes his head and smiles at her, hurries over. "Sorry, sorry, I was just—"

"Oh, I can *see* what you were 'just,'" Mrs. Cardini says, her expression going dangerously knowing. "Your old man used to come in here, you know, back in the day. You look more like him now than you did when you were coming up—it's like that, for some folks. I used to try to tell him." She shakes her head, and then, her eyes sharpening, adds, "Anyway! He'd come in looking just like you, all cheerful, whistling himself a little tune, buying coffee and treats for two. Honestly, it's a little spooky—I think sometimes he was even wearing that shirt."

Will scoffs, rolling his eyes. "Listen—I'm sorry, I don't mean to doubt you, but come *on*. For my mom? I don't think I ever saw him bring her so much as a bag of chips; they weren't like that. Not ever."

Mrs. Cardini wrinkles her nose. "Oh, honey, no. Not for June. Bill and June—well. Nobody ever could have mistaken *that* for a love match, I tell you what. But... Bill never told you, huh? About Lucy?"

"Lucy?" Will says; it comes out slightly laughing, as though he finds this amusing, which he doesn't. There's nothing amusing about this at all; it's that he's realizing, in real time, that his body and brain have no idea how to react to what Mrs. Cardini is saying. "Uh, no, I—can't say that I ever heard him mention that name once in my life. His life. Whoever's, uh, life."

Mrs. Cardini sighs and shakes her head. "Ah. Well. I guess that isn't such a surprise—that was your father. He was how he was. He and my Roger were good friends when they were boys, you know, and he was hard-headed from the first, that Bill. All you Robertson men are made that way, that's my theory. But the way I figure it, Bill opened his heart once in his life, and his daddy couldn't help but crush it. He was never the same, after that. Neither of them were, I don't think."

"Him and... Lucy?" Will isn't sure why he's asking. Half of him is entirely certain he doesn't want to know. "Whoever she was?"

"Bright girl," Mrs. Cardini says, in the tones of a fond reminiscence. "Bill brought her 'round to the house a few times—think he wanted to show her off to us, since he knew his own father wouldn't approve. Whip-smart, she was, and out of his league by a mile. It was a shame. She'd have been good for him, steadied out that temper, balanced out his foolish side. I tried to

216   DYLAN MORRISON

tell Old Bill, but he never did take anybody seriously, especially back then. No talking to him."

"Not to either of them, really," Will says, a little wryly.

"Oh, Bill wasn't so bad," Mrs. Cardini says, waving a hand. Then, at the expression on Will's face, she says, "All right, all right, I'll grant you—he wasn't exactly in the running for Father of the Year. But there were times, when he was young, when he might have gone a different way. I prayed on it, but... oh, you never know, do you? How things'll work out, or why. That Lucy brought out the lighter side in him, I know that. He and June made each other so unhappy, I think, that they both forgot how to get there for themselves."

"Why didn't Old Bill like her?" Will asks. "Lucy, I mean. I think he liked my mother fine, or at least as much as he liked anyone. More than he liked my dad, maybe."

"I always thought so, too," Mrs. Cardini says, with a sad little laugh. "The curse of the Robertson men, though, isn't it? Their own fathers—" She pauses, looking suddenly and uncharacteristically stricken, as the words "don't like them" seem to hang in the air, for all she hasn't spoken them aloud. Will offers her a little nod, both acknowledging the truth of this unsaid statement and, though it's odd to feel like he has this power with her now, allowing it. She lets out a breath, looking relieved, and continues. "Anyway. Lucy was a student in Columbus; I don't remember now how she met your dad, but they made it work almost a year, kept it real quiet. But they kept it quiet because she'd been accepted early to some fancy graduate program— somewhere New Englandy, if I'm remembering right. Doesn't matter, anyway; she was going away and Bill wasn't supposed to. Stupid, since probably she would've been willing to come back if he'd stuck it out with her for a few years up north. Old Bill wasn't a farsighted man, though. He thought Bill should settle down with a nice local girl, grew up here, knew what she was doing, just like he did, and like his father did before him."

FALL INTO YOU   217

Will feels his eyebrows hit his hairline. "Wait, I'm sorry. So —actually, no, you know what, first: Are you *sure* you don't know what kind of graduate program?"

Mrs. Cardini laughs at this, a hard, hearty cackle that makes her throw back her head, although with the slow, careful pace of the brittle elderly. "Oh, honey, I am glad you came back to town," she says, shaking her head as she calms down. "It does an old woman good to laugh like that. You might look like your daddy, but you're your own bucket of fish, and you always were. I should let you get on, but don't you be a stranger now, you hear me? Just because that bridge'll be up again today doesn't mean you can run off for another age."

That's a dismissal if ever he's heard one, so even though he has about a billion more questions, Will nods. "I won't. Thanks for the, um... update, I guess?"

Mrs. Cardini smiles at him and pats him lightly on the arm. "Any time, William. You say hello to Casey for me, won't you?" Will feels himself blush bright red, suddenly sure the old woman can see every last thing he and Casey did to one another last night playing out in his eyes. Certainly she's *grinning* at him like she can, looking abruptly twenty years younger. "Ah, I *see*. So maybe I don't have to worry about you being a stranger after all?"

"Goodbye, Mrs. Cardini," Will says, all in one breath but in a flat, robotic monotone that must tickle her, since her peal of laughter follows him all the way out of the shop.

He must look slightly shell-shocked as he climbs back into the truck, because as Will passes him the maple latte and the turnover, Casey says, in sympathetic tones, "They doing that weird puppet show in there again? I hate the weird puppet show."

"I—it—what?" Will says, badly wrongfooted by this. "Uh, not... as such. No puppets. More of a ghosts of Christmas past situation." When Casey slants him an interested look, Will relates the relevant details of Mrs. Cardini's story, emphatically neglecting to mention what brought the topic up in the first place. When he's finished, a strange, half-irritated impulse compels him to add, "He never, uh... said anything about any of that to *you*, did he? About Lucy, or—I don't know, I guess the other path his life might have taken?"

"Can't say he did." Casey's reply is thoughtful, and he taps his thumb against the steering wheel a few times, thinking. Finally, like he's not totally sure he should be telling Will, he says, "He did mention that name a few times, though. Not *to* me, exactly, so much as at me? He was—" Casey pauses, his throat working as he swallows. "Especially the last few years, he'd lose track of where he was, when he was. We'd have these arguments where he'd think I was other people. And instead of replying to what I said, he'd reply to what they said. Or what they had said, I guess, when it happened originally."

"Oh," Will says, quiet. "Yeah, I—know what you mean, I think. Old Bill used to be like that, towards the end. He and my dad used to have the same arguments over and over, anyway, so half the time they'd already be screaming at each other before Bill realized Gramps was just rerunning a version of it from years before. And God help you if you caught Bill after one of those wrapped up; he'd really let you have it. Probably he just felt guilty or whatever, wanted somewhere to put it, but it was scary, you know, as a kid. Unpredictable." Will realizes he hasn't thought about this in a long time, that he'd shoved it into a room in the back of his mind with which he has done more or less what his parents did to his bedroom: filled it with things he can't bear to look at anymore. "Anyway, sorry you had to deal with it. I know it can get... rough."

Casey's face twists into an expression Will can't quite read, but all he says is, "Sorry *you* did. Probably easier for me; I wasn't related to him. Or a child."

"Thanks." Will's surprised and more than a little embarrassed by the way his voice cracks on it, but Casey doesn't comment, just turns the radio back up and starts singing along.

Maybe it's that, or that story he told about the song, his name; maybe it's the way Will can't stop turning over what Mrs. Cardini told him, the way pieces of that story slot so neatly over his own. Maybe it's just that Casey's rich, warm voice seems to seep into Will's cracks and crevices like so much wet clay, hardening as he sips his coffee into something not unlike resolve.

Whatever it is, when they're about halfway back to the farmhouse, something in Will that has been splintering for years now finally, finally cracks. A bough, perhaps, on the scarred, complicated tree of his life, that he's cut and grafted together mostly by himself, and grown out of spite half the time—it hurts, feeling it break at last, but not as much as the blow that first cracked it did. That blow was the first piece of a story that led him here, to this car and this man and this moment, wondering how on earth to begin telling it; Will had thought it was, anyway. Now he thinks maybe the first blow was years earlier, before he was even alive. Before his own father was alive, maybe. Perhaps it had been the very first Bill who had first lifted the axe, and all of them, ever since, have been telling that same old story he started for the sport of it, handing it down like an heirloom, or a curse.

And none of them, Will realizes, would ever have talked about it. None of them ever had; it was as obvious as anything else about them, that they couldn't or wouldn't engage that way, when the emotional chips were down. It wasn't their way—it Wasn't What Robertson Men Did.

But Will thinks he's had just about enough of being a Robertson man. He takes a breath, and starts talking.

FOURTEEN

It's easy enough to tell Casey the first parts of the story. He thinks, based on the way Casey nods and mumbles, "Mmm," and "Yep," that over the last two weeks, Casey's maybe put a lot of what Will tells him together from context clues. He doesn't seem surprised when Will says that his childhood was less than idyllic, his parents far from warm, which, honestly, is a relief. In spite of everything that's shifted between them, Will had been more than a little afraid that Casey might jump to Bill's defense, tell Will he should have been less selfish, cared more about family and farm. There's part of him expecting that even as he tells Casey the broad strokes of what life was like for him as a kid; that's why he's doing it. He wants Casey to have a grip on that, at least a little, before Will gets into the specifics of The Final Night.

Will's thought a lot about his childhood, over the years. He hasn't talked about it much, though, and most of the talking he has done has been either at the behest of mental health professionals, or while he hasn't been entirely sober. It's harder, by a long shot, to spit the words out here in this truck with Casey than it ever was at the bar with Selma after too much tequila, or

FALL INTO YOU   221

even in a therapist's office. At least, in a therapist's office, you knew you could simply leave and never come back.

Not that Will couldn't leave and never come back here, of course. It's his entire plan, and it has been the whole time. It's just that Will so desperately doesn't want it to be the plan anymore that he's ripping his heart from his chest piece by agonizing piece to place on the dashboard in front of Casey, that's all. Nothing to get worked up about.

It helps more than Will would have guessed, that Casey knew Bill. He'd expected it to go the other way, that Casey's relationship with Bill would complicate this story the way it's complicated so much else between them. Instead, Casey's understanding of Bill, if later in life and from an utterly different vantage point, allows Will to shorthand a lot of things he would have had to explain to someone else—that he *has*, in point of fact, had to explain to everyone else he's ever discussed this with. But to Casey, he can say, "So you know how my father could be when he really had something in his craw, right?" or "You know how Bill could really *yell* when he wanted to yell?" And Casey raises his eyebrows, making it clear that he *does* know even before he nods, which he always does, and...

And it's a *relief*, Will realizes as he skates over being seven and eleven and fifteen, Casey following him easily as he sets this scene with half a dozen smaller ones. It's such an insane, absurd relief to talk about this with someone who *knew* him, let alone to talk about it without being cut off, shut up, told he's wrong. He wants to cackle with glee as he works his way through grim memories, which is an incongruous, almost sick feeling that becomes solely and exclusively a sick feeling when, as they're pulling into the farm parking lot, Will reaches the summer he was eighteen, directly after high school.

"I... met a guy," Will says, and flinches when it comes out, even *now*, in the tones of an *admission*. He tries again: "I met a guy! At a club up in Cleveland that's *definitely* closed now."

222   DYLAN MORRISON

Will sighs, still a little forlorn to think of the whole thing, although it makes him feel more than a little bit stupid. "His name was Brandon, and he was my age, *and* had a car, *and* his parents were a little homophobic, and, obviously, *my* parents were a little homophobic, so, you know, for a while, it was perfect. We'd meet up in out-of-the-way little places, or he'd pick me up outside of town and we'd hang out in his car, or whatever."

"Oh, sure," Casey says easily, waving a hand in acceptance of this. "I had a few boyfriends like that back in the day myself, although I was always the one with the car."

"Increasingly, I'd believe you started driving as a toddler," Will says, smiling slightly in spite of himself. "Sitting on a large pile of dictionaries to see over the steering wheel—"

"Yep, that was me," Casey confirms with a lazy grin. He's put the car in park, and he turns to look at Will, his voice very dry, as he says, "I was on the news and everything. 'Local driving savant, age three, towers over citizens on the freakishly long legs that allow him to reach the pedals—'"

Will snorts, and then lets out a big laugh, and it, too, is a relief. A relief to pause for a moment and feel something good before he plunges into the past, and all the thrashing, dangerous emotion that lives within it. For a moment, he is as a dolphin on a clear, still night, poised on the dark lip of the ocean's surface, pulling in one last long, blissful sip of air before slipping back down to the depths.

"How was Bill about you being gay?" Will asks the question abruptly, like he's pulling off a Band-Aid, and then realizes too late that it's presumptive, even offensive. "Or, sorry—not to just, like, assume that you're gay. You could be bi, or, uh, God, what's the other one—"

"Pansexual is the word you're looking for there," Casey says, with an easy smile that spills into a laugh when Will grimaces at having not been able to think of it when it's, quite clearly, the way Casey does, in fact, identify. "Don't sweat it, man—took me a long time to figure it out. I came out as every other damn thing under the sun first, and honestly, even pan doesn't feel quite right and usually I just say 'queer.' Didn't come up with your dad much; the one time it did, I got the sense he wasn't exactly *comfortable*, but he shrugged and said it wasn't any of his business. 'Live and let live,' I think is how he put it." Perhaps in response to the suddenly thunderous expression on Will's face, he adds, hurriedly, "Most of the time, though, I'm pretty sure he just, uh, forgot. So I wouldn't read into that too much or anything."

"*Live and let live,*" Will mutters bitterly to himself, so far under his breath he's not sure Casey can even hear it over the purr of the still-running truck motor. "Guess that figures." Louder, and maybe a little too sharply, he says, "Well, I'm gay. Known it about as long as I've known anything. I think Bill knew it, too, on some deep level he didn't want to look at too hard." Will swallows, and looks out the passenger window on old habit, his body hoping to see the soothing blur of passing trees even though his brain knows the car is in park. Instead, he's hit with nothing less than a perfect view of the Robertson Family Farms market, and he cringes as he fixes his eyes on the yellow door.

"I was never the son I was supposed to be." Will says this to the cheerful new market door every bit as much as to Casey, as though the wood and glass and paint can hear him, as though it can apply some of the magic it used to change itself to change him, make what he's confessing less true, or at least less painful. "Or... I was never the son he wanted me to be, or he wasn't the father I was supposed to have, or something. We weren't suited; it wasn't a good fit. He wanted Bill Robertson IV, another strong, strapping, outdoor-oriented man to carry on his legacy—"

Will pauses, the words to this old story suddenly alien in his mouth, like when you repeat a phrase so often it loses its meaning and breaks down into a scattered mire of syllables. What legacy, exactly, did Bill have to carry on? Drummed out of the army, never happy in his marriage or in his work on the farm, constantly suffering the disappointment of his own hard-mouthed, disappointed father, and, if Mrs. Cardini is to be believed, heartbroken over a sacrifice he made at that disappointed father's insistence—*was* that a legacy? Could anyone, even Bill, want his son to follow in *those* footsteps? And if that hadn't been what Bill wanted, then...

"God, you know what, it was never about any of that," Will says, his voice dropping to a point barely over a whisper in shock. "All this time, I thought that I just didn't cut it, that I wasn't good enough—but ultimately, I *did* do everything he wanted me to do, all those years, didn't I? Even if I did it a little more slowly, or more thoughtfully, or more *delicately* than he would have, I did it all. As a *child*, I did it. But it wasn't enough, and it wasn't ever going to be enough, because he didn't just want me to be him. He wanted me to be *better* than him, but if it ever looked for a second like I actually was, then... God. Then he hated me for it." Will shakes his head, hardly seeing the yellow door anymore, his mouth twisting. "Mrs. Cardini said it this morning, or she almost did, anyway—that it was the curse of the Robertson men, to be disliked by their own fathers. And he *didn't* like me: That's the truth. He didn't like the ways I struggled, but he didn't like the ways I succeeded, either. He didn't like my personality, or my sense of humor, or the way I did almost anything, even if it was exactly how he'd told me to do it." Remembering it at the last moment as relevant, but feeling it almost incidental, he adds, "Oh, and I mean. He didn't like that I was gay, either, obviously. He never came out and said that, but I never came out and... well, came out, I guess, at least to him or my mother. So, you know, it was all a lot of heavy implication, but there was no missing it."

FALL INTO YOU 225

"Jesus." Casey's voice is low, sorrowful; Will, embarrassed, jolts a little and whips his head around. He almost forgot he was talking *to* someone, let alone to Casey, and he feels a little prickle of anxiety in his stomach to think of how much he's revealed, but it fades at the expression on Casey's face. Casey looks sad, and fascinated, and like he means it when he says, "I'm sorry, Will. That sounds like a... really rough way to grow up."

"Oh, *you* know," Will says, waving a hand, unable to let this land but so grateful for it he thinks his skin will fall off if he doesn't acknowledge it. "It wasn't the best, but we get on with things, right? What else is there?" He swallows hard and then, before Casey can answer, pushes ahead, suddenly eager to be on the other side of this whole discussion. "That's what I did, anyway. With Brandon, that guy I met. I got on with things. And for a while, it was good. Fun. The first time I'd ever been with someone who wasn't..." Will pauses, and allows a delicate little moment to stand in for the broad sentiment "A much older sleazebag, the memory of whom should be left in the early 2000s, where it didn't really belong in the first place, but very emphatically was even so." Casey inclines his head, seeming to indicate, "I, too, participated in club culture during a similar era of the human experience, and we can agree: yikes."

Will allows himself a small, rueful smile before continuing. "Anyhow, like I said, Brandon and I met in secret for a while, but then it got to be August, and he was going off to college in a week—Purdue, I think, though I honestly only half remember now. Anyway, he was leaving and I wasn't going. Hadn't enrolled anywhere."

Casey's brow furrows. "Wait—you didn't go to college? But I thought—the PhD—"

"Oh, I went to college," Will says, shifting abruptly into the wearied tenor of the seasoned academic. "And then grad school, and then even more grad school, and you could honestly make the argument even now that my life is *still grad school*, since it involves teaching and socializing with so many grad students. But all that was after I left; Bill didn't want me to go at all, wouldn't pay the application fees or fill out the forms. Got into a bunch of fights with my teachers about it and everything, it was a whole mess."

"Jesus," Casey says again, shaking his head. "He never said."

Will thinks, *No, I bet he didn't!* quite sharply indeed, but he doesn't say it. It's not Casey's fault, especially since: "Yeah, he was like that, my dad. Everything was need-to-know with everybody, all the time. God forbid he communicate like a normal person even once; the world might have ended, don't you know." Casey's soft snort of laughter is gratifying, and it helps Will take a breath and say: "Anyway, the night I left, I had Brandon meet me here at the farm, because it was his last night and my last chance to see him and I figured it would be fine, my parents would be asleep, it was just the one time. But in the end Bill, um... caught us? In Brandon's car? And the position was, uh... Well. Let's say it would have been incredibly difficult to come up with a heterosexual explanation."

"I see," Casey says, and grimaces a little. "I'm a little afraid to ask how that went, but—"

"Oh, you know," Will says, vague now, far away. He's remembering it as it happened—the edge of the cornfield, the shriek of Brandon's tires as he peeled away, the clear moonlight under the broad canopy of stars. Everything had been so beautiful, this picturesque background like something out of a painting, set against Bill's twisted, red face and hard eyes. "He was angry. He wanted to know why I didn't understand my duty to my farm, and to my family. He said a lot of stuff about how being a man was about doing what was right instead of what you wanted, which at the time I thought was homophobia with like a weirdly religious curveball thrown in, but now I don't know. After what Mrs. Cardini told me—maybe that's really

FALL INTO YOU 227

what he *thought*, you know? That being part of a family meant putting everything else to one side, whatever it meant to you, or however miserable it made you to let it go. After all, that's what *he* did, although personally I think he should have told my grandpa to shove it where the sun didn't shine, but what do I know?"

"Is that what you did, then?" Casey asks, the curiosity evident in his voice. "That night? Told Bill to shove it?"

"Oh, well." Will pauses, and then nods. "I mean. More or less. I said it was my life, and he'd been mean to me pretty much for all of it, and why should I listen to him if he never listened to me? And he said that I *knew* why, that I'd watched my grandfather die the same way he had, that I didn't have time to go galivanting around doing whatever I pleased because *he* didn't have the time to wait."

And for a moment Will's eighteen again, the wind whipping his hair back away from his face, sending flecks of Bill's scream-borne spittle hurtling towards him at punishing speeds. He's eighteen, and his throat is raw from yelling, and every part of him feels sliced open, on display for his furious father to see. He's thinking of all the years he's spent attempting to please this man, and all the brutal, excoriating failures. He's crying, "So that's it, then, huh? That's your big plan for your only son? I'll just spend my whole life here, trying to doing whatever you say, and getting it wrong, and being punished for getting it wrong, and my reward for that, for never doing *anything* for myself, will be—what? To take care of *you* while you lose it like Gramps did?"

And Bill's face is turning purple, and he's screaming, "You ungrateful little—that's what it means to be someone's son! That's being part of a family!"

"No!" God, Will's replayed this in his mind so many times over the years; it shouldn't still have such power over him. It shouldn't still feel so fresh. He shouldn't still be able to feel the

228   DYLAN MORRISON

words, "That's being part of a *tragedy*," scraping against the back of his throat.

"Anyway, he hit me," Will says now, in the present, to Casey. It's flat, matter-of-fact, but that doesn't make it hurt any less to say. "I mean, not—it wasn't totally unprovoked, I said some stuff that was below the belt, for sure. And it wasn't like it was his best swing or anything. He could really fight, when he wanted to; I saw him do it a few times when I was a kid, and he always said he'd get around to teaching me. Probably if he ever had, I would have known how to duck or dodge or whatever, but. He didn't, so I didn't, so he hit me. Not hard enough to do any real damage, but his class ring broke the skin, left an infection that took weeks to clear up. You can still see the scar."

"Christ," Casey says, his eyes wide. "Will—God. I'm so sorry."

Will sighs, touches the little sliver of scar tissue briefly as he says, "Oh, thanks, it—I don't know. I'm not sure either one of us meant it to go as far as it did, and I didn't exactly comport myself well, either." Grimacing, he adds, "For example, at that point, I believe I told him I'd rather be anything but a Robertson, and would be better off with no family than this one. Which wasn't even how I felt, not really; I was just hurt, and sad, and upset, and eighteen, and I wanted to say something that would make *him* feel as bad as he'd made *me* feel. And, I mean, it worked, as least as far as I can tell. After that, he said if I felt that way, I might as well leave, because I was dead to him, anyway, so. That's what I did."

There's a beat. Then, his voice smooth and carefully even, Casey says, "You're a stronger person than he was, then. Good for you."

This wasn't what Will was expecting to hear to such a degree that he can feel his own eyes bug out of his head; it must be entertaining to look at, because Casey cracks a smile, but not a happy one. It slips away, though, into an unhappy little expression, when Will says, "I mean, that's... No. He was... and I'm—"

"Look, I spent my own time with Bill," Casey says, his voice firm. "And I've spent enough time with you, I think, to get a sense of who you are. I'm usually pretty quick off the draw with that sort of thing; in this case, I... let circumstances get the better of me. At first." He gives Will a brief glance under low lashes that Will could, if he wanted to be optimistic, assume communicates certain rather carnal intentions. Will's never been the optimistic type, but it's harder to reach for his usual pessimism after last night, especially when Casey adds, "Anyway, I stand by it. It takes a small person to treat a kid like that—to treat anyone like that, really—and a big one to walk away. It's hard, you know? To walk away." The unhappy smile slips back onto his face, wry this time, as he adds, "I think for a lot of people, it's easier to just live with what hurts than face the effort of trying to change it. They'd rather do what they know, even if all they know is suffering."

Will groans. "I know what you mean," he admits, a little uncomfortably. "Sometimes I feel like I'm—I don't know. Seeking it out, right? Situations that make me feel—well, situations that suck for me, I guess. Just... because it's familiar? Comfortable? Like, okay, a few months ago, I was dating this guy and he had this, God. Just, listen, don't judge me *too* much, but..."

He begins, somewhat relieved to turn the subject to lighter territory for a moment, to tell Casey the story of Anthony and the iguana. Casey's a good audience, better even than Selma—Will loves telling Selma a story, but sometimes she grimaces in a moment that makes him incredibly self-conscious, or raises an eyebrow in response to some action Will took in a way that lets him know, to his bones, that it wasn't the call she would have made. She's not doing it on purpose and Will doesn't blame her for it, but it does mean he holds back details that he thinks

Selma would find particularly egregious. Casey, on the other hand, is incensed for Will and entertained by turns, somehow tuned into every moment of the tale Will is hoping to hear a laugh, or a gasp, or see a horrified shake of the head. For this reason, Will shares details that even Selma doesn't know, like the fact that by the end, the iguana was responsible for roughly a third of Will's grocery expenses, and had peed, at least once, in every pair of dress shoes he owned.

"Only the dress shoes," Will complains, as they climb out of the truck, mostly because it's high time they did; there's only so long two men can sit in a truck in a parking lot before it starts to look like maybe it's a drug deal. At least, that's why Will assumes they're doing it; honestly, he mostly is following Casey, who, laughing at the exploits of the lizard, turned off the engine and hopped out of the driver's seat a minute ago.

"Sounds like that lizard had very expensive taste in toilets," Casey says, with a shrug, as he rounds to the rear of the truck. "Probably he was trying to tell you he wanted you to buy him a lizard bidet." He flips the pickup's back gate down, hops up to sit on it, and then, legs dangling, says, "Come on, come chill with me for a second. I was starting to feel like an idiot, sitting in the cab when it's such a nice day out."

"You're not wrong," Will admits, and hops up next to him. Lifting his arm to block the glare of the sun, he adds, "It *has* always been beautiful here; I missed it. I didn't want to, but I did."

Casey murmurs an assent, and as Will's legs kick back and forth in the air, he's swamped for the second time this morning in a thick cloud of memory. This one is briefer, but older and more weathered, less recently unearthed. To be honest, Will's not sure he's looked at it since it happened, it's so early, and unremarkable, and commonplace.

He was young, young enough to be picked up, and his father had lifted him and plopped him down onto the back of

FALL INTO YOU   231

his old pickup, the one he drove when Will was small. It had been daytime, and they'd been parked in some family friend's driveway, attending a block party for some holiday or another—Memorial Day, maybe, or Fourth of July—but Will thinks he must have been too little to know, even then. All he remembers is that for once, everyone was in a good mood. June was smiling and laughing, and Old Bill was having as cheerful a conversation as he ever did with some old friend, and Will's father brought him a Rocket Pop, which was so delicious that Will didn't care that it left behind a sticky red, white and blue residue as it melted down his hand. Thinking of it now, Will wonders if it isn't a glimpse into what they would have been like if any of them, Bill or June or even Old Bill, even the *first* Bill, had been a little happier with themselves, or with each other. Maybe what had made it all so hard was the ways in which they'd chosen to make it hard, or, at least, refused to try to make it any easier. Refused to do the necessary work, to share the necessary truth, to express the necessary emotion to make "less difficult" even an option.

"I never wanted to come back here," Will says. He's afraid it's going to come out sounding choked, thick with feeling. Instead, he's surprised to hear an edge of weary, raw amusement to it, like some part of him he's not yet ready to face thinks this is all a pretty solid joke. "That night, I packed up my duffel bag with everything that could fit, and I took all my savings from my summer jobs, and I thought: *I'm never coming back.* And I never did come back, Casey. I never did. I found an apartment, and then a job, and then I applied to college, and got in, and found another apartment, and other jobs, and built a whole life without this place. By myself! My mother died and I went to her funeral, up in Canton, but I didn't drive a single mile further south. I told myself it was what I wanted, you know? That I was better off not seeing it; that coming back here would hurt my feelings, and make me feel guilty. I never thought... I

232 DYLAN MORRISON

mean, I was dead to him, that's what he said, so. Might as well
be a ghost, right? I never thought there'd be any *reason* to come
back."

"And now?" Casey's voice is mild, inquisitive. When Will
looks at him, he's looking away, his gaze fixed on something far
in the distance. Will follows his eyeline to the tops of the third
orchard apple trees, leaves still green in a sea of autumn oranges
and maroons, rippling like the surface of a strange, otherworldly
ocean.

"Now..." Will chews the edge of his lip, shakes his head,
sighs. "I guess I just. I didn't know. I hadn't realized that it could
be like this. The way you've made the farm so different from
what it was, and so much closer to the place I used to like to
dream it was, to tell you the truth. When I was small." He swallows hard, *feeling* small, not able to look at Casey or the apple
trees or, if he's honest, himself, as he runs a hand through his
hair and, voice raw, adds, "And the longer I stay, the less sure I
am that I know what Bill meant by leaving it to me at all, or
even, Christ. Even what he meant that night I left. I'm not even
sure I know what *I* want anymore—*is* selling the right decision?
Is going back to Chicago the right decision? Who knows! What
does it matter! It's not like there's anyone else left alive to keep
score!" He presses his knuckles against his forehead briefly,
trying to push off a sharp spike of stress-induced anguish, and
finishes, "Sorry, just. I never wanted to get you, or *anyone*,
involved in *any* of this. I wanted to leave it behind me and walk
away clean, but."

Will takes a breath, his eyes fixed on the rolling sea of apple
trees, the blurred vista of gold and burgundy beyond. This time,
he *does* nearly choke on it, noticing how each word comes out
unmistakably and heavily weighted, like pieces of laundry
pulled, still dripping, from the bucket. Still, he makes himself
say it: "If I'm honest? I never *did* really get clean. Not ever. I
think part of me stayed here, when the rest of me went. It never

left—not the farm, not even that specific night, that stupid pull-off from the road next to the fence by the back field. It stayed right here, where I left it, wandering around like a stupid *ghost*, and I've..." Will stops, and swallows, and steadies himself before he shakes his head, forces himself to finish: "God. I've felt it pulling at me, *screaming* sometimes, all these years in Chicago."

FIFTEEN

Casey is silent for a long time. It's a long enough silence that Will starts to edge into feeling awkward about it, wondering if perhaps he's crossed a line. What line he isn't sure, and it would be maddening to try to guess, but he tries a little, anyway, combing frantically through the last few minutes for anything potentially offensive as his lack of reply stretches away from being a pause and towards being a genuine crisis. Should Will say something? Do something? Selma told him once that the first person who speaks in any interaction, or after any weighted pause, is automatically the loser, but she'd been several drinks deep at the time. And, now that Will thinks of it, several drinks later, she had told him it was something her own dreadful parents used to say, before weepily insisting that he shouldn't listen to her at all, and then that he wasn't truly a friend to her if he did not have, on his person, a taco.

For the second and hopefully final time in his life, Will finds himself wondering if the situation he's in would be improved by his having, at some earlier point in the day, made the decision to put a taco in his pocket. If nothing else, being able to say, "Hey, you want a taco?" would be distracting right now, as would, honestly, just pulling one out from nowhere and eating it himself. Will would find that distracting, certainly, if someone else did it in front of him. And distraction is obviously the name of the game, since if Will sits here in silence for too long with Casey, he's all too likely to tip into nervous, semi-coherent babbling. Either that, or his sheer proximity to Casey will overwhelm logic and reason and thoughts like, *Is this moment, in the direct aftermath of dropping all your childhood trauma in the man's lap, really the right one for attempting to jump his bones? Do you not think he might find it a bit jarring if you were, just for example, to launch yourself at him, shove your tongue down his throat, and push him back across the pickup truck's bed with decidedly filthy intent?* It's a convincing argument; it's just that it's not doing a great job of convincing *Will*. He should, of course, feel terrible right now, after digging up all that old history. But something about the way Casey just *listened* to him, and didn't take Bill's side, and said Will was a *strong person*—it did something to him, fanned what was already a fairly dangerous fire into one he suspects will leave him utterly changed, unrecognizable, when it stops. Or maybe it will never stop: Will's starting to grow concerned that he might spend his remaining years burning, like that coal town in Pennsylvania that's been on fire since the '60s. It's simply not fair, Will decides, for someone so hot and so built and so capable of fireman-carrying him to the nearest mattress to also be so *kind* to him. It should be illegal. There should be a law.

"You know what's weird?" Casey says, in the very final seconds before Will's mouth opens to release some version of this thought, which would have been a disaster. His tone is thoughtful, and he, thankfully, doesn't seem to notice when Will deflates like an untied balloon in relief as he continues. "I know the opposite of nearly all of that. I mean some parts were a little too familiar, but others... In some places, it was like seeing the negative of my own life. Not in the sense that it was

236   DYLAN MORRISON

negative, just—like with film, you know? It's not showing the picture, and it's not quite the reverse." He runs one hand through his thick blond hair, and Will's eyes can't help but follow the motion, the way the sun subtly shifts the shade of each strand as it slides over them. He's so absorbed in staring at it that he almost misses it when Casey sighs heavily and says, "I do know one thing, though. God. I owe you a hell of an apology."

Will blinks, trying to process this. He blinks again. Confused, he says, "Wait, *you* owe *me* an—"

"Apology," Casey says, nodding, "yes. And an explanation. For why I was the way I was. When you got here, and... before."

"Oh," Will says, not remotely sure how to reply to this. "I mean, you don't have to—"

Casey holds up a hand, but it's less that than the pained expression on his face that dries up the words on Will's tongue. "The thing is, man, I do. After the story you just told me? If I want to live with myself, anyway. There're rules."

"Sorry," Will says again, even more confused than before, "there are *rules*?"

"Oh, I don't mean for *you*." Casey makes a frustrated little noise, and then says: "Look, okay. I try to live by a certain code. I didn't have a lot when I was a kid that was... consistent, right? Or mine." He clears his throat, kicks his feet, and reaches a hand around to scrabble next to him in the truck bed. When he turns up a few twigs and pebbles, he starts tossing them towards the end of the parking spot; it seems to relax him as he continues, "I grew up on the festival circuit with my mom; she got pregnant on the road, had me on the road, just kept on going. And because I was always hopping from state to state, no permanent address, it took everyone a long time to cotton on that I wasn't, you know, going to school, for example." He catches Will's slightly stricken expression, and laughs. "Don't worry, it's not as bad as it sounds. Two of the people in the

FALL INTO YOU   237

group we traveled with were ex-Montessori teachers; they made sure I learned to read before the window closed and everything. It wasn't like I was in the forest with wolves."

"Still," Will says, with a sympathetic grimace. "Sounds like it wasn't an optimal growing environment."

Something about this seems to amuse Casey; his expression softens after a second into one that warms Will, for all he hesitates to let himself believe what he sees in it. Then Casey shrugs, and looks away, and says, "Eh, it could have been worse. Parts of it were fun, you know? I ate a lot more pizza and ice cream than the average kid gets to, I'll tell you that, and genuinely saw some musical history happen in real time. That's unreal, you know? And I wouldn't trade it for anything. But parts of it..." He frowns, his eyes going a little hollow. "Some of the stuff that happens at those shows isn't for kids. What people get up to when they're really wasted, or on a lot of drugs, or what happens to them when they've had too much—I shouldn't have been managing that. I should have been... somewhere else."

"I think," Will says, very carefully, "that is maybe a *bit* of an understatement, but: true. I'll give it to you. No doubt there."

Casey shrugs, like he can't quite look this sentence in the face, and changes the subject. "Anyway, around my twelfth birthday, somebody must've cottoned on, or CPS caught up with Mom, or whatever really happened; nobody wanted to talk about it. After that, I lived with my aunt until I finished high school. She was fine, but my uncle was a jerk, and he was never around much, anyway. I never knew my dad—I'm not even sure my mom knows who he was. Anyway, I'm not trying to give you my whole sob story or anything. I'm... Ugh." Casey makes a low, frustrated sound, and then says, "I'm trying to explain why, when I got here, Bill was... God. This is all going to sound so stupid to you, you're his *son*—"

"I mean, right," Will says, and offers Casey a crooked grin.

"I'm Bill's son, so you *know* I have to be fairly comfortable with stupid ideas."

Casey stares at him for a second. Then, covering his mouth with his hand, he lets a few snickers escape before he shakes his head and, obviously trying not to be mirthful at all, says, "I feel bad, I shouldn't laugh, it's just—Christ. The man really did have some godawful ideas, didn't he?"

"Some of the worst," Will says cheerfully. "I once watched him try to light a firework with a road flare. So whatever you're going to say, probably, by my standards, it's going to be fine."

"That's oddly comforting," Casey admits, and takes a breath. "Okay. I just, I never really had a father, or anything. Obviously, Bill *wasn't* my father, he was *your father*, this isn't like—stolen father valor, which, Jesus, is a sentence I never thought I'd say." He runs a hand over his face and laughs, briefly and not very happily. "God. This is ridiculous, the whole thing is *ridiculous*, but I wasn't from anywhere, you know? And didn't have any people. My aunt and uncle are whatever, it's fine but not exactly warm and fuzzy there. After high school, I started—driving around, and then I ended up here—"

"Wait," Will says, blinking, "hold on, you skipped a bit, I think. Unless—you didn't end up here *right* out of high school, did you?"

Casey makes an incredulous face, then laughs. "Are you kidding? No, God. I was *way* too jumpy to settle for even a year or two back then. I couldn't make myself stay anywhere longer than a couple of months. I've been here—God, six years now? Wild." Distantly, and in a hollow tone of voice that makes Will wonder if it's only occurring to him now, he adds, "Longest I've ever lived anywhere. Beats my aunt and uncle's by a year."

"I... see," Will says, doing the math in his head. "And you're in your thirties, so, I mean—must have been at least six or seven years on the road, right? Unless you took a detour for college somewhere in there—"

FALL INTO YOU   239

Casey whistles, but offers Will what seems to be a genuine grin. "No college, but I'm not in my thirties." When Will's mouth drops open, he laughs. "People always look so scandalized; you're not the first person to make that mistake, and I'm sure you won't be the last. Don't sweat it. I'm twenty-eight, so the big 3-0 isn't *far* off or anything, but *technically*..."

"God," Will says, abruptly embarrassed on a few different levels. "I mean, sorry for uh, thinking you were older—it's not that you *look* old, that's not—"

Casey laughs again. "I didn't take it that way, man. Chill. I've always heard it—that I seem a little older than I am. My theory is I had to grow up young, and it confuses the vibe."

"Huh," Will says. He's always thought of *himself* as someone who had to grow up young, but: "When I was twenty-eight, I wasn't capable of much of anything, outside of very specific academic parameters. I certainly couldn't have done all *this*, everything you've managed here—I could have kept it how it was before, if that, *maybe*, but improved it? Brought it back to turning a real profit? No way. Maybe because college sort of didn't end for me until I was older than you are now, but I didn't really have a lot of the, like, basic personhood stuff down? Not until I was at least thirty-one, and, honestly, it's still a work in progress. I was kind of... I mean, okay, so first imagine your average totally useless undergrad was bitten by a radioactive textbook—"

Snorting, Casey says, "Sorry, sorry. Just—you *do* sometimes sound like you've been bitten by a radioactive textbook."

"I wish," Will mutters. "All the powers of a textbook? I'd be unstoppable. Plus, it would get me out of the aging process, because the written word is forever—"

"You're not getting out of it that easy," Casey says, amused, shaking his head. "Not enough time to find a radioactive textbook, for one thing: It's your birthday next week, right? Daphne told me—the town's spooky Halloween baby."

240   DYLAN MORRISON

Will, abruptly distracted from absolutely everything, stares at him. "*What?*"

"Sorry, should she not have said anything?" Casey grimaces, and, hastily, says, "Don't rat me out, okay, if I wasn't supposed to know. She scares the living daylights out of me when she gets into a mood. A person shouldn't be able to zero in on someone else's insecurities like that, it's not fair."

"No," Will says, and shakes his head, torn between surprise and amusement. On the one hand, it's honestly nice, after watching Casey cheerfully drive around like the devil himself was chasing him, and catch and release no less than ten spiders from the house in the last two weeks, to know that there's *something* that freaks him out. On the other hand: "I just didn't know anyone thought of me that way. As a... spooky Halloween baby?" He pauses, and, wryly, adds, "Although I guess it is a pretty small town, and it *would* explain a couple of weird conversations over the years. Honestly, though, I'm surprised Daph even remembered my birthday, let alone told you about it."

"Oh, well, it was that first day you got here," Casey says, casually, like it's nothing. "After you left. And I was, not to put too fine a point on it, *real* mad at you, and I think she was trying to—I don't know, humanize you, a little. She kept saying if you were anything like she remembered, I might not mind you so much with a little time to get to know you. Said you were the type to grow on someone, like a fungus."

"Like a fungus," Will repeats, faintly. "Incredible. Just what I've always hoped to hear about myself. The word in the very center of the vision board for my life? It is, in fact, fungus."

Casey laughs, and then cuts Will a sidelong glance and says, "Fungus or not, she was right," which warms Will enough that he sits in happy silence for a minute, glowing internally from the compliment.

Finally, though, curiosity gets the better of him, and he says,

FALL INTO YOU   241

"Okay, right, but—we were talking about *you*, and how you got here. Were you living out of your car, then?"

"Oh, God, right. Yeah, sometimes, in that first year or two after high school," Casey says, with a little shrug. "But it just depended. Sometimes, I'd stay with friends, or with a partner, or get a motel room for a while, or sublet from a coworker, whatever. It never mattered that much to me, so long as I had something interesting to do, and somewhere comfortable enough to sleep at night. I'd get a contract job, or pick up construction work, and do that until I got bored or it dried up, and then blow town and drive until I found somewhere else that looked interesting."

"*Was* it interesting?" Will wants to know. He couldn't do it himself, but: "It *sounds* interesting."

Casey's eyes widen for a second, just slightly. Then, though he doesn't fully smile, they crinkle deeply at the corners. "Do you know, no one ever asks me that? Even though I always phrase it that way—*yes*. It was *so* interesting. I learned so much *about* so much, I met so many fascinating people, and..." He looks at Will oddly for a second, and then says, "Well. Maybe you know. After you left the farm, did you find yourself feeling that sense of—oh, I'm not sure how to explain this." He pauses, clearly turning the words over on his tongue, before saying, "That sense that all the horrible, hard feelings you were carrying around could just be. Left behind on some curb? Part of a version of yourself you weren't anymore?"

And suddenly Will is eighteen again, the disintegrating vinyl of the Greyhound seat warming slowly under his hands as he clutches it, waiting for Bill to burst through the bus doors and drag him out of the bus station, out of Canton, and back home to Glenriver. God, he can *taste* the cheap cologne the man two seats up was wearing, mixing with a nervous flop-sweat smell he'd end up realizing, halfway through the trip, was coming from himself. The relief of the closing doors, the bus

242 DYLAN MORRISON

lurching away from the station, still hits like a drug even in memory. It was the first slow, sweet taste, of a life outside of Bill and June's influence. Of a life that was about more than being the fourth in a line of similarly named men. Of a life where he felt safe enough to be himself.

"Yes," Will says, after a pause. "I think I do know, yes."

"Well," Casey says, looking pleased to be understood, "it made me feel like that, at first. And for a while, I thought I'd be doing it forever. But when I was about twenty, I realized I wasn't... happy, anymore. That I didn't feel joy when I was driving away, just jealousy of all the local people and the complicated webs of their lives, all their connections and histories and roots. I started to feel like stopping, at least for a little while. I started to feel like if I *didn't* stop, something inside me might turn rotten."

He sighs, and, looking out across the trees and away from Will, says, "I met this girl in Boise, Rhonda. She was beautiful, and smart, and she made me feel—like it was okay, I guess? Like I could tell her about the heavy stuff, about me and my life, and have it be okay. She was so nice about it. *She's* the one who helped me figure out how to do all the basic personhood stuff, as you put it. Certainly, it wasn't my mom, and my aunt and uncle didn't consider me their problem enough to bother, but she knew all that. She came from a big family, good parents who were happy together and pretty well-off, and she'd learned how to be an adult from them when she was a kid, like people are supposed to. So I was grateful, and I loved her, and I thought for a few years there that she loved me, too, that that was it." His voice turning somewhat sour, he continues, "I was so happy to think of having something stable, something real, that I chucked all my eggs right into that stupid basket without hesitating. I moved into her apartment; I got a job working for her dad; he was a nice guy, I liked the work, everything made sense. It was like I saw this whole future setting itself up before my eyes and

FALL INTO YOU   243

I was *ready*. Ready to be a local somewhere, and part of a real partnership. A real family."

"Didn't work out like that?" Will asks, sympathetic, when Casey has to pause briefly, get a handle on some emotion. Could be sadness, but if Will were to guess, he'd say something more along the lines of self-recrimination. It's the same face Bill used to make every time some sleazy salesman had successfully talked him into buying something expensive for the farm that had then, within hours, fallen apart.

Casey shakes his head, and makes a hand gesture reminiscent of an explosion, with an accompanying sound effect. "It all blew up. Turned out everyone in our whole circle—her friends, her family, all these people who'd cozied up to me for years, acted like they cared about me—they all knew deep down, like she knew deep down, that she was going to end up with her high school sweetheart." Making a disgusted face, he adds, "*He* was the quarterback of the football team, of course, and from another prominent local family. *Gary*. It's not even his fault, not really, but Christ, I still hate him." Casey scowls for a second at the thought of Gary and then adds, "Anyway, this is probably obvious, but she left me, and went home to her parents, and then suddenly all my friends, or the people I thought were my friends, were only *her* friends. Had only ever been her friends. And that Monday at work, my boss, her father, who had always been happy to work with me before, couldn't even meet my eyes. And then about a week later, Gary turned up, real polite, at our apartment, to say he was sorry, and he hated to do it, but I wasn't actually on the lease and he and Rhonda were planning on living in it, so if I could just clear on out, that would be real great." He sighs, looking down at his hands. "So I did. I cleared on out. Put all my stuff in my car, and got in the passenger seat, and booked it out of there. I decided to go east because I figured it was the way it would take me longest to hit another ocean, and I wanted to be as far away as I could get."

244   DYLAN MORRISON

Will whistles. "*Damn.* Casey, I'm *sorry*, that sucks."

Casey looks slightly startled to have this clear and obvious fact acknowledged. "Oh. I—thanks. Yeah. I didn't love it."

"Was it weird? To just—pull up roots on your life like that?" When Casey slants him a speaking look, Will holds up his hands, laughing a little, and says, "Okay, yes, I'll grant you, I did famously run away, dooming my family line and ruining the Robertson name, that one time, but it really was only the once. I got on a bus to Chicago, and I still live in Chicago. In the same neighborhood, even, where I got off the bus. Even the place I live—I mean, okay, it's not the *first* apartment I rented, because that apartment was, seriously, very terrible, the stuff of nightmares, full of roaches and previously undiscovered molds and a series of mice who I called Bernard, because calling them all Bernard made it easier to convince myself it was one mouse." Will shudders, briefly, to think of Bernard, and of the morning he had been forced to confront the reality that what he was dealing with was, very inarguably, *Bernards*. "I... moved out of that one pretty fast. But the second place I lived was only better in the sense that it was live*able*, like up to code. It's otherwise grim and dark and empty and I *still* live there. Moving always seemed like too much of a hassle. I've never pulled up and started again as an adult, not even a little. Must've been hard."

Casey smiles, and makes a noise Will's not sure how to parse, a low hum of not-quite-disagreement. "Probably was. I don't remember a lot of it all that well; in retrospect, I think my mental health probably took kind of a nosedive, and I should've stayed put before I went changing my whole life around. But I just had to get *out* of there, so I pretty much drove three days straight across the country. After that I promised myself I'd never do it again, get so attached to the *idea* of something, some possible future." He runs a hand through his hair, shakes his head. "But then I ended up here. If you're trying to get over a young woman, you really *can't* get further away than helping out an old man, so I thought, for a while, that it was all fine. I'd just stick to the farm, and to myself, and help your dad, keep any dating I did out of Glenriver, not that I did much. I thought that way I wouldn't get hurt again." He shrugs, a little despondent. "But then Bill needed *so* much help, and the whole farm did, too, and I'd worked enough construction jobs and handled enough broad-scale projects to see what needed to happen, so I just got to work. It had to get done, right?" He pauses, and, wryly, adds, "My mom always says that's my *thing*, when she sees me. My 'troubled life pattern,' or however she phrases it—feeling like *I* have to be the one to do something, just because it needs doing. Never quite manages to ask herself what might've made me that way, though."

"Oh, of course not," Will says, waving a hand. "Obviously, I'm no expert, but from what I hear, parents rarely do. And God knows mine left me some fun little surprises like that; you should ask my friend Selma about my taste in guys sometime. She'll give you a whole master's-level psychotherapy thesis on how I'm seeking out destructive patterns while the sheer enormity of the embarrassment drives me to drink."

"Spoken like someone *very* committed to disproving her thesis," Casey says dryly.

"You shut *up*," Will says, but undercuts it by smiling at him without entirely meaning to. "But don't, actually, because my *point* is, I get it. Thanks for telling me."

"Oh," Casey says, and blinks, and, to Will's surprise, flushes slightly. "Well, sure. Thank you for... listening, I guess."

"My pleasure," Will says, and waits what he hopes is an appropriate amount of seconds before letting his curiosity get the better of him: "So did you like... *happen* to end up stopping here, in the end? From Boise? That's *crazy*—"

"What? Oh, no," Casey interrupts, shaking his head. "That would be crazy, but, uh, I saw the billboards for Cedar Point—you know about Cedar Point, right?"

246   DYLAN MORRISON

Offended, Will draws himself up to his full sitting height and says, "*Excuse* me? Of course I know about Cedar Point. I *did* grow up here, *nobody* makes it out of Northern Ohio without at *least* one trip to—"

"All right, all right, I get it," Casey says, laughing now. "The point is, I was there, and I saw an ad for this place and—I know how stupid this sounds, by the way, but it's the truth—I liked the name. Robertson *Family* Farms. I know it's dumb, but that's what I wanted, what I felt like I'd lost, and I couldn't get it out of my head." His mouth twists, and he adds, sounding sorry about it, "But then I got here, and the 'Family' in 'Family Farms' was just this one old man, clearly in over his head, couldn't even afford to staff the place because sales were so low. I talked him into hiring me as counter help and just started—fixing stuff. Making it work better." Casey shrugs, looking away. "We... Sorry, Will, but we got on pretty well, me and Bill, right from the start. I don't want to rub it in, that the two of you—that it was so—"

"Oh, God," Will says, waving a hand and pulling a face. "You don't have to do that; it's fine. I figured you probably did." He meets Casey's eyes and, slightly more honestly, says, "Okay, I mean, it might have made me go for your throat two weeks ago, but I don't mind so much now. I guess." Will pauses, chews his lip, clears his throat. "I guess I'm glad he had someone he *did* get along with, in the end. Someone to help." Finally, and so honestly it's a little agonizing, he adds, "And, I mean. No offense or anything, but I'm still pretty glad that person wasn't... me."

This does make Casey laugh, a proper laugh, and when he finishes, he says, "Yeah, that's fair. Probably helped that I wasn't blood—less history, right? And different stakes." He looks at Will, and sighs. "Speaking of which, that's the other thing: the dementia."

"Yeah," Will says, his voice low. "From what you've said,

FALL INTO YOU 247

and what I remember from my grandfather, I kind of figured it probably—came up, between the two of you? I have to imagine at a certain point it would have been impossible for it not to."

"I should have called you," Casey says, quiet. "I'm sorry— the first day I realized Bill had living family, I should have found your number, or your email, or whatever. Before he got diagnosed, probably, right when I first moved in with him to make sure he didn't hurt himself in there alone. But definitely *when* he got diagnosed and I started making decisions. That wasn't right. They were your calls to make, if they were anyone's, and at the very least you had the right to know. But... Bill didn't talk about you, except, uh. Except when he was... a little confused, right, about who he was, and who I was, and when... it was, overall. There were a couple of times he said things to me and I knew he was talking to you. And, well, between that and the people in town I asked about what happened—they were all perfectly polite, you know, but they all said things like, 'Oh, better to leave well enough alone there,' and in retrospect they were trying not to *out* you, probably, but." Casey takes a deep breath, squares his shoulders, and, like a confession, says, "I got the impression that you were, maybe, a mean and spiteful person who willfully turned his back on his family and wouldn't want to hear from me."

"Ah," Will says, surprised to find he feels oddly sanguine about all of this. Perhaps even, dare he say it, slightly amused, if in a grim, maudlin way. "Well, I gotta say: That checks out."

Casey's eyebrows shoot to his hairline. "Really? You don't want to, I don't know, punch me in the mouth for making that decision without you? For deciding you were a jerk and then acting accordingly, without bothering to find out?"

"Nah. I'm not a violence-oriented person," Will says, after a second's thought. "Why attack something when you could put it under a microscope instead, you know? Also, I mean, in the days after I met you, I may or may not have told someone you

248   DYLAN MORRISON

moved here from your previous address of Satan's Butthole, so. I'm not sure anyone comes out of this *totally* innocent."

Casey laughs again, and then surprises Will by saying, "It wasn't my *last* address, but I did live in Hell for about six months once," and they lose about ten minutes to a discussion of Hell, Michigan, a place Will has always wanted to visit. Casey, who had moved there primarily because he thought it would be fun, later in his life, to be able to say that in his youth he'd worked in Hell's gift shop, seems to have wonderful memories. It's nice, to hear him talk for a moment about wonderful memories, the cool people he met, the dear friends he made. Will knows enough—about life, about the people involved, about how these things usually go—to know that what's to come won't be an easy listen.

He wants to hear it, anyway, though; in some ways, he feels like he came all the way down here, got trapped here, spent all this time stuck here, just *to* hear it. So when Casey winds down in his recollections, Will steadies his palms against the sun-warmed metal of the truck bed and, quietly, says, "Will you tell me what happened? With Bill, at the end?"

And Casey sighs, and nods, and does.

Will takes in the story as best he can, although it's a little helter-skelter, both in terms of Casey's telling and in terms of Will's internal experience of the words. He can almost feel some little part of himself running around in the back of his mind, trying frantically to file everything that's coming in and, finding no place to put it, becoming slowly buried in a heap of new information until nothing but one twitching finger is visible. And he knows, even as it happens, that he's putting pieces of it away incorrectly, in places that they don't go. That, weeks from now, he will reach for something little and barely related, like the name of a particular brand of cereal Bill happened to like eating, and be walloped, gut-punched, by a wave of nauseating sadness and grief. It's that kind of story; it's that kind of day. Will thinks that once it would have really upset him, but here in the heart of autumn's vibrant, dying resplendence, he feels calm, at peace. Things hurt, sometimes, even when you don't expect them to, or wish they wouldn't. Things hurt, and you feel it, and you carry on. What else is there? What other choice does life offer?

Casey was helping Bill in a professional capacity, he explains, at first. He helped Bill update the technology, and then do some desperately needed maintenance around the farm, and then fixed the billing system, and then the water filtration system, and then the hole in the farmhouse floor. It was around this time that he asked Bill if he could move into the farmhouse, less because he minded sleeping in his car and more because Bill couldn't explain the hole, or so many of the other problems, and once Casey moved in, it was obvious why. During the middle of the day, he was more with it, but early morning, or later at night, Bill would forget. He'd forget who Casey was, or that he'd moved into the house; he'd mix Casey up with Will, or with his own father, or with people Will might have been able to place in those circumstances, comparing names or details against his own knowledge of his father's life, but who Casey, more or less a stranger, could not.

He muddled through, though, apparently. Casey tells Will, quite earnestly, that for a while it was fine—nice, even. When Bill was lucid, he was grateful for the help, for someone to confide in, and he was lucid more than he wasn't, at first. And for Casey, it was—though Will has to read this between the lines—nice to have someone relying on him, and something around which to orient his own life. A bit of much-needed lead, maybe, in boots that had a tendency to go haring off at a moment's notice.

"But then," Casey admits, on a heavy sigh, "it... wasn't fine anymore. We both knew it; he was getting erratic during the day, and in ways that were dangerous. Dangerous for him, but

250   DYLAN MORRISON

for the farm and the customers, too: One afternoon, he took the tractor out and started trying to clear down the back fields. Problem was, it was the first week of June, and pick-your-own strawberry season. He took out a huge patch of beautiful berries and nearly ran down a nine-year-old, although luckily, she had the good sense to get out of the way in time."

"Jesus," Will mutters.

"Yeah," Casey says, his jaw working; it's obvious the memory still pains him. "Anyway, after that, we had a conversation and made a deal. He said he'd seen all the work I'd put into the place over the years, and that if I helped him, you know, close things out with dignity, or whatever, he'd—he'd leave me the farm." He glances over at Will with an anguished expression on his face, and says, "Please believe me when I say that I— I didn't know about what had happened between you two, all right? Not the real story, anyway. And, regardless, I knew... I knew making a deal like that with someone in his condition was like writing a contract in sand. I *knew*, and I don't expect—" Casey blows out a harsh breath before he finishes, "I'm not telling you this because I think I'm entitled to anything, okay? I just... I want you to know the whole story. After all this, if anyone deserves to know it, it's you."

"Okay," Will says quietly, his mind too overfull to begin to think of saying anything else.

"Anyway," Casey says. He's talking quickly now, like the words are searing his tongue as they land, and he can't wait to get them out of his mouth. "I didn't do it for the farm, I knew it probably wasn't legal, that he probably—forgot, or whatever. I just wanted to help him, because it was sad and he'd been—oh, I don't know. I wanted to. So I found him a nursing home, one that wasn't too far away, and I helped him pay for it—"

"You helped him *pay* for it?!" Will nearly yelps this, and wants to scream, actually scream, when Casey shrugs uncomfortably.

"Oh, sure," he says, like it doesn't matter. "He couldn't have afforded it on his own, and I'm—more or less allergic to rent, honestly, so. I have a lot more saved up than most people do, and anyway, it's not like he lasted that long there. Barely a year. I visited him as much as I could, but the lights were on less and less." Hoarsely, staring down at the gravel, he whispers, "I should have called you."

"*He* should have called me," Will says, abruptly stubborn, crossing his arms over his chest. Then he recognizes the posture and the emotion and cringes entirely away from it, saying, more softly and not at all sure he means it, "Or I should have called him, I guess, although I can't say he ever gave me any reason to want to. It's my personal belief that when you pull the 'dead to me' card, you have to be the one to extend the olive branch, but..." He lets a smile, wry and a little bitter, twist up the corners of his mouth. "Maybe I'm being stubborn, you know? Heritable trait. Maybe when my mother died, I should have— ah, but." He cuts the train of thought off, suddenly and entirely sure: "It doesn't really matter, does it?"

Casey cocks his head. "How do you mean?"

"Me and my dad—we weren't built to communicate with one another." The words tumble out of his mouth like a confession, or a eulogy, too raw to be anything but honest. "Too different in some ways, I think, and in others, I guess..." He grimaces, hating it, but forces it out anyway: "Ugh. I guess too alike? But whatever the reason, my whole childhood we were like—oh, I don't know. Two radio transmitters, maybe, each sending signals to the other in increasing frustration, neither of us realizing we hadn't been equipped with receivers. All these years I've thought I knew who he was, and what he thought of me, and what he wanted from me, and now..." Will sighs, wanting almost to laugh even though it isn't funny. "Now I'm not sure I ever really knew him at all. I know he never really knew me."

252   DYLAN MORRISON

"His loss," Casey says, soft. "In my opinion."

Will smiles at him, although he's sure the expression is at odds with the tears he can feel glimmering, held barely at bay, in his own eyes. He's sad, all of a sudden, in a way he didn't expect to be over his old man, in a way he's surprised to find he's grateful for. "We all lost something, I think," he says, quietly. "All us Robertsons, handing down the same stupid, needless pain across a century. It used to make me so angry, thinking about it—what good did it do anyone? What was the point?" He meets Casey's eyes, warmed by the steady, patient understanding in them, and shrugs. "I thought the only way to win was to stop playing, but. I think... I think the truth is, it's more about changing the rules."

Casey doesn't say anything at first, just considers it for a moment, then nods, sighs. "Maybe there aren't winners and losers, at least not when it comes to this. Just... people being people, and trying their best, and messing it up, same as always. You and Bill—yeah, sure, it's not a nice story, but it's a family story, right? If *my* childhood taught me anything, it's that family doesn't have to be nice to make you who you are." He smiles, and shrugs, and, a little awkwardly, adds, "And I've heard, if you don't like the one you're issued, the option is on the table to go ahead and make your own. No personal experience there, of course, but. Rumor has it."

A train whistle screams in the distance as if to underscore his point, low and mournful and impossible to miss, startling the birds from the trees. Just for a second, as he watches them climb, Will thinks he feels a similar shift within his heart, a susurration rising as if from nowhere to seek new skies.

SIXTEEN

In the end, after several minutes of companionable silence and then several more minutes of slightly awkward silence, it becomes apparent to Will that they need—or, at least, *he* needs—to get off the truck bed and do something physical. If he doesn't, one of two things is going to happen. The first, likeliest, and worst option is that the weight of what's been said in the last few hours will come crashing down, and Will just doesn't think he can take that right now. On top of everything else, being flattened like a bug under the enormous, crushing shoe of his own emotions seems a bit too much.

The second option is that—faced with nothing left to say to one another and the nearly empty, perfectly serviceable bed of Casey's pickup behind them—they might succumb to temptation, and try out the practicalities of the phrase "A roll in the hay." Granted, it wouldn't exactly be a roll in the hay so much as a roll in the hay, mud, twigs, leaves, dirt, and various tools, but Will doesn't actually think that would be their biggest problem. Their biggest problem would be that this is the *market parking lot* and it is *Saturday morning*, so anything they got up to would be giving the good citizens of Glenriver quite the

254   DYLAN MORRISON

show. Even the ones who weren't here to see it would have heard about it by the time Will next talked to them, and every one of them would have something to say, some joke to make, some comment about how Will's the one who finally bagged him, eh? The thought of that, just at this moment, is stomach churning, and yet Will is upsettingly sure that if he sits here much longer, he'll lose sight of it entirely, too distracted by Casey's gently parted lips, the jut of his square chin, the curve of his jaw.

Casey must come to a similar conclusion, because after a long, charged look at Will, he glances away and, somewhat sheepishly, says, "Hey, not to thank you for telling me all that with asking you to do a bunch of manual labor, but any chance you might, ah. Be willing to help me break that fallen tree down into mulch? I went and got the woodchipper from Greg three days ago, but it's just sitting back there, next to where we hauled the stupid tree last week, because... well, because I've been lazy, mostly."

Will groans, but good-naturedly, not meaning it, as he hops off the back of the truck. "I swear to God, nobody back in Chicago is going to believe me when I tell them how much of this trip I spent using a chainsaw."

"Are you kidding? They'll probably be jealous," Casey says. He hops down, too, closing the truck bed up before starting off in the direction of the outbuildings, glancing back briefly to make sure Will is following him and grinning when he is. "I'd want to get my hands on a chainsaw if I spent all day in a cubicle."

"My coworkers don't spend all day in a cubicle!" Will says, and then, in the tones of an admission, has to concede, "But, it is. You know. A lab, so. A little sterile, I guess. And some of them probably *would* like to get their hands on a chainsaw, although... it might better if they very emphatically did not, especially in, uh. A few... notable cases."

"Mm," Casey says, and, only half-jokingly, "sounds serious," and Will, more or less accidentally, finds himself telling Casey about the flaws and foibles of his various colleagues as they walk to the far corner of the farm. Casey's just... upsettingly easy to talk to, that's the problem, and before he knows it, they've reached the tree and the woodchipper and Will's told Casey all of his fears about what his second-in-command, Bartholomew, gets up to while he's away, but has not once cycled back to:

"Catherine Rose," Will remembers, with a groan, as Casey reaches towards one of the chainsaws to start breaking down the tree trunk, which he more or less strapped whole to his truck and dragged down the road last week. "God, I forgot to—look, I've been dodging her calls for the last two weeks, all right? I don't know *what* I'm going to do, but I know I don't want to... well, to screw you over, or anyone else, either. I just need some time to think, and talk to my friend Selma—she's a lawyer, you know—and I *tried* to talk to Mere and some of the other business owners in town, but—"

"All clammed up on you, right?" Casey says, and shakes his head. "That stupid company—I can't prove it, but I'd bet anything they got the locals to sign something, promising them some payout if they go along, and making sure they know they'll feel it if they opt not to. When they first rolled into town, a lot of folks around here were on my side—Mere and Sandy, Noah Anderson, a lot of the older guard. They said they didn't want some outside corporation having such a significant stake in the town any more than I did, and if Nimbletainment did try to make an aggressive move for the farm, they'd vote down the business license when it came before the council." He sighs, rolling his shoulders back. "But, you know. Suddenly they were getting visits from your buddy Catherine Rose, and one by one, they all kinda faded out on me. Real awkward, every time, even with Mere—*still*, sometimes, you notice that? After everything?"

256   DYLAN MORRISON

"Yeah," Will says, because he has. "Sometimes, it's like she's —embarrassed, I guess, is how it comes off."

"I wish she wouldn't be," Casey mutters. "It's not her fault, and I don't blame her. I don't blame any of them, you know? They've got kids and livelihoods, and they don't know what I know; I couldn't expect them to. But if they did know, they wouldn't accept the payout—it's worthless in the long run."

"How so?"

"Oh, the festival will come in and take it all over," Casey says, waving a hand. His tone and body language are light; only the grim twist to his mouth, the tightness in his jaw, betrays how angry the very idea makes him. "Seen it all before, in other little towns. They get enough space that it's a big-deal venue, and suddenly, it's, hey, why stick to holding a little festival once a year when they could have music playing here every weekend? And, hey, that's a cute local restaurant, but it's a little far from the venue; why don't they open one almost exactly like it, just a little bit worse, right on the venue grounds? And, hey, it seems like the locals aren't loving the constant congested traffic through town, and the way no one wants to bother coming out to Main Street on a night with a venue show, and people are starting to shutter their businesses after all—might as well buy that real estate up cheap, right? Turn some of it into short-term rentals for festival-goers, and otherwise sell it out to big-name retailers, who don't live and die on their weekly sales the way smaller operations do? And hey, while we're at it, who needs these old apple trees, anyway, right?"

Casey's breathing hard by this point, and he seems to realize it; he cuts himself off, and Will can almost see him reeling himself back in to say, trying unsuccessfully for nonchalance: "Or, at least, that's how I've seen it go in the past. Maybe it'll be different this time! But I doubt it."

"Jesus," Will says, alarmed. "Why didn't you just *say* that two weeks ago?"

FALL INTO YOU   257

Casey shrugs, discomfited. "Would you have believed me? Nobody else does, and they're my friends and neighbors! You were a stranger, and I had a... let's call it an incorrect impression of you, on top of it." He casts a slightly helpless look at Will and adds, "And then I realized pretty quickly that I'd maybe gotten the wrong end of the stick from Bill, but I didn't want to—I don't know. It felt like if I said something, it would all go wrong; it was all a lot more fun than I expected, honestly, and I couldn't bring myself to ruin what I thought was—ugh." He scowls, and mutters, "Jesus, this isn't coming out right. In a lot of ways, we hardly know each other and I don't want you to think I'm, Christ, *expecting* anything from you because of last night. If it was just a one-off for you, a bit of fun before you go, then that's—"

"It wasn't," Will says, very quietly, because even for him, it's hard to interpret that particular statement in a way that doesn't line up, quite precisely and on a number of the more vulnerable particulars, to Will's own reasons for not wanting to talk about it. "Or, I mean... it *was* fun, it was *really* fun, but it wasn't, uh. Just fun. I—understand what you're driving at, I think. I've felt... similarly."

"Do you?" Casey says this sharply, and whips his head around to look at Will with such intensity that Will flushes. "*Have* you?"

Still, flushed or not, Will can't *entirely* help being his father's son: His chin lifts defiantly, of its own inherited accord, even as he swallows hard and admits, "Yes."

For a moment, they stare at each other, small in comparison to the corpse of the tree sprawled in front of them, and yet each of them seeming slightly larger, more substantial, than they did just a moment before.

Then Casey grins, wide and slow and lazy, and says, "Well, okay, then. I guess we should get to cutting this tree up, huh?"

"That mean I can stay?" Will asks this before he can even

258   DYLAN MORRISON

ask himself if it's what he wants; he knows it is, though, the minute the words hit the air. "Until I decide what I want to do, anyway? I promise I'm not going to screw you over, at least not on purpose."

"It's your house," Casey reminds him.

"I don't know that it is," Will says, shrugging. "Not by rights, anyway. You could make the argument that Bill promised it to you long after he told me to stop thinking of myself as his son—there's a lot of people, I think, who'd hear this story and say it was yours."

"Well, regardless, you stay as long as you like. As to your argument—" Casey chews his lip for a minute, considering, and then says, "I think we should talk to some chainsaws about this, really. See what they have to say about it."

Will grins brightly back at him; the truth is, Casey was right earlier. His coworkers back in Chicago *should* be jealous about the chainsaws. "What a truly *excellent* idea."

Around noon, Casey steps away a few feet to the nearest apple tree, a Fuji with a branch hanging out over past the fence. He plucks two apples from it and tosses one to Will, calling, "We'll go back for lunch soon, but until then!"

Will catches the apple, and leans up against the nearest fencepost to eat it. Fuji has never been his favorite—mealy sometimes, and too sugary—but this one is good and crisp, plucked just at the right moment, the punch of honeyed sweetness welcome after so much physical strain. As he chews and swallows, he lets his gaze dance across the nearby third orchard, and cut back to what little he can see of the first and second, beyond it. Even the younger trees have been alive longer than Will has, and some of them have been here long enough to see every William Josiah Robertson come and go—or, in Will's case,

FALL INTO YOU   259

come and go and come back again. He wonders, knowing even as he does it that it's inane, unknowable, what they think of him.

"You wanna go back?" Casey asks, coming over to join him. "Track down some real lunch? We can finish this up later."

"Yeah, all right," Will says, though it pains him a little to leave a job half-finished, especially here; even now, as sure as he's ever been than Bill's stone-dead, Will half expects to find himself in trouble for walking away from something undone. In some ways, he thinks it's what drove him to science, where the whole point is often to walk away from something while it's still in progress, and see what it does on its own.

Still, as Will follows Casey back across the property, he finds himself relaxing, soothed by the now-familiar sound of his footfalls. What's past is past; what's here, now, is a sunny day, and a strapping man, and, if he's lucky, time enough for Will to do what he likes with both.

It's a good feeling. A singular one. Will folds it up small and careful, like a paper airplane, and places it, for safekeeping, in one of the lesser-used rooms of his heart.

As they approach the farmhouse, he jogs a little and catches up to Casey. Will's opening his mouth to ask Casey what he wants to do for lunch when he notices the little gaggle of people standing on the porch.

Mere Gunderson he places first; he waves at her, his mouth dropping openly slightly when he recognizes the person next to her as her husband, Sandy. So he knows what she's going to say even before she opens her mouth and calls down, "Will! There you are! We came to tell you they fixed the bridge, and Sandy wanted to say hi, and thanks, and—"

"Casey, my dude!" The speaker is a tie-dye-wearing young woman of approximately college age, who is unfamiliar to Will, but Casey is sighing a resigned, knowing sigh even as she says, "I was trapped on the other side of the bridge, you see, and

260 DYLAN MORRISON

anyone you might have seen these last two weeks who maybe could've looked kinda like me in the right light was just—"

"Samantha, I made direct eye contact with you at Mike's like three days ago," Casey says wearily. "And I know it *was* you, you don't have a twin, there wasn't a hologram; let's not do this. You can just work your next scheduled shift, which is, I believe, in twenty minutes. Okay? But Will's reorganized some stuff in the back so it works better, might be good if he took you through that first, assuming he doesn't mind walking someone else... Will?"

But Will's not listening to Casey, or to Meredith, or to Samantha's vaguely entertaining excuses. He's looking past all of them, to where Catherine Rose is standing, slightly apart from everyone, arms crossed over her chest, tightly tapping one foot.

There's always a moment for Will, right before his brain pitches him into a real panic attack, where everything goes... still. For some years, he's operated under the belief that this is, ultimately, nothing more than the obvious result of many millennia of compounded human evolution: If panic is his body being flooded with adrenaline for survival, then surely these moments of frozen horror serve an equally salient purpose. In the event Catherine Rose *were* going to, say, jump off the porch like a prehistoric predator, with every intention of eating Will for lunch, then the moment of frozen horror certainly would be helpful. He'd have a chance to come up with an exit strategy, at least, and the best way to execute it.

Catherine Rose is not going to jump off the porch and eat him; Will knows this logically, rationally. Illogically and irrationally, however, he knows that Catherine stands as a glowering beacon of every decision he's not ready to make yet, every complicated angle cutting into his conscience, every pressuring force bearing down on him like a lowering blade. If Will's not careful here, he's going to put himself through the woodchipper,

FALL INTO YOU 261

or Casey, or both of them, and he finds abruptly that he can't bear the thought of it, the waste of it, the shrapnel of yet another needless interpersonal tragedy woven into the bones of this place. How many of those can one place hold? Is it so much to ask that Will have a chance to think about this, really *think* about it, with more information to hand and a clearer sense of the picture? Is it so terrible to want a little breathing room, a single minute to parse everything Casey's told him, and everything he's told Casey, and whether or not he even wants to sell the stupid place, and—

Oh. Will finds, a bit embarrassed by it, that he *is* running away, without having quite decided to. His feet, impatient with the decision-making process and certain that they wanted to be anywhere else, have simply taken off without him.

"Will!" Two voices call it in unison—Casey sounds concerned, and Catherine sounds like a bloodhound who's just caught her first scent in days. He ignores them both, except to pick up the pace, hurrying as quickly as he can towards his rental car.

Will should stop. He should say something—he should explain himself—he owes them more, these people, than to turn tail and run away the second things get real. But a little part of him, old and bitterly cold, can't help but mutter: *Ah, but that's all you know, isn't it, Will? The worn, familiar pattern? And it feels good, doesn't it, a little? To feel bad in such a comfortable way?*

The thought's an upsetting one, so he tries to ignore it, too. As he approaches the car, though, he is painfully aware that the number of things he's trying to ignore is reaching a critical fail-point, and any second now, one of them might slip through and—

A warm, calloused hand encircles Will's wrist only two steps from the car door. Damn, damn, damn.

"Will, wait." It's Casey when Will turns, because of course

it is—he knew it the second Casey touched him, familiar already with the way the fluttering veins of his wrist feel against one of Casey's broad, steadying palms. Will looks up at him with all that he's feeling naked on his face; it must look as much like animalistic desperation as it feels, because Casey winces, drops his voice low, like he's soothing something dangerous and wounded he found in the forest. "Okay. Okay, I can see you're— maybe freaking out a little, right? But you don't have to do this, I promise you don't. Take it from me: You can try to run from your problems, but your average problem moves quicker than your average person, so it'll just beat you wherever you're going more times than it won't. Just stay, okay, like we talked about? You can think; we can tell Catherine Rose to screw off. You don't have to panic—"

"Oh, I don't have to *panic*, well, great, thanks so much," Will snarls. He tries to jerk his wrist back out of Casey's grip, but somehow can't quite bring himself to do more than half-heartedly pull his arm in towards himself; Casey doesn't let go. "That's easy for you to say, isn't it! *You* don't have to make any decisions here, *you* aren't going to disappoint anyone, and *you* probably have a single objective thought left in your skull, too! *You* haven't been living at the mercy of someone else's hospital-ity, away from home, without a single thing you own or any way to get out! *You* haven't spent the last two weeks walking around either in your *dead father's* clothes, or the clothes of a man you were *already* half in love with *before* you slept with him—"

Will slaps a hand over his mouth, realizing what he's said half a second too late. Humiliation and horror rise like bile in the back of his throat and then—

God, and then Casey is stepping forward, and letting go of Will's wrist, and pulling Will's hand away from his mouth, and —oh, and then Casey is kissing him.

Will's mind goes briefly, blissfully, beautifully blank, every iota of agita abruptly and utterly wiped away. He is a clean, clear river that has never known the churn of silt he is a new tree in strong soil, roots relaxing luxuriously down into the earth; he is folded piece of paper that somehow sails, anyway, further and faster than anyone would have expected, a miraculous agreement between sharply defined angles and the unknowable whims of the wind.

He would have expected himself to freeze, if he'd been expecting it. He doesn't freeze. Will throws himself into the kiss like it's his last chance before death takes him, like he's been drowning nearly thirty-five years and Casey is his first taste of air. He kisses Casey with an abandon that will embarrass him later, like he's never known the sick humiliation of heartbreak, like—like a teenager, Will realizes, flushing, as he and Casey pull apart. The last time he kissed someone like that it was... well, here. Not *right* here, in this parking lot, but around the corner, in Brandon's ancient Pontiac, right up until the minute Bill came knocking on the window.

Will stares at Casey, startled and breathing hard and caught between panic and something a lot closer to ecstasy. Casey's looking at him like he did last night, like he thinks this is one of those problems that you don't solve with talking. But even if Will let Casey sweep him up in another kiss and take him back to the attic, or the truck bed, or the hayloft, or *wherever*, it wouldn't *change* anything about his objectivity or his life in Chicago or need for some time *away*, somewhere *neutral*. He can't be expected to think clearly, to make smart decisions, in such an inherently vision-clouding situation.

He opens his mouth to say as much to Casey, but before he can, Catherine Rose rounds the corner and points at him, her stilettos clacking ominously against the pavement. "I saw that!" she calls, stalking over to them. "And I tell you what, if some ill-conceived *romance* is really why you've been ignoring my calls for the last two weeks—"

"God, I can't," Will says. He's so overwhelmed it comes out

264   DYLAN MORRISON

strangled, nearly sobbed; he backs away from Casey, unlocks the car door, and opens it, as he repeats it loud enough for Catherine to hear it, too: "I can't, I can't, I *can't*."

Then he's behind the wheel of the car and, thankfully, it's easy from there. Although Will braces himself as he turns the engine over, whatever Casey did to it worked beautifully: It purrs to life happily, not even a hint of a whine to suggest it ever troubled him in the first place.

That would be satisfying, if Will didn't catch, in the rearview mirror, the look on Casey's face. It makes him lift two fingers to his lips, where he can still feel the ghost of Casey's kiss lingering, and haunts him all the way out of Glenriver: the sharp lines of Casey's frown, the dismay and disappointment in his eyes.

It consumes his thoughts so completely that it takes Will nearly an hour to notice that he is, without meaning to, returning the way he came. He's back in downtown Cleveland, hopping onto Route 90 heading west, when it clicks for him that he is going back to Chicago.

God, he can't just keep *finding* himself doing things, stumbling around like the right answer is going to land at his feet. It's not *dignified*, for one thing, and it's not the better part of adulthood, either. Adult life, *personhood*, is about making decisions, and taking actions, and doing what you can to make your life the one you want to live.

Will's father lived his whole life in service of someone else's vision for him. That he'd wanted that for Will, too, was wrongheaded, certainly, but it was understandable, the way wrongheaded things often are. What other understanding of personhood did he have to work with, after all? What other lesson could he possibly have taught?

But Will thinks, as he drives past what he hopes will be the day's final NEED TO CLOSE? CALL CATHERINE ROSE! billboard, that maybe this is like the nitrogen in the soil, and harvesting strategy for the apples, and so much else: Just because his father insisted on doing it a certain way doesn't mean that way was right.

If Will wants to be his own person—if Will wants to make the decision here that a Robertson wouldn't make—then he has no choice but to face the music, turn his open eyes towards the truth, and let the chips fall where they may. The time for the soothing balm of denial and fantasy has come and gone; what he needs now is reality. The harsh kindness of brutal honesty.

Will sighs, and shakes his head, and does what he was always going to have to do eventually. He calls Selma.

SEVENTEEN

Will doesn't reach Selma.

Or, well, that's not *strictly* accurate. He reaches Selma for a rushed, whispery forty-five seconds, in which she manages to communicate that she is in court, that she can't talk to him now, that he'd better be on his way back to Chicago, and that she's planning on very thoroughly killing him when he arrives. The bulk of the forty-five seconds, in fact, is spent on her laying out that final point in some detail.

About fifteen minutes later, however, he gets a call back from Selma's assistant, which makes him wince out at the road because, while yeah, okay, he deserves it, she must be *really* pissed at him. Still, after a few very pointed comments about the value of Selma's time and how *some* people don't seem to understand what an important person she is, Alexandra, who Will has always suspected of harboring a bit of a crush on her boss, does deign to inform him that Selma expects to see him tonight, and where, and when. Will rolls his eyes—usually he would refuse to play such games with Selma at all and send her a text begging her to climb down off her high horse enough to meet him at one of their usual dinner spots. She's not

FALL INTO YOU 267

usually this mad at him, though, so Will agrees to an oddly late dinner at the sort of fancy restaurant in which she will swan elegantly around and enjoy being seen at heartily, while he struggles with which fork he's meant to pick up with less and less grace.

This takes, roughly, six minutes. It's not long enough, and, despite his best attempts to claw himself out of it, Will spends the remaining four and a half hours of his drive in a dragging, cavernous pit of self-loathing. It's almost like a shampoo, washing the good parts of Glenriver out of his hair as though they were never tangled there at all, asking him what he'd been thinking, and what he could possibly have thought would happen, and how he could be so stupid: lather, rinse, repeat.

Will certainly feels in a lather by the time he crosses the state line into Illinois. He'd thought at the beginning of the drive that maybe he'd prove Casey wrong and outrun the haunting image of his face in Will's rearview mirror, that obvious, crestfallen heartbreak—no dice. Even two states away, it seems to be overlaid across the windshield, or maybe Will's *retinas*, for how persistently present it's been since he pulled away from Robertson Family Farms. Casey might as well be in the passenger seat, his presence in Will's mind is so heavy, so palpable.

It's damning, Will thinks, gnawing not for the first time at his too-recently- and too-well-kissed lips, that he wishes Casey *was* in the passenger seat. It would defeat the whole purpose if he was—Will has to get some distance here, he *has* to, it's the only rational way to approach this and he'd always wonder if he didn't, but—God. He wishes Casey were here, anyway, this man he's only known two weeks, singing along with the radio and taking a turn at the driving. He just likes the person he is when Casey's around a little better, maybe. Maybe it's just easier to like the person he *always* is with the proof that Casey does.

Or did, anyway. Will has to assume, though it twists his

268   DYLAN MORRISON

stomach to do so, that Casey is not feeling particularly fond of him anymore.

The thought is so upsetting that Will presses his foot down a little harder against the gas pedal, as though leaving it behind is simply a function of reaching his apartment. Though he speeds the entire way there, he feels no further away from the terrible, ruinous idea when he sighs, parks the rental car, and steps outside. He stares at the car for a moment; is he supposed to return it somewhere? Someone dropped it off for him when he left two weeks ago, obviously at the behest of the irascible Zane the Assistant—is that guy going to come back and get it? The thought of calling Zane and asking is even more bloodcurdling now than it was before, which is really saying something. He's half-afraid, given the way he left things with the sale, that the man might send snipers to his location.

Eventually, he decides the rental is Catherine Rose's stupid problem, pockets the keys, and starts walking. He's about a block from his building—after long experience with the parking around here, he hadn't even bothered to make the frustrating and almost always fruitless attempt to find a closer spot—and he makes the journey slowly, looking around. Though he hadn't set out for a vacation when he got in the car two weeks ago, he is, in a strange way, returning from one. Certainly, these last two weeks were the first time in years he's spent more than a few days outside of Chicago, and those times it had been on business, or to bury his mother. So this is, in a very real sense, the first time Will has ever *returned* from a vacation to see this place, where he's lived all this time, with the fresh eyes of someone who has allowed himself to briefly grow comfortable somewhere else.

The cement sidewalk is smooth and flat under the treads of Will's shoes; he hadn't realized how used to the uneven gravel he'd become. He nearly trips more than once, his feet compen-

FALL INTO YOU   269

sating for something that isn't there as he cranes his neck and looks around.

Will likes this neighborhood... doesn't he? Likes living here? Certainly, he's lived here a long time; why would he do that, if he didn't like it? Why would anyone? He likes these... well, these slightly drab and boring buildings, if he's honest—but still, they're buildings! Familiar ones! And he likes them! And the... the sad wispy trees the City Works Department seems to have given up on, that look as though they've never heard of chlorophyll, let alone managed to produce any themselves. Well, Will likes those, too. Who wouldn't like those? It's not as though it matters, anyway, like Will needs to live in some fancy neighborhood with great curb appeal and lots of amenities. He can make almost anything work. He prides himself on it.

And as for his building itself, Will thinks as he steps into the lobby that it's... fine. It's perfectly fine. After all, who wouldn't be happy with the creaky, upsetting elevator and its orchestra of unsettling sounds? Or the increasingly dark hallway, because the bulbs have been burning out one by one for the last year, but the super won't replace them until they all go, which Will knows from the last time this happened? He slides his key into the lock under the flickering light of one of the two remaining bulbs and, looking at the cheap wood-print laminate surface of his own front door, thinks again of the yellow one into the farm market. Pushing that door open the first time, before it all went wrong, and then more wrong, and then weirdly right, and then *hideously* right, and then somehow wrong again—it had been such a rich, warm surprise, to expect the market of his childhood and find, instead, Casey's version of it.

Walking into his apartment is the opposite of that.

It's exactly as he left it; that's not the problem. Looking around, a lump rising in his throat, Will almost wishes someone would have come in and tossed the place while he was gone. Realistically, at least in his life at present, the only people likely to have done that would be Catherine Rose or Bartholomew from work—either prospect is horrifying, and still, he'd take it over having to face it like this.

It's a perfectly fine apartment, of course. It's always been perfectly fine. Will's pretty sure that's even what he said when he'd first toured it: "Well, this looks like it will be perfectly fine." But as he stares around his living room, and then, walking around in a blank, glazed headspace, takes in the rest of the apartment, he realizes that in all these years, he's never made it his own. His office at work has personality—a few pieces of artwork along with his diplomas on the walls, a photo of him smirking while Selma laughs framed on his desk, a variety of little oddities he couldn't quite leave behind at flea markets sitting on bookshelves and surfaces, for guests to examine or fidget with as they will. Someone who walked in could get a sense of Will, if only a broad one, even if he wasn't there to greet them. And being in that office makes him feel calm, happy, in a way he's realizing only now that being here never quite has.

Because this place—God help him, it reminds Will of his *father's* bedroom, minus the sad, indicative Post-its. The books on the shelves tell a story, of course, and there's a little of him in the kitchen, although admittedly mostly what's in the kitchen right now is the series of unfortunate discoveries left for any regular home cook who has unexpectedly left said kitchen untouched for two weeks. But otherwise, anyone could live here; there's very little evidence that *Will* does.

He returns to his living room, sits down heavily on his couch—beige, here when he moved in—and puts his head in his hands. At eighteen, he'd been so determined to get out of Glenriver, to build his own life, to make things work whatever the cost. He'd wanted to prove that he *could* do it; he'd wanted to know, for himself, that he was *right* to walk away, to seek a world beyond the river that ringed his hometown. And he did it, didn't he? Whatever it cost him, however he had to, he'd put his head down, and gritted his teeth, and made it work. He first got good at that, after all, back home on the family farm, one long, heavy day after another.

But he never stopped to ask himself whether he *should* make it work, just because he *could*. Or whether there wasn't a difference—a whole world of a difference, even—between making something work and being... being...

There's a knock on the door at this point, which is a relief. If Will had been forced to confront the end of *that* thought, he might really have lost it.

He's surprised, and happy, to see Selma on the other side of the door. Still, suddenly suspicious of Alexandra, who he knows has never understood Selma's continued friendship with him, he holds up his hands and says, "She told me we had a reservation! I was going to leave in fifteen minutes!"

"Oh, I cancelled it," Selma says, scowling at him. "I wasn't *really* going to make you embarrass yourself with the cutlery, I just wanted to know you *would*." She pulls him into a tight hug then, and, in his ear, mutters, "Ass."

"Yeah. Sorry," he mumbles back, and then, as they pull apart, opens his mouth to say more, but—

"Ah," Selma says, holding up a single finger to silence him. "I'm so sorry to break this to you, William, dear, but when you ignore my calls for two entire weeks, you forfeit the right to any control over the evening. What I would like you to do, now, is follow me. On our journey, I will catch you up on my *own* last couple of weeks; you will listen, and nod politely, and ask no questions. When we arrive, you will order some food and eat it immediately. When it's gone, and you have thus already run through all your likeliest avenues for deflection, you will answer every question I ask you to the best of your ability. Do you understand the terms and conditions of this arrangement as I have presented them?"

272   DYLAN MORRISON

Will blinks at her, trying not to let his amusement show on his face. "You understand that this *isn't* court, right? We're at my apartment, Sel, and I don't even own a gavel—"

"Sass me right now," Selma says, in a dangerous tone, "at your genuine peril," and then she simply turns around and walks out of his apartment. Will has been friends with Selma a long time; he sighs, and follows her, knowing that's what he's supposed to do. She does, at least, deign to wait at the stairs while Will locks the door behind him, though she starts down them the second he finishes, making him scurry to catch up with her.

She does, as promised, spend the entire walk to the bar that ends up being their destination filling him in on the last two weeks of her own life. It's not particularly surprising stuff. Selma, unlike Will, has a rich and thriving social life outside of their tight, unusual little bond, and though the details change, the broad strokes stay the same. Selma's life, Will's always thought, is a bit like a sitcom: there's always some bizarre situation at work, an unlikely source of interpersonal conflict that would, coming from anyone else, sound made-up, and a love interest with energy that suggests the writing and/or casting department didn't think things through. This time, for example: At work, there's a petty thief swiping office supplies and other things of little value but driving the already tightly wound lawyers to insane lengths to catch the culprit. On the unlikely interpersonal-conflict front, an old nanny has reached out, some thirty years on, looking for Selma's testimony to aid her in suing Selma's mother for emotional damages. And in the arena of love interests, she appears to be wooing a nonbinary theater technician who moonlights as a shock jockey, and is only available from midnight to 3 a.m. for most of the week.

To this last, Will can't help but ask: "Where do you *find* these people?" But, because he wasn't supposed to talk, this earns him only a glare and a slight increase in Selma's volume as

FALL INTO YOU 273

she walks him through the various emotional pitfalls of dating Riley, which is apparently the theater tech/jockey's name. Will doesn't bother committing it to memory—Selma rarely settles down with anyone, and when things do get serious, it's easy to tell, mostly because she stops wanting to joke about it.

Still, he listens dutifully as she leads him to the Rowdy Elephant, their local for so long now that Will can barely remember a time before it opened. The drinks are good and the food is surprisingly solid, and even on a Saturday night like this, there's always a table for the two of them. At Selma's insistence, Will orders chicken wings and fries along with his gin and tonic, and after a single bite realizes that he's barely eaten today and is *ravenous*. He devours the meal in short order, and it's only then, holding her own cocktail in front of her like a talisman of strength, that she says, "All right, then: Spill it."

Wincing, and in spite of her incredibly detailed and painstaking efforts, Will lets her down immediately and tries to deflect. "I mean, what do you want to know, exactly? It's not... There's a lot—"

"I would like to know," Selma says, a razor's edge appearing in her tone, "*everything*. I mean, *please*. Don't act like you don't know me—all of it. Right now. I'm not screwing around."

"God, fine," Will mutters, and, at last, tells her.

It takes him... a long time.

When he's done, Selma is quiet for several minutes. She stares at him; she stares at the ceiling; she stares out the front window of the bar, grimy and smudged, and watches people walk past outside. She drums her fingers against the countertop. She narrows her eyes at him.

Eventually, silently, she stands up, walks to the bar, and orders two shots of good tequila in a ringing tone. She accepts them when they're poured, walks them back to the table without spilling a drop from either one, and then, without offering Will one or indeed speaking at all, takes them both

274   DYLAN MORRISON

herself, one after the other, as though they're nothing more than water.

"Will," she says, when she's put the second empty shot glass down on the table. "I have to ask you a question now that I have wanted to ask you for many, many years. I don't think you're going to like it, but. I'm going to do it, anyway."

"Oh, God," Will says, grimacing, but: "I mean, I probably owe you that much, honestly, after vanishing on you like that, so. Shoot."

"Are you aware," Selma says, cocking her head like she genuinely wants to know the answer, "that you're not a happy person?"

"What?" Will stares at her; this is not what he was expecting at all. Feeling uncomfortably pinned by her sharp stare, he adds, "Don't be ridiculous. Of course I am. What are you talking about?"

Selma sighs, pinches the bridge of her nose, releases it, and says, "Will, look. You are, in many ways, a very irritating and stressful human being, but you are, for my sins, my best friend. And because of this, the advice I want to give you is to stay in Chicago forever so we can keep getting brunch and laughing at the drunk people falling asleep in their pancakes. I want to do that so *badly*, Will, but you're *not* a happy *person*."

She holds up a hand to stop his protests as she continues, "You live this sad, miserable little life—no, shut *up*, okay, don't argue with me, you *do*. You never take vacations or mental health days or the afternoon off to see a *movie*, even! You just work and work in that little lab, or sit in your apartment watching documentaries and reading, or, when I can *drag* you, you come out with me." Selma's voice is climbing in pitch and intensity now, to Will's mild shock; he hadn't realized she cared this much. "You date these guys who treat you like dirt, who let their *animals* loose in your *apartment*, who take your time and your money and your energy and then leave you in pieces for me to pick up, every time! Which I do, because you are my best friend, but I'd be lying if I told you I loved it."

"Oh," Will says, after a long moment, because. Well. Because he's not sure what else to say.

"So," Selma continues, her tone taking on a dangerous edge again now, "even though I have watched one hundred Lifetime movies and thought, every time, that the stupid best friend who says, 'Upend your whole life for someone you met two weeks ago!' must be taking downers *and* uppers and getting confused in the middle, I gotta say—you sound happier and more engaged talking about this farm and this town and this guy than I have *ever* heard you. Look at you! You're carrying yourself different, did you know that? And this guy... Will, he sounds like he was *nice* to you. Do you know how long I've waited for you to be into a guy who was nice to you? Even one?"

"I've liked guys who were nice to me!" Will protests, somewhat desperately.

Flatly, Selma says, "Name one, Will. Name one guy."

"I mean," Will says, floundering slightly, "there's always— uh, Roger—"

"Roger who filled your bathtub with Monopoly money for an art project and then left it like that for a week and insisted no one clean it up? That Roger?" Selma sounds incredulous, and Will can't exactly blame her, because:

"Yeah, he did do that," Will has to admit. "Um, twice, because the first time he didn't... have any film in the camera." Selma's glare at this is so intense that Will feels compelled, in spite of knowing himself to be beyond the point of no return, to add, "What about Jake? Jake really wasn't so bad, he—"

"Will," Selma says, in a pained voice, "wasn't Jake the one from my office Christmas party five years ago? The guy who got his tongue stuck? To the ice sculpture? Because he wanted to see if the ice on the top of the sculpture tasted like the shrimp at the bottom of the sculpture?"

Will blinks at her for a moment as the memory swims back to surface. Then, grinning a little in spite of himself, he says, "Do you know, I'd forgotten about that? The look on your boss's face—"

"Oh, God, don't remind me," Selma says, and then they're both laughing, leaning into one another in that semi-hysterical way of two old, drunken friends who don't really need to talk to revisit their shared past.

"See," Will says, when they've both calmed down a little, "I can't move to Ohio, what would I do without—"

"Oh, don't start any of that up," Selma says, waving a hand. "Nobody says you have to *move*, you know. Don't do anything crazy, just take some actual vacation time, maybe? A sabbatical? Go deal with your life and your real estate issue and see if this is something real, I guess, is what I'm suggesting."

Will groans. "Sel, I have *no idea* how to deal with my real estate issue." Realizing it only at this moment, he drops his head into his hands and adds, "Jesus *Christ*, I can't even keep track of my belongings—you know I drove all the way back here and I'm just realizing I never went back to my *hotel*. My laptop is there! And my second-best duffel bag!"

"Oh no," Selma says, mock-solemn, "not your second-best duffel bag."

"My *point* is," Will says, ignoring this, "I should not be trusted, okay, with something as serious as a land deal. I am not equipped. I am not prepared. I am not suited for solving a problem of this nature. Also, I mean, I think it's even odds Catherine Rose is going to roast me on a spit, so—"

"Did you know, 'I'm about to be roasted on a spit' is one of those sentences that tends to just summon lawyers out of the ether," Selma says, offering him a small and promising smile. "And this Catherine Rose sounds... *fun*. Here's another question for you: Have you ever found yourself with any interest in showing me your hometown?"

EIGHTEEN

Two days later, Will once again finds himself cruising down the long, lazy stretch of Route 90 towards Cleveland, this time in the passenger seat of Selma's cherry red convertible. It's a nice day, sunny and in the high sixties; they've made the bulk of the journey with the top down, at Selma's enthusiastic insistence. Will is 90 percent sure that Selma's love of open-air driving is less about the air and more about feeling like she's Audrey Hepburn, since, with her hair tied back under a scarf and a pair of enormous sunglasses on, she does look a bit like Audrey Hepburn. Audrey Hepburn's scarier, more scandalous cousin, perhaps. Tawdry Hepburn.

Will shares this thought with Selma, who laughs, looking quite pleased by it, and then says, "Tawdry Hepburn should be your drag name, you know."

"Please," Will says, rolling his eyes. "First of all, I would be terrible at drag; I can't sing, I can't dance, and I have no rhythm to such a horrific degree that I can barely clap along to a beat. Remember when you tried to teach me to do the Electric Slide? At that wedding?"

278   DYLAN MORRISON

Selma grimaces dramatically out at the road. "Who could forget?"

"Well, exactly." Will shakes his head, adding, "And that means if I *was* going to do drag, I'd have to lean into the camp thing, be as over the top as possible, which isn't exactly my vibe. I'd have to base it on someone, and the campiest person I can think of is—" Will glances out at the road, considering, and then catches the single eye of one of Catherine Rose's large billboards and shudders. "God. *Her*."

Selma glances at the billboard, the fourth or fifth they've passed, with an unimpressed expression. "You know, this is starting to get grating. Is it just going to be like this the whole way? Signs with her eyeballs?"

"More or less," Will admits, with a sigh.

"Tacky," is Selma's verdict; her mouth twists in distaste. "It's not that it doesn't *work*, you understand—if I put up eight thousand billboards along the side of the highway that said, 'Think you got screwed? Call Selma Mahmoud,' I would get hundreds of calls a day—"

"That's actually a good slogan," Will says, turning in his seat slightly to grin incredulously at her. "Oh my God, have you *thought* about this?"

"Of course I've thought about it, William, everyone thinks about it," Selma snaps, glancing away from the highway for an unsettlingly long time to roll her eyes at him dramatically. "You clean up, generally, if you do it. It's just, you know, not tasteful."

"Yeah, well. I wouldn't call Catherine super tasteful in general, to be honest," Will mutters. As they pass a billboard with her full headshot on it, it makes cheerful and unpleasantly direct eye contact with him, her frozen gaze following him briefly up the road before, thankfully, the car pulls out of its range. Still, it makes the look on her face the other day swim before his eyes again, and that seems to follow him up the road every inch as much as the billboards. He shudders.

FALL INTO YOU   279

"God," Selma says, eyeing him. "You're really freaked out by this woman, aren't you? She's just a *consultart*, Will. She can't do anything, you know? And honestly, like I said at brunch yesterday, I'm sure she has a personal stake in it. Or, at least, she's certainly *acting* the way I know people to act when they've overpromised something to a corporation like this: panicky. Sloppy. But that's what you get when you bite off more than you can chew, at least with any company that classes in the 'ruthlessly evil' category—"

"And you're sure," Will says, not wanting there to be an inch of room for doubt, "you're *sure* Nimbletainment falls into that category?" He'd said the same thing yesterday at brunch, when Selma had pulled out a manila envelope marked, WHY WILL SHOULD NEVER AGAIN STOP TAKING MY CALLS FOR TWO WEEKS WHEN DEALING WITH ANY LEGAL MATTER and started laying out her case against Nimble-tainment.

Or, well, okay. First there had been several foldable brochures, of a type Will recognized from Selma's office; typically when he's seen them before, they've said things like, PROPERTY TAXES AND YOU or COPYRIGHT LAW: WHAT'S ALL THE FUSS ABOUT? These were not like that. Selma had clearly made someone in her office print them up special, as they said things like, THINGS YOUR FRIENDS WILL CONVINCE THEM-SELVES HAVE HAPPENED TO YOU and LETTING YOUR PALS MICROCHIP YOU LIKE A DOG: IT'S MORE LEGAL THAN YOU THINK!

"It's not, actually," Selma had told him, stabbing a potato, when Will asked about that last one. "But I wasn't going to do it anyway; I was just really mad at you that afternoon, and there's good gossip in the copy room if you're careful about where you stand." Then she'd passed him a beautifully spiral-bound presentation entitled GUILT GIFTS YOU SENT ME, RATED BY HOW MUCH I ENJOYED THEM, which she explains she had made the same afternoon, and suggests he file away to refer to at Christmas.

Those essentials settled, she'd gone on to explain about the company's long history of doing more or less exactly what Casey had said they'd do, not to mention leaving behind them a string of lawsuits, ruined lives, bitterly unhappy ex-employees, and evidence of deeply questionable business practices.

Still, even now: "I mean, they've got the whole town behind them," Will says, the wind whipping his hair back as Selma speeds recklessly down the road. "Wouldn't someone have noticed if they were evil? And made sure they didn't get away with it?"

Selma stares at him incredulously for so long that Will starts to genuinely get nervous she's forgotten she is driving and they're both going to die. Then, turning her head back to the road and shaking it slightly, she says, "Christ, Will. Sometimes you're so smart and sometimes... sometimes I forget that you're basically a science hermit, and you don't know *anything* about the real world. Need someone to tell you the protein structure of a molecule, you're the guy, but—companies do stuff like this all the time. If there isn't someone like Casey to put their foot in things, it mostly... goes ahead, honestly. Even *with* someone like him, it tends to go ahead."

"Oh," Will says. He considers this for a moment. "But surely some intrepid local journalist—"

"Nope," Selma says, shaking her head. "That only happens in the movies, at least these days. Local papers are mostly dead, and anyway, even if someone does run a story, things *usually go ahead*. There also isn't going to be a last-minute vote by the town council, or a moment where the CEO of Nimbletainment has a change of heart due to being overcome by the Christmas spirit—"

"It's October."

FALL INTO YOU 281

"Well, exactly," Selma snaps. "*Exactly* my point. It's October, it's Monday morning, Nimbletainment knows what they're doing—this is all business as usual. The only way it ever *isn't* business as usual is if one person, or ideally several people, take a look at the opportunity to be given a big pile of money in exchange for signing something they don't totally understand, and instead say, 'You know what? I'm good. You keep the big pile of money; I'm all set.'" Selma casts a sidelong glance at him, and sighs. "You're still worried about people being mad at you, aren't you? For getting between them and their big piles of money?"

"Yeah," Will admits, with an uncomfortable little shrug. "It's not that I don't think it's the right thing; I mean, your case was very convincing. The stuff on the other towns..." Will grimaces. "I don't think anyone will want to think of us husked out like some of those places looked, and the stories about ruined business and people getting bankrupted by legal fees were. Grim."

"You know, some of that," Selma says, very casually, "may just have found its way to distribution amongst the townspeople of the good village of Glenriver yesterday. Who could say how that happened? Maybe there was some random email address that, if anyone bothered to trace it, would route to a remote village in Switzerland; maybe that email address happened to pass some information along to the maintainer of a certain town message board. Hard to know what goes on, you know, in these tiny Midwestern towns."

"You didn't!" Will says, after a beat.

"Of course I didn't," Selma says calmly. "That would have been in violation of the Prime Directive."

Will furrows his brow, but not seeing any way around it, asks: "Uh. Isn't that 'Don't interfere with the natural development of alien civilizations,' more or less?"

"Not for lawyers," Selma says cheerfully. "For lawyers, it's

282   DYLAN MORRISON

just 'Don't interfere.' People are going to do what they're going to do; we're just here to clean it up and get paid."

"Hmm," says Will, who has, over the years, determined that while Selma talks a big game, the vast majority of her work is fighting for the rights of the little guy. "Well, I'd be grateful to anyone who *did* do that. If someone had. Would make the whole thing feel a little less daunting."

"Duly noted," Selma says, "though irrelevant," and flips on the radio.

They drive in comfortable silence for a while, Will staring out the window and gnawing at his lip as they pass through Cleveland, wincing away from every Catherine Rose billboard they see. He's nervous about the town hating him, sure, and about regretting the choice he's made—about to make—whatever. He's nervous about Catherine Rose murdering him in cold blood, and also about her then making a billboard out of the crime scene photos as a warning to other potential obstacles to her closing process; whatever Selma says about how she's bound to be more bark than bite, Will is reasonably sure that's a real concern for him here, at least if the voicemails of the last few days are anything to go by.

But mostly he's nervous about seeing Casey, who hasn't called, or texted, or emailed. Will's not even sure Casey *has* his email address, but he's refreshed his inbox four hundred times over the last two days, hoping against hope to see something pop up. Will knows this is ridiculous, not fair; the ball is so emphatically in his own court here, and he's the one who should be doing something. He's the one who ran off, drove fully out of the state without even stopping by his hotel for his things, after Casey put it all on the line and kissed him so thoroughly and passionately that a little part of Will is still there, locked in it, wholly unwilling to *ever* come up for air.

The rest of him, however, has to face reality, and so he swallows down his nerves, drums his fingers against the passenger

FALL INTO YOU   283

side door, and asks Selma if she minds swinging by the hotel for his laptop.

It takes a few minutes to get that laptop, largely because the employee at the hotel desk is quite amused by Will's attempt to explain, poorly, why he left his laptop behind. After a fumbling explanation that involves a lot of hand gestures and apologies and saying Casey's name rather more times than is appropriate, the woman tilts her head, looks at him, and, sounding like she's trying very hard not to laugh, says, "You understand that I don't need to know any of that, right? Just your room number and ID should do it."

The whole experience is humbling, but it doesn't take that long, either, and soon they're in the last fifteen minutes of the drive, the aggressive Catherine Rose billboards seeming to appear every mile or so now.

"Do you know what, I actually think it must be an intimidation strategy," Will mutters, after what has to be the twentieth board they've passed today; Will's half-convinced she's had new ones put up since the last time he drove this way, two weeks ago. "Like a threat display or whatever. Nothing to unnerve your enemy like making them stare at you anew around every bend!"

"It never means anything good for your headspace when you start using words like 'anew,'" Selma comments, but lightly enough. "It seems like this woman genuinely scares you, Will. Why? She's just a consultant; it's not like she can force you to sign."

Will shudders slightly, not totally sure how to put it into words. "She's just—ugh. She's so aggressive, and she'll never take no for an answer, and it can only be her way, and she doesn't listen to anything I say, and if I don't do what she wants she'll just keep *hounding* me and *belittling* me and *screaming* at me and making me feel like—" Abruptly, Will hears himself and flushes. "Oh. You, uh. You... think this is about my dad?"

"I," Selma says, smirking slightly, "am a lawyer, not a thera-

284   DYLAN MORRISON

pist, so I'm going to go with: You said it, I didn't." But she slants him a sidelong look that says more than enough, and Will sits in slightly embarrassed silence for a few minutes, processing.

He groans when they pass another image of Catherine Rose, towering over the road. "Okay, look, maybe it is about my dad, but still, it's too many billboards! I swear to God it's like she's *following* us."

Selma laughs, glancing jokingly in the rearview mirror. Then, sounding lightly surprised, she remarks, "God, actually, weirdly enough, there's a woman who looks like her in the car behind us. What are the odds, right?"

Will freezes. Then, very carefully, he turns in his seat as slightly as he possibly can, so that just enough of his face is tilted past the headrest for him to glance back to the car behind him.

Catherine Rose, scowling in irritation, her hair bigger than Will has ever seen it, makes direct eye contact with him and bares her teeth. Will's not proud of it, but it's so unsettling he nearly yelps.

Instead, heart pounding, he slams himself back to facing forward and hisses, "That's *her*, Sel. It's not *like* she's following us—the lunatic is *actually following us*."

"Good Lord." Selma's voice is casual, unbothered; her gaze, when it flicks back to the rearview mirror to assess the situation behind her, is utterly calm. "People do not have enough to *do* down here, if this is what they're getting up to. Honestly. Does she have nothing more urgent to attend to than stalking you? No other clients to see? Park benches to paper with her own face? Really, it's embarrassing."

"Your professional standards aside, what do we *do*?" Will hisses, peeking back over his shoulder again and regretting it. "God, she saw me *see* her—"

Selma, on the other hand, laughs. "What do you mean, what do we do? We do exactly what we were already doing—

FALL INTO YOU   285

head to the farm. GPS says we're close, and we were going to have to call her once we got there, anyway. Let me handle her, though; I'm not sure the necessary conversational grace is, ah... entirely in your wheelhouse."

"You can just say, 'I think you'd put your foot in it, Will,'" Will mutters, trying to glance behind him without turning his head at all and failing quite miserably.

"I think you'd put your foot in it, Will." Selma says this with a solemnity that is either slightly mocking or upsettingly sincere —Will can't quite tell. She turns the radio back up, and adds, "Look, try to stop thinking about her, okay? We're only a few minutes out; you should use this time to make sure you're good with what we talked about, what you decided. If you want to change your mind, this is final notice that the window is closing."

Will nods and goes silent as Selma winds the car down the last few roads before the new Glen River Bridge appears in front of them. He hadn't bothered to look at it while he was haring out of town on Saturday, but as they cross over it, Will decides that it's a good bridge. It's not as ornamental, maybe, as the one that washed away, but it looks stronger and sturdier, engineered to survive more serious weather than its predecessor. Like much of what they pass as they drive up Main Street and down the twisting residential blocks that lead to Will's childhood home, time has played its favorite trick: taking what once was and replacing it with something almost like it, but not quite.

Catching a glimpse of his own pensive expression in the rearview mirror, Will thinks wryly of looking at himself from this same angle as an eight-year-old, in his father's old truck. He'll be thirty-five in just a few days—the face he's wearing lately bears only a passing resemblance to that little boy's; it's been so long since Will lived through being him. And yet that child sits here still, tucked up within the branches of the gnarled

286   DYLAN MORRISON

tree of Will's life, looking out from behind Will's eyes with his own smaller, more trusting ones.

"No," Will says, very softly. "I don't think I would like to change my mind."

"Okay, then," Selma says, and grins. "Then this should be a *riot*."

She pulls into the parking lot of Robertson Family Farms, parks the car, and then smirks slightly when Catherine pulls to a stop directly behind them, tires screeching. Will, himself, has never quite understood this aspect of Selma; he's always hated nearly all forms of confrontation, done whatever he could to avoid it. Setting aside a few particular moments—screaming at his father in the cornfield, for example, or yelling at Casey in the rain—he's generally a quiet, unassuming person, the kind who will go along to get along, because it's not worth the trouble.

Selma, on the other hand, often enters, incites, or otherwise engages in confrontation just for the *fun* of it. Out of *boredom*. It's something Will's admired about her from the first day they met, although she's always refused to give him any advice on it, and, mystifyingly to Will, doesn't seem to consider it one of her better qualities.

Now her face splits into a grin that reminds Will of nothing so much as an ecstatic piranha when she gets out of the car. In spite of himself—in spite of the nervous glances he can't help casting at the market door every ten to fifteen seconds, wondering who's working today, and if it's Casey, and if it *is* Casey, how long it will take him to come outside and see what's going on, and if he *does* come outside, what he'll *say*—Will starts to feel a little better about the business side of things. It's true that Catherine Rose looks as though she's considering mailing different parts of Will's body to various countries across the globe, to be disposed of by a network of trained agents who understand the importance of closing, but Will thinks, on reflection, that if push does come to shove here, his money is on

FALL INTO YOU   287

Selma. He knows (nearly) for sure she doesn't have a network of trained agents across the globe, but he's also quite certain she doesn't need them.

"Will," Catherine says, as she climbs out of the car. Her once-polished demeanor has tarnished, somewhat, though it's hard for Will to quite put his finger on why. Little things, he thinks, adding up to a larger picture. Her hair has always been big, for example, but last time they met, it looked *intentionally* big, shaped and crafted into something closer to a helmet than a hairdo. Today, the edges of it are fuzzy and slightly askew, as though said helmet is desperate to give up the charade and admit to being hair after all; it's an odd effect, as is her slightly uneven makeup, not quite concealed under her oversized cat-eye glasses. Something about her outfit, too, is off, though Will honestly doesn't know enough about women's clothing to put a finger on what it is.

Regardless, it's not a big deal, except that Will can tell from the moment she shuts the car door that Catherine *herself* is conscious of it, and irritated. She's pulling at the side seam of the dress she's wearing, and at the hem of the blazer thrown over it, even as Will swallows and says, "Catherine, hi. Sorry, I know I've missed a few calls from you—"

"Oh, *have* you?" Catherine's eyes, Will notices, have picked up a wild, dangerous edge since the last time he encountered her in person. "Have you missed a few of my calls, Will? Because, you know, I've only called you three or four times—*a day*! Sometimes *an hour*, what could you *possibly* have been—"

"Oooh," Selma says, in cheerfully scandalized tones, and raises a hand to her mouth in a pantomime of shock. "Harassment! Right out of the gate, too, what fun—"

"Excuse me," Catherine snaps, turning to glare at Selma, "but I was speaking, all right, about a very important business deal. Didn't anyone ever teach you it's rude to interrupt?"

"It appears no one taught *you* that it's rude to chase people

288   DYLAN MORRISON

down the road like a cartoon villain," Selma says, arching an eyebrow and offering Catherine an unpleasant smile. "If we're asking *that* question. But, if you're so bothered, you have my apologies for interrupting you. I just like to keep score—you were describing harassing my client, so I wanted to note it. Just the kind of thing that might come up later, you know?"

"Your... client," Catherine says, glancing from Selma over to Will, and then, in tones of great betrayal, hissing, "You hired a *lawyer*? I thought we had an agreement!"

Will knows that they did not, in fact, have an agreement; being friends with Selma all these years has had its advantages. He's careful about verbal contracts, so he knows he didn't agree to anything the first time he met with Catherine, and he'd certainly remember and have kept copies of anything printed or written down. And yet, even though he knows this must be a tactic, her trying to trick him into siding with her out of guilt, he *does* feel guilt flare within him, a sense that he owes it to her to deal with her one on one.

And then, God love her, Selma says, "Hired me? Ha. I mean, technically, okay, I made him give me the traditional dollar as a retainer and, yes, that means that he hired me by the letter of the law, but this man has been my best friend for many years, and if hadn't brought me in on this, I would have murdered him." She pauses, pulls out her card, and, her eyes hardening, passes it over to Catherine as she adds, "There was, and is, no version of this deal that doesn't go through me. Sorry you're the last to know, but facts are facts."

Catherine's face puckers up as she glances over Selma's card, as though reading it has filled her mouth with lemon juice. Her voice is very dry and flat, however, when she says, "Oh."

It is at this point, out of the corner of his eye, that Will sees the market door open.

It's Noel who appears first, sticking just their head out. Will, turning helplessly to look, is expecting or at least hoping to see Casey, and feels his face flush slightly in embarrassment when he meets the teen's eyes instead. Noel looks shocked for a second; then they grin; then they let out a whooping noise and disappear back into the market.

Not fifteen seconds later, the door opens again. This time it flies fully open, as though the person opening it has all but ripped it away from the frame; this time, that person is Casey.

Will swallows, or tries to. He finds that his throat and mouth, however, have both gone suddenly bone-dry, as though the sheer intensity, the heady, half-panicked heat, of the blood pounding through his veins has evaporated all the moisture within him. A little part of Will, the bit that started turning to comforting facts instead of processing overwhelming situations as a very small child, begins to list plants that could survive such a temperature shift, and for how long, and in what kind of initial condition, and what type of soil, and—

God, Casey is *looking* at him. Casey is looking at him and his face is not collapsing into anger and rage like it had that first day, in the market, after that stupid, inexplicable, perfect moment of connection that Will has never quite stopped thinking about. He's... well, he's staring, mostly, his mouth dropping open, his eyes widening, and then narrowing and just for a second, Will thinks he's going to scowl and turn around and slam the yellow door shut behind him, before—

Casey's face breaks into a grin, and he starts to run.

"Okay, Will," Selma says, very low, just for him to hear, putting a hand on his shoulder, while Catherine is distracted by turning back to her car, opening the back driver's side door, and digging around frenetically for something in her briefcase. "Stay focused. I understand that you're experiencing the end stages of a Midwestern courtship ritual and that's very distracting, but there's *work* to be *done* here. Give me three more minutes of even your most half-assed attention and then, I swear, the two of you can run off into the corn together and, I don't know,

290 DYLAN MORRISON

commune sensually with the woods while wearing as much flannel as possible, or whatever people do down here—"

"You've lived in Chicago for more than two decades," Will hisses, without actually looking away from Casey, who is approaching quickly. "Technically, *you* are a Midwesterner, however West Coast your roots may be, so I think the David Attenborough routine is maybe a *little* over the top—"

"You bite your tongue," Selma chides. Then, in a rather different, more evaluative tone, she adds, "He looks strong. Like the kind of guy who could help a girl move several large pieces of furniture from one side of her apartment to—"

"I'm literally not even dating him, Sel. I think maybe you want to keep your plans to make him cross state lines and do manual labor for you under wraps a bit longer, yeah?" Will's heart is barely in this—Casey is nearly upon them—God, this close Will can see he hasn't *shaved*. Will's never actually seen the man with more than a five o'clock shadow before, but he's past that point now, a scruffy but undeniable beard that runs a shade or two darker than his blond hair unmistakable on his face. He looks tired, Will thinks. And—nervous. And... happy.

"Hi," Casey says, when he reaches them. Though he's stopped running, he seems to be bouncing on the balls of his feet, as though staying still is too much to ask in this particular moment.

Will thinks maybe he, himself, is experiencing the reverse feeling; he feels crystalized in time, frozen stiff and still, his lips barely moving as he replies. But his voice, at least, comes out warm, rich with that same heat that burned the moisture from his mouth, as he says, "Hi."

"HI!" Catherine Rose nearly screams this; it's so jarring that Will physically jumps, an all-over shudder he can't fight or conceal. He turns to her, aggrieved, and gives her a dirty look, but this time she hardly notices; she is bearing down on Casey instead, brandishing what appears to be a newspaper at him in

FALL INTO YOU   291

fury. "It was you, wasn't it? Who did this? That's what I *came* here to do, to ask you how you plan to pay the enormous sum you'll owe me in *damages* for this—"

"Owe you?" Casey says, and laughs. "What could *I* possibly owe *you*? Lady, I had nothing to do with this. It's not *my* fault if, every once in a while, somebody wants to get up to some actual journalism around here."

"Oh, a likely story," Catherine snaps. She takes another step towards Casey; Will, feeling a thrill of daring, leans forward and plucks the paper from her hands. She doesn t notice, too fixated on Casey to change course, and Will looks down with interest to see a copy of the *Glenriver Gazette*. It had been a weekly paper when he was a child; now it's a monthly, and he knows from talking to the editor a few times over the last couple of weeks that it's struggling even to manage that.

But the headline makes the intended impact in bold black and white all the same: FROM TRANQUILITY TO TURMOIL: CONTROVERSIAL PLANS THREATEN COMMUNITY'S FUTURE. Will skims the story below, glancing over the photos, and finds he recognizes both details and images.

He looks at Selma, who is gazing innocently down at her nails. She doesn't meet his eyes, but, when she realizes he's glancing her way, she does smirk, which is as good as a confession. He bites down on his smile—really, he should have known. She did say, or at least imply, that she'd disseminated the information, after all.

"Why would I do this *now*?" Casey's asking, sounding bewildered, as Catherine stalks towards him. "If I'd had this info all along—why sit on it? What would be the point?"

"I don't know, to *ruin my life*?" Catherine cries, clearly at the end of her rope. "To ruin this *deal*, to ruin my *year*, to carry on Bill stupid Robertson's infuriating legacy of making every visit to this *armpit* of a town my *living nightmare*? Do you have any idea how long I promised these people I would deliver them

292   DYLAN MORRISON

this deal, okay, it was *years* ago, and when that old bastard finally went into that home, I was sure! Sure that I could get it to them in time, but you got in my way, and you made everything so difficult, and you made sure no visitors were ever allowed in, so I had to wait until he *finally* bit the big one and *then*—"

Seeming to remember Will exists for the first time in several minutes, she turns to him, realizes he's holding the paper, snatches it out of his hands and snaps, "Don't look at that! Don't read that; you don't have to worry about any of that at all." Her voice abruptly shifts tone and register, into one Will thinks might be trying for soothing, though it's definitely, definitely not achieving that, at least for him. "You *want* to sell, right? Of course you do. You hate this place, and hated your childhood here, and you hated him"—she points to Casey without looking at him—"the second you met him, so. No-brainer, right? Help out your old buddy Catherine, and just sign the paperwork right now, and then we can—"

"I'm sorry," Will says, cutting her off, his voice cold, "I'm just processing—you said Casey made sure there were no visitors. Were you trying to... what, trick my father? My dementia-riddled, dying father? Into selling our family farm?"

"'Trick' is such a harsh word," Catherine says, her tone quite careful now. "I just wanted to have a conversation where he was a little more receptive, maybe, to other points of view—"

Will snorts. "Well, yeah, I'll grant you, you would have had to wait until he was dead for that, but—Christ. That man never liked me, and to tell you the truth, I never much liked him, either. Terrible mess of a father, I'm sorry but unafraid to say, just as I'm sure he'd've been happy to tell you I was a real failure of a son. But you know what? If I know anything, I know that he'd rather the old place ended up with me—even estranged from him, even gay, even though we never spoke another word to one another after the day I left—then snaked

FALL INTO YOU   293

out from under him by somebody like you." He lifts his chin; he takes a breath.

It's maybe the most Robertson act of his life when he says, "Anyway, even if I do, in general, hate doing what my old man would've wanted: It's over, Catherine. I'm not selling."

There's a long, stretched-out beat of silence; Will can hear his own heart thudding in his ears as he waits for a reaction. But it's not Catherine he's looking at, for all the comment was addressed to her; he's looking at Casey, who is staring back at him, his mouth open.

Then: "*Really?*" Casey's voice is almost a whisper. "You're... I don't have to... You're *really* not going to sell?"

But before Will can reply, a... noise... begins to emerge from the general area of Catherine Rose. It's a high-pitched, nearly inhuman whining sound, just on the edge of hearing; for a real moment, Will thinks it's maybe a car alarm, or a bomb, and looks around wildly for its source. But after a second, as it increases in volume and pitch, he realizes it is coming *from* Catherine, and is the windup to a brief, wordless shriek of frustration, which she tips her head back and releases up towards the sky.

Then, with a truly wild energy slipping into her eyes, she drops her head back down to Will's eye level and yells, "You little *twerp*! Do you have any *idea* how much *trouble* you've caused me? Why couldn't you just *go along* like a *normal person* and accept the deal two *weeks* ago? Hell, even if you'd told me *no* two weeks ago, that would have been better. You're—you're a disgusting, time-wasting—um—ingrate! Is what you are!"

"Hey, now," Casey starts, in a warning tone. This makes something embarrassing and infantile occur somewhere deep in the recesses of Will's heart, but he doesn't actually need his honor defended; Selma had warned him this might happen, and told him to let her tire herself out if it did. Her exact words had been, "The more upset people are, the more they reveal." Will doesn't think it's necessarily the most morally upstanding approach in the world, but does seem like it might yield results, and he has to assume Selma doesn't want Casey interrupting things, however noble his intentions.

Sure enough, Selma casts a sharp look at Casey and, her voice so low she's basically mouthing the words, says, "Be cool, man." This does seem to immediately pacify Casey, but it's such an un-Selma thing to say that it makes Will suspect her of having researched him like a potential juror and said that specifically because it's the sort of thing someone on the festival circuit might say. He glares at her; she ignores him.

Catherine Rose, for her part, appears to be nearing the end of her rope. The anger in her voice is already starting to slide into panic and desperation when, jabbing a finger in Will's chest, she says, "All I wanted to do is help you make a lot of *money*, you bastard, and, okay, also make me a lot of money, and Nimbletainment *so* much money—oh, God, and I told them it was a sure thing. I told them to go ahead and start selling those *tickets*."

"By tickets, you wouldn't happen to mean that Autumn Harvest Experience being hawked as a pricey add-on to this year's Shiver?" Selma's voice is smooth and calm, the complete opposite of Catherine's panicked whine; perhaps it's that, how even and prepared she sounds, that makes Catherine's mouth snap shut. "Because I'm quite certain the owner of this property didn't agree to that, so I was interested to note this very address listed on your website." Widening her eyes with mocking innocence at Catherine's caught expression, she adds, "Gosh, I sure hope your corporate overlords are the forgiving type. I mean, aside from the bad PR and the wasted money, you've made them potentially liable for *several* different lawsuits to be brought. Are they low-key, usually? About that kind of thing?"

"No!" Catherine snaps, turning pleading eyes on Will. The desperation in them is naked and obvious, and it makes her look,

FALL INTO YOU   295

suddenly, smaller to him. Less powerful; less frightening. As ever, maybe Selma had a point about his fear of her, and its true source. "I know I've been, ah, a little aggressive, but—oh, can't we work *something* out?"

"To be honest," Will says, with an uncomfortable little shrug, "I might have been more open to that before, like, the tenth voicemail you left me? But at this point—"

"Will's very close to this," Selma interrupts, her voice honey smooth all of a sudden. Fixing a very fierce look at Will, one which is completely at odds with her sugary tone, she says, "And he wants to step away now, right, Will? You and Casey have a lot to talk about, I'm sure? Casey, by the way, I'm Selma, I'm sure Will's told you so much about me, and if he hasn't, you have a little time to come up with a convincing way to lie to me and say he did—we'll meet properly in a bit."

Then, in spite of being neither the owner nor the manager of the property, she shoos them away with one hand as she puts the other arm around Catherine's shoulder and says, "Now, the way I see it, you have a real opportunity here. Maybe you shouldn't have sold those tickets—but does Nimbletainment need to know that? What if you went to them with a new proposal; say, having someone who already knows a lot about events like this put it on for you? For a fee, of course? I think I know just the guys."

She winks at Will and Casey over Catherine's shoulder, then jerks her head in the universal gesture for "Now, get lost." And, what's worse, they *go*, both of them automatically taking a few shuffling steps away from her glare and then falling, more out of habit than anything, into an ambling walk back towards the house. Though he has so much to say to Casey it's hard to contain it all, they walk in silence for a few minutes, Will unable to figure out where to begin and Casey seeming to be waiting for him. Impatience seems to get the better of him, though, because as they near the grove of trees in front of the house:

"So—that's the scary lawyer best friend, then?" Casey sounds casual, or at least, he sounds like he's *trying* to sound casual. "She seems... well, scary, actually, but not in a bad way, I don't think."

"That's Selma for you," Will agrees, wondering nonsensically if Casey can hear his heart thudding, sense the way his stomach is flipping over and over. "You don't want to cross her, that's for sure. But, you know, she's a good friend to have, especially if you, uh, decide you want to back out of a real estate deal at the last second."

"Yeah, about that," Casey says, and stops under a large, wide-branched buckeye tree, the ground around it littered with the large nuts it drops around this time of year, some cracked to reveal the chestnut-brown, inedible seeds within. The whole tree is poisonous from root to fruit, but Will's always loved them, anyway, the way they stand tall and unabashed, their enormous, unmissable leaves, the disruptive, spiked missiles they drop from above in the fall. If the apple tree is gnarled and fickle, changing mood and energy by season, holding itself small and taut, then the buckeye is its opposite: taking up space for the sake of it, just because that's what it was born to do.

God, Will is thinking nonsense about trees again; while that might be the best possible summary of his life, it doesn't mean this is the moment. So:

"Yes," Will says, taking a breath. "To answer your earlier question: yes, really. I really am not selling the farm."

Casey's eyes, which had been focused anywhere else, abruptly meet Will's, wide and wondering. "*Why?* Or did you mean that you don't want to sell to Catherine, or to Nimbletainment, but—"

Will holds up a hand, smiling at him. "I don't want to sell the farm to anyone, Casey. Not Nimbletainment or anyone else.

I thought..." He pauses, biting the inside of his cheek, but: This is what he came here to do, isn't it? This is the plan he discussed with Selma, what *he*, Will, wants to do, or at least wants to do today; it's just a matter of doing it. He squares his shoulders, sets his jaw. "I thought it might be cool to, uh... set up a lab here, actually. These trees have been growing a long time, and there's plenty of them to work with, and I'd have a lot more leeway than I do with the orchard I work with in Illinois—it'd be easier to get to, too, at least if I was living down here. I thought I might stick around a bit, do some thinking, put a funding proposal together. But, you know—" Will finds he can't actually look at Casey for this part, even though—perhaps because—he means it so desperately, and with so much of himself. "I don't think I'd be able to do, ah, both, so. I'd be looking for—partners, you know. Or, uh. Partner. To go in on the business with me. Someone to manage the farm, keep things running. What you already do now, basically, to be honest."

"Oh?" Casey's voice is so controlled that Will can't help but look at him after all. There's a fire winking in his eyes, Will thinks, but it's banked, still smoldering; maybe it's just a trick of the light. "And when were you planning on holding interviews for that position?"

"Uh," Will says, and winces. "Right now? Because, I mean, if you don't want it, I'm not hiring—I'm not interested in anyone else." He swallows hard, and, weakly, trying for casual now himself, adds, "Though of course, I'm not trying to, like, force anything on you here? If you'd rather... I could always be a, um, a silent partner, if that would be better. I mean, I'd need to set up the lab, obviously, and mark some of the trees for experimenting, but I was thinking back of the third orchard, anyway, so you wouldn't even have to see me if you didn't want to, and—"

Will's voice dies in his throat as Casey smiles, and shakes his head, and steps closer, his right leg slipping into the space

298 DYLAN MORRISON

between Will's as though it was always meant to be there. He braces himself with one hand against the rough bark of the tree, and uses the other to lift Will's chin, so their eyes are meeting.

Very seriously, Casey says, "Listen to me, Will: If anyone calls our names, or one of the goddamn teenagers appears from thin air, or the local water main explodes, or *whatever*, we're going to ignore it, okay? I think, after all this, we've earned a few minutes to ourselves."

Breathlessly, Will says, "Yeah, I won't fight you on that one," and then Casey's kissing him.

Their last kiss was desperate, and pleading, and intense. It was a great kiss, one whose memory, hand-in-hand with an endless photo reel of choice moments from their night together, chased Will all the way to Chicago, and all the way back. But this kiss is *filthy*, so rich with promise of the things to come that they might as well be doing them. Will loses himself a little in the sensation, dizzily trying to catalogue the places Casey has touched him and, for once, finding the fine details too arduous to be bothered with; wherever Casey touches him, it sends sparks of white-hot electricity through Will's every nerve ending, so the minutiae doesn't seem important. When Casey tilts Will's head to deliver a series of kisses along the side of his neck, Will lets out a groan that he would, normally, be a little embarrassed to release even alone in the privacy of his own apartment. But somehow today, even under the buckeye tree in front of his parents' house, even in earshot of every ghost that's ever haunted him and probably also, God help him, Daphne, he doesn't care who hears him. It could be that he's growing as a person, but Will suspects it has rather more to do with the way Casey chuckles against his ear, says, "Oh, so you like that, then? Okay. Noted."

"God," Will says, and catches Casey's mouth again so he won't have to say anything else. He can't quite remember most of the words in his personal dictionary right now. His world has

FALL INTO YOU   299

narrowed down mostly to sensations: the warmth of Casey's hands against his skin, the weight of Casey's body against his, the soft cracking and crunching of buckeye nut shells being crushed under the soles of his shoes. What words he can call to mind are hardly descriptive enough to do the situation justice, and are instead the basic, simple, bedrock ones, like "good" and "wow" and "yes."

When, eventually, Casey pulls back, it's only a little; he allows Will to remain in the circle of his arms, which Will thinks is good, because he's not totally sure he trusts himself to stand on his own in this critical moment. Half of him is almost *blissed out* to a degree that's a little frightening and another third is scrabbling to get back to the unresolved conversation and whether or not being kissed nearly to death counts as agreeing, and the awkwardly sized sliver that remains is thinking ridiculous thoughts like, *I should send Anthony the Lizard Man an anonymous telegram that says "In the time since we parted, I have grown reasonably sure you're NOT actually good in bed,"* which, while entertaining, isn't productive. Will's not even sure how he'd go about sending a telegram at this particular moment in human history, nor how to contact Anthony, who had communicated largely through a series of burner photos and via a social media account, from which Will has since been blocked, for his lizard.

God, and Casey's just *looking* at him, warm and smiling, eyes crinkling at the corners, and...

"Oh my God, man, you have to *say* something," Will groans. "You can't just kiss me like that and *look* at me after I make a proposal like that, are you *in*? Does that mean you're *in*? Or do I need to, like, read it from your mind while you stare into my eyes—"

"Yeah, see, I just don't think you have it in you to be a *silent* partner," Casey says, grinning at him now, his eyes dancing. "Not really how you're wired, is it? So I'd say I'm in, but, you know. Only for the version where you talk." Smiling down at Will, he adds, "It's your name on the building, after all. It's only right."

Will smiles back up at him, brimming suddenly with so much happiness he feels like it might just spill out of him, bubble over like a pot left too long on the stove. "Eh," he says, feeling a little laughter slip out on the words. "A name's just a name. It's what you do with it that counts."

EPILOGUE
FIVE YEARS LATER

On the last day of October and the first day of his fortieth year, Will arrives, six-pack in hand, at the cemetery. It's an awkward place to be on Halloween, to be sure—Will passes several clusters of uncomfortable-looking teens, who scatter like cockroaches at the approach of a card-carrying adult. It reminds him, with a pang, of Noel, off at college for a few years now, replaced by an equally bizarre youth called Dakota of whom Will has, in the end, also grown quite fond, and who he will be sad to replace in her turn when the time comes in a few months.

Time keeps rolling on, no matter how much you might like to catch it between your palms like a firefly and keep it still—nothing says that quite so succinctly as teens in a cemetery on Halloween. Will smiles wanly at them, the passive, "Please, God, let's not interact, I'm trying to be polite, but for the love of all that is holy, do not attempt to speak to me," message seeming to land every time, and keeps his distance. He's relieved to find the corner of the cemetery he's headed for empty when he gets there; it would have been a bummer, honestly, to have to shoo children away from the area. On theme for the errand, certainly, but a bummer just the same.

302 DYLAN MORRISON

Will sits down, at last, in front of a headstone that reads WILLIAM "BILL" JOSIAH ROBERTSON III. It's buttressed on either side by headstones that also read WILLIAM "BILL" JOSIAH ROBERTSON, jammed in between the other two when it was obviously intended to be the third in the line—Will asked about it, a few years ago, and was told the cemetery had done it to save space. They'd offered to alter it for a fee, but Will had told them to leave it; it was fitting, really. The whole thing was fitting, down to the fact that the three of them were stuck with each other in the end; Will had always found it telling that none of the Robertson wives had wanted to be buried here in the family plot. His own mother, who had done her hard, complicated, miserable best at least some of the time, had started telling him when he was only ten or eleven, her voice very serious: "When I die, don't you let them bury me here, Willy. You make sure they take me back home to Willow Brook, and put me with my own parents, and Grandma Dottie, and Aunt Grace."

He had, too. He'd made sure; he hadn't spoken to his father, but he'd called, and double-checked the arrangements, and confirmed that his mother's burial was exactly as she'd wanted it. He'd felt he owed her that much. Maybe that's what he's doing here, this odd, macabre little birthday tradition: Will doesn't feel he owes his father anything, necessarily, but a little part of him can't quite let go of the idea that coming here feels... good. That, paradoxically enough, it feels like letting something go.

Will cracks the bottle cap off his beer on the top of Original Bill's headstone and, smiling slightly, says, "Hello, boys."

None of them answer him, which in a way makes these meetings the best conversations he's ever had with at least two of the three deceased participants. He never actually spoke with Original Bill, who was dead long before Will showed up, but he does feel he met the man in absentia. His ghost did its haunting somewhere in the ways Old Bill hurt Will's father, in the ways Will's father hurt him, although Will does understand that maybe he hasn't seen the man's best side.

"Farm's good," he tells Bill's headstone, taking a long pull from his own beer and sprawling out as comfortably as he can amongst the somewhat unkempt grass. "Turning a nice profit this year. Casey's ice cider's really taking off, and the tourist traffic has been higher than ever, so. And the lab's doing well, too, not that you'd care. I know all you ever wanted was for me to put the books down and be more like you, but we're making breakthroughs that a normal parent would have been proud of."

He sighs, and then frowns, just slightly, at the carved lettering of Bill's name. Of course, in this form, in this place, it reads very nearly as Will's might have one day: just that old yolk of a name, with no other inscription besides the years of his birth and death. "I couldn't think of what to put," Casey had admitted, clearly embarrassed, when Will asked why there wasn't an epigraph. "I asked him once and he said, 'Guess you might as well put, "Here lies Bill, who was over the hill."' It *was* just about the only time I ever heard him tell a joke, but still. Didn't feel tasteful."

Of course, Will is Will Reeves now. He sold Selma the rights to decide what words go on his grave more than fifteen years ago, in exchange for her never again mentioning a particular incident involving a risqué costume party, a very ambitious and ill-thought-out outfit choice, and the sentence, "Well, how hard could it be to shave my legs," so. Maybe he's never been at that much risk of a sparse tombstone; after all, setting the name aside, it's not as though he and his father were ever much alike.

In any case, Will can't blame Casey for being unable to come up with an epigraph for the man. Will wouldn't have been able to, either, despite sharing his DNA and spending most of his childhood with Bill. The situation is too complex to explain on a headstone, and, anyway, Bill wouldn't have wanted it explained. Bill would have preferred, Will thinks, this blank rock to one that revealed too much, or that made him look like a different man, softer or warmer than his reality. For all his flaws, for all his problems, he was—Will has to give it to him—who he was. Subterfuge had never been his style.

Sipping his beer, Will lets his gaze unfocus for a minute, staring out into the middle distance. After a while, motion catches at the corner of his eye, and he looks over to see three cardinals swoop down into a nearby tree. It appears, to Will's surprise, to be something that could pass for a family grouping— a showy, bright red male, a more demure brown female, and a juvenile male, still growing in his crimson plumage, and looking a little awkward next to the splendor of the older birds. They're probably not a family—just three separate, unrelated animals who have landed here together by coincidence—but Will still finds himself staring, oddly transfixed.

All three are silent for a moment; then the older male trills sharply at the juvenile, who balks at once and flits away, vanishing into the nearby tree line. The remaining male, smug, hops closer to the female, trilling at her too; she ruffles her feathers, annoyed, and takes flight, leaving the small red bird to puff up in victory and then, at least to Will's eyes, deflate a little, as though realizing that, through his own familiar folly, he has found himself alone.

That's not what's happening, Will knows. Really those birds were having a conversation of their own, probably on the topic of hunger, territory, or mating, in a language Will would be a fool to imagine he could begin to understand. He could call up maybe a dozen former classmates or colleagues who broke towards fauna instead of flora, and they'd all confirm that the state bird of Ohio probably was *not* inclined towards playing out intricate family dramas to mirror Will's own.

Still, he can't help but smile at the cardinal, who stares back at him, fixed and unblinking, and doesn't fly off even when Will

FALL INTO YOU   305

stands up, stretches, finishes his beer, and cracks open a second one.

"Here lies Bill," he intones, in his most serious voice, "who was over the hill," and slowly, he pours the beer out onto the grass, staring at the bird all the while. He'd like to tell himself he doesn't know why he does this every year—it's not as though he owes his father anything, after all—but he can't. Every time he tries, his mind crowds up with images of the last five years, of Casey and the life they've built together, of his work and his lab and his beloved grove of testing trees, of the friends who have become like family, of the farm that's become something more than it was when Will was a child. None of it would have happened if Bill hadn't left Will the property, even though he'd promised years before, in no uncertain terms, that he'd do no such thing. That choice, if it had even *been* a choice, as opposed to decades of the sort of inertia that might motivate someone to fill up a room with junk—that *action*, whether Bill meant to take it or not, changed Will's life. It brought him to love and happiness; it brought him home, to a version of this place that could *be* a home for him, instead of a trap, or a cage, or a millstone.

Smiling up at the cardinal, as the last drop of beer lands, Will adds, "I can't say much about the old bastard, but he got one thing right."

The cardinal trills and, at last, takes flight, its bright red plumage a streak of crimson through the air before it's gone. Will sighs, and smiles, and shakes his head, and starts the long walk home.

He doesn't mind the walk. In fact, he'd had Meredith drop him off here with the goal of walking, after a leisurely birthday lunch and a long chat in the upstairs office at Gunderson's. It's become something of a tradition in the last few years, for his birthdays and hers, to do a bit of a Year in Review; the results are always hilarious, and often oddly heartwarming, and it reminds Will of their teenage years in a way that brings him a

306   DYLAN MORRISON

small, almost comforting pang. Back then, every birthday had felt like turning a page in a new, exciting book, breathless with excitement to see what was going to happen, and they'd celebrated together by imagining what the next chapter would hold. Now that Will's reached that awkward point in his life where he's probably read at least as much of the metaphorical book as there's remaining to go, it's nice to look back on the year he's left behind him, savor it for the utterly singular delicacy it was.

Will takes, now, the route he would have taken as a teenager, ignoring the various objections his adult self has woolgathered over the years, to petty things like "trespassing" and "traffic laws" and "not climbing the fence into someone's vegetable garden just because it will save you .27 seconds of walking time." He cuts across the Northside Creek, and walks briefly the wrong way up Poplar Road, before he grins and, for the first time in twenty-plus years, cuts through what used to be old Mrs. Quincey's yard. No one's lived here since before Will left, Mrs. Quincey having died sometime around Will's fifteenth birthday and the house having slipped into the kind of chaotic mess of disputed wills and mismanaged estates that leads a place to fall to ruin. Her farmhouse, which had been cut from a similar cloth to Will's own home, is dilapidated now in a way that would have horrified the old woman. Will hadn't known her well, but what impression she did leave was all rooted in the pride she took in keeping her home and garden pristine. Well, that and the truly pervasive, utterly inescapable scent of mothballs.

Feeling slightly guilty about the mothballs thought, Will smiles to notice that the old woman's prize-winning rosebushes are still here. They're wilder and more unkempt than Will remembers them, certainly, but they've survived all the same, the fancy varietals cross-pollinating with one another to create all sorts of interesting one-off blooms. Intrigued, Will can't help but pull out his pocketknife—an anniversary gift from Casey, a few years ago now—and take a couple of cuttings, careful to carry them without gripping the thorns. The blooms are lovely, and Will's interested to see if he can reproduce them if he plants these at home, or if they'll just default back to whatever their base varietal was once separated from the thicket.

He turns before he carries on and looks back at the old place: the holes in the roof, the broken glass in the windows, the way nature is creeping up, as she always does eventually, to reclaim whatever territory humanity will cede. This might have happened to his own farmhouse, once a prison and now a paradise; it might have happened to the ancient barn, now a beloved local petting zoo, or to the collection of ill-maintained outbuildings, replaced now by Will's perfect, exactingly constructed laboratory. The thought twists Will's heart in his chest, but even as it does, the vines crawling up the support beams of the porch, the grasses shooting up from between the floorboards, bring him solace. The apple trees, at least, would have figured it out.

He walks the rest of the way home humming, an old song he hardly remembers the words of, but that he'd liked when he was young. As he goes, he can almost imagine the teenage version of himself walking with him, slouched and awkward, cringing away from the world before he could disappoint it; the Will of today walks with his shoulders back, his head high, an ease in the swing of his arm and the bend of his leg that's hard to quantify, but undeniable. He wishes he could reach through time and speak to that version of himself and offer—well—*anything*. A glimmer of hope; a glimpse of a better future; a good long hug, maybe, if nothing else.

On the other hand, he'd had to live through that part of his life to get to this one. So maybe better to leave well enough alone.

Twilight's starting to fall in earnest when Will gets back. The Robertson Family Farms sign is lit up tonight, in prepara-

308   DYLAN MORRISON

tion for the Halloween Fright Night event Casey cooked up a few years ago; as he always does, Will gives it a slightly wistful smile. He'd thought so hard about changing the name that sometimes he still expects to see Reeves Family Farms, or just Reeves Farms, or even R&R Farms, which had been the top three contenders.

In the end, though, Will had decided maybe it was better to let it stand with a name no one carried anymore. The place itself could be the storied Robertson upon whom expectations and demands were heaped; it was safer, that way. A place was better equipped than a person to bear them.

Will's a better Reeves than he ever was a Robertson; he proves it as he walks around the front half of the property, checking in on employees setting up for the event, and customers heading out for the day, and making sure everything's all right at the market before he actually goes home. That wasn't the Robertson way; the Robertson way would have been to bellow that everyone better be doing their jobs before sitting to sulk on the porch. It's a wonder to Will these days that *anyone* could have spent so much time sulking here, in this place, where joy seems to flutter out of every crack and crevice if you just know how to look for it. But then, Will knows, they *hadn't* known how to look for it, or how to cup it gently in their hands when it did dare to approach them, instead of stomping on it or scaring it off.

As he walks through the little grove of trees that separates the rest of the farm from the house, Will looks for his own joy, and finds it. Casey is backlit in the kitchen window, aproned and streaked with something that looks like chocolate; Will grins, biting down on a laugh, and shakes his head. Casey's no chef and even less of a baker, having grown up nearly entirely on things like TV dinners and Hot Pockets and pizza; he'd confessed to Will, sometime around the six-month mark of their relationship, that he'd been in his early

FALL INTO YOU 309

twenties before he realized that cake did not, traditionally, come from a box.

But in spite of this, every year he determinedly pulls up a recipe—never, Will has noticed, the same recipe twice, not that he's judging or complaining in any way—and attempts to make Will a birthday cake. It's never once been a beautiful birthday cake, and the first two years it was neither beautiful nor edible, as in the first case Casey had mistakenly used salt for sugar, and in the second, he'd forgotten it in the oven until it was more or less charcoal. But these last few years he's managed to produce something that tastes quite good, provided you don't mind that it looks as though it was assembled by a couple of half-drunk raccoons.

Will doesn't mind if his cake looks like it was assembled by a couple of half-drunk raccoons. He hadn't even minded the inedible ones; blowing out the candles on that charcoal cake, gripping Casey for dear life as they both howled and wheezed with laughter, was and remains one of Will's favorite birthday memories, something he reaches for in moments he feels grim about getting older.

It's why he's so sure that whatever Casey's made, this will be another of his favorite birthdays, as all his birthdays with Casey seemingly are. They'll have dinner, and cake, and the dinner might be a little over-seasoned and the cake might be a little malformed and that will be lovely, and perfect, and just right. Casey will tell him some absurd story from his day and Will won't be able to help laughing; Will's own stories, which Casey will be genuinely interested in, will fall out of his mouth without his even meaning them, too, pulled loose naturally by Casey's easy, comfortable curiosity.

And then, afterwards, they'll go back down to the front of the farm and join their friends and neighbors, who will be singing, and laughing, and dancing. They'll build a bonfire, a local tradition of sorts since the flood that had the good grace to

310   DYLAN MORRISON

trap Will here and force him to see what was in front of him; in the flickering orange glow of the firelight, Casey will wrap an arm around Will's waist, put his chin on Will's shoulder, and let Will lean back against him. Together, they will exchange greetings and pleasantries with the people they've come to know and love, who have come to know and love them. Some of those people will say, "Happy birthday, Will!" and some of them will just smile and nod, but no one, not one of them, will look at him like they were hoping to see someone else.

As Will stands there, Casey, in the kitchen, looks up, sees him, and grins. He lifts his spatula to his chest in mock-shock and waggles his eyebrows salaciously, as though he's caught Will doing something scandalous; Will snorts, and rolls his eyes, and grins back at him as he starts walking again, eager to get inside.

And as he takes the porch steps two at a time, a memory springs up like the grasses bursting from between the cracks in Mrs. Quincey's rotting wooden floorboards: that night in the bar with Selma, half a decade ago now, where she told him he wasn't a happy person. At the time, Will hadn't quite been able to believe her, although he hadn't quite been able to mount a defense, either—it had just seemed like such a ridiculous notion, such an absurd, impossible thing. *No one*, he'd been sure, was *really* happy, was walking the world with a song in their heart and a spring in their step every bright blue day of their blissful, blessed life. Even Selma wasn't happy, at least when she'd asked —these days, two years into a serious relationship with someone she met on a lesbian cruise, Will thinks maybe she is. But back then, at least from where he was standing, happiness wasn't realistic, and so, as far as Will had been concerned, the idea that it might be achievable simply wasn't a hypothesis that merited further study. After all, Will encountered miserable people every day: in his job and daily routines, in the halls of his apartment building, in passing on the street. The world was brimming with miserable people; miserable people had raised him. It had just seemed like the better part of rationality, at least in that arena, to avoid shooting for the metaphorical moon.

So Selma had been right, at the time. She'd been right about William Josiah Robertson IV, who'd been *unhappy* so long as to have confused despair for neutrality and loneliness for safety, who was comforted by the familiar touch of a harsh word. He had, no doubt, been an unhappy person. Probably, if Will could go back in time and ask them, it would turn out that *none* of the previous William Josiah Robertsons were happy people—that they were all lugging along the same old, tired sack of broken garbage, insisting that it was their treasured birthright.

But Will hasn't answered to that name in years. He's Will Reeves, and he isn't happy every minute of every day; life's still harsh and bitter sometimes, overwhelming, exhausting, hard to bear. He still wakes up some mornings with dread thick in his throat, anticipation for a punishment that isn't coming pounding in his ears, and has to wince his way gingerly into his day.

But no matter how complicated, or unanticipated, or downright screwed up that day happens to be—no matter how irritated Will ends up, how physically spent, how twisted up in the sweaty bedsheets of his own anxieties—Casey's still there, offering a hand or a smile, whistling a tune under his breath. There's still a chance for Will to reset, to take a beat, to hear that smooth, beloved baritone remind him that he's not alone. There's still the way Casey always grins and shrugs like it's nothing, whatever's gone wrong, and says that they'll figure it out together. That there's going to be another opportunity, when the sun breaks in through their bedroom window tomorrow morning, to run at it all again.

In five years, Will can't remember a day he hasn't laughed.

He hasn't bothered asking Selma lately if she thinks he's a happy person; though he's sure she'd be thrilled to offer an opinion, he's pleased enough knowing the answer for himself.

A LETTER FROM THE AUTHOR

Hello, dear reader!

I can't thank you enough for reading *Fall Into You*; I hope you had as much fun following Will's journey as I had writing it. If you want to join other readers in hearing all about my new releases and bonus content, you can sign up here:

www.stormpublishing.co/dylan-morrison

If you enjoyed this book and could spare a few moments to leave a review, that would be hugely appreciated. Even a short review can make all the difference in encouraging readers to discover my books for the first time, and I'd be so grateful for any words you can spare. Thank you so much!

This story is about love and connection, but it's also about growing up queer in Ohio, something I did long before Will turned up in my mind demanding to be written down. I wrote it for the complicated, messy teenager who still looks out of my eyes some mornings, and for everyone who carries such a passenger with them through adulthood. May we all know comfort, safety, happiness, support, and the joy of a *really* good apple.

Thanks again for being part of this amazing journey with me and I hope you'll stay in touch—I have so many more stories and ideas to entertain you with!

Dylan

www.dylanmorrison.net

facebook.com/dylanjstrand

x.com/dylan_thyme

instagram.com/dylanthyme

linkedin.com/in/dylan-strand-92aa43219

tiktok.com/@dylanthyme

ACKNOWLEDGMENTS

Writing acknowledgements for a novel is essentially an impossible task—I think that's why they're usually (sorry to say it) so boring. The author, faced with the unclimbable mountain of recognizing everyone who has contributed to the work, has no choice but to do their best to make things basically unreadable in order to obscure their own shortcomings with the written word. I mean, how wide do you go? In a real way, I could thank everyone I've ever met, especially the people in and around Cleveland, Ohio, where I was born and raised. Glenriver is fictional, but my well of love for Northeast Ohio and the ways it can be amazing is both deep and very real, and I drew from it extensively in writing.

But presumably you, the reader, do not have it in you to browse the Cleveland phone book, so I'm going to try to keep things as brief as possible.

Of course, I have to start with thanking Kathryn Taussig for being interested in my book in the first place, and for putting so much work into bringing it to life! The entire Storm team has been an absolute joy to work with, and I couldn't be happier, or more grateful, for their help.

I also have to thank my parents, Pam and Adam, and my brothers, Scott and Ike, for being so unlike the Robertsons in so many ways, including being open and accepting of my own queerness. I couldn't list everything they've done for me here, but I'm so grateful for all of it. (And of course, I must also thank

Bob the dog, their tiger-sized English mastiff, whose good vibes improve the world daily without his even knowing it.)

To ALL my friends who have all let me ramble about my various ideas for years, read a variety of my writing, and provided guidance on a wide variety of topics: You're the best. And to Shea, Ritz, Lily, Lena, Sophie, and Kaye, who were so kind and so patient with me as I was cranking this story out, I really can't thank you enough.

To my spouse, Rowan Morrison, I owe thanks that go beyond this book—I could not have written this without them, because without their kindness, support, insight, and love over the last eight years, I would not be the person I am. Thank you for finding my lost objects and navigating my choppy waters and bearing the way I thrash around at night like a seal on a lawn chair; thank you for having weird conversations with me when we should both be asleep; thank you for being yourself, and making it more fun to be me.

To Hannah Bond, who found me on the internet when I was truly, deeply certain I didn't have the chops and I'd never be able to write a book I was proud of, let alone sell one: I can't capture my gratitude here for a million reasons, not the least of which is that there is too much. So I'll thank you for *everything*, very much *including* proving me wildly, madly wrong. In so many ways, I could never have managed this without you.

Finally, I'd like to take a moment to acknowledge everyone who has, over the last twenty years, read, enjoyed, commented on, podficced, translated, created art based on, or otherwise made my fanfiction a part of their lives. Writing for you and with you has been a joy, and every one of you helped shape me as a writer and person. Thank you for taking the time, and for being so kind about my work over the years. I will never stop appreciating you.

Printed in Dunstable, United Kingdom